HOLIDAY NOVELLA SERIES
BOX SET

Books 1 to 4

A BUCKSKIN CHRISTMAS
MY EASTER MIRACLE
INDEPENDENCE DAZE
GIVING THANKS

HOLIDAY NOVELLA SERIES BOX SET

four novellas

by

Bruce K Beck

New York

This is a work of fiction. Names, characters, businesses, places, events, and incidents are either the products of the author's imagination or used in a fictitious manner.

This is a first edition from Audacity Books.
Please visit us on the web at www.audacitybooks.com.
For information about rights or purchases,
please email us at info@audacitybooks.com.

For updates, and for occasional gifts and offers, please subscribe at:

www.audacitybooks.com/#subscribe

Many thanks to Walter Maas for his generous wisdom. And to Richard Kutner for his classy edits. Tim Barber of Dissect Designs (*www.dissectdesigns.com*) signed on as a cover designer for my first novel and then became a friend. You're Sure to Fall in Love, indeed. This journey would not have been possible without the example and the teaching of Joanna Penn at *www.thecreativepenn.com*. I am delighted, Joanna, to add this volume to your long list of books you have enabled. No doubt you will hit your one million mark any day now!

Bruce K Beck is both a writer and an accomplished chef. His novels—including the **Love Trilogy,** the **Obsession Trilogy**, and the **Tolerance Trilogy**—are available online and wherever books are sold. Before turning to fiction, Beck authored ***PRODUCE: A FRUIT AND VEGETABLE LOVERS' GUIDE***, which was called "gorgeous" by ***The New York Times***, "a dazzler" by ***Bon Appetit***, and "the most spectacular food book of the year" by ***The Boston Globe***. His next book was ***THE OFFICIAL FULTON FISH MARKET COOKBOOK***, which was called "invaluable" by Jacques Pépin, and "a treasure" by Irene Sax of ***Newsday***. And Rex Reed said, "... you'll love this book. It's like a movie!"

These books are dedicated to all who
believe in holiday miracles.

A BUCKSKIN CHRISTMAS

BRUCE K BECK

A BUCKSKIN CHRISTMAS

a holiday novella

by

Bruce K Beck

New York

What did I know about cowboys? I didn't even like Westerns all that much. John Wayne was always a big turnoff for me. Now, Guy Madison—he was my idea of a proper hunk. No, Rory Calhoun was the hunk. Guy Madison was the tender Western beauty in my fantasies. But then, I watched a lot of old movies. And a lot of old TV reruns. There didn't seem to be all that much else to do for a gay kid growing up in a small New Jersey town.

When my boss asked me to host his new "star writer," I felt mostly annoyance. I had an extra bedroom, true. My roommate had headed home to Arkansas, and I had decided to keep the apartment that was a little bigger than I needed. But the rent was reasonable. I could have been paying the same for a large studio. So I kept it. Wise choice? I had supposed so until I was asked to board a stranger from Montana.

"Look, Daniel, we want to get this book right, and you know how tight budgets are." This from my employer, Jim Stevenson, who was so tight he squeaked. "If you'll let him stay with you, you'll get extra face time. Extra editing insight. And you can take him to dinner every night for less than the cost of a hotel room. What if we send someone in to clean once a week?"

"How about twice a week?"

"Done," he said.

"You know me, Jim," I said. "I'm nothing if not a team player. Just tell him horses are not allowed in New York City apartments."

"I think he knows that. Thanks for being a good sport, Dan. What do you think of the manuscript—so far?"

What indeed? I thought it was better than it had any right to be. I thought it could be shaped—that I could shape it—into a credible story. I thought it lacked a certain sense of heart. I told Jim as much. What I didn't tell him was that I also thought our cowboy was hiding something. Did I want to learn what it was that he was hiding? Maybe. If I had to fix his book, then I'd have to know him better.

"Caleb gets into Kennedy Thursday evening," Jim said. "Harvey's going to meet him. They should get to your place by about ten.   Thanks again, Dan. We'll make it up to you."

"I'm sure you will," I said. I got on with my work. I liked my position at Scrive. The house was big enough to have some clout in the publishing industry—what's left of it—and small enough to give truly personal attention to every manuscript. I normally shepherded maybe three or four projects a year. Jim was smart about what to buy and how to package it. The in-house cover designer was excellent. It was a quality operation.

In the five years I had worked for Jim, he never asked me to wash garbage. And as we all know, the problem with washing garbage is that when you finish, it's still garbage. I feared that Caleb Bromley's manuscript might be Jim's first slipup. And yet, once I started reading it, I understood why Jim had acquired it. Some of the sentence structure was clumsy—easy enough to fix—but the basic story spoke to me. And that's what the reading experience is all about, after all.

My work life was going well. My personal life was a disaster. I hadn't been in love in several years—not since Steve took a job in San Francisco and headed west. Did I miss him? Terribly. Did I beg him not to leave me? Not a chance. Maybe I sensed our affair had run its course. The new coolness of my bed was the hardest part of adjusting to Steve's departure. I had grown accustomed to his warm body touching mine all through the night. I didn't sleep much the first month after he left New York.

Sex helped. It's easy enough to find, of course. There are millions of horny gay men in the City—or perhaps it just seems that way. I intersected with at least a hundred of them in the years after Steve moved West. My place, his place. I was flexible. I was also empty. And I never asked a trick to sleep over. It would have been too cruel—sharing another man's warmth without wanting more. Sharing bodily fluids was easy. Warmth was a different matter. Overnight in my bed was strictly for the beloved. And I hadn't seen one of those in far too long.

I came to a realization that summer before Caleb's arrival in New York. I decided that what I really needed was a relationship, and that I wasn't going to find one on Grindr. So I canceled my account and stopped looking for quick, anonymous sex. It took a few weeks to adjust to the lack of little vibrating notifications on my phone. The new stillness was disconcerting—as if I had ceased to be hot meat. But adjust I did. The celibate me was the version Caleb would meet on Thursday.

I told my friend Letisha Carmichael about Caleb's imminent arrival, of course. I told her everything. Nearly. She had seen me through more than a dozen years of stupid choices and heartaches. And I had made my shoulder available whenever she needed to unburden. Tisha had seen all of my heart, and all of my body, too. As I think I had seen all of hers. We fell into bed together often when we were under-grads.

It was Tisha's skin that first attracted me—silky, caramel colored. It was her fierce physicality that kept me coming back. I always knew I was gay. From birth, I think. But friendship can be a powerful force, and a powerful aphrodisiac—for twentysome-things, anyway. It took us a while to find our true paths, but I'll never regret a single moment that I spent in bed with—and inside—Tisha. I think she felt the same way about me. I hoped so, anyway. She said as much. But I started dating men, and she started dating *black* men.

I always thought that black men are deadly at-tractive. Don't get me started on how much big black cock I've serviced—some of my favorite memories of mindless sensuality. Tisha agreed with my sensibil-ity. But the men she chose were always just as deadly as they were attractive. Definitely *not* hus-band material. I worried about her choices, while at the same time I reserved the right to swim in the same risky waters.

"My, my, Danny," Letisha said, "a cowboy in your spare room! How ever will you manage to keep your hands off him?"

"That should be easy, Tisha," I said. "We don't like each other very much, Caleb and I. It's typical of the writer/editor relationship. Most writers can't take criticism, and it's annoying to have to read prose that I could write better in my sleep. I don't lust after men I don't like. Normally. And I'm assuming he's straight."

"A straight cowboy?" she asked. "What will we hear of next? All those long nights out on the range and up in the mountains. What do you think those boys do for warmth and companionship? I'll bet you can guess."

"You have a vivid imagination, dear," I said. "That's part of what I love about you. Another part is your kindness. If you want to practice *that* trait, then you'll drop the subject of cowboys."

"Yes, dear," Tisha said. "Just promise me you'll be careful. I know what happens when your heart gets involved."

"Promise. Where are you taking me for dinner?"

"*Chez moi*," she said. "A woman I work with has been teaching me about Ethiopian cooking. She also told me where to buy *injera*, because there's no way I'm going to attempt to make an edible tablecloth. I think you'll like it, Danny. Come at 7:00."

"With pleasure," I said. "I'll be your guinea pig anytime. I still remember that Brazilian *feijoada* you made last year. Will you make it again some time?"

"Of course, dear," she said. "But I'm working on a shrimp thing from Bahia, with coconut milk and *dende* oil."

"Yes, please," I said. "I'll peel the shrimp."

"Deal," she said. "Danny, what are you going to feed your cowboy?"

"Yes, well, Caleb is not my cowboy, Tisha. He's my client. And I don't know. I doubt I'll cook for him. There's a dining budget. We'll go out. Steaks and burgers are usually safe. Or maybe he's into New California Cuisine, I don't know. Will you help?"

"Of course, darling," Tisha said. "We'll see that he doesn't starve."

"He might just fancy you, of course," I said. "All straight men do. Plus the occasional faggot. You have evidence of that. What if he wants to become *your* cowboy instead of *mine?* Will you revive your taste for white meat?"

"Don't be crude, dear," Tisha said. "You know I consider men on a case-by-case basis. We'll take care of your—*our* cowboy. Not to worry. But I'm flying to Chicago two weeks after Thanksgiving. What are you going to do with him over Christmas?"

"Caleb. He has a name."

"What are going to do with Caleb?" she asked.

"I usually spend Christmas with Mom and Dad. They have plenty of room. I guess Caleb will have to come with me—unless he wants to spend that time alone in the city. It will be up to him. I can exert some influence when it comes to his sentence structure, but I can't tell him what to do. Let me go, Tisha. I'm trying to work. Can we talk about this tonight?"

"Of course," Tisha said. I was apprehensive about hosting a houseguest, but Jim was right, of course. The extra face time would improve the editorial process. Our relationship had consisted entirely of weekly emails. Soon we'd be able to communicate in person. But that proximity inspired a touch of apprehension I had not shared with anyone, not even Tisha. Maybe not even with myself. Caleb had sent the design team an author photo, for the book jacket. He was obviously gorgeous, my cowboy. How would I handle a month or two with that kind of beauty in the next room? Hands off, of course.

Chapter Two

"Caleb Bromley, meet Dan Blackwell," Harvey said. I liked Caleb's handshake. It was firm and warm. I hated to release his hand. But I didn't over-extend our contact. I wanted to be careful not to do anything pervy on our first meeting.

"How was your flight?" I asked.

"It was fine," Caleb said. "I'm used to little prop planes. I fly one, actually. Oh, you know that. Jumbo jets are a different breed."

"Welcome to Casa Blackwell. I hope you'll be comfortable here." Was I coming on too strong? I'll admit the reality of Caleb Bromley in my apartment was a bit disconcerting. He was slightly taller than I had imagined, and even handsomer than his photo. Slightly rugged features. Piercing brown eyes. A sexy beard, just a little scruffy around the edges. Broad shoulders and a lean body that had obviously been toned through hard work rather than gym time.

"Thanks for looking after our favorite author, Harvey," I said. _Definitely_ coming on too strong. "Tell Jim we'll stop by the office tomorrow afternoon. I want Caleb to sleep late and take the morning off, his first day in New York."

"Sure. Thanks, Dan," Harvey said. "I'll leave you two to get settled in."

I reached for Caleb's bag, to carry it to his room. "I'm good," he said, as he took the bag from me. I led the way.

"Let me know if there's anything you need. Are you hungry?"

"No, they gave us something on the plane that was sort of like food. I'm good."

"How about a nightcap?"

"Sure," he said.

"I'll be in the kitchen. Come out when you're ready." It was worse than I had ever imagined. Not only was Caleb a glorious hunk of manflesh, but he was also charming—in a very laid-back way. I was head over heels and well on my way to feelings I would never allow in a business arrangement. I was a lost boy.

"I have beer, wine, tequila, and brandy. What'll it be?" I asked Caleb after he had changed into shorts and a T and come to join me in the kitchen. I liked him even better without a hat. I knew I'd like him best in nothing at all. But I didn't dare to consider the possibility.

"Tequila, I think," he said. "I don't drink much, but I also don't fly to New York City very often. Like, never."

"I hope you'll like it," I said. "I couldn't live anywhere else—I and eight million other New Yorkers. You're not the only cowboy in town, you know. I could take you to Times Square to meet the Naked Cowboy. He has a way with a guitar."

"Look, Dan," he said. "I know you're making fun of me, and I don't mind. Especially tonight. I need some sleep. Can we talk in the morning?"

"Of course," I said. Caleb headed to his bedroom. He looked just as stunning from behind as from the front. "Don't set an alarm," I called after him. "Just get up when you want to. I'll have coffee made, and I can always scramble an egg, or something." Caleb disappeared behind a closed bedroom door. I wanted to say other things to him. I wanted to say, "I don't know what you like, Caleb, but I'd like to find out." Things like that.

Instead, I brushed my teeth and headed to bed. Alone, of course. I read for twenty minutes—one of our new titles I had not yet gotten to. And then I turned out my light. I lay there in the almost-darkness of my room feeling sorry for myself because I was alone. I was aware of an intense ache that started in my heart and then spread all over my body. I suspected the ache would never end unless I could lie beside Caleb. Fat chance.

"Sleep well?" I asked him when he surfaced in the morning—only an hour after I did.

"Yeah," Caleb said. "Nice pillows. Duck or goose?"

"Goose, I think," I said. "I'll call Bloomingdale's right after breakfast and ask them. How do you want your eggs?" Caleb gave me a sort of half smile instead of saying, again, "I know you're making fun of me."

"Over easy, please," he said.

"Coffee?"

"Milk, no sugar." I could remember that. In fact, I would remember every moment of the first morning

I shared with Caleb. Every detail of his sleep-tousled hair and his smile and his eyes in the morning sunlight and the way he cradled his coffee cup and the little divot below his Adam's apple that peeked out from the frayed lapel of the old robe I left on the bed for him to wear—every detail was burned into my brain.

"We should put in an appearance at Scrive this afternoon," I said after we had eaten. "Jim will want to know that his investment is safe. But you don't have to tap-dance, Caleb. You just have to show up and maybe smile a little. Or not. Sullen writers are a thing, you know."

Caleb said, "Look, Dan, I think you're a nice guy. I haven't always been happy with your editorial suggestions, of course. But, I'm pleased to be working with you. Actually, I have to admit that you're always right when you tell me what's wrong with my story."

Fuck! I thought. What I said was, "Thanks for that, Caleb, but we don't have to talk business until Monday, really. Let's get that audience with Jim out of the way, and then you'll be free to enjoy your first trip to New York. Until Monday, of course. Then we'll crack the whip. What do you want to do? What do you want to see?"

"Dan, you don't have to entertain me."

"Of course I do," I said. "Don't the laws of hospitality apply out West? You're my responsibility, Caleb. You're my brother as long as you're under my roof." I couldn't believe I said that. I felt it, of course. Intensely. Caleb seemed to recoil ever so slightly. I had never spoken to another man that way, so I had no reason to think he should accept my declaration. I waited.

"I thought New Yorkers were supposed to be gruff," he said.

"Well, you thought wrong. Let's get our asses in gear. There are plenty of towels in your bathroom and shampoo and conditioner and all that. Let me know if you need anything else. I don't want to rush you. Meet me back here in, what, forty-five minutes?" Caleb laughed at me—with his eyes. For the first time. I was stunned.

I'd have died happy if I had been struck down, just at that moment, while a beautiful man favored me with his trust and his smile and a glimpse of his perfect body as my old robe opened just enough for me to know that the ache in my heart was entirely justified.

📖

"Welcome to New York. Welcome to Scrive," Jim said as he rose from his desk chair to shake Caleb's hand. "Dan is taking good care of you, I trust. What are you going to do today?"

"Touristy stuff, I guess, Jim" I said. "We haven't set our agenda, but I'm sure we'll end up at the observation deck at the Empire State Building. That's a view that never disappoints."

"Well, enjoy yourselves this weekend," Jim said. "And I'll see you both bright and early Monday morning." The audience was over. We stopped at Harvey's desk to say hello to him, and then we headed out into the crisp autumn air. Yes, it was a good day. I had a beautiful companion to share New York City with me on a perfect afternoon in my favorite season. Who could ask for more?

My heart asked for a lot more, but it would have to settle for what it got. "What if we just get the Empire State Building out of the way first thing?" I suggested. "It doesn't get more iconic than that."

"Sure," Caleb said. We headed to Fifth Avenue and walked downtown to 34th Street. Along the way I gave Caleb a little history. I told him that the building was planned before the famous Stock Market Crash at the end of 1929; that it was finished in 1931 as the Great Depression raged on; that the building shares New York State's official nickname, but that when it opened for business the economy was so bad that the building earned its *own* nickname, "The Empty State Building." But, of course, it's a survivor, like the rest of us New Yorkers.

We made our way up to the observation deck. The air was crystalline. I was delighted that the city put on such a show for Caleb's first visit. He seemed—not exactly enthusiastic, but properly impressed with the majesty of the city and its setting. It was so clear we could see parts of New Jersey and Long Island and most of Staten Island. Caleb smiled at me. Several times. That was worth all my pains. I started planning the rest of our day while Caleb drank in the view.

When we were back at street level again, I said, "It's too early for dinner, of course, but I have an idea. It's near here, actually. I'll see if I can get us a table at six or so. We can walk around the city until then. It's a famous old steak house. My uncle took me there when I was a teenager, and I've never forgotten it."

"Sure," Caleb said. I checked online for a reservation at Keens Chophouse. Done. I steered Caleb in the direction of Broadway, and we reached Macy's in two or three minutes. I would have taken him east instead, to the Morgan Library. But passing the old B. Altman building—which had been such a treat when I was a kid—was always a little depressing. And I wasn't certain if Caleb was the Morgan Library type. I wasn't certain *what* type he was, of course. Macy's seemed safe.

"Would you like to go inside the world's largest store?" I asked him.

"Sure," he said. We took a quick tour. The men's department looked a little cheesy, but there were some lightweight cashmere sweaters that were inviting.

"Here, hold this up," I said, handing him a sweater that was turquoise blue. I checked it with Caleb's coloring and decided it was not quite right. Then I spied one in a sort of moss green. "Try this one," I said. He held it up, dutifully, and it was perfect. His eyes sparkled; his cheeks took on a new healthy glow. "I think Jim wants you to have that sweater," I said. "Medium or large?"

"Dan, you don't have to do that."

"Of course not," I said. "Don't fight me, Caleb. You're going to lose."

Caleb considered the situation and said, "Large, I think. More comfortable." That was done. We headed back to Broadway and walked north to Times Square. I wanted him to see the bustle of the Theater District. I wasn't sure if we'd see a play while he was in town. I didn't bring it up then—our first day together. There would be time for all of that. And

Caleb was free to tell me what he wanted. But would he ever say what he really wanted? I wondered.

We wandered the city for hours. I showed Caleb my favorite—and unfavorite—architecture. He spent much of his time looking up. As tourists do. We stopped for a coffee at a Starbucks—so Caleb would know we're not all that different from the rest of the world. The conversation was sparse. I didn't push him. I didn't want to chatter on and make him uncomfortable. I'd have been very sad if I'd seen his eyes glaze over as he tuned me out. I did not.

Inevitably it was time for dinner. We made our way to Broadway and West 36th Street. The host led us to our table past all the racks of meerschaum pipes that had been smoked—and autographed—by guests through the decades. Quaint relics of the past. I like a little history. As always, I couldn't tell what Caleb liked. When we were seated and I had ordered some red wine that was entirely too expensive, I said to Caleb, "They're pushing their steaks these days. I'm sure they're good, but the signature dish is the mutton chop. It's not really mutton, but it's a huge, super thick loin lamb chop, and it's delicious, if memory serves."

The waiter asked, "And for the gentleman?" indicating Caleb.

"The mutton chop, medium rare, please," he said.

"I'll have the same," I said. Some vedge, and we were all set. That was easy. I couldn't explain to myself, at the time, why I felt so happy when I was with Caleb. He certainly didn't go out of his way to be agreeable. And yet he never fidgeted and looked as if he'd prefer to be elsewhere. He was always present. And, after all, what more could I expect?

The weekend seemed to fly by as Caleb and I explored the City. We took the bus that goes all the way up Madison Avenue to the Cloisters, the Met's medieval museum. The trip is nearly as interesting as the museum. Caleb took it all in. I made a mental note to take him on the 7 Train some weekend. Our journey would start at Grand Central and continue through half the world's cultures on our way to Main Street, Flushing—the city's other big Chinatown. Great Korean food, too.

I still wasn't certain what pleased Caleb, so I just took him to places I liked and to restaurants I liked and hoped I was being a competent guide. And I hoped I was getting to know him. I also hoped he was learning to like me. He played his cards close to the vest. No, it wasn't that he was secretive. It was just that he possessed a certain modesty that drove his natural reserve. I wondered if I hadn't maybe broken through it now and then. Pure fantasy?

Chapter Three

Getting back into the workday routine was a little strange. We had a meeting with Jim on Monday morning. All business, of course. Jim laid out a revised production schedule for Caleb's book. He delivered our marching orders, really. Essentially, Jim said, "I want a finished manuscript, ready for proofreading, on my desk by February 1."

We were both fine with that. It seemed doable. We returned to my office, where Harvey had set up a small desk opposite mine for Caleb to use. Facing him all day was a distraction, but a most pleasant one. Had we been working in my apartment, I doubt we'd have gotten much done. But the office setting felt like business. Gazing at Caleb over our computer screens created just enough distance to make it possible for me to edit.

I wasn't so sure about the working title—*ABOVE THE CLOUDS*. It may have been appropriate enough for a story about a young guy living in the Rockies who falls in love with flying small planes. Still I thought it lacked specificity and heart. But as long as we were all on the same page, the final title was the least of our current concerns.

And we were on the same page, I felt. I told Tisha as much when I spoke to her noontime, while she was on a lunch break. I always thought *GLITZ* magazine was exceptionally fortunate to have Tisha and her unerring fashion sense on their team. She helped to keep the publication on the cutting edge of lifestyle trends. And because I lack the fashion gene, Tisha had also kept me from making sartorial blunders on several important occasions through the years.

"So when do I meet your—our cowboy, Dan?" she asked.

"How about tonight?" I suggested.

"I don't have any food in the house, really. Couldn't we make it later in the week?"

"You don't have to cook, dear," I said. "Let's go out, someplace fun, the three of us. Will you choose a restaurant? You know everything."

"There's a newish place in Brooklyn, in Gowanus, if you can believe it. Sort of modern American cooking, mostly small dishes to share, open kitchen, cool vibe. I know the host, so I'll bet he can seat us. What time shall I tell him?"

"We have to get to Brooklyn," I said. How about 7:30? Caleb and I could pick you up in an Uber about 6:45, if that works."

"Perfect," Tisha said. "I'm dying to meet him! Have a good afternoon, darling."

"And you. Thanks, Tisha!" I said. I smiled as I thought of the two of them meeting. I knew Tisha would be charming and seductive and that Caleb would be reserved—to begin with. But Tisha would surely warm him up, and in a way I had never been able to. And it would be delightful to watch. "I made a dinner date for us," I said to Caleb when I returned to my desk. "Are you okay with that?"

"Sure," he said. We made some important revisions in Chapter Three, and then we headed home for a twenty-minute nap and a quick shower. "Does it matter what I wear?" Caleb asked.

"Not really," I said, "but why don't you wear the new sweater? With nothing under it. And you'll be ready for anything." He disappeared into his room. I headed to mine. I imagined how Caleb would look in a V-neck pullover that draped softly over his lean body. Nice. Throat a little naked, I thought. I went to my jewelry box. I had one, though I rarely wore anything other than a ring my parents gave me when I was a teenager.

I knew I owned a delicate gold chain or two. One had a little heart suspended from it. That was the one I most wanted to see Caleb wearing, but I didn't dare go there. Instead I chose the one with a little gold nugget on it. Yes. Subtle, handsome, quiet. Like the man himself. Caleb and I met in the living room at 6:30. "You look good," I said. What he actually looked was stunning.

I hated to fuss over him, but I had to get the chain around Caleb's neck. So I said, "Hold still for a moment." He did. I fastened the delicate chain in place. It was short, and the tiny nugget fell right into the lovely divot above his collarbones that I admired our first morning together. Perfect. Caleb didn't rush to a mirror to see what had happened to him. He simply touched his throat to get some idea of what I had done, and then he put on his jacket. We headed out.

"We have to get the pork belly," Tisha said. "They're famous for it. And the grilled octopus. Since there are three of us, let's start with six plates. That should do it. But we can always order more." Tisha smiled at Caleb. He smiled back, ever so slightly. "Choose something," she said to him as she gazed into his eyes. Caleb blushed faintly. I saw it, of course. I'm sure Tisha did as well.

"Why don't you and Dan choose. I like everything," he said. Tisha and I did choose—some veggie and salady things, and a vaguely Mongolian beef preparation with a sweet glaze. Nice variety. The wine was good, if overpriced. But then where isn't it? Dishes began to arrive. We were off to a great start.

"So what do you think of New York?" Tisha asked him.

"It's a little overwhelming," Caleb said. "But everyone has been very kind to me."

"That's our secret weapon," Tisha said.

"I like New York," he said. "I didn't expect to, but I do."

"Good," she said. "That makes you one of us. How do you like the octopus?"

"Very much. Should we order another one?" Tisha and I both laughed and suggested that we had probably ordered enough food.

"We could get one to go," I said, "if you want it for breakfast."

"Maybe another time," Caleb said as he smiled—not broadly, exactly, but he gave me a smile nevertheless.

As we were ordering coffee, Tisha said, "I don't know how you feel about sweets, Caleb, but I'm going to order the sticky pudding with dates and figs. It's heavenly." Caleb and I both begged off dessert, so Tisha ordered the pudding with three spoons. And then Caleb excused himself to go to the men's. "Don't talk to strangers, Cowboy," Tisha called after him. He smiled.

"Danny, oh, Danny Boy!" she said to me. "This is even worse than I imagined. If I set out to conjure up the perfect mate for you, he'd end up being Caleb. What are you going to do?"

"Good question," I said. "I'm taking it one day at a time. I'm in pain, darling, but I'm dealing with it. Thanks for your support." She took my hand and squeezed it. Caleb returned to the table just as the pudding arrived. As predicted, it was dense and sweet and irresistible, especially with a spoonful of cinnamon ice cream. I was glad to have a taste. So was Caleb.

Over coffee, Tisha said, "Gentlemen, we have to discuss Thanksgiving. My place, I think. Any input?"

"If you want to host, darling, that's great," I said. "Just give us assignments. Caleb, do you cook?" He shook his head no. "No matter," I said. "I can follow directions. And I can shop like a pro. We'll be fine. You decide on the menu, Tisha. You're so smart about these things. And then just tell me what to do—as if you haven't been telling me what to do for the last fifteen years."

"I like an obedient man," she said. And then she said, looking at Caleb, "And I also like a man who knows exactly what he wants." It was the only slightly awkward moment of the evening. But it didn't last long. We were soon piling into an Uber for the trip home. Traffic was light. The view from the

Brooklyn Bridge was breathtaking, as always. We dropped Tisha at her place and headed on to Chelsea and my apartment.

"I like Tisha," Caleb said as we took off our jackets. "And she obviously loves you. You must be a very good man to deserve her love, Dan."

"I don't know about that, Caleb," I said, "but we have some history. Get some rest. We want to be sharp tomorrow."

"I nearly forgot," Caleb said. He unfastened the chain around his neck, took my hand and pressed the jewelry into my palm with his other hand. He lingered, briefly, looking into my eyes, with both his hands enveloping one of mine. "Thank you," he said. And then he headed for his room. He paused at the bedroom door, turned back, and asked, "Do you think Tisha would go out with me?"

"I wouldn't be surprised," I said. "Ask her." And then I headed to my room. I started some deep breathing exercises as I stripped and prepared for bed. Tisha was right, of course. It was worse than any expectations. How ever could I survive a few months with Caleb in the next room instead of in my arms?

Chapter Four

On Saturday morning, as I was making coffee, my phone rang. Caleb wasn't up yet. "Hi Mom," I said. "How are you two?"

"Old," she said. "Other than that, we're both great. How are you, Danny?"

"I'm just fine, Momma. I was thinking about you."

"That's nice to hear. At least you were thinking about me, even though you didn't call."

"I guess I was thinking about calling you," I said. "I have a favor to ask. It's about Christmas."

"I'm calling to ask _you_ about Thanksgiving, and that comes first. Will you join us? We'd love to see you."

"Oh, thanks, Mom, but I've got a lot on my plate at the office. I don't feel like I can really get away. Tisha's cooking on Thursday. It should be a nice day off. Is Mary Ellen coming?"

"No, she and Hank are moving into a new house. You know your sister. Everything always has to be bigger and better. The Harrisons are joining us. It will be fine. But it would be even better with you at our table, Danny."

"Thanks, Mom, but we'll do it next year."

"I'm sure Tisha will take good care of you. We liked her, very much," she said. "But you know that.

When we thought she might be our daughter-in-law, we wanted to get to know her. It had never occurred to us we might welcome a person of color into the family, but we were ready to do it. I hope you know that, Danny."

"Yes, Momma. And I love you both for that. I'm wondering if you and Dad would mind if I brought someone with me for Christmas."

"Is my little boy in love?" she asked.

"You don't mince words, Momma," I said. "It's complicated. It's about work and it's also about love and that's all I have to say on the subject this morning. Is it okay?"

"Of course, dear. I'm sure you father will be pleased. I'll put your guest in Mary Ellen's old room. It is a man you're bringing, isn't it? I'm sure he'll be very comfortable there. She had to have the finest mattress money could buy. Some things never change."

"Thanks, Momma," I said. "I'll tell you more about it when I know myself." Indeed.

I was sitting at my desk a few mornings later when I had a sudden question. I looked up at Caleb and said, quietly, "I just realized I know next to nothing about your childhood. Will you fill me in?"

"Not here," he said. "At your place, maybe tonight."

"Okay, let's do that," I said. "We could order in pizza or something and make it an early evening.

"Sure." We headed home after work, changed into robes, and ordered in. The pizza was decent. The salad was more crunchy than flavorful. The wine was the best part of our meal. We decided to skip coffee, so I poured shots of brandy. I waited. Caleb would get to his story at his own pace.

"No one talked much about my folks except to mention how much they hated each other. Maybe always, except for the night I was conceived. Dad split, and Mom dumped her baby with her sister, Marie, who had children of her own. So I grew up in the care of a woman who didn't like me much. I survived. I had some really good teachers who encouraged me to read books and learn everything I could.

"When I was fifteen, I got a job working on the town newspaper. It was grunt work, but it was in the room where news came together. There was a reporter and an editor and an ad manager and a type setter, and they made the paper happen, every day. The publisher liked me. He offered me the little attic room that had once been used for paper storage. I went home and got my things. There weren't many— just a few clothes and a couple of books. And I moved into the newspaper building.

"I didn't bother to say goodbye to Aunt Marie and my cousins. There didn't seem to be any point in it. I haven't seen any of them since, except for once or twice by accident, in town. I managed to finish high school. And then, well, Dan, you know about my first job at the little airport. I think that's about it."

We sat quietly for a while. Caleb declined more brandy. I poured a splash for myself. Eventually, I said, "Thanks, Caleb, for sharing that with me. I'm honored by your trust." I didn't tell him how much more I loved him because he introduced me to the hurt little boy who lived within. I couldn't go there.

Instead, I let the editor in me surface. I said, "Caleb, you were hiding from me, and now you're not. That's a good thing. But you're still hiding from your readers." *Shit!* I thought, *did I really say that?* "Look, Caleb," I said. "You know your story. Whatever I think I know about you or whatever John Doe thinks he knows, it's your story. And if you don't tell it, then no one will care."

I felt like a rat. We were quiet for a while. And then we stood, put the supper things away, and got ready to end the evening. Caleb suddenly enveloped me in a bearhug that lasted for nearly a minute. Then he said, "'Night," and headed for his room.

I called after him, "Speaking of families, I want you to come with me to my parents' house in New Jersey for Christmas. *They* want you to come."

"Sure," he said. "That sounds nice." And he was gone.

📖

"I'll give you a shopping list and detailed instructions on Saturday," Tisha said when she phoned the week before Thanksgiving. "So you can get organized on the weekend. Maybe your cowboy will help you carry things."

"In his saddlebags?" I wondered.

"Or he can just be decorative, if you prefer. He's very good at that."

"No question," I said. "Tisha, I'm so grateful you're doing this for us."

"Shut up, Danny," she said. "Just try not to fuck up the side dishes!"

"Yes, dear. We'll stop by Wednesday after work with everything prepped. What time do you want us on Thursday?

"Three o'clock, maybe. No, let's make it four. So everyone can sleep late. Have fun, darling."

I got on with my day. I'm not certain how much Caleb and I accomplished that week—with his manuscript. But we showed up at the office as expected and put in our time. And afterward, we wandered the city as it performed its annual transformation into a holiday wonderland.

Caleb seemed to grow more comfortable with New York City. And with me, I hoped. We fell into a routine. Food shopping, restaurants, the drug store, the wine shop, the dry cleaner on the corner, the best cup of coffee. My neighborhood became Caleb's. He did begin to feel like my brother, just as I had predicted. Only I'd have preferred to have a brother with benefits.

"If you can fly a plane, you can peel a sweet potato," I said to Caleb on Tuesday evening. He could, of course. He could also trim brussels sprouts. I loved our kitchen time together, following Tisha's instructions.

We had already started to put together suppers in my kitchen for the two of us. Nothing too ambitious—a steak, a chop, a salad. It was a warm and happy time, except that I had no idea how I'd ever adjust to *not* having Caleb in my life, once it was time for him to move on.

📖

"You two look delicious," Tisha said as she greeted us. "I can't decide which of you I want first."

"Don't decide now," I said. "There's plenty of time for that later. Thank you dear." We presented the wine we brought and a few other goodies—crystallized ginger, mango ice cream, rolled almond cookies, and a bottle of Williams pear *eau-de-vie.*

"You know Lisa, from the magazine, don't you?" Tisha asked. I did. Caleb didn't. Introductions were made. I kissed Lisa and commented on how fortunate we all were to have Tisha as a friend. I was glad it would be just the four of us. Somehow a large, loud gathering would have seemed daunting. Tisha's apartment smelled heavenly. Instead of a traditional roast turkey, she had taken the bird apart and braised it in a Thai red curry. There were festive twists on all the usual dishes.

Once when Tisha was flirting with Caleb, Lisa said to me, "I'm glad to finally meet your cowboy, Danny. Tisha was right. He certainly is gorgeous. How's that going?"

"Yes, well, today I'm focusing on gratitude for what I have. And I'll leave regrets for what I don't have for tomorrow."

"Wise choice!" she said. "Do you believe all those aromas coming out of Tisha's kitchen? I hope she freezes the leftovers and brings them to the office."

The food was exceptional. The conversation sparkled. How could it not with Tisha at the head of the table? Caleb seemed to warm to the occasion. It wasn't that he was effusive. Just participatory. I wondered if it was new territory for him—a festive dinner with interesting people who found him charming and beautiful. There was a lot to wonder about in the handsome man across the dinner table from me.

Lisa said, "Tisha, I think we should shoot a fashion spread in Montana. Especially if we can convince Caleb to model for us. They have summer in Montana, don't they? Caleb would be a great addition to the swimsuit section." He blushed crimson. Even Tisha had never flirted her way into that kind of reaction from him.

"Lisa, I knew there was a reason I keep you around me," Tisha said. "That's brilliant. Let's start booking it first thing Monday morning. Caleb, when are you available?"

"Not until spring, dears," I said. "He's committed to his publisher. And I'll be committed to an institution if he doesn't deliver."

Caleb smiled and said, "Yes, spring, I think. You'd like spring in the Rockies. It's a little cool for swimsuits, though."

"Not to worry," Lisa said. "The lights will warm you up. And so will the production assistants. Leave everything to me, Tisha." It was that kind of evening.

When we had all overeaten and overindulged in quality beverages, we were lingering over coffee when I decided it was time for the going-home-train. I stood and said, "Amazing, Tish, as always. I've never been more thankful for you." There were kisses and good nights all around. And then Caleb and I headed out into the bracing cold of a late November night. The air was like a slap in the face. In a good way.

Chapter Five

It was late when we got home from Tisha's. Lots of good food. Lots of good wine. Neither Caleb nor I was feeling any pain. I poured two brandies, and we settled on the sofa to unwind and digest our feast before bed. It was instinctive, really, the way I leaned in toward Caleb's body, as if we were accustomed to cuddling. I gave him the opportunity to put his arm around me. He didn't. It still felt nice to be so close to him.

I knew better, of course. I had promised myself it would never happen. But I turned and moved in to kiss him. Just as our lips met, Caleb pushed me away with such force that I fell back and hit my head on the edge of the sofa arm, which was firm and angular. "Oh, shit!" Caleb said. "I'm so sorry, Dan. I wouldn't hurt you for the world."

"I'm fine," I said. "No harm done."

"You could have a concussion or whiplash or something. Let me see." He fussed over me and felt my skull, then turned my head gently in all directions. He looked me over for signs of trauma. "Are you sure you're okay?"

"Positive," I said. "Caleb, please stop worrying. It was nothing." Caleb knew better, of course. Violence is always significant, even when it's merely reflexive. And then he did something I found quite surprising. He embraced me. Caleb held me tenderly in his arms, as if I were his beloved. As if I were something rare and fragile. I half expected him to go into a cowboy lullaby. He didn't sing, but he did rock me slightly from time to time.

When Caleb released me, he said, "I'm so ashamed. I don't know what to say. I'm going to bed." Caleb couldn't bring himself to look at me, but I could tell that he had been crying. I wanted to call after him—to comfort him, to tell Caleb everything would be all right. Surely I believed that, didn't I? But I couldn't find words. Imagine that—a New Yorker with no words. I let him go. I took our drink glasses to the kitchen and then took myself to bed.

It looked as if it would be a gray holiday weekend—in the apartment, that is. The city was glorious in the late November sunlight. I couldn't decide how to handle the fact of Caleb's lashing out at me. He didn't seem to know how to handle it either. Friday morning, I made coffee and put out some little pastries Tisha had sent home with us—some savory and some sweet. When Caleb emerged from his bedroom dressed in my old robe, he looked sullen and puffy. He also looked intensely beautiful.

"Good morning, Cowboy," I said. Better to keep it light, I thought.

Caleb managed a weak smile and "Thanks for the coffee."

"What would you like to do this weekend?" I asked. I suppose I had decided to pretend that nothing had happened the night before.

Caleb avoided my gaze. "I thought I'd work on some revisions, mostly," he said.

"Sorry," I said, "that's not allowed on holiday weekends. Will you come with me to the Met Museum? There's a temporary show on African art I want to see."

"Sure, if you want," he said. I did want. We finished our breakfast, pulled on some clothes, grabbed our jackets—and Caleb's hat, of course—and headed out.

"If we take the C Train to 72nd Street, we can walk across the park. It's still beautiful this time of year, and it's not too cold today."

"Sure," he said. "I can use some exercise."

"We can always stop off somewhere for coffee or mulled cider or something if we feel chilly. I think your jacket is plenty warm." Caleb's jacket was distressed leather with a shearling collar. It screamed cowboy and sex at the same time. Is there much of a difference? Caleb was always hot, but that November morning as we set out to enjoy New York City, his beauty clutched my heart and my crotch with equal grip strength.

We didn't talk much as we waited on the platform for the next arrival. And then the train sped us five stops to 72nd Street. We also didn't talk much as we walked into the park. I watched for signposts that would head us in the direction of Fifth Avenue. The paths and the roadways meander somewhat in Central Park, but I wasn't worried about the possibility of getting lost with Caleb. Surely I'd have no such luck.

We also didn't talk much as we enjoyed the autumnal beauty of the park. A couple of times, Caleb seemed to want to reach out to me. But he always censored himself before any words emerged. I couldn't push him, of course. I smiled a lot. I introduced Caleb to the angel who guards Bethesda Fountain. He was suitably impressed. I told him about the Biblical connection that the city fathers felt when the new Croton Aqueduct brought clean drinking water to New York City for the first time. He got it.

It didn't feel as though it was the right day for lunch at the Boathouse, charming as the setting is—overlooking the little lake behind the Fountain. But there's a small carryout bar in the back where park goers can grab refreshments. And they had mulled cider! I bought two, and we sipped a while before we secured the lids and headed on our way. They made good hand warmers. Caleb was quiet. Nothing unusual there.

We exited the park onto Fifth Avenue and walked north to the Met. Caleb looked a bit dazzled. It is, after all, one of the world's great museums. I made a beeline for the African show. It's always a little confusing trying to find the entrance to the temporary exhibit gallery on the main floor, hiding in plain sight in the middle of Greco-Roman marble splendor. I found it, and we went inside.

The show was about religious art from the Kongo people. Reliquaries, mostly, in the form of fierce-looking men staunchly guarding the treasures in their care. I had seen some examples before, but I was unprepared for the haunting beauty of the hundreds of pieces that the Met had assembled. Caleb seemed awed. We both were, really. When we exited that gallery, we were suddenly in the middle of brighter lights and European culture. It's only a short walk to the Canova Perseus. Now there's male beauty for you—unblushing and unapologetic. And it isn't even ancient!

Caleb studied Perseus from all angles, as all visitors do. Just when you think his butt is your favorite part, his dick calls to you and you want to caress—visually, of course—the front of him instead. It's a delicious dilemma. I let Caleb have his fill. And then I suggested he come upstairs with me to see a few of my favorites in the permanent collection. We looked at some Whistlers, some Sargents, some Goyas, a Vermeer or two. And then I said, "How about a beer?"

"Sure," he said.

"The Met isn't going anywhere. I hope you'll return often. In fact, I hope you'll return often with me." I let it go at that. I didn't want to push Caleb. We left the museum and headed to a bar nearby. "So what shall we do for dinner?" I asked. "Jim gave us a budget, you know. So we should take advantage of it."

"Whatever you want, Dan. You know the city and I don't. You choose."

"In that case," I said, "there's a French bistro on 86th Street I've always liked. You okay with that?"

"Sure."

"Let's do it," I said. We headed back out into the last moments of that November sunset. As we walked to the restaurant, I had a keen desire to hold Caleb's hand. I didn't, of course. But when our hands brushed against each other, he didn't recoil. I took that as a good sign. We reached the restaurant. We got a table. We ordered. Caleb was quiet. We ate. We drank a decent French red. I ordered coffee. Dinner was fine. I asked for the check. And then I asked Caleb, "Shall we?"

"Sure," he said, and we rose to leave. Going home on the subway from the Upper East Side would have been a little complicated, so I hailed a taxi. Traffic was lighter than usual, because of the holiday. We got home in good time. I let us in, and Caleb headed for his room.

"Some TV?" I asked him before he disappeared behind his bedroom door.

"Sure," he said. "I'll be out in a minute." I was feeling at loose ends. I prided myself on being a good communicator, and yet I didn't feel I was getting anywhere with my new audience. For just a moment, I resented the complications that Jim had tossed into my life. It wasn't that I was blissfully happy before Caleb showed up. But at least my life was ordered and reasonably predictable and free of drama. More or less.

I got over my negativity, even before Caleb met me in the living room. He looked like a little boy in his old hoodie and sweat shorts. He also looked irresistible. I melted. "What would you like to see?" I asked. "We can watch CNN, or I can stream a movie—even a Western. I'm sure I could find one. Somewhere."

"I don't care," he said. "Dan, do you mind if we make this an early night? I've got a headache, and I'd like to just read for a while and then turn in."

"I have the perfect headache remedy," I said. "Come with Dr. Blackwell, and he'll prepare an ancient elixir that cures all ills." Caleb followed me warily into the kitchen. I poured a tall glass of club soda with a few ice cubes and several generous dashes of Angostura Bitters. I poured one for myself while I was at it. I said, "Drink this down with two ibuprofens. Recovery will be nearly instantaneous. You need looking after, Caleb. You're neglecting yourself."

Caleb took my remedy—reluctantly, as he seemed to approach all my suggestions—and then he said, "Thanks, Dan, but I don't need a nursemaid. I'm capable of looking after myself. I've been doing it for thirty years."

What I wanted to say was: *No, Caleb, you don't need a nursemaid. You need a partner.* What I *actually* said was: "No, Caleb, you don't need a nursemaid. But you *do* need people around you who love you. Don't fight it. And please don't fight me." We stood quietly for a while in the florescent glow of my kitchen, finishing our bitters and soda. I wanted to talk about plans for the rest of the holiday weekend. I decided all that could wait until morning.

"I feel better already," Caleb said. He gave me a quick hug and a peck on the cheek. "'Night," he said, and he was gone. My, my, that man could throw me off balance! I put our glasses and the breakfast things into the dishwasher, and then I headed to my room. Two more days. Two more days of holiday joy with Caleb. How would I survive them?

I made coffee on Saturday morning, but we decided to go out for breakfast. Just a coffee shop, but a very gay one. Caleb drew a great deal of attention from the other patrons. I would have felt proud to be his tablemate if I had been his boyfriend. But under the circumstances, I felt mostly sadness that I was not.

Over Belgian waffles with strawberries, I said, "I had an idea for this afternoon, if you approve. I think we should take a cruise around Manhattan. It leaves from the West Side and heads south into New York Harbor, past the Statue of Liberty, and then north into the East River and around the island. It gives a different perspective of the city from anything you see on land. How does that sound?"

"Sure," Caleb said. Enthusiasm didn't seem to be his long suit. So I decided to have enthusiasm for two.

"Good," I said. "We can order sandwiches to go, before we finish here, and we can stop at the liquor store for a bottle of wine with a screw cap and a couple of plastic glasses. Then we'll be all set for an open-air luncheon on the water. Caleb brightened just a little. I knew he wasn't resistant to the idea of spending time with me. He was simply deeply unhappy. And I had no idea why and no way of helping him out of his funk.

The Circle Line's Best of NYC cruise is great fun, and yet New Yorkers rarely take it unless they have out-of-town guests in tow. Pity. It's always cool and breezy on the water, of course. We were lucky to be on one of the last boats of the season that was wide open. Bracing, I'd call it. Caleb took it in his stride. He also smiled occasionally, which was a treat for me. We ate—and drank—our lunch up at Spuyten Duyvil. And then we sailed down the majestic Hudson for our return to the dock.

There were taxis queued up at the landing to meet our boat. We hopped into one and headed back to my place. "How about a nap?" I suggested after we got in and peeled off our outerwear.

"Sure."

I called to Caleb as he headed to his room, "Why don't we stay in tonight? We could order in something when we get hungry."

"Sure," he said. At least he wasn't picky. And still, entertaining Caleb felt a bit like hard work. Fortunately, I had never shied away from hard work. "Thanks, Dan," he said before he disappeared into his room. That was something, anyway. I headed to my room and stripped. I didn't spend a whole lot of time looking at myself in the mirror, but I couldn't help but notice that spending the afternoon with Caleb had given me what felt like a permanent erection. *Not a bad package,* I thought. *And not a bad body, if I do say so myself. I'd be proud to offer it to him. If only I could convince him to want it!* Oh, well.

Sunday morning, over coffee, I said, "Well, Cowboy, we have to get back to the daily grind tomorrow, so let's make the most of today. How about the Bronx Zoo, before they take all the animals indoors for the winter?"

"That sounds like fun," Caleb said, "but could we stay nearby, instead? I keep hearing about the High Line. Is that worth seeing?"

"Sure," I said. "We could enter at the top, which is only a few blocks from here, and then walk down to the south end and have an early dinner on Gansevoort Street." Caleb had obviously heard about the disused rail spur on the West Side that was in danger of being torn down until a group of people dreamed up a way to repurpose it. And now it's a park.

"What's Montana like?" I asked Caleb as we strolled the High Line. "I've never been there, and I have no sense of it."

"Very different from New York, I can tell you," he said. "It's rugged country, a lot of it. The mountains are very beautiful in all seasons, but I like them best in winter. There's also huge acreage of pastureland with lots of cattle—and cowboys, by the way. There aren't that many cities, and people are mostly spread out. That's why my air courier business works well. When people need to get something somewhere in a hurry, I can fly into a small, private airstrip, or even onto a cow pasture if they move the cows out of the way."

"I love Montana. I love my house. It's small and kind of rustic, and it's been my home for the last five years." Caleb became distant, and then it was as if the door shut and the light went out. We continued our walk, but I no longer had a companion on the journey. We got a table at one of the trendy eateries that have materialized in recent years. The food was fine. I was more interested in the wine. Caleb didn't seem to be interested in much of anything.

"We have to go to the new Whitney soon," I said. "Maybe next weekend." I started to say, "And we have to talk about Christmas. It's only a few weeks away." But I didn't go there. One thing at a time, I decided. We finished our dinner and headed home in silence. When we got to my apartment and took off our jackets, I headed to the kitchen to sit for a few minutes. Caleb joined me.

"Could I have another Dr. Blackwell remedy?" he asked.

"Of course," I said. I poured two glasses of the greatest *digestivo* ever devised. We sipped in silence. I wanted to leave it at that. But I couldn't do it. Instead, I said, "When you talked to me about Montana this afternoon, I almost felt that I knew you. And then you stopped, Caleb. You shut down. I don't want to talk business tonight, but I have to tell you that it's the same thing I see in your writing. You give and give, and then you suddenly freeze. You leave the reader dangling, yearning for a connection with your heart. Just as you left me dangling on the High Line this afternoon. Figuratively speaking, of course."

I couldn't believe that I had really been that—confrontational? But it was said. The ball was in Caleb's court. He gave me an "I'll be right back" sign and went to his room. He returned dressed in my old robe. I also changed, into a nightshirt Tisha had given me. Caleb said, "Could we go to the living room? I can think better in softer light." We picked up our glasses of bitters and soda, and Caleb led the way to the sofa.

"I had one great friend in my life. You probably saw his name in my dedication. You don't miss much, Dan." I decided to take that as a compliment. "Jesse and I went to school together and grew up together, really. And then we started the air courier business together. I couldn't have done it without him. It was his idea, really. He liked flying as much as I did. We were making a living.

"One night he was at my place. We had had a few beers at a tavern nearby. It was chilly, so I started a fire in the fireplace. Just as the flames danced and the room was starting to warm up a little, Jesse embraced me. And it was not a "Yo, bro" hug. He was genuinely reaching out to me. I was surprised by the urgency of his connection. His friendship had been the most important part of my life ever since I could remember. But this was new territory. I didn't mind it. I just didn't understand it.

"Jesse held me for a while. I gave no resistance until he looked into my eyes and moved in to kiss me. I pushed him away and said, 'What are you doing, man?' He looked so sad, so humiliated. Jesse grabbed his jacket and headed out the door. It had started to snow lightly, and I was worried about him driving home on slick roads. I called after him, 'Jesse, don't drive tonight. Stay here. Your room is always ready for you. Jesse, don't be a fool!'

"He ignored me. He gunned the engine of his pickup and screeched out of my driveway and then down the little road in front of my house. There didn't seem to be any point in going after him. What could I have done? Instead, I went to bed. I didn't learn until morning that Jesse had spun out on a tight curve and ended up at the bottom of a ravine, where his truck burst into flames.

"I killed him, Dan. I killed my best friend. My only *real* friend, actually. I killed him, just as surely as if I had put a bullet through his skull. And I've been living with that for the last three years. I think of him nearly every minute. I haven't had a really good night's sleep since his death. I don't expect to, ever. I'm resigned to that. You don't want to know about the nightmares or the bouts with nausea."

Caleb grew silent. I didn't know how to comfort him. I didn't want to do anything physical that could make things worse. I waited for a while. Eventually I said, "Caleb, I don't know how to comfort you. I'd like to. I'd like to share your pain and help you relieve it. But I don't know how. You'll have to show me. I'm here. I'm not going anywhere." Caleb looked at me, deeply, as if for the first time.

"Could we share a hug?" he asked. I fell into his arms, of course. I let Caleb's warmth wash over me. *That* time it was offered, not stolen. *That* time we met as equals and for mutual support. *That* time I had the man I loved right where I wanted him because he was right where he wanted to be. The rest of it—the future—would have to sort itself out. "Will you kiss me, Dan? I know I have no right to ask anything from you."

I nearly creamed in my nightshirt, but I drew back and said, "Caleb, are you sure it's what you want?"

"Certain," he said. I always thought kisses were significant, but *that* one seemed laden with import. Our first kiss had to be perfect, didn't it? I was quite nervous. Maybe even more nervous than Caleb was. After a silly hesitation, I simply kissed Caleb as tenderly as I dared. He kissed me back. So far so good. When we surfaced from that kiss and looked at each other, Caleb said, "Will you kiss me again?"

"Whenever you like," I said. We did kiss again. And again. And again. Eventually, I said, "Caleb, we don't have to pack a lifetime into this one evening. We could take it slowly. I don't want you to regret anything. I'm hoping you'll learn to feel as close to me as I feel to you." I *didn't* say, *I hope you'll learn to love me as much as I love you.* I didn't dare go there. I just put on the brakes. Lightly.

Caleb said, "Dan, you're a great editor, but I'm not so sure about how you're handling this story. I think the protagonists should make love."

"You're spot-on, Caleb," I said. "But let's work on the timing. If you come to me in some quiet, sober moment and say, 'Dan, I want you,' then I will be yours. I'll give you anything you want. And maybe some attentions you didn't even know you wanted. But I won't let you do things that are not right for you, just because you feel close to me tonight. I won't risk our friendship, Caleb. If I lost it, it would break my heart." Shit! I said that right out loud.

"I don't know, Dan," Caleb said. "I think you're wrong about this, but I don't want to argue. Could I have a good-night kiss?" I did kiss him, of course. We melted into each other as if we had always been lovers. It was warm, it was comfortable, and at the same time it had the urgency of shared passion. It wasn't easy for me to break away. But I did it. I stood up, and Caleb did, too. We both rearranged our erections in futile attempts to mask them. "One more kiss?" he asked.

"Of course." One more kiss, and then I slapped his perfect butt and said, "Sleep tight, Cowboy." Caleb went to his room, dutifully. And I went to mine—alone, sadly. But I knew I had made the right choice. Or at least I hoped I was right. I sensed that Caleb wasn't ready for his feelings for me. I wanted him to adjust to them. Gradually. I wanted him to accept that he had feelings—beyond friendship—that he had never really allowed himself before. "Don't fuck this up!" I said to myself.

Chapter Seven

The next weeks seemed strange, like being under water half the time. I did more second guessing than anything else. What if I got it wrong? What if Caleb thought I was rejecting him? What if the door was open and I missed my chance to enter? What if Caleb gave up on me and his heart moved on? What if?

We had work to do. That provided a little emotional stability for me. And we had our routine. That helped, too. I realized shortly after our Thanksgiving weekend that Caleb was taking all of my text suggestions seriously. His revisions began to show a new honesty, a new transparency. Heart maybe? It made me very happy to see it, personally and professionally. It also made me love Caleb even more. Which was not so happy.

"Why don't you come out on Wednesday so you can spend a few days with us," Momma said when I made my Christmas-planning call to her. "Will you stay for New Year's? We'd love to have you."

"Thanks, Momma, but we'll have to get back to the city. Deadlines and all. What can we bring?"

"I can't think of a thing, unless it's mistletoe," she said. "Farmers around here try to kill it off."

"I think I can handle that, Momma. I have to tell Caleb what to pack. We're not going to dinner at the country club or anything, are we?" I asked.

"No, we'll keep it casual, I think," she said.

"Good. Thanks, Momma. I'll talk to you soon. I love you."

"Take good care of my little boy," she said. "I'll never have another."

When I went off to college, I was so glad to get out of New Jersey I could hardly stand it. And yet it had been like a magnet to my soul ever since. I didn't tell Caleb about my feelings for home. It didn't seem fair, considering that I had a family and he didn't. Instead, I tried to include him—to ease him into the circle so gradually that he didn't even see it coming.

At supper that night, I said to him, "Mom wants us to come out the Wednesday before Christmas. Are you okay with that?"

"Sure."

"She asked us to stay through New Year's, but I told her we needed to get back. We're not going out for a fancy dinner or anything, so just stick a few comfortable things in a bag. Which reminds me, I have a small wheelie you can use. I'll get it out after supper."

"Thanks, Dan," he said. "That sounds good."

"I booked a Zipcar after I talked to Mom. I figured it's only for a few days, and it makes better sense than trying to go out on the bus with luggage and packages and all."

"Sure," Caleb said. "Just let me know my share of the car rental. I'd like to take gifts to your parents, but I don't know them. What do you think?"

"That's very kind of you, Caleb. It's not necessary, but I'm sure they'd be touched. Mom has lots of interests. Gardening, most of all, I guess. It's kind of off-season for that. I don't know. Let me think about it. Dad used to be a fisherman, but I don't think he does that anymore. Even so, maybe we'll find something at Orvis. I'll help you. Caleb, it just occurred to me that Dad always wanted to be a pilot and never did anything about it. I bet he'll want to take you to the local airstrip. Are you okay with that?"

"Sure," he said. "I always have my license on me. I don't know what the facilities are like there, but if they have rental planes, I could take him up for a spin."

"You'd do that?"

"Of course, Dan," he said. "I'll do anything that makes you happy." I was stunned. Literally. I froze for a few seconds. And then I finished my supper in silence.

After we straightened up the kitchen, I said to Caleb, "Let me get that wheelie, so I don't forget." I pulled it down from the top shelf of my bedroom closet and brought it to him. "You only need two or three changes of clothes, so this should be plenty big."

"Thanks, Dan," he said. "What do you want for Christmas?"

I was stunned again and at a loss for words. My first thought was: *All I want for Christmas is you.* I didn't go there, of course. Instead I said, "All I need is a promise that we'll meet our deadline."

"Done," he said. "Maybe I can think of something else, too."

"How about you, Caleb? What do you want for Christmas?" I asked.

"I have everything I need," he said. "I have the chance to make my manuscript the best it can be, and I have a new friend. So, I'm good. 'Night." A quick peck on the cheek and he was gone. I poured myself a brandy and sat at the kitchen counter for a while. I started to create an elaborate scenario that began with my knocking on Caleb's bedroom door. Surely he would invite me in. And then surely he would invite me into his bed. And then surely he would make tender love to me.

And surely it was not going to happen. Not that night, anyway. Some other night? I didn't dare go there. It was too cruel.

Tisha and I met for a quick lunch before she left for her holiday trip. I brought along the Christmas gift I had chosen for her—a silk scarf with splashes of color like a Cézanne. Tisha gave me an alpaca scarf in a wonderful shade of toasted orange—persimmon maybe? "When inspiration strikes twice," she said. I told Tisha that Caleb and I had kissed, of course. "And?" she asked.

"And then I told him I wouldn't make love to him until I was certain he was ready for it."

"'Right out of the age of chivalry, that boy,'" Tisha said. I probably looked puzzled. "Lee Patrick in *NOW YOYAGER*, one of my favorite films. Look, darling, I think you're stellar, and I think Caleb is stellar, and I think you two are destined to enjoy a long life together. How you get there is none of my business. Just don't wait too long, sweetie. There's always low hanging fruit available."

"Thank you, dear," I said. "You've always said how much you hate Chicago. Why do you go back every year?"

"Danny, I always thought that you had an easier childhood than I did. I've met your parents, after all. Say hello to Elaine and Richard for me, please. They were very kind to me. Don't think I've forgotten that. The rest of it doesn't really matter, and I refuse to compare battle scars with anyone. But I think you know, Danny. I'm certain you know. There's a pull, like the fucking moon on the fucking tides."

Tisha grew silent. I knew exactly what she meant, of course. I said, "Do what you have to do, darling, and then hurry home to us. But don't make any plans for me for New Year's Eve. I'm keeping my options open."

I got through the weeks leading up to Christmas with the help of our routine. Caleb was always pleasant, but we never seemed to regain the closeness we had felt that one Sunday night. I was resigned—or nearly so—to the notion that I had mishandled the situation. That the chance was gone. It was not a nice feeling.

We did some Christmas shopping on the last weekend before our trip. We went in a different direction for Momma, away from gardening and crafts. Caleb spied a silk dressing gown at Bergdorf's in lovely rose and mint-green stripes. It was frightfully expensive. "I think I have to get this for your mother," he said.

"Out of the question," I said. He gave me his best "I'm going to do this whatever you say" look. I relented. I said, "Will you share it with me? The expense and the gift?" He indicated that he would. I said, "Then let's get it and get out of here before we get into more trouble."

We headed to an antiquarian bookstore that was a favorite of mine. Caleb was like a kid in a candy store. I spied a signed copy of Alan Davidson's *NORTH ATLANTIC SEAFOOD.* I hoped Dad would appreciate it. I had already chosen a gift for Caleb and secreted it away in my room. Caleb found a biography of Amelia Earhart—also a signed first edition. I assured him it would make a fine gift for Dad. We paid for our treasures and headed home.

With shopping out of the way, it was just a matter of getting through the next few days before our holiday. I started to dread the trip because it meant spending several days next to Caleb but with a thin wall between us. Would the wall come tumbling down? Who knew? I was mostly on autopilot. Caleb seemed fine, as always. If he was suffering even half as much as I was, he certainly didn't show it.

Chapter Eight

We arrived in Ridgewood just after three on Wednesday afternoon. The folks came out to greet us. "Mom and Dad, this is Caleb Bromley. Caleb, please meet Elaine and Richard Blackwell." There were greetings all around.

"Come in, come in," Mom said. "It's cold out here."

"Thanks for the invitation, Mrs. Blackwell," Caleb said as we picked up our bags and headed inside.

"Call me Elaine. And we're pleased to have you. Take off your coats and I'll hang them here, by the door."

"I'm Richard," Dad said. "How was the drive out?"

"Not bad," Caleb said. "Dan's a great driver."

"He had a great teacher," Dad said. "Let's get you two settled in your rooms. Then come downstairs. I'm tending bar."

I put our Christmas gifts on the sideboard in the dining room, and I gave Mom the little things we had brought—mistletoe, a bottle of port, some chocolates made by a little chocolatier in the Village, and a bottle of Mom's favorite after-bath splash. I led Caleb to the staircase. "I still remember the way," I said to my folks. "You don't have to come up." We headed upstairs. I took Caleb to Mary Ellen's old room and said, "You can unpack if you want. Then come get me—just across the hall—and we'll go downstairs to-gether. Thanks for coming, Caleb."

Before I could turn and head to my room, Caleb put his beautiful hands on my shoulders, drew me to him, and kissed me. I kissed him back, of course. "Welcome to New Jersey," I said. "I hope you enjoy your stay."

"I'm sure I will," he said. My head was spinning, but I managed to get to my room and to head to my bathroom to pee and freshen up a little. Caleb came to my room in a few minutes, and we headed down-stairs together and settled in on the sofa.

"I'm sure the sun is over the yardarm some-where," Dad said. "What can I get you to drink?"

"A glass of white wine, I think," I said.

"Caleb said, "I'll have the same, please."

"Coming right up." Dad poured drinks, and we sipped them. We made small talk. Caleb was quiet but present. And then Dad said, "Caleb, why don't you let me show you the property? We have nearly four acres here." *And a toolshed/workroom*, I thought.

"Sure," he said. They got their coats and went out the back door.

When Mom and I we were alone, she said, "He seems like a very nice young man, and he's certainly easy on the eyes. But, I don't know, Danny. He's not your usual type."

"I don't have a type, Momma. I fell in love with *Caleb*. Maybe he wants me, too. It's possible. And if he does, then I'll never let him go. It's that simple. And I hope you and Dad will be happy for me."

"Of course, dear. It's just that Steve was ... more like you, I guess. Educated, urban professional. You and Steve looked like a couple."

"Well, Momma, maybe Caleb and I will grow to look alike, in time, like you and Dad."

"I suppose I deserved that," she said. "It's just that people with more in common seem to be more comfortable together. But what do I know?"

"Momma, you should be writing romances. Your stories would be super easy to edit. I've always found real life a little more complicated. Caleb has never been in love before. No, that's not the truth. He loved his childhood friend with his whole heart. But he wouldn't allow himself to express that love physically. Now, maybe, he'll find the freedom to love me completely. I don't know yet. But I'm willing to wait to find out."

Mom embraced me and she said, "How did you get to be so smart?"

"Good DNA," I said. "What's the plan for the rest of the day?"

"Not much," she said. "I have a pork roast in the oven. You always liked that. After dinner we can watch TV or talk or whatever you like. Would you mind if I show Caleb our picture albums?"

"Thanks for the heads-up on that," I said. "I suppose it's inevitable. Humiliating your kids by showing off their most awkward moments seems to be in the *MOTHERS' HANDBOOK*."

"The *SONS' HANDBOOK* calls for respect for parents, as I remember. Or did they change that?" she asked.

"No, Momma, the respect part is still there," I said. "I'm sorry I was snippy with you."

"Forgiven," she said. "Why don't you grab your coat and join the boys? Caleb can probably use a breather by now. Tell them dinner is at 6:00."

"I love you, Momma," I said as I embraced her. And then I headed outside to rescue Caleb. I found him and Dad down by the duck pond. The ducks were going about their ducky business and looking very handsome in their winter plumage. They would be fine until the pond froze over, at which point they'd have to move into the shelter on the side of the pond and we'd have to bring them food from the feed-and-grain store. Yes, duck feed is a thing. Or, rather, *Dad* would have to attend to all that because I no longer lived there.

There were floods of memories, of course. I remembered how I refused to eat duck when Mother roasted two for our dinner. Until I was a teenager, I guess. And they weren't even our ducks! Caleb looked wonderful in the late afternoon cold. His cheeks and the tip of his nose were rosy. And his eyes sparkled in the horizontal sunlight that caressed his face just before it moved on to the next time zone that needed its blessing.

"Mom says dinner's at 6:00." I delivered my missive, dutifully. And then I said, "Are you guys warm enough? You could come back inside and add a sweater, you know."

"I'm good," Caleb said. His smile told me that he was fine with the tour. I left them to it. When Caleb and Dad came back indoors, they had already planned a trip to the community airstrip for the following day. Dad seemed delighted. And so did Caleb, really. He hadn't been aloft in weeks, after all, and the air was his natural habitat.

Mom was busy in the kitchen, as she so often was. I asked if I could help. "No thanks, dear," she said. "You didn't inherit the culinary gene. But then neither did Mary Ellen. I expect you'll both survive. You could set the table, though." I did. Dad opened two bottles of a rather nice red. We were on our way.

Dinner was delicious, really—if a little retro. I had forgotten about Mom's roast loin of pork with a few gingersnaps in the gravy. It was quite wonderful. One meat, one starch, and two vedge—one green, one yellow. All the major food groups. Tried and true. And immensely satisfying.

After dinner we had coffee in the living room. Dad offered to open the port we had brought. I suggested he save it for Christmas Day. I accepted a cognac, but then there's no surprise there. And so did Caleb. Mom brought out the photo albums, of course, and Caleb got to laugh at one dorky stage in my development after another. I asked for more cognac. And then I followed Mom to the kitchen.

"That was delicious, Momma," I said. "But it's so much work! Can we take you out to dinner, maybe tomorrow night?"

"No, dear," she said. "You can take us out when we come to visit you in the City. I don't think I trust you to cook my dinner."

"Wise woman," I said. "I'm so grateful for this, Momma. I always love coming here at holiday time, but this year it's ... it's ... I don't what it is. I love him so much, Momma. Thank you for welcoming him."

"Hush, baby," she said as she embraced me. "It will all work out. My little boy turned into the smartest man I know. And the best man I know—after your father, of course. You'll deal with it. Why don't you get some rest? I think all New Yorkers suffer from sleep deficit."

When we headed upstairs, Caleb followed me into my bedroom and said, "Dan, you grew up with all this?" I gestured to my desk chair. He took a seat. I sat on my bed and started untying my shoes.

"As Tisha would say, 'I refuse to compare battle scars.' My childhood was what it was. Some of it was great. Some of it was intensely painful. I'm more interested in the present."

"I like your parents, Dan," Caleb said. "They've both been very kind to me, of course, but what I like best about them is how much they love you. Maybe I've never seen that. I'm not talking about what I didn't get when I was a child. I mean that I've never seen two parents who love their son so unconditionally." Caleb grew silent.

I didn't know where to go with our conversation. I stood and said, "Get some sleep, Cowboy. We have a big day tomorrow. Christmas Eve and all." Caleb stood and embraced me. I was in my stocking feet and he still had his boots on, so he was considerably taller than I was. I liked the perspective. Caleb looked at me intently. I had only seen that look once before. And then he kissed me.

Caleb looked at me again and said, "Dan, I love you." I was speechless. He gave me another kiss and said, "'Night." And he disappeared into Mary Ellen's old room. *Fuck!* I thought. *Did I hear that right? Did Caleb Bromley just declare that he loves me?* I can't say that I trusted my senses, exactly. But I floated to bed and got on with something that was a little bit like sleeping.

I was slightly groggy in the morning. But I got myself up anyway and took a long shower. That helped a little. Caleb, on the other hand, looked bright as a button when I threw on my robe and walked across the hall to make sure he was up. "Good morning, Cowboy," I said. "How did you sleep?"

"Great," he said. "This mattress is amazing."

"Suburban living obviously agrees with you," I said. "Hungry?"

"Sure."

"Give me five minutes to throw on some clothes," I said, "and I'll come get you." I dressed, and we headed downstairs, where Mom had morning in full swing.

"Come to the kitchen," she said. "Caleb, sit there. I'll bring you some coffee. There's milk and sugar on the table. How do you like your eggs?"

"Over easy, please," he said.

"Danny, I'll scramble yours, unless you've changed your ways. Richard!" she called. "Come join the boys. We see so little of Danny, let's not waste a moment." Dad did come to the kitchen, and he sat next to me. I was unused to the proximity, but I liked it. It felt natural. After all the friction—

especially in my teen years—we had come to an understanding. More than that, really.

I had dropped all my negative feelings for him—for both of them. And I think he had done the same. And what remained was simply love. Yes. "So, you two are going up into the wide blue yonder today," I said. "Are you getting a flying lesson, too?"

"I doubt it," Dad said. "But we're never too old to learn, Danny, as I hope you have the good fortune to experience. What are you and your mother up to today?"

"Not much, I think," I said. "I'm going to drive Mom into the village to do some food shopping. Put in your order before you head to the airstrip. And then I'm planning to take a nap. I'm not used to the quiet here, but it's coming back to me."

"Good," he said. And then he looked at me, carefully, in a way that was unfamiliar. And Dad said, "I'm glad to have you here, son." I can't remember having teared up at breakfast before. I embraced him. That was not such a familiar occurrence either.

"You two be careful," I said. "I want both of my men home in one piece." Did I really say that? Apparently. And no one batted an eye. We finished breakfast. And Mom started cleaning up, of course.

Dad said to Caleb, "The reservation is for 10:00, so we should head out shortly."

"Sure," he said. "Wear a sweater, Mr. ... Richard. It gets cold up there, in all kinds of weather."

"Done," Dad said. "I'll meet you at the front door in twenty minutes." He and Caleb headed to their rooms to dress for their adventure. I lingered over coffee.

"Momma, please join me," I said. She paused her work, picked up her coffee mug, and came to the table. "Thank you," I said.

"For?"

"For everything." We sat quietly for a while. And then I said, "Last night Caleb told me he loves me."

"Isn't that cause for celebration?" Momma asked. "You seem very quiet this morning, Danny."

"I suppose I am," I said. "It all seems so complicated—not as simple as two people who love each other. Caleb lives in Montana and I live in Manhattan, for instance. How will that work?"

"I expect it will work however you two decide to make it work," Mom said. "You're too smart to let logistics get in your way, Danny. For what it's worth, I think Caleb is adorable. And I think you'd be a fool to let him get away." I teared up for the second time that breakfast. "Now, why don't you run along and play, dear. I have work to do. Let's go shopping at 10:30. I want to be sure the fish market isn't sold out."

Mom had an Italian-American neighbor once who always cooked lots of seafood on Christmas Eve. Seven varieties, actually. Momma never went that far, but she liked to serve a fish or two. And I knew there would be lots of other goodies as well. The shopping expedition went smoothly. Mom made her selections with a trained eye. I hauled the bounty to the car.

Mom chose everything she would need for dinner that night, plus the Christmas ham and all the fixings that would accompany it. It seemed like enough to feed an army, but I suspected the four of us would manage to put a healthy dent in it. I helped Mom put everything away. Dad and Caleb returned from the airstrip shortly thereafter. Dad was flushed and effusive. Caleb looked—beautiful.

"I think we've earned a hot toddy," Dad said. "You too, Elaine. It isn't Christmas every day." He went about the business of making drinks for all of us. I started a fire in the fireplace. And then Caleb and I headed upstairs to change into comfy clothes. I saw that Mom had hung mistletoe just above the bottom step. I gestured to Caleb to join me under it. The folks were both in the kitchen. I put my arms around Caleb and kissed him warmly.

"Merry Christmas, darling," I said. I had never called him darling before. I liked the sound of it. He smiled broadly. We headed up, changed, and went downstairs to join the folks. Hot buttered rum, I think, was what Dad concocted. "So, Dad," I said, "are you ready to take up flying?"

"If Caleb will take me up now and then, I think that will do it." Caleb assured him he would be happy to do just that.

"So, Caleb," I said, "what do you think of New Jersey?"

"I don't know what I was expecting, exactly," he said. "But I didn't expect apple orchards and horse farms and so many trees. I like it. On the ground, too." The folks smiled. I melted. It was a warm, quiet afternoon. I tried to help Mom with her dinner chores. As usual, she allowed me only the safest tasks.

Dinner was delicious, as expected. And Dad served good wine, as expected. We had coffee in the living room, as before. I stoked the fire. Everything felt warm and festive. And I had my Christmas cowboy next to me on the sofa, after all. Instead of cutting a tree, Dad had strung lights on trees outside the living room window, and outside the dining room window as well. Mom had toned down her decorations since Mary Ellen and I left home. But it still felt like Christmas. The small clusters of jingle bells hanging on the door handles made me a little misty.

"What time do you want us to appear in the morning?" I asked.

"I don't know, 9:00?" Mom suggested. I looked toward Caleb and he seemed fine with that.

"Done," I said. And we headed up to bed. We kissed, at the top of the stairs, and then we turned to our separate rooms. I was giddy with the pleasure of knowing that Caleb had real feelings for me and with the anticipation of how we would act on them. I didn't know what else to do, so I brushed my teeth and turned in.

An hour or so later, Caleb came quietly into my bedroom and sat on the side of my bed. I was only half asleep, and suddenly having Caleb sitting beside my naked body was enough to wake me thoroughly. He said, "Dan, you told me I could come to you some quiet, sober moment. Well, it's *very* quiet in New Jersey, and I'm reasonably sober. And I have to tell you that I want you so badly that I can't bear to be without you, Dan. Please let me love you."

"Get in," I said. Caleb stood and dropped his sweatpants. I pulled back the covers in a gesture of invitation. He slipped in beside me. I rearranged the bedclothes to give both of us some warmth. Caleb's kiss I understood. I had been there before. The warmth of his hands on my body and the feeling of his bare chest against mine were all new sensations. I reached for his buttocks and pulled him tightly to me. Our erections fit nicely side-by-side.

Caleb seemed a little tentative about where he wanted to go with our first union, so I took charge. I rolled on top of him, kissed him deeply, and then began to explore his chest. He shivered when I nibbled his nipples. He let me continue down his torso. Every inch was sweet and inviting. When I reached Caleb's crotch, I buried my face in the warmth between his legs and drank in his scent.

I wanted to move in. I began to cry, softly. I'd have been happy to spend the night—and the rest of my life—right there. I nuzzled Caleb's balls. They offered themselves to me. I took them into my mouth, alternately. And finally I explored the treat that had long fascinated me. How can I describe Caleb's dick? It was perfection, really. Straight and proud; ample but not scary. A dick for every day and twice on Sunday—and thrice on holidays. With foreskin, too!

I tried to honor Caleb with my mouth. I must have gotten something right, because he rewarded me shortly with a flood of precious sweetness. I savored every drop. Perhaps another time—if we had other times—I would save some of the bounty to share with him. But not that night. Not our first time. I needed to have Caleb's gift all to myself. When he had recovered a bit, he pulled me up so that he could kiss me.

"Dan, that was amazing," he whispered. "I don't know what to say."

"Then don't say anything," I suggested. Instead of speaking, he rolled us over so that he was on top. Caleb proceeded to give my body a quick tour before he ended up in the male department. I needed nothing more from him than the closeness we had already shared, but I gladly accepted Caleb's attention to my dick. He seemed tentative at first, but then he relaxed into it. The warmth of Caleb's mouth and the fact of his hands on my body pushed me right over the edge.

We lay quietly together for a while. And then I whispered, "Merry Christmas, Caleb. I love you so much I can hardly stand it." Caleb began to snore very softly. I wrapped my arms around him and gave in to sleep.

In the morning, as we stirred, with our bodies still entwined, Caleb said, "Dan, this is the best Christmas ever. Can we share lots more of them?"

"That's my plan," I said. We sat up in my bed and looked at each other in the morning sunlight. "How do you manage to be so beautiful, Caleb?" I asked. He blushed.

Caleb said, "I've wanted you since the moment we met, Dan. It seemed awkward—business and all. And I didn't know—I still don't know—how to love you properly. I don't know how it's supposed to work, between two men."

"I wouldn't worry about that. You have excellent instincts, Caleb" I said. "I'm way ahead of you, by the way. I've wanted you since your author photo arrived at Scrive. Truly. Since my first glance. And the real thing is even better." We kissed for a while. Then Caleb reached for my dick—which responded instantly. He was like a child with a new toy.

He said to me, "You know, I never thought too much about it, but I always liked my dick, I suppose. But I like yours better. Dan, it's so beautiful. And it's so like you—it's strong, and sweet, and generous. I could play with it forever."

"Good," I said. "I'll hold you to it." He started to speak again, but I stopped him with a kiss. Then I said, "Look, Caleb, if I get any happier, my heart will burst." Caleb had been so reserved the previous weeks, but once he started to speak it was difficult to stop him. I kissed him again—morning mouth and all—and then I said, "Mom likes to make a nice Christmas breakfast. We should probably put in an appearance."

Caleb got out of bed to slip back into his sweatpants. The beauty of the body I had caressed the night before—now seen in the winter morning sunlight—astounded me. The perfection of his ass as he lifted first one leg and then the other to step into his pants was heartbreaking. I wanted to tell him, but I didn't dare go there. Instead, I said, "You have beautiful legs, Caleb. I thought cowboys were supposed to be bowlegged."

"Well, I'm not a cowboy, Dan. I don't mind when you call me that, but I'm actually a sky jockey. I know you like editorial accuracy." I threw my pillow at him, and Caleb dove back into my bed and threw his arms around me. "I love you, Dan," he said. "I want to hold you forever."

"Good thinking," I said. "Let's arrange it. Right after breakfast."

Christmas breakfast was delicious, of course. Sausages and eggs and sautéed apples. And Mom toasted some wonderful challah from the Jewish bakery in the next town. "Delicious coffee, Momma," I said. "I don't remember coffee this good when I was growing up."

"No, I get this blend mail order. They still had A&Ps when you were younger, so I just bought their Bokar. It seemed good enough at the time. But now we're spoiled. Should we open gifts? Bring your coffee with you." We did as we were told, of course, and headed for the dining room.

First thing, Caleb and I gave Mom the dressing gown we bought for her. She ooohed and aaahed and went right to the kitchen to take off her robe and put on the new one. She looked terrific in it, and we told her so. I was relieved that we had gotten the colors right. Tisha always said I lack the fashion gene. True, but I have a color sense I can usually trust.

Mom gave me a package to open. It was a merino sweater in a bulky knit with a front zipper—like a jacket with a hood. Navy blue. "Because you don't dress warmly enough," Momma said. I thanked them both. We traded our other gifts. Dad claimed he loved the Alan Davidson seafood book I bought him and the Amelia Earhart biography Caleb brought. The folks gave Caleb a bolo—a vintage Navajo silver one with a lovely piece of turquoise in it. He was speechless. But he embraced each of them.

I gave Caleb a rare, signed first edition of Zane Grey's *RIDERS OF THE PURPLE SAGE*. Caleb embraced me. And he kissed me. In front of my parents! Their holiday smiles never wavered. Caleb gave me a Mont Blanc pen. "Try it," he said. "They have other nibs." We found some paper for me to test the pen on. It was silky smooth, and the ink was red! I would have loved to wrestle Caleb to the floor and have my wicked way with him. But I settled for a thank-you embrace.

"Let's have a splash of Madeira with the last of our coffee," Dad said. "Elaine, is there maybe a little more?" She assured him there was, and she came back from the kitchen to warm up our cups. Dad poured Madeira all around. We sat in contented silence for a while.

Dad said, "We always thought we were creating this place for our two kids, didn't we, Elaine?" Mom looked to be in at least partial agreement. "But I'm not so sure these days. There's nothing here that Mary Ellen wants. And it doesn't seem to really work for you either, son." I probably looked a little frozen. "Your Mother and I have decided to take an apartment in the village. If you want this house, it's yours, Danny. We'll work something out with Mary Ellen's inheritance so there's no friction. And if you don't want it, then we'll sell it, I suppose."

You could have knocked me over with a feather, as they say. I embraced Dad and held him longer than I ever had done. Finally, I managed to say,

"You've thrown me a curve ball, I think it's called. I don't know what to say, Dad. It never occurred to me that you and Mom would want to downsize, and it never occurred to me that I could live anywhere but Manhattan. But I'm more touched by the offer than you'll ever know. I get it. I know this isn't easy for either of you. Will you give me some time to consider it?"

"Take all the time you need, son," he said. "The offer stands." I looked at Mom, hoping to gain a little perspective. She seemed comfortable with the situation. I looked at Caleb, who seemed just as dazed as I was. I had had that same deer-in-the-headlights look, surely, the first time I met Steve's parents. Ah, families. God bless 'em.

"Why don't you boys go outdoors and enjoy this beautiful afternoon?" Mom said. She didn't need to add, "and let me clean up this mess." We all knew that was part of it. I kissed both of my parents, and Caleb and I headed upstairs to bundle up. I took my new sweater along. I asked him to come to my room and help me figure out the situation.

We sat on the side of my bed for a bit. "If you don't kiss me immediately, I'll probably die," I said. Caleb indicated that he didn't want to see that happen. He kissed me. And then he held me as I shivered and twitched and tried to figure out what life had just hurled in my direction.

We only began to talk about it when we were walking the grounds. "This is crazy," I said. "I've spent half my life trying to get out of New Jersey. Why would I want to come back?"

"Because you love it?" Caleb wondered. "You seem comfortable here," he said. "Dan, I've never seen you so relaxed as you've been since we arrived on Wednesday afternoon." I took my time trying to process that information.

"Caleb, we have enough to deal with already," I said. "We've got Manhattan and Missoula, to begin with. I want to spend my life with you, Caleb. I want us to be together. I'm not sure I could share you with Montana or any other place. And you like to be up in the air. I'd just as soon not get any higher than the twelfth floor. What are we going to do about this?"

"If you let me love you, Dan," Caleb said, "we'll figure it out. I have some decisions to make. I think I want to become a full-time writer. I've found more joy in it—and in meeting you—than in anything else in my life. The guy who's running my air courier business wants to buy it. I'm probably ready to sell." Caleb grew silent.

"But, Caleb," I said, "could you really give up Montana? It seems like such a part of you."

"Well, you heard Tisha. She says I'm a New Yorker now. I could let go, with you at my side, Dan. I can do anything if you'll stay with me." I pressed Caleb against the first tree we came to and kissed him. Hard.

"What about your house, Caleb?" I asked. "I know you love it."

"Yes, well, I won't give it up until you come to stay with me there for a week or two, Dan. In February, maybe. Jim won't mind. You've earned a vacation. If you come with me and help me make some new memories there, I'll be ready to move on." I started to get weepy, or maybe it was the wind in my face.

"Have we just solved the first part of the equation?" I asked.

"I believe we have," Caleb said.

"You're good at this," I said. "What next?"

"Dan, you can work from anywhere there's a decent Internet connection. And so can I. We could live here part of the time, because you love it and because it would give me a chance to fly. I might even convince you to let me take you up some time."

"I want to share everything you love, Caleb," I said. "Of course I'll go up with you—as long as it isn't for too long or too often." Caleb kissed me.

"Dan, will you marry me?" he asked.

"Whoa, Cowboy," I said. "I mean, whoa, Sky Jockey. I'd marry you tonight, Caleb, but I need to be certain you're certain. Let's let our feelings grow and develop for a while. We have so much to learn about each other."

"You don't have to decide today, Danny. You don't have to feel rushed. Not about me or about this house. But I'm hoping you'll come to me some quiet, sober moment and say, 'Caleb, I want you.'" I chased him through the trees in the back yard, just above the duck pond. We'd have thrown snowballs at each other, had there been enough accumulation of snow. Even without, it was still a winter wonderland.

We stopped and caught our breath. I looked closely at the exquisite creature who loved me—who just proposed marriage to me. He looked radiant. I said to him, "Yes. Yes, I'll be honored to marry you, Caleb. Just give me a month or two."

"We'll do it your way," he said.

"Yes, dear," I said. And that time it was *Caleb* who chased *me* around the yard until he caught me and embraced me with such force that I feared for my ribcage. "Caleb, you've practically killed me with joy already. Please don't finish me off." He relaxed

his grip into something more manageable. "Perfect,"
I said.

"There's plenty of time before dinner," Caleb said.
"Do you think your folks would mind if we went up
to your room—or my room—for a while?"

"I think they expect it," I said. "I'll race you to the
house." And that's what we did with our afternoon.
Delicious.

Chapter Eleven

Driving back to the city on Sunday afternoon was mercifully uneventful. The goodbyes were the hardest part. I had experienced it before—a sense of longing when leaving my parents. It was more intense this time. It was a combination of factors, I suppose. They were both in robust good health but undeniably older. I wouldn't have given it much thought had they not decided to move into an apartment. Mortality, anyone?

And then there was the matter of the house. I was still shocked that the folks were willing to entrust to my care the product of decades of life and work and dreams. Was I even up to the challenge? Would I be able to honor their gift properly? Did I even want to? Who the hell knew? Caleb beside me in the front seat of our Zipcar helped to ground me.

I glanced at Caleb frequently, maybe trying to convince myself he was real. Every time I glimpsed him, he was looking at me and smiling. I said, "I love you," several times, for no particular reason other than that I did. Caleb put his hand on my leg. The sensation went right to my crotch. It was so distracting I had to ask him to remove his hand. It would have been a shame to spin out on Rte. 17 with so much future ahead of us.

When we got back to the City, we returned the car and headed home. We were down to one wheelie each after having parted with all the Christmas goodies. It was only a few blocks, so we walked. I smiled a lot. So did Caleb. Two new men entered my old apartment that evening. It welcomed us just the same. I looked around and realized that I had done next to nothing to spruce up the place in recent years. That might have to change.

"You know, we could turn the second bedroom into an office," I said. "If you even want to stay here."

"Of course I want to stay here," Caleb said. "I love this apartment. And most of all, I love you, Dan." That got my full attention. I interrupted our undressing and unpacking long enough to wrap myself around Caleb and hold him as if my happiness depended upon him—as indeed it did.

Caleb returned my embrace. "You feel so good," he said. "You give me everything I need, Dan. Please let me hold you always."

"Petition granted," I said. "On the condition that these embraces include kisses. Otherwise, you'll be in default." Caleb stopped my foolish prattle with a long, slow kiss. Perfect. "Why don't we order in something light?" I suggested. "Something mostly salad, maybe? Or how about Japanese? We could order soup, salad, and sashimi."

"I'd like that," Caleb said. Done. We hadn't shared a meal—just the two of us—in days. It would be a different experience, sitting across from Caleb at my dinner table now that he had given himself permission to love me. Everything would be different, really. And everything would be better, surely. Wouldn't it?

The food was good. The company was better. But Caleb was not the same man who had sat opposite me the previous weeks. He was just as handsome and just as gentle and winning. But Caleb had acquired a new glow. He seemed always on the brink of a grin. In short, he was visibly in love. I wondered if I gave myself away with the same foolish face. Probably.

After dinner we straightened up a bit. I said, "Caleb, please come to my bed. I need you there."

"Sure, Danny," he said, "but let me grab a shower first. I feel a little sticky."

"Forget it," I said. "I want all of you. Don't edit a thing for me, Caleb." We laughed. We kissed. We tumbled into my bed. We didn't need to actually *do* anything. But I wanted to express my love for him, and actions speak louder than words, after all. I was dying to rim Caleb—had been ever since Christmas morning when he showed me his perfect ass in the early sunlight. But I didn't think he was ready for that. And I didn't want to spook him. It could wait, surely.

Instead I explored other regions. When I got to his armpits, I said, "Caleb, please stop wearing deodorant. I want to taste *you*, not a chemical factory." He smiled broadly. Caleb had ten fingers and ten toes—all delicious. Nice feet, too. I took my time. When I finally reached Caleb's glorious cock it was more than ready for my attention. I savored the slight muskiness and made a mental note to ask Caleb how he had managed to escape the scalpel.

So much to learn about him. *I'm going to marry a man with a beautiful body and a beautifully natural dick,* I thought. *Life is sweet.* I did my best to honor Caleb. I got my reward. And as I had promised myself, I saved his gift until I could share a big, cummy kiss with him. Caleb seemed surprised but not alarmed.

"How did you do that?" he asked.

"Ancient family secret. But if you're a careful student, you'll learn."

"Yes, Master. Please teach me," he said.

"Anything, Grasshopper." Every moment with Caleb was bliss. I got weepy a lot those days during and after Christmas. It seemed cruel that we'd have to go back to work in the morning. But we'd be together, after all. So, it was still good. "Choose a side," I said to Caleb, indicating my bed. "I'm used to sleeping here," I said, pointing stage left (or house right). "But I really don't care, if you have a preference. Caleb, I'll sleep anywhere as long as I have you in my arms."

"Dan," he said, "I'm so used to sleeping alone that I never thought too much about it." He paused and got a little misty. And then he said, "Danny, will you really sleep with me every night? Will you hold me and keep me safe?"

"Hush, baby," I said as I embraced him. "I'm here, and I've got you, and that's the story. And there's nothing to edit." Caleb laughed. We got on with the business of brushing teeth and getting into bed. When we had snuggled together and kissed goodnight, I turned out the last light and spooned Caleb. He took my left hand in his. His breathing became regular and audible. And I said to myself, "Daniel Nathan Blackwell, you are home."

📖

Tisha got home from her Chicago trip on Monday night. I phoned her at lunchtime the next day. "I missed you, darling," I said. "How was it?"

"Like swallowing razor blades, as usual, but never mind that. How are you?"

"Tish, Caleb asked me to marry him, if you can believe it."

"Ooooh, Danny Boy. You work fast! I always thought you were hot, but not *that* hot. How did you manage it?" she asked.

"I don't know," I said. "Maybe it was about getting out of the city and sharing Christmas. Mom and Dad knew what was happening. They were great about it. That had to be a factor. But I don't know why Caleb gave himself permission to love me—and to make love to me. But he did. And I won't question it."

"And nor will I," Tisha said. "I'm so delighted, Danny! Why don't you two come for dinner? On Wednesday, I think. Lisa gets back in town this evening, and I'm sure she'd love to see you both. We'll celebrate *amour*. Before New Year's Eve madness sets in."

"Thanks, darling," I said. "I'll check with Caleb. What should we bring?"

"Wine is always nice. Funny how it never goes out of style."

While we were dressing for dinner, I finally got around to asking, "Why is that perfect cock of yours uncut, Caleb?" He looked a little puzzled. Young men in his world were probably not obsessed with foreskin the way so many gay guys are.

"Oh, that's simple," he said. "I was delivered by a midwife, and there wasn't a hospital nearby. No one cared about those things. Do you hate it, Dan? Because I'll have it fixed."

"No, darling," I said. "I love your dick just the way it is. And you should never edit yourself—unless I suggest it, of course." Caleb kissed me. It would be a good evening, surely. We headed to Tisha's.

As she let us in, she called out, "Oh, Lisa, the two handsomest grooms in New York City have arrived!" There were hugs and kisses all around. I gave Tisha the wine I had brought. Caleb had decided to bring some flowers, and he had the bright idea of making it an orchid plant—lovely magenta-colored blooms, defiantly tropical in the face of Old Man Winter. Tisha thanked us for the gifts and put the orchid plant on the coffee table, where it looked perfect.

"We're eating a little heavy tonight, but it's that time of year," Tisha said. Her trip to Chicago had reminded her of ethnic favorites. I always thought that while New York and Chicago both have huge immigrant populations, New York seems—to me, anyway—more of a melting pot, while Chicago is more about ethnic enclaves. Whether that's true or not, Tisha had been to Chicago's Little Poland for dinner one night, and that was the inspiration for her menu.

We started with tripe soup—which always seems to be wonderful, whether it's Polish or Mexican or Chinese or whatever. The main course was a vast *bigos*—hunter stew—full of fresh and smoked meats and mushrooms and sauerkraut. So satisfying on a cold winter night. Nearly as satisfying as sharing a meal with trusted friends whatever the season.

"I want to hear everything," Tisha said. "Don't edit a word." Polite titters.

"It's obvious that something important happened," Lisa said. "You two are not the same boys who sat at this table last time." Caleb and I both blushed. I could feel it. I looked to him for help with the explanation we needed to share with our friends.

Caleb said, "It's simple, really. Dan and I both knew about our attraction, from the day we met. But I held him at arm's length as long as I could stand it—because we had business obligations and because I didn't think I could give my heart to another man. When I realized my mistake, Dan refused to make love before he was certain that I could handle my feelings for him. He made me wait until Christmas Eve!"

"How romantic!" Tisha said. "Christmas in New Jersey, at Elaine and Richard's. Isn't it a beautiful house, Caleb? You've never seen it, Lisa. It's one of those big old places in upper Bergen County, nestled into horse country. WASPy as hell. Inviting, anyway. So, Dan, your folks were very kind to a little brown girl a while back. How did they deal with our cowboy here?"

Caleb answered for me. "The Blackwells welcomed me into their home as if I were family. As I told Dan at the time, I was mostly shocked to see two parents with such unconditional love for their son. But I don't think I told him that it helped me find my way to that same kind of love for him." Caleb fingered the Christmas bolo that was around his neck. I was speechless for a while. And misty.

"Let's keep the story moving, here," Tisha said. "I heard something about a wedding."

"Yes, well, it's complicated," I said. "As if the thrill of making love to Caleb for the first time wasn't enough, after breakfast on Christmas morning, Dad told me they're downsizing, and they want me to have the house."

"No way!" Tisha said.

"Way!" I replied.

"And?"

"And Caleb is much smarter about planning than I am, I learned." He smiled. "Caleb thinks we can pull this off. He thinks he can give up the West, gradually, and that I can learn to divide my time between Manhattan and Ridgewood. I believe in Caleb, so I believe in his vision. I'm probably going to have to accept the house—with all its responsibilities. Soon, I think."

"But what about the wedding?" Tisha demanded to know.

"Yes, well, Caleb and I were down by the duck pond. You remember the duck pond, Tisha. The ducks certainly remember you. They send best regards."

"This is my home," Tisha said. "And I'm going to clear the room if I don't get some information!"

Caleb jumped in. "I asked Dan to marry me. He said, 'Maybe.' And then he said, 'Yes, but give me some time.' I suggested we go to Montana in February so Dan can see my old life firsthand. That's all I need. I just want him to know me better, and then I'll be ready to move on."

"Tisha, I can see the whole thing," Lisa said. "Montana rustic, springtime in the Rockies, a gay wedding with two grooms who are so handsome it's hard to pick a favorite. Can we get a photographer in the cockpit—pardon my French—of a single engine plane, to document your first flight as husband and husband?"

"Lisa, I think that's brilliant," Tisha said, "but I think you're scaring the boys. It's a thought, though, guys. *GLITZ* would pay for everything—wedding wardrobe, transportation for friends and family, hospitality. It might even be fun. I always wanted to see Danny in a custom Valentino suit. I don't know if we should put Caleb in Zegna or some new line. Maybe some hot downtown designer. I'll work on it. Anyway, there's time to make those decisions. And, by the way, Lisa and I would guarantee that no one treads on your privacy."

I looked at Caleb. He looked at me. I said, "Could we sleep on it?"

"Of course," Lisa said. "Take all the time you need. I'll draw up a contract in the morning. Tisha, this is going to be wonderful. We never do anything about the West that isn't LA or San Francisco. We haven't even been to Seattle in *years*. This feels like a scoop, somehow. I can't wait!"

Caleb and I said our thank-yous and good nights and Happy-New-Years and left Tisha's building. We were both a bit dazed. Caleb said, "Well, it makes better sense than the swimsuit edition."

I stopped us right there on the sidewalk and said, "Do you have any idea how precious you are to me, Caleb?"

"I think I do," he said, "if it's anything like my feelings for you." We kissed, under the harsh rays of a streetlight. And then we hailed a cab to get us home.

Chapter Twelve

New Year's Eve had long seemed an overrated holiday. Steve and I used to go away someplace quiet—like the Adirondacks. There's real quiet for you. In recent years Tisha had dragged me to lively parties with lots of glamorous—and drunken—people. I asked Caleb if we couldn't do something simple that was mostly about the two of us at home. He agreed enthusiastically.

I still wanted to take Caleb out for a bit of New York City fun, and I remembered the Turkish restaurant on Second Avenue that had a holiday package at a reasonable price. "Lots of good food and Turkish wine, music, belly dancing," I told Caleb. "If we go for the early seating, we can get the full treatment and still be home by 10:00 or so—before the crazies make the city a little scary to be out in."

"That sounds great, Dan," Caleb said. "I'm glad you thought of it. I don't know anything about Turkish food—or Turkish music or belly dancing, for that matter. This sounds like a good way to learn." I embraced him warmly and then made a reservation. Done. We could have gone to a dogfight and had a great time just because we were together. Luckily, we had much more civilized plans.

Dinner was festive, but not raucous. Caleb loved the food, and so did I. The belly dancer gave Caleb an especially passionate performance. He blushed crimson. I could see it even in candlelight. The food and wine coupled with the entertainment put us in a genuine holiday humor. When we were ready to leave, I found an Uber driver cruising in the neighborhood who got to us in about three minutes—an occurrence that would have been impossible at 12:15, for instance. It was good to be early and to be on the East Side, far from the Times Square madness.

I suggested he drive straight down Second Avenue and then west on 14th Street—well south of the congestion. Smooth trip. We were home! We changed into robes, and I poured us a cognac. We sat and looked into each other's eyes, mostly. I couldn't help grinning with delight, and neither could he. About 11:30 I suggested we go to bed. Caleb agreed. We brushed our teeth and then settled in.

I wrapped myself around Caleb and kissed him warmly. Then I did something I'd wanted to do for weeks but hadn't dared to consider actually doing. I prayed that Caleb was ready for it as I straddled his pelvis and pointed his perfect dick toward my interior. I hadn't had anything up there in a long while, so I knew I'd be tight. And I knew I would have to accept an ample visitor. And I knew love would find a way.

I never took my eyes off Caleb's eyes as I eased him inside. He seemed ready. That helped me relax into our union. It was gradual, but I accepted him. And when the penetration was complete, I reared up, threw back my head, and whooped. Caleb laughed loudly. It was a joyous sound I'd never heard before.

And it was music to my ears. At first we were still, and then Caleb began to move inside me. I continued to study his eyes, when I wasn't kissing him, that is. He seemed blissful.

I'm not much of a talker during lovemaking, but I made an exception that New Year's Eve. I said, "Caleb, I don't need any Macy's fireworks. I only want yours." And sure enough, just at midnight, Caleb launched a series of rockets that lit up my body and my soul. I came, too, of course. How could I not? I was in a state of ecstasy. That's the only way I can describe it. And Caleb seemed to join me there.

When we were mere mortals again, Caleb said, "Danny, I didn't know I could feel so close to anyone, not even you. I had no idea." I was still speechless, so I embraced him and held him against my heart. Later, he said, "I've wanted to do that, Dan, but I was afraid of hurting you. I couldn't stand that."

I stopped him with a kiss. And then I said, "You couldn't hurt me, Caleb. Not while you're beside me." I felt a sudden chill, and I said, "Please stay with me, Caleb. I couldn't bear to lose you."

"Hush, Dan," he said. "I'm not going anywhere. Not tonight, and not anytime except when you come with me."

I dreaded the conversation, but I knew it had to happen. I phoned Ridgewood on Sunday. I asked Mom to have Dad pick up an extension phone, so the three of us could talk. "I've taken this week to consider your offer, and yes, I'd like to accept it. I'm a little frightened of the responsibility of caring for that house, but I want to try it. Actually, *we* want to try it. Caleb asked me to marry him. And I accepted. We're going to do the deed in a couple of months. You have to come, of course."

"Danny, that sounds wonderful," Momma said. "And it seems so smart for the two of you to breathe young life into this old house. We've experienced a lot of joy here, and you'll make your own. I couldn't be more delighted."

"Congratulations, son," Dad said. "I love a good wedding. Mary Ellen's a busy woman, you know. Be sure to give her plenty of advance notice." We all laughed. "On a sober note," he said, "I want you to know that we'll help you with the legal things and property tax and upkeep as long as you need it. And I want you to remember it's just a house. If you can get a decade or two or three of pleasure out of it, then great. But don't think you owe us anything. When you're ready to move on, do it." I was well on my way to becoming a weepy mess.

"Is Caleb there," Mom asked.

"No, Momma," I said. "He went out to run some errands. I'll tell him you asked for him."

"Danny, your Dad and I fell in love with Caleb during your Christmas stay. I wanted you both to know that. Am I right, Richard?"

"You're always right, Elaine. But in this case, you're *especially* right. I'll be proud to have Caleb as part of our family, Danny." I was about to pop. "Never thought I'd have a pilot for a son-in-law. Hmmm. Isn't life full of surprises?"

Indeed! I thought.

Tisha called to invite us to join her for dinner at a new Azerbaijani restaurant in Queens. "I'll bring the wine," she said. "They don't mind as long as they don't have to touch it. You'll love the food, Danny. It's like Mediterranean and Arabic and Russian all rolled into one. Tell Caleb to skip lunch. They'll keep feeding us until we burst."

At dinner, she said, "I think I have the May cover of *GLITZ* for the two of you. **East Meets West**. I can see the whole thing. I'm not sure if it will be the cockpit shot or the marriage ceremony, but it will be fabulous! Everyone in the office is excited. We all need a springtime lift. And you boys are going to bring a lot of lift into a lot of lives." I was certainly more interested in my own life than in the lives of Tisha's readers. I think Caleb agreed. We both tried to be grateful.

Then, Tisha said, "I had a brilliant idea this afternoon. Drum roll, please. We'll dress Caleb in Ralph Lauren, because they have wonderful menswear, and because they have an incredible collection of vintage Southwestern jewelry—and they will lend me whatever pieces I need for the shoot. Caleb, how would you like to be married in a $10K concho belt?"

"That's fine, Tisha," he said. "I'll be married in anything you like, or nothing at all. I really don't care."

"That brings me directly to my next question. Is there a hotel in Missoula, or nearby, that has a hot tub on the roof? I know that's very Telluride, but I don't know anything about Montana. I want some shots with the happy couple unclothed. Don't worry,

Danny, I can't show your cock, but I'd put it on the cover if I could get away with it. Now, that would sell magazines!" Caleb laughed.

"Tisha, please," I said, "Caleb doesn't know everything about my checkered past."

"Well it's time he did, dear. But not to worry. We'll get you two into a steamy hot tub under the stars even if I have to manufacture one. Leave it to me. Did Lisa email you the schedule, Danny?"

"No, dear."

"Well, I'll see that she does—in the morning. I know you need to invite people. And I'll invite some people, too. It's going to be such fun! Would you mind having a lesbian rabbi officiate? She's very progressive. You'll love her."

Caleb and I looked at each other and said, in unison, "Yes, dear."

A few evenings later, I said to Caleb, "What do you think? Are you ready to submit the manuscript to Jim?"

"What do *you* think?" he asked. "Isn't that more to the point?"

"No, darling," I said. "You're the climber. I'm merely the Sherpa."

"I know you'd tell me if it wasn't good enough, Dan."

"Correct."

"I think I should let go of it."

"Good," I said. "Let's ask Harvey to print it out in the morning and put it on Jim's desk. I had a thought about the title, by the way. It's entirely up to Jim, of course, but if I were publishing it I'd start with the working title and add a subtitle. I'd call it, *ABOVE THE CLOUDS: A Journey to Freedom.* What do you think, Caleb?"

"I think you're an amazing man, Danny. I can't imagine my life without you."

"You don't have to," I said.

"Hold on a moment," Caleb said. "Let me pull up the top of the manuscript. I want you to be the first one to read the new dedication." He retrieved his laptop from his bag and opened the file. When he had cued it up, he handed it to me.

> With deepest gratitude to my editor, Daniel Blackwell, who not only taught me what I needed to learn about storytelling but also taught me everything I will ever need to know about love.

I nearly creamed in my pants, of course. I reached for Caleb and held him as tightly as I dared. "I think it will be a lovely wedding," I said, "provided you don't kill me with happiness before we can get to the altar. Or the huppah, or whatever the hell Tisha cooks up."

"I don't think it much matters," Caleb said.

"That's so smart," I said. "I love smart men. It all started with my love for William Shakespeare. There have been other smart men along the way, I confess. But it was always, always leading to my love for Caleb Bromley. My heart is full to bursting, darling. Please use it gently."

"Hush, Danny," he said. "Let's get some sleep. We have a big day tomorrow."

The End

HOLIDAY NOVELLA SERIES
BOOK TWO
MY EASTER MIRACLE
BRUCE K BECK

MY
EASTER
MIRACLE

a holiday novella

by

Bruce K Beck

New York

It was hard to believe I was flying to Missoula, Montana, to photograph the wedding of two men I'd never met. And yet, I was on the plane. The pay was good, and I loved working with Letisha Carmichael from *GLITZ* Magazine. Her shoots were always pleasant, and the results always gave me quality images for my portfolio.

I preferred to create murky, ambiguous photos. My favorite series of mine was a collection of drag queens at their makeup tables. Black and white— the photos and the subjects. I was moved by Josef Sudek's vision most of all. Velvety cityscapes and gardenscapes, even still lives and portraits with heartbreaking sadness just beneath the quiet sur- face. My nudes ended up looking a bit like Arthur Tress—only better, I always thought. But I was in the habit of eating daily, so—to pay my bills—I took jobs that were light and frivolous.

So that's how I came to play wedding photogra- pher that spring weekend. The plane touched down, and I hefted my gear—nothing compared to what I'd have needed even a decade before—to the ground transportation area. Tisha had arranged a car for me. It whisked me to a large Hilton near the airport. I had never been to Montana, so I didn't know what to expect, really. I didn't see much of the city on my way to the hotel. And if you've seen one airport you've seen 'em all, of course.

I did notice the setting, however. The hotel was planted on the edge of a valley surrounded by impressive snow-capped peaks. Do you suppose that's how it got the name Montana? The air was bracing and crystal clear. I always liked the smell of New York City, but the hint of evergreen in the air made Missoula smell even better. Like Christmas all year round, maybe? I checked in and got a bellman to guide me to my room. I tipped the very cute young guy, who smiled appreciatively. So far, so good.

I know there's more space in the West than back East, but the dimensions of my room were staggering: a huge bed in the middle of a massive space with the usual hotel furniture and a long wall of windows that looked out over the city—with a glimpse of the mountains on the other side of the valley. Quite lovely, really. The bathroom was bigger than my Brooklyn apartment. And this was a single room! A couple of rollaway beds and it would easily have accommodated a family of four.

I stowed my gear, freshened up a bit, and headed downstairs to the restaurant just off the lobby. Tisha was right where she had told me to find her. She was shepherding wedding guests and crew with equal efficiency and warmth. "Kenny! How was your flight? Why don't you have dinner with Lisa? She's right over there." I had met Lisa Turner at the *GLITZ* offices in Manhattan, but we had never actually worked together.

Lisa smiled sweetly. "Kenny! Come, sit here. Let me pour you some wine. This is going to be such a fun weekend!" She looked me straight in the eye and said, "I'm a big fan of your work. I told Tisha it had to be you. I'm delighted you could join us. It wouldn't be the same with any other photographer." Lisa kissed me warmly and said, "Please, sit. Let's get some food in you—something to replace the taste of your flight. I'd order a steak, if I were you. I'll find the waiter." And she was off to her next project.

The red wine was good. The steak was even better. Lisa returned to the table now and then to check on me. I don't know how those *GLITZ* women do it. Boundless energy and effortless charm. Wouldn't it be fun to *have* that combination—instead of just experiencing it? After dinner I ordered a fancy bourbon and a coffee. I was well mellowed when Lisa returned to the table with a cute guy in tow. "Kenny, please meet Matt Flowers—your video assistant. Matt, Ken Garda."

We greeted each other. "Please join me, Matt," I said. "There's plenty of room at this table. Are you hungry?"

"No, thanks, Ken," he said, as he took a seat at the table. "I already ate. I just wanted to stop by to meet you."

"Well, I'm glad you did," I said. "Isn't this an amazing hotel?"

"They reserved a room for me, but I live in town," Matt said. "I'll move in tomorrow morning—so I'm totally available for the shoot this weekend. You live in New York City?"

"Brooklyn, currently," I said. "I love it. Have you been there?"

"Not yet," he said. "But I've wanted to live in New York since I was a child."

"We have that in common," I said. I didn't tell him that I grew up in Boston. I didn't tell him much of anything. There was a lot to like about Matt Flowers. He had a boyish face, a great smile, a superlean body, and flaming red hair. I've had a soft spot in my heart for redheads ever since I got my first case of crab lice from one. The memory was bittersweet—but sweet, nevertheless.

"I don't want to keep you," Matt said.

"Not at all," I said. "Do you like bourbon? This one is delicious." I convinced Matt to order a shot my way—with one ice cube and a splash of plain water. He agreed that it was tasty. We sat together for a while, often in silence. I smiled a lot. So did Matt. "Have you met the grooms?" I asked.

"No, not yet. Tisha said tomorrow morning. At 10:00?"

"I believe so," I said. "I've seen a picture of Bromley, actually. He's a writer, you probably know. Great-looking. If the new hubby is half as hot, this should turn out to be fun."

"I'm sure it will be," he said. I liked the quietness of Matt's nature. His modesty. I liked *him*, of course. I hadn't felt that kind of warmth—in my heart—in a long time. Four years, to be exact. Matt stayed at the table for nearly an hour. We ordered a coffee for him and another bourbon for each of us. We shared small talk, mostly. Odds and ends of getting-to-know-you. "What do you think of Montana so far?" and "Is spring always so cold here?" and "Can you believe the images we can get with tiny devices these days?"

Just as we were about to say good night, Lisa stopped by with yet another man in tow. "This is Harvey Letterer, from Caleb's publisher, Scrive." She introduced us all around. "Harvey wants you two to have copies of Caleb's new book," Lisa said, "so you feel closer to him and his story." Tisha and Lisa and *GLITZ* always thought of everything, of course.

"We're excited about the wedding," Harvey said. "If you two can get the book cover into a shot now and then, we'll be grateful."

"Harvey," I said, "sit down and try this bourbon. Matt and I can both recommend it."

"Oh, thanks, Ken," he said, "but it's been a long day, and I'm dead on my feet. Have one for me. But only *one.* We want sharp focus from both of you tomorrow!" Harvey said good night and dashed off to finish his evening. *Pleasant guy,* I thought. *Nerdy-but-nice.* Matt and I looked at each other for a while.

I sensed that perhaps I should ask Matt to come up to my room, and I sensed that he would accept my invitation. And yet I knew that I couldn't do it. Instead, I said, "Matt, it's getting late. I've loved meeting you. And I'm looking forward to working with you this weekend." I rose and shook Matt's hand and said, "Get some rest, Cowboy."

As I walked to the elevators, I didn't dare look back to see Matt's reaction to my departure. Instead, I zeroed in on getting to my room and getting my teeth brushed and getting into bed. I looked at the copy of *ABOVE THE CLOUDS* that Harvey had just given me and put it on my night table. I picked it up—briefly, before I turned out the light—mostly just to refresh my memory of the author photo. Yes, it would be a good weekend. Wouldn't it?

I met the grooms in the morning. The slightly shorter, slightly older one had a handsome face—not to mention a great body—and an easy warmth about him. Tisha said, "Gentlemen, please meet your photographer, Ken Garda. Ken, this is Dan Blackwell [the one I had exchanged smiles with] and Caleb Bromley [the slightly taller, slightly younger one, who was pistol-hot and blessed with a face with equally fine angles.

Tisha made a fuss over them—and me. It was pure Tisha. I was relieved to see that both men were easy on the eyes. It would make my job easier. I knew about Bromley, of course. His recent novel was getting splashy press all over. His author photo didn't do him justice, however. I knew he'd look much better when I finished with him. Matt arrived a minute later, and Tisha introduced him to the grooms.

The boys seemed slightly apprehensive about the wedding circus that swirled all around them, and yet they both glowed with an intense love for each other that would make shooting them a breeze. "Ken and Matt are going to follow you two around today," Tisha said, "to get some background images. Please let them observe your day, everything except lovemaking. Unless you want that for your private archives.

I can't use it, unfortunately. Except for a little miniature for my night table. I'm just saying."

"We'll behave, Tisha," Dan said. "They seem like nice guys." Great smile. "We'll try not to be difficult," he told me.

"I love you," she said and kissed both Dan and Caleb. "Have fun today, boys. Think of Ken and Matt as your new best friends." That time I got a smile from Caleb. Great teeth. This would prove to be a pleasure, yes? It was spring, but there was still lots of snow not just in the mountains but in the hills that surrounded the town. Everything seemed very quiet—compared to New York City—but there was a nice energy.

A car took the four of us into the middle of town. "Just ignore us," I told the grooms. I said to Matt, "Please just shoot anything you think has potential in motion, and I'll focus more on still moments." Matt knew exactly what I needed, of course. And he also looked especially delightful in the morning sunlight, I noted. Yes, it was a good day.

Matt and I followed the grooms for several hours while they wandered around the city. I had Googled downtown, so I could suggest some places for them to visit. Caleb had some ideas of his own, of course. We took lots of shots of the boys sharing a bite of lunch at the diner, the boys in the park, the boys in the museum, at a ski shop, trying on Western hats. The one obligatory stop was a bookstore with Caleb's book in the front window. Check.

It was an easy day. Matt and I became a perfect documentary team in no time. And the grooms were quietly cooperative. When we headed back to the hotel, Matt peeled off because he had some commitment in town. I went to my room and reviewed the images I had captured so far. I was satisfied we were off to a good start. So I took a nap.

Matt and I joined the grooms for dinner in the rooftop restaurant. All perfectly pleasant. Matt was even more fetching in candlelight than in daylight. Like the rest of us, I suppose. While we were sharing a too-sweet dessert, Tisha arrived and said to the grooms, "Now, boys, I know I promised you a hot tub on the roof. *That* I couldn't manage, but I found the next best thing. And our team will rock it."

She explained. The grooms looked a little skeptical, but their smiles never entirely disappeared. "You two decide when you want Ken and Matt to come to your room. Let's do it tonight, though. There's so much going on tomorrow—with the airstrip and all. Let's get this one out of the way." Tisha sprinted off to her next project.

Caleb said, "There's no time like the present. Shall we?" Dan agreed. The four of us proceeded to their suite. I thought *my* room was big. The bridal suite was even more massive. The grooms ushered us into the bathroom, which was twice the size of mine. "I should start the bath water, I guess," Caleb said. We'll be right back."

The bathtub—with jacuzzi—was big enough to accommodate at least a half dozen bathers. Two young lovers would have the whole thing to themselves that evening. As the tub filled with steamy water, the whole situation began to feel more inviting. Matt and I stowed our gear in a corner. We only had to worry about my camera, Matt's iPhone, and a pop-open reflector I always carried in my bag—in case I needed to redirect light. No tripods, no lighting instruments. Low-light camera technology made everything simpler.

One thing that never changes, however, is the human element. When the boys joined us in the bathroom—now that they were dressed in those triple-thick terry robes hotels like to supply—they did not look so eager to jump into the situation. Caleb, especially. It's my job to put subjects at their ease in front of the camera. Otherwise, I don't get my shot. I smiled a lot and tried to do some fast thinking.

"What if we all strip?" I asked. "Would that make you more comfortable?"

"No," Dan said. "But it would certainly be more fun. What do you think, Caleb?"

"I think we should get on with this shoot. Sounds fair—having everyone strip." And that's what we did. So there were *four* erections in that colossal king bathroom as we fired up the whirlpool, added a drop of bubble bath, and got the boys into the tub. They both had such pretty bodies that it was an effortless exercise—worshipping them with my camera. I also took a strong interest in my new assistant. The first thing I noticed when we all stripped—besides how hot the grooms were—was Matt's amazing color combination of ginger pubes and a bright pink glans. Add the delicate blue veining of the shaft. Festive, indeed.

We snapped away. The grooms ignored us, really—which is what subjects should do. Matt held the reflector so as to bounce the light a little, now and then, when I felt I needed it. And I did the same for him. The boys would look deliciously oblivious to the seeing eyes—I was certain—in my stills and in Matt's video as well. I was satisfied that we had everything we needed. Plus a little something extra for Tisha—with the boys' permission, of course.

I even thought I might have some images for my own use. For my personal portfolio. Not dark and brooding, exactly, but quiet and unrehearsed. There were a few unguarded moments between the boys—with tiny, intimate gestures—that I found heartbreaking, really. I looked forward to seeing what I could do with those images once I got back home.

The boys got out of the jacuzzi and slipped into their huge robes. They thanked us and headed to their bedroom. As Matt and I were putting our clothes back on, I said to him, "Buy you a drink, Cowboy?"

"Sure," he said.

"Then meet me in the bar in fifteen minutes. If that works for you."

"Which bar?" he asked. "There are so many." We both grinned.

"The one off the lobby is fine with me. We could maybe save the rooftop bar for another time. When we know each other better."

"Fifteen minutes," Matt said. And we finished up.

As I was leaving their suite, I said to the grooms, "Thanks, guys. You're both beauties, and you're making our work easy. What time did Tisha say our call is tomorrow?"

"10:00, I think," Dan said. "Thanks, Ken. That shoot was not painful after all." He embraced me and gave me a peck on the cheek. "Sleep well," he said.

Caleb also embraced me and said, "Thanks, Ken. Are you looking forward to the flight tomorrow?"

"Are you?" I asked.

"I look forward to every flight. I'm not used to having passengers, but I think this will be fine." Caleb kissed me, full on the lips, and then Matt and I left the boys in peace.

We made our way to the elevator in silence. We got in and pressed our floors. When Matt got out, he turned to me and said, "See you in a few." As the door closed, I felt, keenly, the loss of Matt's smile. I wanted it back. I wanted to own it, really.

And then we met for drinks in the lobby bar. "Who are you, Matt," I asked, as we sipped big, overly sweet house cocktails, "besides an exceptionally pretty young man?"

Matt blushed, modestly. "Ken, you don't have to flatter me," he said. "I'd gladly get into your bed, no questions asked." It was my turn to blush.

"I want to know you, Matt," I said. "Let's put the rest of what I want on hold for the moment. Will you share?"

"Of course," he said. "I was born in Billings. My parents moved here when I was ten. I suppose I'm a Montana boy, but I never felt quite at home."

"Do you suppose that has anything to do with being gay?" I asked.

"I think it has *everything* to do with being gay," Matt said. We looked at each other for a while. I was every bit as smitten with Matt even when he wasn't smiling. I began to wonder how his kiss would taste. I began to lose my reason, really.

"Sorry. I interrupted you," I said. "It's a habit of mine. Will you get this story back on track?"

Matt smiled. I melted. He said, "There's not much to tell, really. I decided while I was in high school that I wanted to be a nurse. Instead of going right to nursing school, I got a job with an EMS unit. It was tough, at first. It's always tough, really. But most of the guys—and some of the girls—are burly machos, so I had to earn respect. I had to be the strongest and the bravest. And I did it. I haven't heard a catcall in the last year, anyway."

The ginger beauty across the bar table from me seemed an unlikely hero. And yet I felt his strength as keenly as I felt my desire for him. "Why did you take up video?" I asked.

"Hard to say. I've always been obsessed with technology," Matt said. "And lately I've felt restless. I've been shooting pics on my iPhone for years now. I experimented with video. I have a following on Instagram. And that's how Tisha found me, as far as I know."

"I'm glad she did," I said.

"And you, Ken?" Matt asked. "I've seen your website and I've seen you. But I don't think I know you."

"That's fair," I said. "But I think it's getting late, and I think we should get some sleep. Will you let me off the hook until tomorrow? Tomorrow evening I could make my life an open book."

"Is that a promise?" Matt asked.

"Yes," I said. And I meant it. At the time. We finished our drinks, and we headed back to our rooms. Reluctantly, I think, both of us. When the elevator arrived at my floor, Matt suddenly got off with me.

He quickly led me into a quiet corridor and put his arms around me—his EMS hardened limbs—and said, "Will you kiss me?"

"With the greatest pleasure," I said. Matt's kiss was even more than I had imagined. Our mouths were a perfect fit. I wanted to own Matt's mouth. I wanted to have it for my personal use, only. I wanted to move in, really. We might still be kissing in that corridor, except that another hotel guest got off the elevator and headed to a guest room near where Matt and I had sequestered ourselves. "Good evening," the three of us said, politely, as he passed us. The spell was broken.

"Matt, I'm a little overwhelmed," I said. "Could we continue this—conversation—tomorrow?"

"Of course," Matt said. He looked a bit sad. I felt sadder than he looked, but I just couldn't invite him to my room. I couldn't go there, as much as my body had started to ache for the chance to be close to Matt, to hold him in my arms, to taste his entire body, to go deep inside him, to possess him, really.

I watched Matt get back on the elevator. And he was gone. I went to my room. I said to myself, "Kenneth Michael Garda, you're a fucking idiot! This kid is glorious. And he wants you. Why won't you let him in?" I had no answer. I got ready for bed. I downed a shot of scotch from the bottle I had picked up in our travels that afternoon. I set an alarm for the morning. And then I turned out the lights and sank into the overstuffed oblivion of hotel bedding.

Chapter Three

I wasn't much keener than Matt was on going up in a single-engine plane. But it was all part of the job. On Sunday morning, I put on an extra sweater and headed to the lobby restaurant. Matt was already there. I served myself a buffet breakfast and joined Matt. "I like the way you look in the morning," I said to him.

"I like the way you look all the time," Matt replied.

"I'm glad we've established that," I said. Matt grinned. So did I. We finished our breakfast and poured ourselves a little more coffee. We were early enough that we didn't have to hurry to make the 10:00 rendezvous. Matt and I looked at each other. A lot. He blushed slightly. I probably did, too. And then Tisha came by with an older couple in tow.

"Elaine and Richard, meet our photographers, Ken Garda and Matt Flowers." We sprang to our feet. "Gentlemen, these are Dan's parents, Mr. and Mrs. Blackwell." There were greetings all around. Tisha hurried on to her next project.

"Richard, why don't you sit there?" Mrs. Blackwell said. "I'll get us some breakfast." She headed to the buffet. Mr. Blackwell joined us, of course. He smiled warmly. We poured some coffee for him.

"First trip to Montana?" Richard asked.

"For me, yes," I said. "But Matt's a native." We made some small talk. Elaine returned with plates for each of them.

"Richard, they don't have the kind of yogurt you like, but I got some cottage cheese that looks okay." She settled into her chair. I poured her a coffee, as well. She smiled broadly. "Are you guys having a good time?" she asked. "I never expected to spend Easter in Missoula, Montana, and yet, why not?"

I hadn't really thought too closely about the timing. I knew that people don't normally get married just before or just after Easter. And yet, the demands of publishing sometimes trump those niceties. To make the May issue of *GLITZ*, the wedding festivities needed to happen at least a month in advance.

I hadn't paid much attention to the Christian calendar since I was a child. I had a Jewish boyfriend once, in college, so I was vaguely aware of how Easter and Passover sometimes align. But he was no more observant than I was, so neither of us gave much attention to holidays. "Mrs. Blackwell ..." I started to say.

"Elaine."

"Elaine, I think your son is a fine man. And I can see where he gets his good looks, as well as his character." I meant it, of course. The last thing I needed to do that Easter Sunday was to bullshit the parents of one of the grooms.

"Thanks, Ken," she said. And she reached over and took my hand. "We think Danny's wonderful, of course."

"And Caleb runs him a close second," Richard said. "He's a fine pilot, by the way. You can feel safe when you're up in the blue with him today. And I'll bet the view will be staggering."

I'm looking forward to it," I said. Now, *that* was a lie. My first of the day? Or the only one?

Matt stood and said, "If you'll excuse me, Mr. and Mrs. ..." They stared him down. "Elaine and Richard, I'm going back to my room to make sure I have everything I need for today. I'll see you shortly." Matt squeezed my shoulder as he passed me.

"Ken, is Matt your boyfriend?" Elaine asked. "He has a very sweet nature."

"No, actually," I said, as I no doubt blushed at least slightly, "we only just met Friday night. Matt lives in Missoula, and I live in Brooklyn." That put some perspective on things, saying it out loud—for me, anyway.

"Geography is only a word, Ken," Elaine said. "Don't stumble over it."

"Elaine is a famous matchmaker," Richard said. "If I were you, Ken, I wouldn't try to resist her advice."

"I wouldn't consider it," I said, "but we're all here to honor your son. Why would you take an interest in me—and Matt?"

"Because we've been celebrating love for a lot of years—am I right, Richard?"

"You're always right, Elaine," he said. "Ken, listen to her. Don't miss out on a chance for real happiness. We've all seen too many victims of that mistake. Don't be one of them."

Fuck! I thought. *I came to Montana to make some money, and now I'm about to have my heart turned upside down? No, that was never part of the deal.* I tried to smile and be gracious. But the Blackwells had shaken me to my core, really. "You two have given me a lot to think about," I said as I rose from the breakfast table. "May I?" I asked as I raised my camera.

"Sure," Elaine said as they moved in closer together to pose for my lens. A few shots, and I had everything I needed to document Dan's half of the new family the boys were forging. I wished the Blackwells a good morning and headed for the lobby. Matt arrived shortly thereafter, followed by the grooms. Just as we were about to get into the car that would speed us to the airstrip, Dan's parents walked into the lobby.

Elaine embraced Dan and said, "Did you get some breakfast, Danny?"

"Yes, Momma," he said. "We ordered room service. It was good."

"I'm glad you're wearing your Christmas sweater. Your dad says it gets cold up there. You have the hood. You may need it. But don't put it up until after the boys have their pictures! We don't want to hide your beautiful face." Dan embraced his parents, who then embraced Caleb. We headed for the car.

I grew up in a big, noisy ethnic family where everyone professed love for everyone else. And yet I had occasionally wondered if my parents really loved me any more than was strictly required of them. Watching the Blackwells interact, I was revisited by that nagging sense of having missed out on something. Before he got into the car, Dan called back to Elaine and Richard, "Have fun today. There won't be much open in town, but I'm sure you'll find something to do."

"I'm sure we will, Danny," she said. "Be safe!" And we were off. I had decided to just deal with the airplane shoot. It would all happen on the fly (sorry about that). Camera angles, lighting—it would be what it was, and I would have to be smart about capturing the most interesting images that presented themselves to me. Matt, too, of course. But that's what photography is all about, after all—lucky surprises and what we do with them.

It was a tight fit—Matt and me in the back of the cockpit. Luckily, neither of us minded being pressed together. Caleb seemed very professional as he started the engine, went through the safety protocols, and radioed the little tower for permission to take off. So far so good. I had probably never flown in a prop plane, so I had no idea what to expect.

The takeoff was fast—much faster than jets do it. We were quickly aloft. It was exhilarating, really. I experienced a hint of the feeling of freedom—of being able to fly like a bird—that aviators crave, I would imagine. The engine was very loud, however, and the vibration was intense, compared to a jetliner. Matt and I looked at each other and smiled a lot. Conversation would have been difficult at that noise level, even with our proximity.

I studied the grooms as we flew. They looked at each other often—fortunately for my photo needs. Caleb so obviously loved being airborne, and Dan so obviously loved Caleb that my work was easy. Once we were above the clouds, the sunlight that streamed into the cockpit was intense. So my challenge was to find the right moments when the plane dipped or banked and presented me with views of the boys at their best. Even for beauties who can't take a bad picture, it's still all about light.

Matt seemed more comfortable with the whole thing than I was. I trusted him not only to document the event but also to capture the texture of the experience. And that's exactly what he did. Up until that point, I had only just tolerated the notion of adding video to our coverage of the wedding. But when I watched the "rushes" that afternoon, on Matt's iPhone, I became a believer.

I had believed in Matt since we met, of course. I just hadn't believed so strongly in the importance of his contribution to the project. I had to go up in the air with Matt to get there. It was worth the flight. We were sitting on the edge of Matt's bed that afternoon, looking at raw video footage, when Matt said, "Ken, you promised to tell me about you. Today. Is this a good time?"

"I think I need a good dinner and a couple of glasses of wine before I can go there," I said. "Will you wait until tonight?"

"Sure," he said, "as long as you kiss me now."

"That's fair," I said. Matt fell into my arms. We easily recreated the warmth and the urgency of our kisses the night before. Joined-at-the-mouth is what we were. I paused long enough to say, "Matt, I could kiss you forever."

"Sounds good," Matt said. And he kissed me again. There was no hotel guest getting off the elevator to interrupt us that afternoon. We could quite easily have stripped and slipped into Matt's bed to continue our explorations. We both wanted it. Intensely. But I couldn't go there.

Fortunately for me, I had an excuse. "We have to be at the rehearsal soon. Can we continue this after dinner?"

"Of course," Matt said. We pulled ourselves together and headed to the pool area, where the ceremony would take place the following day at noon.

Harvey's a minister?" I heard Dan ask Tisha. "What happened to the lesbian rabbi?"

"She decided she couldn't get away so close to Passover. But Harvey's ordained, actually. By some church or other. He registered in Montana. We're good. Harvey will be there at the far end of this patio. The hotel staff will set up seating for the guests in the morning. They'll make a center aisle, and you two can walk up it together just at noon. We've got music, we've got flowers, we've got everything. Harvey!" she called, "are you ready for the boys?"

He waved to indicate that he was ready, and the boys walked slowly toward Harvey, along the path that would be an aisle the next morning. The grooms never stopped holding hands. I got a few shots that were brilliant, if I do say so myself. The view of the mountains behind the celebrants was stunning. And then the couple met briefly with Harvey so he could tell them what to expect from the service, I assumed.

Tisha indicated that the rehearsal was over. She embraced me and said, "Kenny, isn't this fun? Are you happy with the images you're getting?"

"I am, Tish," I said. "The grooms are lovely, the air is clear, and the sun is bright. Who could ask for more?"

"And how about your assistant?" she asked. Matt had just headed inside.

"Tisha, I'll admit I didn't quite get it before," I said. "But I think Matt's videos will add real value to your website coverage and your Instagram feed."

"And what value is Matt adding to your life, I'm wondering?"

"You're always so subtle, Tisha. Matt's a charmer, isn't he?" I said.

"Indeed. What's next, Kenny? You've been alone too long, I think. Just saying."

"Yes, well, thanks for taking an interest, Tish. I'll keep you posted." I kissed her and headed indoors to make dinner plans with Matt. And then I went to my room and took a very welcome nap. Happy Easter to me!

Chapter Four

At dinner that evening, I was glad Matt and I had a table to ourselves. The grooms and Dan's parents were nearby. Harvey joined them. Caleb didn't seem to have any family with him. I wondered about that, but it was none of my business, after all. Tisha and Lisa and the rest of the *GLITZ* team were circulating, mostly. They must have paused to eat something, but it didn't seem so. Again, none of my business. I focused on Matt.

"Thanks for being so easy to work with," I said.

"I feel like I've been damned with faint praise," Matt said. "You know I want more than a working relationship, and I'm guessing that you do, too. What's going on here, Ken?"

"Will you come to my room after dinner?" I asked.

"Of course."

"Good," I said. "Dessert?"

"No, thanks."

"Smart. Why don't we say goodnight to everyone and head to my room?" And that's what we decided to do. The grooms smiled warmly. Harvey seemed somehow more substantial—I suppose that's the word—than he had seemed when we first met. Elaine and Richard were cordial. Matt and I waved to Tisha and the others. Tisha waived back. It felt like permission to withdraw.

We were nearly out of the restaurant when Elaine suddenly called to me. I stopped and turned around. She walked over and embraced me. "Ever heard of an Easter miracle?" she asked quietly, in my ear.

"Not since I was a child," I said.

"I think you're due for one, Kenny. Don't fight it." She patted my cheek, smiled at Matt, and headed back to the grooms' table.

When Matt and I reached the elevator, he asked me, "What did Dan's mom say?"

"She has a silly notion in her head that I'm in love with you. Can you believe it?"

"Why, yes, actually." Matt said. "Sounds reasonable to me. Is there any truth to it?"

"We'll find out," I said. "I promised to tell you my story. If you can stay awake through the whole thing, then who knows?" I let us into my room and put on a few lights. I had two super-thick robes in my room, too, just as the grooms did. I could have suggested that we change into them. I didn't. It felt too obvious. Instead, I poured some scotch for each of us—along with a splash of water and one ice cube—and we went to sit across from each other at the table near the windows. I opened the drapes to reveal a vista of starlight in a clear night sky, just above the shimmer of civilization.

"I grew up in Boston's North End. It feels like more of a melting pot these days, I think, but when I was growing up it was still Ultra-Guinea. And there was an Ultra-Mick neighborhood that bordered it. Not exactly West Side Story, but everyone knew their place. Patrick Nolan and I didn't meet—wouldn't have been likely to meet—until college. We met our junior year at UMass.

"Patrick was not only great-looking—his coloring was a little bit like yours, Matt—but he had survived childhood with a wonderful sweetness about him. He made me want to lose the hardness I had fought to cultivate. He disarmed me—there, I said it. I was never the same after Patrick came into my life. And I was never happier.

"We moved to New York City after graduation. Patrick got a job on Wall Street—in the mail room, as they say. I took some temp jobs. I had some computer skills. You've never lived until you've transcribed legal papers on the over-night shift. I take it back, Matt. You can live quite happily without that experience, I'm sure.

"I took a few photography courses at the New School. It was sad, really. They had recently ripped out Berenice Abbott's darkroom, for instance. And the darkroom at Parsons was just about to receive the same fate. I got an important education in Photoshop in one weekend session. Other than that, I had to mostly learn my way around a camera on my own. But I did it. And I started to get work.

"We had a dozen good years together, Patrick and I. *Great* years, actually. We were both looking forward to decades more. And then one evening Patrick came home from work and said, 'Kenny, you won't believe this, but I was sitting in the lunchroom today; I stood up, and I fainted. We have a little infirmary, and two guys walked me there. The nurse checked my vitals, and he made an appointment with a doctor. I'm seeing her tomorrow. I don't want you to worry, Kenny, but I can't pretend this isn't happening.'

"So, what did they look for first? HIV, of course. That's what gay men get, isn't it? Only Patrick didn't have HIV any more than the Pope did. What he had was a fucking aneurism in his brain." I grew silent. I went to get my scotch bottle. Matt declined another splash, and then he changed his mind and joined me. "By the time they figured out the problem, Patrick had already had a few episodes. It was terrifying for me and confusing for him, of course. There were consultations with surgeons. Conflicting opinions, but none of them promising.

"I can only imagine the fear that Patrick experienced, but what I *saw* was his intense sadness about leaving me alone. I'd have gladly switched places with him, if it had been possible, except that the cruelty of abandoning Patrick would have been even worse than.... Well, after Patrick's death, I was unable to complete the grieving process. I went through anger and bargaining and most of that other shit, but I never got to acceptance. Never have. Patrick lives in my heart. The blood that courses through my veins is Patrick's blood. I forgot how to tell the two of us apart years ago. Still can't. When I get up in the morning, I'm never sure which of us I'll see in the bathroom mirror. And if I stop seeing him there, I'll know I've lost him forever."

Matt walked over behind my chair and put his arms around me. We were silent for a while. I was weepy—surprise, surprise. Eventually, I said, "Tisha knew Patrick. She adored him. Everyone did. Matt, I wish you could have met him." That seemed a stupid thing to say. "Matt, I want you to understand that since Patrick's death I've had sex with dozens of men. But I've never made love to a man with a face and a name. Never. I don't know if I can do it."

"Oh, is that all?" Matt said. "I was afraid you didn't like my dick." I laughed, in spite of myself. "Kenny, I'm grateful that you shared your story with me. I feel honored. I'd like to stay over tonight. I won't pressure you. I just want to hold you. I don't think you should be alone." I embraced him.

"Yes, please," I said. "Should we turn in now?"

"Sure," Matt said. "Big day tomorrow. Why don't we put in our breakfast order now, so we won't have to scramble around in the morning?"

"Good thinking," I said. We filled out the room service "key" and hung it on the outside door handle. We stripped. It was my second chance to see Matt's very nice body with the dramatic coloring. I liked everything I saw. Again. It occurred to me that while Matt was boyish and cute, he was also intensely masculine. He wore his strength like a badge of honor. He had earned his position as a man among men, after all.

Matt hung up his clothes, since he'd have to wear them to his room in the morning, to change for the wedding. I turned out most of the lights and slipped between the sheets on the left side of the bed. Matt joined me on the right—Patrick's side. I didn't dwell on it. I simply let him hold me. "Matt, you're so young," I said.

"I'm thirty-three, Ken. Definitely post-adolescent. I think Jesus wrapped up his entire ministry at that age. I'm hoping for a lot more time, but who knows?"

I turned out the light on my night table, snuggled in closer to Matt, and said, "Thanks for being smart, Matt. And thanks for being kind."

"Hush, Kenny," he said. "Let's get some rest."

As I lay there in the dark, I thought, *Well, Elaine, I think you're onto something.* And then I conked out.

Bruce K Beck

Chapter Five

When I woke in the morning, Matt was still holding me. I hated to disturb him, but I really needed a pee. Matt stirred as I disentangled myself. It was still dark in my room. The blackout curtains were highly effective. I wished that mine at home were so efficient. I hoped Matt would go back to sleep for another half hour or so. When I returned from the bathroom, Matt said, "Any chance of a little light here?" I turned on the night table lamp. Matt had raised himself up on his right elbow. He lay there looking at me and smiling.

"Matthew Flowers, you're the best-looking thing any morning could produce," I said. "Any chance of a repeat production?"

"I think your chances are excellent, Mr. Garda. But let's get through this day before we tackle tomorrow. What time is it?"

About 7:30, I think. Breakfast should be here shortly. Why don't you get a little more sleep?"

"Because I can't see you so well when I'm sleeping. And I love looking at you, Kenny."

"Even in the morning?" I asked.

"*Especially* in the morning," Matt said. "You're always handsome, but I like you best before you've put on your business face.

"The gentleman likes mornings. So noted," I said. "What else does the gentleman like?"

Matt beckoned to me, and I fell back into bed and into his arms. Matt kissed me. I kissed him back, of course. "That's what the gentleman likes," he said. We were still kissing when the room service waiter knocked on my door. I quickly grabbed one of the oversized robes and slipped into it.

"Where would you like this?" the waiter asked. He was a hot little Latino kid with a great smile.

"On the table, I think," I said. I quickly opened the drapes and let the morning in. The waiter set up our breakfast, I signed the check, and he was off.

He paused at the door and said, "Have a wonderful day, gentlemen." He flashed that great smile, and he was gone.

"Alone at last," I said. "Let's eat something before this gets cold."

"So smart," Matt said as he put on the other robe and joined me at the table. "I love smart men. In fact, I'm sapiosexual, mostly. But body heat is nice, too. And you have plenty of that, Kenny. Fortunately." It was a delightful breakfast. It was shaping up to be a terrific day. The sky was clear except for a few puffy white clouds. The perfect day for an outdoor wedding, surely. We didn't have to rush to make our call. So we found lots of time for kisses—at breakfast, back in my bed after breakfast, and even in the bathroom as we started our routines.

Two sinks allowed us to shave in unison. I always travel with a second razor, just in case. It's not easy to shave and grin at the same time. We managed it. After we had showered—together—I handed Matt some undershorts and said, "Try these. I think you'll fill them out nicely." He did. I dressed in my dark suit—so I'd fit in with the wedding guests—and Matt headed back to his room to dress. "Don't be too long," I said. "I've grown accustomed to having you beside me." Surely I didn't deserve Matt, I decided, but I vowed to accept him anyway.

Our call was 10:00, even though the wedding wasn't until noon. The hotel had set up a huge canopy as a just-in-case measure in the event of rain. It didn't diminish the sense of being outdoors, fortunately. But it would soften the midday sunlight just enough to make our work easier. Matt and I documented the arrival of the flowers and their arrangement. It let us shoot close-ups without spooking any wedding guests. The sound man set up his system. The hotel staff cleaned everything, including the pool. The catering staff arranged the buffet tables with plates and glassware for the party after the ceremony. The string chamber ensemble set up just to the side of the pool.

Tisha brought us a glass of champagne at 11:00. "The boys will be down in about a half hour," she said. "Wait till you see them! Dan's in Valentino Couture—and his Dad, too—and Caleb's in Ralph Lauren. *Don't miss the jewelry!* You won't get another chance to see vintage silver and turquoise of that quality, I can guarantee you. And it's meant to be worn, of course. I saw Caleb try on one of the pieces last week, and it suddenly came alive. You'll see. And Elaine's in Vera Wang. She outdid herself. You'll see. Don't *miss anything*, boys," she joked.

"We can only run this wedding once!" And she was off.

"I like weddings," I said to Matt.

"So do I."

"I think I like weddings because I admire commitment," I said.

"So do I."

"So, we have that in common," I said. "Good." We got on with our morning. Guests began to arrive just after 11:30. Some of them were Tisha's *glitterati* who had flown in the night before. Some of them looked very much like friends and family, even though they were probably not. Tisha even managed to round up some adorable children, including a flower girl and a ring bearer. What a production!

"If I ever get married, I want Tisha to arrange it," I said. Matt smiled broadly. I loved his smile. I loved *him,* of course. I hadn't wanted to admit it to myself. But the truth of my love for Matt was inescapable. *One more heartache?* I wondered. *We're talking New York and Montana, here. Surely, it's impossible.* But then I remembered that the grooms had managed to bridge that same gap. And for just a moment I felt young and alive and full of hope.

Matt and I were in the staging area when the wedding party arrived. Tisha was right, of course. The grooms were both stunning, in their different ways. I made it a point to catch close-ups of some of the jewelry they had draped on Caleb. The concho belt was breathtaking. He wore it well. And it did indeed come alive as it encircled his beautiful waist.

"Kenny, I like you in a dark suit," Elaine said. "But I like you even better dressed in love."

I blushed slightly. "Elaine, you look terrific," I said. "Will you wear that dress to *my* wedding?"

"I'll probably have to return it when we get home," she said. "But God bless Vera for not wrapping me in mother-of-the-bride mauve. If I have to put on a dress, I want to feel glamorous in it."

"And so you are," I said. I kissed her. Elaine looked at me, carefully.

"Yes," she said. "You received your Easter miracle. I'm delighted for you, Kenny." She put her gloved hand on my cheek. I started to get a little misty. So did she. "Wait till your only son gets married," Elaine said. "See if you can get through the day without tears." We embraced, carefully, so as not to disturb our wedding finery.

"Kenny, you look good!" Dan's father said.

"Thanks, Richard, "I said. "Very spiffy!"

"Yes, well, just when you think you never have to put on a suit again, things change. But I prefer this to wearing a suit when they carry me out feet first. Oh, look! The princess has arrived! That's Dan's sister, Mary Ellen, and her husband, Hank." He went to greet them, as did Elaine and the grooms. Matt and I followed.

"Daddy, you look so handsome!" Mary Ellen said. "And young!"

"Yes, well I am," he said. "Your mother and I are delighted you could make it, Elly, and so is Dan. You haven't met Caleb." There were introductions all around. Mary Ellen and her husband were decorative additions to the wedding party. I couldn't help but notice that Elaine's greeting for her daughter was a bit cooler than her husband's and her son's. Families! Still more none-of-my-business. All the guests were seated.

Harvey arrived looking very ministerial, indeed. He was wearing a robe and a stole in vivid purple with bands of gold lettering—Alpha and Omega, I think. Vaguely religious but not sectarian. A good place to be, I thought. Harvey made his way to the front of the aisle. When he turned to face the audience, the chamber group took that as their cue. They began the processional. Bach, I think. And the grooms began their march. Matt and I followed them as much as possible. They both radiated such warmth that it was difficult for me to concentrate on my work. But I did it, of course.

It was a delightful wedding. And everything went off without a hitch, because Tisha and Lisa were in charge. The party afterward was great fun. Matt and I got all the usual shots, including the grooms feeding each other wedding cake. I wondered if I hadn't just snapped the *GLITZ* cover photo. It was full of joy and play, and the grooms managed to look handsome and stylish as well as foolish. And Caleb's jewelry was clearly featured. Don't think *GLITZ* wasn't careful to keep Ralph Lauren happy.

Richard seemed to be having the best time of all. He wasn't used to seeing both of his children at the same time, I gathered. His daughter worked the Daddy's girl thing. Her husband indulged her. They were a handsome couple and ideally suited to each other, I guessed. But I wondered if they had ever experienced the joy that Dan and Caleb shared. Even *more* none-of-my-business.

Elaine had that both-of-my-children-happily-married contentment about her. She wore it well. I said to her, "Elaine, I loved meeting you this weekend. Thanks for being such a willing subject, and thanks for taking an interest in me. And Matt. I probably won't see you in the morning, at the airport. You two are flying into Newark, aren't you?" I gave her my card, which she tucked into her purse—a vintage Judith Leiber, surely.

"I hope you don't mind if I put you on my Christmas card list, Kenny. Old habits die hard."

"I'll be honored," I said.

Elaine looked into my eyes and said, "Follow your heart, Kenny." We embraced, and then we parted. I wondered if I'd see her again. It didn't seem likely. But then, what in life is likely? The grooms stopped to thank Matt and me on their way upstairs.

"Ken, I think you got the Momma treatment this weekend," Dan said.

"Thanks for sharing her, Dan. I loved it."

"We live in Chelsea. You're in Park Slope? We're not so far apart. Maybe dinner, some evening soon?" Dan suggested. "We'd love to see you." Caleb joined him and flashed his delicious smile. "Both of you?" Dan wondered.

"What a good idea," I said. "I'll let you know." There were embraces and kisses all around, and the grooms were gone.

Matt asked me, "What are you going to let Dan know?"

"He asked me, pretty much, if you would be in New York with me when we all meet for dinner. Matt, we haven't discussed this, but I just finalized my plans. Just this minute. I'm going to trade in my ticket for two seats in coach. And you're coming to New York with me tomorrow. I want you there forever, but if you only give me a week, I'll take what I can get. But I won't discuss it. It's a done deal. You have a few hours to make arrangements."

"Do you always make decisions for other people's lives?" Matt asked.

"Only when I'm cornered," I said. "Only when my future depends on it. This situation qualifies."

"In that case, I guess I'd better get busy," he said. Matt embraced me. We made certain Tisha needed no further images, and then we headed to our rooms.

"Matt, will you check out of the hotel and go home to pack a few things for the trip? You won't need much. A few shirts and jeans, maybe. I intend to keep you naked as much as possible." I was sputtering with excitement. "You don't really have to bring anything but your toiletry kit, Matt. You can wear my clothes. I'd love to see you in them. I'd love to see you in my bed, most of all."

"Kenny, let me get on with this," he said. "I have to make a phone call, to get some time off. And I'll pack. I'll be back for dinner. How's that?" The elevator arrived at his floor.

"It's perfect, but I expected nothing less, Matt." He was off to accomplish his portion of the plan. I sprang into action, too. As soon as I had gotten back to my room, taken off my suit, and hung it up, I phoned the airline to make the switch. There was a fee. I couldn't have cared less. The only thing that mattered was that Matt was coming to New York!

There was a strange moment when I was dressing for dinner, just before Matt arrived with his wheelie. I stood in front of a mirror to make sure I didn't have toothpaste on my collar or an open fly, and Patrick appeared just behind my right shoulder. He smiled at me as only Patrick could smile, and then he waved goodbye. I nearly reached for him, but then I

stopped myself. It didn't seem fair—to either of us—
to keep him chained to me any longer.

When Matt tapped on my door, I was a different
man. A free agent maybe? Except that my heart was
already no longer my own.

Chapter Six

Matt and I floated through dinner. We had chosen the most secluded restaurant in the hotel in the hope of having some privacy. Not a wedding guest in sight! I don't remember what we ate. The food seemed irrelevant. I do remember we drank a bubbly rosé. Lovely. And then it was back to my room.

"Cold feet?" I asked Matt.

"Let's find out," he answered.

We were long past the nervousness of "Will he or won't he?" and the anticipation of our first kiss. We even had some shared knowledge of our bodies. And yet I had never given myself permission to make love to Matt. And I knew that was about to change. Matt had a face—a wonderful face—and a name—a delightful name. And I was ready to embrace him fully.

We began to shed our clothes. I knelt at Matt's feet to untie his desert boots. From that vantage point I couldn't resist reaching for his legs and pressing my face against his torso. Matt's impressively colored—and sized—cock was already standing at full attention. I took it into my mouth for the first time. Delicious.

I could have happily spent the night worshiping at that altar, except that Matt reached for my shoulders and encouraged me to stand. He looked at me carefully and then kissed me deeply. "Please come to bed, Kenny," he said. I didn't need to be asked twice. We sank into my bed and continued with the first tastes I had already begun.

I liked everything about Matt's body—the texture of his skin, the slightly salty taste of his armpits, the way his nipples hardened when I nibbled them. I had somehow not noticed before what beautiful hands Matt had. And feet as well, I discovered. Warm feet, at that. But the treasures I most wanted to explore were between his legs. The delicate blue veining on the shaft of his penis was repeated in his scrotum. I might have played with Matt's balls for hours except that the area below them beckoned to me.

I eased Matt's legs over his head and dove for the sweet spot. I had always known that Matt had an exceptionally cute butt, but I was unprepared for the thrill of actually tasting it. I was like a starving man at a banquet. I *was* a starving man, actually. Had been for four years. I tried to measure my pace, without much success.

Matt knew exactly what he wanted, which was more than my lips and my tongue could provide. Again he reached for my shoulders, and again he urged me to align our bodies. When I kissed Matt there was a new urgency in his kiss. He smiled and said, "Yes." That was all the encouragement I needed.

I tried to be gentle and respectful, but my body was in a frenzy. When I presented my dick for entry, Matt smiled broadly—he invited me in. I was so afraid of hurting him, and yet he seemed more than ready. As I eased myself in, Matt winced once, early on, but his smile quickly returned. And then it never wavered. Some people have a sex face that's a little scary. Not Matt. He looked positively angelic the entire time our bodies were joined.

I had nearly forgotten the rush of emotions that accompany inhabiting the beloved. I started to weep softly. Matt welcomed my tears as easily as he welcomed the rest of me. He held me, and I knew I was home. I have no idea how long our union lasted. All I remember is when Matt gripped me, whispered, "Kenny, please don't stop," and then splashed wave after wave of sweet pearlescence onto his chest.

I felt his spasms, from within, and they pushed me right over the edge. I erupted as deeply inside Matt as I could manage to be. We clung to each other for a while, until our breathing had nearly normalized. And then we started to laugh. Matt first, I think. I wanted to stay inside him—forever, really. But it doesn't work that way, of course.

We lay together for a while, sharing more kisses. Eventually, Matt said, "Kenny, that was even better than anything I hoped for. Thank you."

"Elaine was right, you know," I said. "I'm in love with you, Matt. I want you with me always. I want to build a new life with you. I want it all." We were silent for a while. And then I asked him, "Matt, what do *you* want?"

He seemed to understand that I had considered the question, and so he considered his reply. Matt said, "Look, Kenny, I've done a lot of stupid things in my life, but I'm not about to miss the chance to love you. That would be insane. I want the two of us as much as you do. I want to hear you say, 'I love you,' every night before we go to sleep and every morning when we wake up. I want to know more about you than you know about yourself. I want to know every inch of your body better than I know the back of my hand. I want to hold you for the rest of my life."

That shut me up for a while. Eventually, I said, "I thought you were a visual artist, Matt. What's this with the words?"

"I have my moments," he said. "And so do you. Kenny, could we maybe not have any more questions tonight?"

"Great idea," I said. "They interfere with kisses." We did kiss for a while, and then we brushed our teeth and settled in for sleep. Matt took the same side of the bed as before, and he spooned me, as before. And I felt warm and safe, as before. Even with all the excitement of our new union and our life-changing trip coming up in the morning, I slept like a baby.

📖

I don't mind long flights. I figure if I'm going to get on a plane, I might as well get my money's worth. A thirty-minute flight feels like: "Why didn't I just take the train?" Connecting flights and layovers, however, can be a bit trying. I wasn't anxious that Tuesday morning, because I had Matt by my side. He was just as beautiful and as cheerful as he had been the previous mornings we shared.

I couldn't quite let go of my fears, however. As we were sitting in the flight lounge at Chicago O'Hare, waiting to board the final flight of our journey, I said to him, "Matt, I promised myself I wouldn't push you for details, but I'm dying to know how long you'll stay—how long you'll let me hold you."

"Hush, Kenny," he said. "Let's deal with it as it comes. I don't know yet if I can just walk away from my past. You're asking me to give up my life and create a new one with you. I cherish the invitation. But I need a minute to consider all the ramifications."

"Of course you do," I said. "I won't pressure you about this again, Matt. Because I know you'll make the right choice, and because I know you'll be gentle with my heart, however it goes."

Matt said, "Look, Kenny, I'm not exactly a kid. I've had a few boyfriends. I like being in love, and I like having really good sex. But I've never experienced *you* before. And I've never wanted anyone the way I want you, Kenny. Please, let me figure this out." Matt looked serious and fragile and ethereal, all at the same time. He let me shoot a few frames.

"In your own time," I said. We were quiet for the rest of the trip. We smiled a lot. I was glad we were flying into LaGuardia. It makes it so easy to get home—except for New Yorkers who live in far eastern Queens, I suppose. Since I had moved to Park Slope in Brooklyn, I was probably equally close to JFK. And yet it still felt remote to me, after years as a Manhattanite. I booked an Uber as soon as we landed.

It was Matt's first trip to New York City, of course. I warned him not to expect much from our drive through Queens on our way to Brooklyn. If you've seen one expressway, you've seen 'em all. I hoped he would like my neighborhood. I had fallen in love with my tree-lined street with its carefully maintained brownstones. I felt fortunate to have found a ground floor apartment—with a garden! Had I waited a year before changing boroughs, I would never have found anything affordable.

"Come in, Matty," I said. "Follow me." I led him to the bedroom, of course. "There's plenty of closet space. I've never had a houseguest before. But then I don't suppose that's what you are. You'll love waking up in the morning to the sound of birdsong in the garden. The summer birds are making their way back right now. The snowbirds have already flown wherever they fly for the summer. Spring is a beautiful season here—and everywhere, I suppose. I don't spend all that much time in the garden, but I love looking at it from my bedroom window. Nature parades before my eyes. I think I'm babbling," I said.

"I like it when you babble, Kenny. It shows that you care."

"Well, there's a lot I care about. But today, most of it concerns you, Matt. Let's stow your gear and head out, so I can show you my neighborhood." And that's what we did. I was never much of a clotheshorse, and I was good at culling the older things I'd never wear again, so there was plenty of room for Matt's clothes. I smiled a lot. So did he. It was a bit cloudy, but otherwise a nice day. Perfect for photography. I grabbed my camera. We went out to the shops that were only a block-and-a-half from me. So convenient.

"Buy you a coffee, Cowboy?" I asked. Matt smiled. I steered him to my favorite coffee shop—the one that also roasted and blended the beans I brewed at home. I greeted the counterman, Omar, and ordered two Americanos. "The cleaners is around the corner," I told Matt. "The wine shop is in the next block. There are three or four decent restaurants nearby. The people at the Greenmarket are very nice. I can always grab a quart of milk at the deli, and for serious grocery shopping, there's a Whole Foods within walking distance."

"It's a real neighborhood," Matt said. "I didn't know what to expect, but then I can't imagine you not grounded, Kenny—not rooted in place. I'm like that too. I still feel tied to places I hate." Matt had a faraway look in his eyes. I tried to capture it with my lens. Middling success, I decided. But something to remember him by. I didn't ask Matt to explain. I didn't want to intrude. I figured anything Matt wanted me to know he would tell me—in his own time.

"So, what would you like for dinner, Cowboy?" I asked. "I think we should go out on our first evening here together. I'll cook for you tomorrow. Italian, probably. My grandmother was an awesome cook. I learned a little, even though boys weren't supposed to be in the kitchen. There were lots of things boys weren't supposed to do. I mostly did them anyway."

"How did I know that?" Matt asked. He smiled broadly.

"I love your smile, Matt," I said. "But then I love everything about you. Do you suppose Omar would mind if I stretched you out on this table and had my wicked way with you?"

"Ask him," Matt said. "I don't normally have sex in public places, but I'm game. Should I strip?"

"I don't want to share you with anyone. Not even the prying eyes of strangers. I do, however, have an intense need to make love to you, Matt. Could we go home?"

"An excellent idea," he said. On our way out, I introduced him to Omar, since Matt was now part of the neighborhood—I hoped. And then we raced home, stripped as quickly as we could, and fell into bed.

"Yes," I said. "Matt, you're the best feeling thing in the world. And the best tasting. I can't get enough of you."

"Hush, Kenny," Matt said. "I can't kiss you when you're talking." I became silent, of course. And Matt did kiss me. He also kissed a number of my body parts. I usually prefer to be doing something, rather than being done. But I was eager for anything Matt wanted. We bounced around my bed like a couple of teenagers. I hadn't felt so acrobatic since I-couldn't-remember-when.

It was the joy, really—the sheer joy of being together. I'd have done anything that brought Matt pleasure. I'd have gotten on all fours and barked like a dog if he had asked me to. I'd have let him inside me if he had wanted it. No man had been there since a bad experience when I was seventeen. I was ready to release that memory and make new ones. Yes, I would be ready if the situation arose. I wanted it. Intensely. Yes. I wanted Matt any way I could get him.

Eventually, Matt lay face-down, spread eagle on my bed. I covered his torso with mine and matched him limb for limb. We clasped hands as I entered his perfect body. He welcomed me like a flawless host. I explored his interior. I wouldn't have believed that anything could feel warmer than the rest of his body. But his interior did. I moved in, really. I wanted to own Matt, one hundred percent. He granted my fantasy. He surrendered to me, body and soul. I took possession of both.

I had never—not even with Patrick—felt so close to another human. Never mind the tears I shed, which mixed in with our kisses. It couldn't last forever, of course, as much as I wanted it to. The sensations crescendoed until there was no turning back. Just as I was about to erupt, Matt shouted, "I love you, Kenny!" and then all hell broke loose. We gradually came down from our high. I'm sure I started to laugh first, that time. Matt joined me.

"Matt, I'm speechless," I said.

"You expect me to believe that?" Matt asked. More laughter. We lay together in the late afternoon sunlight that steamed in from the garden along with a robin's song. I didn't release Matt for a very long while. I continued to lie on top of him for as long as I dared. He seemed comfortable with that arrangement of our bodies. He drew my left hand in close to his face and kissed it.

Eventually, I had to give up possession. Reluctantly. "I'm going to pour some wine," I said. "Red or white?"

"White, I think, if you have some open."

"Always," I said. "Here, take this robe. Come see the rest of the apartment, Matt. I can't very well expect you to spend all your time in the bedroom, as much as I'd like it." I poured two glasses of chardonnay, and we took them to the living room. We smiled a lot. Eventually, I said, "Matt, that changed my life—making love to you just now. I'm a different man. I hope I'm a better man. Talk to me."

"I was there, too, Kenny," he said. "I've never felt sensations like that before. Maybe I've never really been in love before. It's possible. You're a hot guy, Ken, but that's only just part of it. I've gladly shared my body with lots of hot guys who wanted to use it.

And I've enjoyed lots of orgasms in the process. It was all good fun. But you showed me something different, Ken. No man has ever wanted me so completely. I think that's it. No man has ever honored me as you do. And my head is still reeling from it."

So, that's how it happened that *two* heads were reeling that spring evening in my apartment in Park Slope. We decided not to go out for dinner after all. We spent the rest of the evening in robes, looking at each other, mostly. I ordered a food delivery from my favorite Greek restaurant. It was adequate. Looking at Matt was better.

At bedtime, I began to feel sad about sleep robbing me of the ability to see Matt. But as we settled in and I felt him holding me—as our bodies pressed together and our left limbs entwined—I gave in to the sweetness of innocent slumber.

In the morning, I uploaded all my wedding images to my laptop and began the process of selecting the ones I wanted to submit to Tisha. Matt had brought his laptop, of course, and so he did the same. It was fun sitting across the dining table from him while we worked. I could imagine many mornings like that—two visual artists plying their craft in perfect harmony. In my apartment. I didn't ask Matt if he had the same imaginings. I didn't want to disturb him. I do sometimes know how to shut my mouth at the right moments. Sometimes.

By noon we were both ready to upload our results. I went first because still images are so much less data-rich than videos. I asked Matt, "How about some lunch, Cowboy?"

"What did you have in mind, City Slicker?"

"What I had in mind is what I always have in mind. But I think we should eat something, too. There's a little deli that makes great Cuban sandwiches. Why don't we head there as soon as we get you uploaded?"

"Sure, but I don't know what a Cuban sandwich is," Matt said.

"You will soon enough," I said. We scheduled Matt's upload. My Internet connection was on its good behavior. In fifteen minutes, we were ready to pull on some clothes and head out into the early spring sunlight. "I had a thought, Matt. We could pick up some sandwiches and some water and a bottle of wine with a screw cap. They have plastic cups at the deli, and paper napkins, of course. We could have a picnic in Prospect Park."

"Whatever you think," Matt said. "I'm all yours."

"Good," I said. "Let's keep it that way." We gathered the elements of our picnic as we worked our way east. Matt put his arm around my waist as we walked along. "I love Central Park," I told him, "but I almost like Prospect Park better. It's slightly less grand, I suppose. Same design team. Maybe Brooklyn was still a separate city at the time. Competition, you know. But don't quote me. History is not my forte."

After we had entered the park, we stopped at the first picnic area we encountered. There we unpacked our goodies in a shady spot. "It's a little early in the season for sunbathing," I said, "but then you don't look like much of a sun worshiper."

Matt laughed. He didn't need to say, "With this pale skin?"

"I don't sun either," I said. "Used to when I was twenty. In Provincetown. Patrick loved the sun, even though he got nasty burns. We used to douse him with vinegar and then baby oil, and then we'd make love. Carefully. Those were sweet times." Did I become a little distant? Probably. Matt was patient with me.

"Great sandwich," he said. "What makes it Cuban?"

"It has all the major Caribbean food groups—white bread, fresh and cured pig, cheese, pickles.

They started grilling these things in Havana in the '30s, I think," I said. "But again, don't quote me. Get your history from Mr. Google, Matt. And please come to me for love."

"So smart," Matt said. "And speaking of love, do we have a date this afternoon, or did I imagine that?"

"Let me check my calendar," I said. We finished our picnic, dropped all the disposables in the proper trash bins, and headed home. I wanted Matt just as much as I had wanted him for days, but there was less urgency in our homeward trip than in previous anticipations of going to bed. It was more … comfortable. Being together was nearly enough. Matt and I held hands the whole way. We both smiled a lot. It was lovely.

When I turned my key in the bottom lock to complete our entry, I said, "Come in, Matty. I hope we're not late for our appointment."

"I think we're worth waiting for," he said. No question. We put the remains of the wine and the water in the fridge, and then we headed for the bedroom. Surprise, surprise. I had been craving Matt's kiss all afternoon. He gave me exactly what I needed. We slipped out of our clothes, gradually, and eased our way into bed.

"I love the way you warm my sheets," I said. "But then … no, I won't say it."

"Say what?"

"How much I love everything about you, Matt. You'll grow tired of it. And I couldn't bear that."

"Hush, Kenny," he said. "There's nothing about you I could grow tired of. Do you need to hear every little thing I love about you? Are you that needy?"

"Yes," I said. "I need to hear everything."

"Okay, but let's pace ourselves," Matt said. "How about if I tell you how beautiful your throat is? I think maybe I noticed your Adam's apple first—the way it leads the eye down to the perfect modeling of your collar bones and up to the tiny dimple in your chin. It's sculptural perfection, Kenny—your throat—and it would be easy to get lost in its combination of strength and vulnerability, masculinity and delicacy, armor and invitation."

We were silent for a while. I got so much more than I requested. Eventually, Matt said, "I don't have any more speeches in me today. Could we make love, maybe?" I became instantly nonverbal as I reached for Matt. He fell into my arms with a perfect combination of submission and intent. I responded in kind, really. I wanted whatever he wanted. And what Matt wanted was to be in charge. No problem there. I had always considered myself a top, but domination never interested me. If I can bring my partner pleasure, then I'm a happy man.

Matt eased me back onto the pillows as he kissed me sweetly and held my head in his hands. First he visited the throat he had professed admiration for. And then Matt began to pay calls to other regions. He found body parts to nibble and caress that I had all but ignored my entire life. I knew I wouldn't make those mistakes again.

In time, Matt settled into full-on cock worship. I was awed by his devotion. Most men enjoy a good blowjob, I suppose. I was never really one of those men. But that Wednesday afternoon I submitted to Matt's desire. I accepted his attentions in the spirit in which they were offered. I assumed the role of Priapus. I became an erection in search of someone to satisfy. My someone was closely monitoring my pleasure.

As I got close to an eruption, Matt held my balls tenderly in his warm right hand and my right buttock in his warm left hand. The combination was irresistible. I relaxed, as much as possible, into the inevitability of an orgasm that was devoted entirely to my beloved. It was all for Matt, surely. Every pulse. Every drop. Was I having an out-of-body experience? Maybe. But I can swear I watched Matt—from some vantage point above my bed—as he received everything I had to give him.

As soon as Matt was certain he had offered me every possible oral pleasure, he straddled my pelvis, reared back, and stroked his own priapic perfection for a few seconds before he gifted me with a lava-flow of living essence. It seemed to go everywhere, Matt's fluid offering—onto my chest, onto my face, into my hair. I didn't mind the wave that landed in my left eye, even though we all know how much it burns. A small price to pay.

Matt roared with pleasure and satisfaction as he sprayed me with his best. We gathered up every drop that landed in an accessible zone. I knew how sweet Matt's semen tasted, but I was unprepared for the experience of sharing it with him. I was largely unprepared for a lot of our experiences that week. I figured it out as I went along. He did, too, really.

I beckoned to Matt, and he fell onto my chest. As I wrapped my arms around him, I think there was a bird fight going on in the garden. Everyone gets upset when bluejays appear. Other than that, we were mostly oblivious to anything negative. We lay together for many minutes. I tried to just be quiet. That didn't last for long. I said to him, "Matt, I can't do this. I can't fall in love and then lose you. I'm not built that way. I don't have the strength for it."

"You have the strength for anything, Kenny," he said, "but I'm not going anywhere. Soon. We don't have to deal with loss. Not now. And if we do, we'll manage it together." Was I reassured? Partially, I suppose. But the thought of losing Matt still horrified me. I vowed to enjoy every moment we shared.

"I know I said I'd cook for you, Matty, but not tonight, please. I can't bear to let go of you long enough to shake pots. We'll do it soon. But I can pour a glass of wine with one hand and hold you with the other. What do you say to that?"

"So sapient," Matt said. "And after you've plied me with wine, how about I take you to dinner?"

"*Che saggio*," I said. "*Io sono molto contento.*"

"I don't savvy your lingo, but I think that was a yes," Matt said. "What should we eat?"

"Well, you know my favorite food," I said. "But maybe we should vary the diet. How do you feel about Puerto Rican cooking?"

"Don't tease me, Kenny. Just feed me," he said. And that's what I did.

Chapter Eight

I phoned Tisha in the morning. "Kenny, I was just about to call you," she said. "Everything looks great, and I wanted you to know that you were spot-on: The art director chose the wedding cake scene for the cover! It's going to look terrific."

"Glad to hear it. It was a fun shoot, Tisha. Thanks for thinking of me."

"I'm always thinking of you, Kenny," she said, "which is why I wanted to ask you to come to dinner, maybe on Monday? Dan and Caleb are available then, and I know they'd love to see you."

"Tisha, that sounds lovely. Well, I'm sure you know that Matt flew to New York with me."

"Hey, Kenny, you're talking to *me* now. I know everything. I was just about to ask you if Matt can join us."

"I'll ask him," I said. "I'm sure he'd love to. If he's still in town."

"I won't touch that," she said. "Just get your pretty ass over to my place on Monday, and you'd better have the squeeze in tow. It's going to be a celebration. No tears allowed."

"Got it," I said. "Thanks, Tish. Talk soon."

"What did Tisha say?" Matt asked me. "I only caught, like, every other word."

Bruce K Beck

"She said the artwork looks great—that includes yours, of course—and she wants us to come to her apartment for dinner on Monday. I said I'd ask you." We hadn't yet had 'the talk' about how long Matt was staying. I grew quiet. It seemed time to acknowledge the elephant in the room.

"I can't just disappear from Missoula, Kenny," Matt said. "I have a life there. A job. An apartment. A few friends. Even some family I rarely see. I have to go back. On Wednesday. That's all I know, Kenny. I want to share my life with you, but it has to be done properly. I can't leave loose ends out West. Please trust me."

"I do trust you, Matt," I said. "I just can't imagine my life without you in it. I won't pressure you. Just come back to me as soon as you can. That's all I ask." Matt embraced me warmly. We held each other for a while. He kissed me. That helped. "So, I'll tell Tisha yes, for Monday?"

"Sure. Sounds like fun." And that's what I did.

Tisha's apartment smelled wonderful. I knew she liked to cook, but I had never had the pleasure of sampling her kitchen efforts. I should have assumed that Tisha could cook as competently as she did everything else. "Come in, boys," she said. "You both look so edible I can't decide which of you I want first."

"How about both of us? At the same time," I suggested.

"An excellent idea," she said. She kissed me, and then she kissed Matt. "Come in, men. You know everyone. I'll bet Lisa will pour you a glass of wine."

I gave Tisha the little box of cookies I had brought, and Matt gave her the bottle of brandy we had selected. More kisses. Lisa was just as lively and fun as she had been in Montana. She poured us glasses of a delicious red.

"We're not supposed to talk shop tonight," Lisa said, "but I just have to tell you both how much I love the work you did for the shoot—the stills and the video. You exceeded my expectations, and I expect nothing less than perfection. And I love working with artists who make me look good. Enough of that. Matt, how do you like New York?"

"I love it," Matt said. "I wasn't sure what to expect, but Kenny is a great host."

"I'll bet you can get him to take you to the Statue of Liberty—*someday*. Meanwhile, I'm sure he has a very comfortable bedroom." We all laughed. Tisha had planned a Filipino feast for us. It started with some snacky things—empanadas that looked for all the world like Hispano-Caribbean treats, except for the bean sprouts and eggs and dry sausage inside. Vinegar-based dipping sauce. Delicious.

Dinner started with a seafood soup—rich and hot and spicy. Mains included roast pig and a braised chicken dish called adobo—not Mexican in the least but nicely seasoned with East-meets-West ingredients. Vegetables—and rice, of course. Flan for dessert. A feast, indeed. "Tisha, this is an amazing meal," I said. "I don't know if I've ever dined this well. How did you manage it?"

"I had the weekend to prep," she said, modestly. "Let's have coffee in the living room." Before we left the table, Dan proposed a well-deserved toast to our hostess. We all joined in enthusiastically. And then we dispersed. I took a seat, and Dan joined me. Matt and Caleb began to converse nearby. The ladies were doing a preliminary straightening-up of the dinner things.

"Dan, please say hello to your parents for me," I said. "I loved meeting them."

"And they loved meeting you," Dan said. "Elaine was about to start adoption proceedings until I said to her, 'Momma, you already have Caleb and me. Aren't we enough?' She conceded that we would do nicely. But, Kenny, if you want to stay in touch with them, I'm sure they'd be delighted." Then Dan said to me, quietly, "And what about Matt? Is he staying?"

"He's flying home on Wednesday. Maybe to finish up his life in Montana, and maybe to stay there. I don't know. He'll break my heart if he doesn't return, but it's not really up to me, after all."

"Maybe Caleb can help," Dan said. "I'll ask him. I could be an idiot, but I suspect Caleb will have some perspective on this. Leave it to me."

I thanked Dan for taking an interest in our futures. Tisha and Lisa rejoined the gentlemen. We all sat contentedly, enjoying the buzz that can only follow a fine meal enjoyed in fine company. When Dan and Caleb rose to leave, I took that as my cue. "Tisha, this was amazing. I'm speechless." Matt chuckled.

"I loved having you two here tonight," Tisha said. "We could make it a weekly thing, you know." That was directed at Matt. He got it, of course. He embraced her warmly. But he offered no info about his future availability. I kissed the ladies good night, and Matt and I followed Dan and Caleb to the elevator.

When we reached the street, Dan said, "I wish we could give you a lift, but since we're headed in opposite directions...."

I embraced Caleb. I hadn't really spoken to him that evening. I said to him, "So how's married life treating you?" He flashed his wonderful smile at me, there in the harsh streetlight in front of Tisha's building. The wattage of Caleb's smile brightened everything.

"Kenny, I knew I wanted to share my life with Dan," he said, "but I was unprepared for the experience of marriage. It's a spiritual thing. I can't describe it, but I hope to find the words some day. Meanwhile, I can recommend it highly." Another smile. Another embrace. I kissed Dan and said good night, and they were off. I looked at Matt, who had his own wattage, of course, there in the greenish light of a nighttime sidewalk. I pressed him close to me. Our car arrived and sped us home.

When I let us into the apartment, I was quiet, to begin with. After we had taken off our clothes and slipped into Ts and shorts, Matt said, "Kenny, I don't have any friends like that in Missoula. I don't think Montana makes people that energized and loving."

"Montana made you, Matt. And Caleb. And you're neither of you chopped liver, if you'll excuse the New Yorkism. Stay with me, Matty. There are eight and a half million New Yorkers. And we can always use one more. No pressure. I promised myself I wouldn't bring it up. I want you to do whatever you need to do with your life. It's just that if that doesn't include me, then I don't know how I'll ..."

"Hush, Kenny," he said. Matt embraced me. He said, "Can we turn in now? I want to hold you, Kenny. All night long if you'll let me."

"So smart!" I said. "Let's do it." And that's what we did.

Chapter Nine

I was mostly quiet that Tuesday, the day before Matt's flight to Montana. I needed to ready some photos for a show that was opening in June. The exhibition was timed for Pride Month. I'd have preferred to be thought of as a photographer rather than a _gay_ photographer, but I was proud to be included in that collection. My gallerist had asked me for twenty images. That would give me a generous amount of wall space. I was eager to get it right.

I had made most of my choices before Montana. Many of the images were already finalized. I was working on the ones that were still raw, which included three new ones from the trip. It was a process—completing the edits and submitting the files to my printer, followed by approving the prints, signatures, and mounting. I had just enough time to make it work.

I was glad for the distraction—especially for the chance to work on a portrait of Matt. It was a shot I grabbed in a quiet moment at the airport, in Chicago. It seemed to me at the time I photographed him that Matt looked like a sad little boy who had been offered a ray of hope. Or was that wishful thinking? Or was I delusional? The portrait would end up as _I_ wished it to be, of course. Isn't that the very nature of portraiture? Life, however, can be quite different.

Matt was quiet, too. He made a little lunch for us. I poured us a glass of wine. I stopped my work long enough to join Matt for a bite and to stare into his eyes. I wanted to be certain I had memorized his face on the chance that I might not see it again. I was also keen to talk to him, of course. "Matt," I asked, "what do you most want to do—professionally, I mean—when ... if you come back to New York?"

Matt smiled thoughtfully. "I like my video work," he said. "It feels satisfying. I taught myself to edit, and so I can create now. I've learned how to present information and entertainment, I think. And there's so much more to learn. And so much new technology every day. I want to be part of the future."

"Do you mind if I speak to Tisha about it?" I asked. "They have so many video needs at *GLITZ* these days—as their online presence grows. And, of course, she knows everybody."

"Thanks, Kenny," Matt said. "That would be great." We went back to being quiet.

I completed my work. I was satisfied that if I spent another moment on Matt's portrait, I'd only screw it up. I surrendered to the need to finish things and move on. I poured a glass of wine and said to Matt, "I'm going to phone Tisha to thank her for dinner. I could ask her advice about your future, if you want. Matt, please, I'm not trying to pressure you."

"Hush, Kenny," he said. "I know you want to help, and I love you for it. Thank Tisha for me."

I placed the call. "Tisha, what an extraordinary dinner!" I said. "We had a lovely time. I don't know how you do it."

"Well, Kenny, you didn't grow up on the South Side of Chicago, so maybe you'll never know how I do it."

"Boston's North End doesn't count, I suppose. But I hope it gives me some perspective. Tish, could we just talk about the present?"

"God, yes!" Tisha said. "You and Matt are both charming guests. Let's do it again soon."

"Love to!" I said. "I have a request: I spoke to Matt a little while ago about his career plans, and he has strong feelings about his video work. I told him I'd ask you for guidance."

"Interesting timing," Tisha said. "We just had a meeting this afternoon about our video program. When our online presence became more important than print, we hired a small video start-up to plan and execute our needs. They're competent, if not inspired. But today we talked about doing that work in-house, so that everyone can be on the same page minute to minute. Matt's wedding coverage was perfect for our style. He seemed to know exactly what to shoot and how to edit it for maximum impact. Put him on."

"Sure. He's right here," I said, handing the phone to Matt. Tisha's voice was clarion enough that I overheard much of their conversation. Essentially, Tisha invited Matt to interview for a position at the magazine, maybe even Video Director. She also told him it had to be within the next week or two. Matt's part of the conversation was mostly "Yes" and "Thank you." After "Thanks, again, Tisha" and "Goodbye," Matt returned my phone. He looked a bit dazed.

I let him sit with the news, to process it in his own time. He asked, "Did you hear...?" I gave him a nod.

"It's crazy—a job opportunity like this. I'm over-whelmed."

"Well, I'm overjoyed, if it's what you want," I said. "Sleep on it. Meanwhile, I have an idea to take your mind off business. I think we should make love."

Matt said, "I think you're right." I gave Matt my hand, which he took, and I led him to the bedroom. We peeled off our at-home clothes in seconds. Matt's embrace was heavenly. I wondered if I could live without it. Most of all, of course, I wondered if I'd *have* to live without it. Matt's kiss relieved some of my fears, and he gave me the gift of his sweet body. I took it with the reverence of a man who believes he has found his one chance for redemption.

We were mostly still for the rest of the day. We never stirred from the apartment, ordering in a just-okay food delivery for supper. I vowed to be cheerful and not to drink too much. I mostly kept my vows. Mostly. Matt threw the last of his things into his bag—everything but his toilet kit and the clothes he had decided to wear on the flight.

I wanted to help, but my heart wasn't in it. So I mostly stayed out of his way, except for handing Matt a bikini brief of mine and asking him to wear it home. I wanted to be able to think of his perfect buttocks cradled in long-staple Egyptian cotton, and not too much of it. Matt agreed. He also kissed me.

My sleep was fitful, even with Matt's arm around me. I've rarely welcomed the dawn so eagerly. The chirps and (real) twitters in the garden gave me a lit-tle perspective. I rose carefully, without disturbing Matt, and went to the kitchen to make coffee. I took some eggs, butter, and good bread and marmalade out of the fridge. I had some sausages in the freezer.

I figured if I had to send my man off on a journey, I could at least fill his belly first.

Matt was beautiful—as always—when he wandered into the kitchen a little while later. I sat him down and tried to pamper him. I watched him sitting at the kitchen table in my old robe, and I began to weep softly. I turned back to my cooking chores. It's good to be busy. After breakfast, Matt took a quick shower and dressed for his trip (starting with my shorts). He wheeled his bag to the front door. "That time" was fast approaching.

I slipped into Matt's bag a package of *Sevillanas*—Mexican sweets made from *cajeta* (*dulce de leche*) sandwiched between sheer wafers. "Call me often," I said. "Remember, we have 'unlimited talk and text.' I don't know what you'll be doing, so I'll try not to bother you." I wondered how good I'd be at not bothering him. Matt embraced me with reassuring tenderness. A genuine kiss, a genuine "I love you," and he was gone.

The emptiness I felt was no surprise. It had begun to set in days before. I sat at the breakfast table for a while, drinking coffee and studying the plates and utensils that Matt had just used. I would wash them and put them away, of course. The only shrine I'd build would be my bed. I refused to change the sheets until Matt returned. And if he didn't return? I supposed I'd become Miss Havisham.

I stopped in at my coffee place the day after Matt flew home. Omar knew my blend—mostly Sumatra and French roast Colombian plus a few little tweaks he had recommended. I usually bought two pounds and put it in the freezer. "Where's your friend?" he asked while he was blending and grinding.

"Matt had to go home to Montana," I answered. The reality of it was like a leaden weight in my stomach.

"But he'll be back, right?" Omar asked.

"I hope so," I said. That was certainly the truth.

"Are you going to marry him, Kenny?" he asked.

I think I blushed a little before I said, "Omar, what a question! Why would you ask that?"

"I've known you, what, three years now? I've never seen you in love, Kenny. Never. You can't hide it, you know. What are you going to do?"

"I wish I could tell you, Omar. It's up to Matt now. I can only make so many decisions for him. He has to want it as much as I do. I thought *bartenders* were supposed to be amateur shrinks. Now it's baristas, too?"

Omar didn't often grace me with his wonderful smile. He did that afternoon. Just when I needed it. "Do you know how many people I see every day? I'm an excellent judge of character. Kenny, he's a nice guy. Trust your young man. He'll come back to you. Now, go home. I have work to do!"

I got on with my life, as much as possible. I could take photographs and plan the images I wanted to create from them. I could make sure I ate reasonably well and exercised reasonably often. I could do lots of things while wallowing in self-pity. I did speak to Matt often. Our phone conversations mostly skated cheerfully over the surface of the situation. "When are you coming home?" was my only real question, and the only one I couldn't ask. I waited.

Did I reopen my Grindr account? Mindless sex is an excellent way to lighten the sadness—and the anger—of being abandoned. I considered it. I wanted it. I might have started fucking around, except that Matt was the only man allowed in my bed. And coming home with another man's scent on my body would have defiled my shrine. A long hot shower and all the perfumes of Arabia would not have sweetened my body enough for me to lie in the sheets that Matt had consecrated with his presence.

So, celibate me got through the days and the nights. I accomplished some new work, and I stopped by my printer every other day to approve prints and sign them for the gallery show. It was not exactly my favorite definition of life, but it was productive. And it was the only way I knew to do it— just as surely as Matt was on the only path he knew. I tried to be generous. I tried to remember only the love. Sure.

It was nearly a week and a half into Matt's absence when he finally had some real news for me. "I never meant for this to drag on so long," he said. "For one thing, I thought I should see my mother before I leave—I'm leaving Montana, Kenny. I'm coming to you—if you'll have me." Great shouts of joy don't communicate so well over the phone.

"I had nearly given up hope, darling," I said. "No, that's a lie, Matt. Let's not start our new life with a lie. I always knew you would return. I just didn't know when and how long I could survive your absence. Speaking of which?"

"Mom was visiting her sister in Idaho. She's back now. I had lunch with her yesterday, and I'm flying tomorrow. I should get in about dinner time."

"Perfect," I said. "I can just about last another day without you. Hurry to me, Matty. We still have so much to learn about each other. I'm more than ready to start."

"Good, Kenny," he said. "I've missed you more than I thought possible. I love you, you know."

I was pretty much speechless. There was an awkward pause, and then I said, "Get here fast, darling."

"I have an appointment with Tisha at *GLITZ* first thing Monday morning," Matt said. "They haven't made decisions about staffing yet. There's still a chance for me. Think good thoughts."

"Always, Matty." It was time for our conversation to end. I was all abuzz with the excitement of Matt's return. I spruced up the apartment—which had suffered a little neglect in recent days—and I did some laundry. I also spruced up my appearance—which had also suffered a little neglect recently. I planned what I would cook for Matt to welcome him home. I made a shopping list. I bustled.

With the shopping done, I was free to start cooking and to exult in the anticipation of having Matt back in my arms—back in my bed. While I baked a ricotta cake, I sang—a little Puccini, a little Verdi, a little Billie Holiday. My singing was always long on passion and short on technique, not to mention talent. But it amused me. And no one else had to suffer from the sounds produced in my throat.

Matt phoned me early in the morning to tell me his flight had been canceled—due to lack of interest, most likely. My heart sank. "There's a later flight they can get me on," he said. "But it means a redeye out of O'Hare. I'll only have time to shower and change before I go to meet Tisha. And if the flight is late, then I don't know what I'll do. Anyway, I booked it, and I'll see you as soon as possible, Kenny. I'll text you the flight numbers."

"Sorry, sweetie," I said. "Get as much sleep as you can on the flights. You'll be fine. Just get home to me as soon as you can." It was not the way I most wanted to spend my Sunday—alone. But I did things. I made my version of my nonna's Sunday Sauce. I had better olive oil than she used, and I would stir in some shreds of fresh basil leaves before dressing the pasta. And I would serve it with grated *reggiano parmigiano.* Nonna couldn't find anything finer than *grana padano*—nice enough, but not quite the king of cheeses.

In the afternoon, Caleb called to ask if the four of us could get together for dinner soon. He seemed to know that Matt was on his way home. Odd. "Give me a couple of dates, and I'll run them by Dan," he said.

"Absolutely," I said and pulled up my calendar. I suggested a Friday and a Saturday in the near future. And then I asked, "How did you know Matt would be here?"

"We Montanans have to stick together," he answered. "I spoke to him last week. And again yesterday. Kenny, I don't want you to worry if Matt's homecoming is delayed. Tisha will understand. We're all at the mercy of an airline now and then. Dan will smooth it over however it plays. He's very good at that. Very smart. Very patient. Very kind. And also relentless."

I laughed in spite of myself. "You should be in the PR business," I said. "I'm ready to hire Dan and I don't even know what the position is. Thanks, Caleb. You've been very helpful. I'd love to meet soon—the four of us." We agreed to speak again in the near future—sooner if Matt's flight plans derailed, and later if he got home and off to his interview on schedule.

I was grateful to Caleb, of course, but I couldn't help but wonder at his involvement in Matt's homecoming. Did I work up a slight case of jealousy? Nearly. I finished up my prep for what would become our Monday supper, and then I read for a while, watched some CNN, and turned in early. I was just about to drift off to sleep when Matt phoned to tell me the red-eye was overbooked and they had bumped him to a morning flight that would get him to LaGuardia in the early afternoon.

"*Coraggio, il mio amore,*" I said. "This will all work out somehow. Dan and Caleb are on the case. But you know that. Capable guys, I'd say."

"Thanks, Kenny. I'm trying to be optimistic, but mostly I'm feeling exhausted."

"Of course you are," I said. "Get some sleep, Matty, the best you can. The boys will start the process here. They'll let you know the plan, I'm sure. Put it out of your mind for now. Just sleep—and have a dream about me sucking your cock. May I share that dream with you?"

"I think we should share everything," Matt said.

"Good," I said. "I love you so much my heart is almost bursting. Sleep, baby." I hated to hang up and leave him stuck alone—but not quite alone enough—in an airport for the night. But we had no better choices in the matter. I slept a little.

📖

In the early morning it was Dan who phoned. "Sorry to wake you, Kenny, but I thought you'd want to know that I spoke to Tisha. She's locked into Matt's 9:30 interview. It's the only time that the whole committee can assemble. I told her to be creative. I told her to make it a remote interview. I think she'll take the ball and run with it—make it look like a refreshing idea. Anyway, that's what's going to happen this morning."

"Thanks, Dan," I said, "for taking an interest in Matt's future. For everything."

"Nonsense," he said. "I like bright people. And attractive people. And I also love seeing a perfect couple get the chances they need to make it work. Kenny, I adore both of you—individually and together. Caleb feels the same, by the way. He even.... Never mind. That's for him to tell. I'll let you go. Don't worry!"

I did worry, of course. I also got up and made coffee and pretended it was just another new day. I took my coffee—and my phone, of course—into the garden. There was a little morning haze that would probably burn off. It was a good day. It would have to be. It was the only one available. And I was the only one in the garden preoccupied with outside matters. The sparrows and the bumblebees were doing exactly what they always did on a warm late spring morning.

I hoped Matt would phone me before his interview—however it shaped up. I also hoped he'd use the time to compose himself and put me totally out of his mind. He did call. I shushed him and sent him back to the project at hand. And then I waited. Impatiently. The sparrows and the bumblebees couldn't have cared less.

I tried to imagine what was going on—a virtual interview while Matt was sitting in a flight lounge at O'Hare. An event like that would seem commonplace today, but it was rather exotic in the recent past. From what Dan said, I suspected it was all his idea. I think he suggested—firmly—that Tisha turn the conference room into a media space. They had the technology for it.

"It went well," Matt said when he phoned me after the interview."

"Good," I said. "Now get home where you belong. I'll feed you, if that's any incentive."

"You're the only incentive I need, Kenny," he said. And he ended the call so he could head to the gate for his homeward flight.

Dan phoned minutes later. "Tisha said Matt was brilliant. She said the committee will meet in a few days to finalize the staffing. She's confident." Dan also explained some of the details of the interview. Some of it was fascinating, and some of it I'd have preferred to hear from Matt face-to-face. Apparently they projected the signal Matt sent from his iPhone to the largest screen in the room. That gave Matt a certain immediacy—I'm told. I wasn't there.

And he was prepared, Dan said. No surprise there. Matt presented some ideas for regular video features for the magazine's media outlets. I had seen Matt when he was like a little boy, and I had seen him when he morphed into a man of substance. There was no doubt in my mind which iteration of Matt showed up for that interview.

I survived the afternoon, of course. And I welcomed Matt home. I melted at the mere sight of him. He fell into my arms and gave me the gift of his warmth and his sweetness—his love, most of all. "Please don't go away again," I said. "Not unless you take me with you. And not unless you take me some place that has an excellent bed."

We shared a good dinner, we talked and laughed and drank wine, and then we headed to *my* excellent bed. "Kenny, let me grab a shower," Matt said. "I'm sure I stink."

I went through the motions—theatrically—of smelling Matt's body before I said, "In my opinion, you smell like paradise. No shower for you, young man." I pushed him gently onto my bed and dove in beside him. It was having Matt in my arms again that made me tingle. He had some reactions of his own, of course. I needed nothing more than his kiss and his proximity. I received a whole lot more.

Tisha's committee decided to create a new video department with two supervisors—one to oversee the website and the other to manage social media. And they offered Matt the website post! He was delighted. I was euphoric. It would be good for him and his career path—and his bank account, of course. And it also felt as though he was laying down roots. We went out to dinner to celebrate—to a trendy place in nearby Gowanus.

Open kitchen. Good ventilation, of course, but even so, the dining room smelled wonderful. We ordered a series of small plates for sharing. New American, I suppose—with lots of international influence. Matt had never eaten octopus, so we ordered that for sure. Greek style, more or less. Garlic shrimp, a salad with slivers of duck crackling on top, steak tartar with avocados and blue corn tortilla chips, pulled pork splashed with a spicy vinaigrette. Like that. Festive.

Matt and I would have been happy sitting at my kitchen table and eating peanut butter sandwiches, but going out was even better. And the inflated wine tab seemed worth the price of being fed and pampered so richly. Over coffee and a shot of añejo tequila, I said to Matt, "I think you're a Brooklynite now, but we have to turn you into a New Yorker. I'll work on it. I lived in Manhattan for, what, a dozen years? I love it, and I want to show you my favorite places. I'm less familiar with the Bronx and Queens, so we'll have to get some help there. Staten Island we can save for another day."

Matt laughed. "What's that about?" he asked.

"Someday if we own a car, we should drive to Staten Island to see some of its historic sites. Other than that, let's take a pass." It was such a beautiful evening that Matt suggested we walk home. "Lesson coming," I said. "Matt, New York is the safest big city in the country. In the world, maybe. But don't go walking at night in neighborhoods you don't know. Any questions?"

He laughed. We took a car service home. I let us in, and we changed into robes. We sat in the living room for a while, mostly just looking at each other. And then I asked, "What made you decide to come back to me, Matt? Other than the lure of a job offer, of course."

"That's cruel, Kenny," he said. "Take it back."

"Gladly," I said. "What's the truth?"

Matt said, "I realized I couldn't imagine my life without you, Kenny. It was as if my old existence was black-and-white, while you offered me all the colors of the rainbow. I could see it the moment I stepped off the plane in Missoula. And yet I hesitated at first to make a clean break with my past. Caleb helped me get there."

"What is this about Caleb?" I asked. "Dan mentioned it, too. I'm confused. Please don't dangle me, Matty. I don't like being in the dark."

Matt embraced me. He said, "It's simple, really. Caleb phoned me after I got back to Montana. We talked for a while, and then he said, 'I'm going to send you an email. It will give me a minute to gather my thoughts. Watch your inbox.' And that's what he did. Will you read it, Kenny? I'd like that."

"Of course, darling," I said. Matt cued up the email:

Dear Matt,
Dan and I grew very fond of you and Ken on our wedding weekend—each of you and the two of you together. Ask Dan. He'll tell you. I don't know exactly why I think I know you, Matt. Maybe it's something about Montana, but I don't want you to make the mistake that I almost made. A big difference in us is that until I met Dan, I had never allowed myself to be totally at-tracted to another man. Correct me if I'm wrong, but I don't think that's your issue. And still, I think we're more alike than different.
Even when I accepted my feelings for Dan, I still fought the notion of giving in to them, for fear of being hurt, I suppose. It took me nearly a month to learn that I could trust Dan with my life. But now I do. And I think you can find that same trust with Kenny—if you let yourself go there. I could see it almost from the moment I met you two. Maybe I misread things, but it seemed to me that Kenny knew—and that you didn't.
Don't hold back, Matt. Don't waste the chance you've been given. Embrace it with both hands. A gift like this from the Universe is rare. Accept it. Cherish it. Nurture it. Kenny is bright and talented and kind, and he's also a very hot man, Matt, in case you didn't notice. You can't expect him to put his needs on hold any more than

you'd be willing to ignore your own needs. Let him love you, Matt. Let yourself love him with your whole heart. You'll never regret it. And you'll never be truly happy until you give in.
Yours,
Caleb

I reached for Matt and he snuggled in beside me, with his head on my chest. We sat quietly for a while. I had always loved the smell of Matt's hair. He let me savor it. After a while I said, "It's been a long day, darling. Come to bed." And that's what we did.

In the next two weeks, the days were about work and the nights were about Matt and me. The office culture at *GLITZ* was decidedly casual, but Matt had to look hip. No hayseeds allowed. I lent him some of my trendiest clothes—skinny shirts and tight slacks from Dries Van Noten or Brunello Cucinelli, mostly—and he filled in with Western things of his own. I also owned a Tom Ford suit that looked great on Matt. There are business occasions that just call for a suit, no matter how casually it's accessorized. It would all do until after my opening, the first week in June. And after that we'd go clothes shopping.

Matt seemed to love his new life, and I loved everything about our new life together. Every day was productive, and every night Matt came home to my arms and my bed. I cooked now and then. He mostly didn't, but he promised he'd learn to cook my favorite foods. We ordered in, we went out, we drank wine, we made love. We lived.

One Thursday evening Matt came home and told me, "Tisha is throwing a little cocktail party tomorrow at 5:00, to welcome the new video team. Will you come?"

"Of course, darling," I said. And then I began to worry if I had anything chic enough in my sparse closet that they hadn't already seen on Matt's back. But I reminded myself the party was all about Matt and not about me. I relaxed. I'd look fine—as a background figure, of course. A slim black T and tight black jeans work for 'most any occasion.

📖

I hadn't been to the *GLITZ* offices in years. It was fun returning. Tisha was welcoming, of course. "Hi, handsome," she said when I arrived. She kissed me and embraced me warmly. "Come in, sweetie. Let's get you a glass of wine. You don't know everybody, but we'll fix that. Have I told you what a great job Matt is doing? Best choice we've made in years. Lisa," she called, "look who's here!"

Tisha passed me off to Lisa, who greeted me warmly and headed me to the bar—since I was empty-handed. "Matt's good for you," Lisa said. "You've gotten younger, Kenny. I won't say better looking. That would be impossible. But younger, for sure. Please eat something. The tuna with a dab of wasabi mayo is fabulous. Is there anyone you haven't met you'd like to?"

"Oh, thanks, Lisa," I said. "I'm good. I'll just go and see Matt, for now."

She paused for a moment, put her hand on my cheek, and said, "Yes, Matt's good for you. And he's good for us. Let's keep it that way." Lisa was off to her next hostly duty, leaving me slightly off-balance. Matt was across the room, talking to a very hot guy I'd never seen before. I approached them. Matt looked terrific in a vintage Versace shirt I had given him. It made his hair, skin, and eyes sparkle.

Matt kissed me on the cheek and said, "Meet Steve Preston, the new Social Media Director. Steve, this is Ken Garda, my partner." We greeted each other. All very civilized. There was no apparent reason—none whatsoever—for my back hairs to bristle, and yet they did. The three of us made some small talk about photos and videos and magazines. Perfectly pleasant. I can bullshit with the best of them when called upon to do so.

I was fine until Tisha swept by and said, "Matt, I need to borrow you. I need you to meet our printer. He has some ideas to run by you. Sorry, gentlemen. I'll return him in good condition." And they were off. That left me alone with Steve Preston. We smiled. We also had nothing to say to each another, except "Another glass of wine?" It seemed an eternity before Tisha and Matt returned. It was probably all of ten minutes.

"Great party," I said to Tisha. "Will you let me steal Matt away? I was hoping to have a little supper with the honoree."

"Of course, darling," she said. "Get some rest, Matty. We have the August issue to plan tomorrow." We said our goodbyes. I even managed to smile and shake Steve's hand again. And we were off. And not a moment too soon, as far as I was concerned. Matt and I stopped for a simple dinner on the way home. I said all the right things about how proud I was of his new success. He said all the right things about how any happiness he had found was due to me.

When we got home, we changed, met in the living room for a nightcap, chatted briefly about the day, and then headed to bed. All very usual—and comfortable. And when we turned in, Matt enveloped me in his arms. But even when he had told me he loved me; even when his presence filled my bed with my perfect complement; even when I should have felt totally warm, I sensed a slight chill.

I didn't realize until morning, after Matt had headed to work, that the Green-eyed Monster was gnawing at my heart. I had never been there. Never thought I would be. And yet I felt it. A new sensation: Jealousy. What if Matt fell in love with Steve? What if Matt left me? What if he had an affair with Steve and tried to pretend it wasn't happening? What if? I had plenty of what-ifs that morning.

It wasn't until lunchtime, when I went to sit in the garden for a while and answer some emails, that I started to get some perspective. Sunlight is a powerful disinfectant. I realized that most doubts and fears come from a lack of information. I vowed to talk to Matt that evening. To clear the air. To restore my happiness, really. If possible.

"So what brilliance did you invent for the August issue?" I asked while we were having supper.

"I wouldn't call it brilliant," he said, "but the whole issue will have a nice Summer in the City feel to it, and my video program will reinforce that and be very, very sexy."

"If anyone knows sexy it's you, darling," I said. "And speaking of sex, it was interesting meeting Steve last evening. He's a hottie. How are things working out with the two of you?" The words just tumbled out of my mouth. But my question could easily have been construed as a business query, so I left it alone.

"I think Steve's very smart about how to exploit the different social media platforms. I used to post videos on Instagram that people liked to watch, but it was all instinct. He knows exactly what he's doing and why. I respect that. So far we've worked very well together."

I said, "Not *too* well, I hope."

"And what does that mean?" he asked.

"It means that I worry about you being so close to such a hot guy every day. I couldn't bear to lose you, Matt."

"Hush, Kenny. Nobody's going to lose anybody. Steve and I have a business relationship. Nothing more. You're the one I love. Speaking of which, will you come to bed?"

I did, of course, and Matt made love to me with perfect tenderness. It was almost enough to relieve my fears. Almost.

Chapter Twelve

Openings are always exciting—like all beginnings, really. I was confident about the new work, and yet I was the only one who had clapped eyes on it—except for my printer, of course, and she was famously nonjudgmental. And my gallerist, Tim Hart. He had a perfect eye for composition, and I was always impressed by the way he could visualize a wall or an entire room and assign works to just the right places.

By the time Tim finished planning and hanging an exhibition, viewers saw each piece to its best advantage, and each work looked as if it had been created precisely to occupy that particular space. Being a guest at one of Tim's Chelsea shows was like walking through a candy store and thinking, "Oooh! I'll have one of each!" No other gallery sold my work as successfully as Tim did. And that's why I had given him exclusive representation for years.

I was happy with the new collection. Some of the works from earlier in the year were dark, even by my standards. I always see at least a ray of hope in even my bleakest representations of the human condition. I hope my viewers do as well. But that's none of my business. It's my job to create the image, and that's where it stops.

I was especially pleased with the new portrait of Matt—from a frame I shot at the airport. I titled it *Potential.* Indeed. I hoped Matt would love it. I had avoided showing it to him. So, he would see it for the first time when he walked into the gallery, just like everyone else. I also loved my portrait of Dan's parents, from a shot I took after breakfast on Easter morning, when Richard instinctively reached for Elaine's hand. I titled it *Partnership.*

And I also had a soft spot for my portrait of Dan and Caleb, from the shoot in the whirlpool at the end of a long day of scrutiny. It was a private moment when their foreheads met and their eyes closed. I titled it *Union.* Yes, I was satisfied with the work. As much as possible. And I was in excellent company. The other four artists Tim had invited to show were talented and professional, with visions quite different from mine. All of us LGBTQ and all highly individual. Perfect.

Matt and I arrived a little early, of course. Tim seemed relaxed and prepared, as always. He greeted me, met Matt, and asked the bartender to open the first bottle of bubbly in our honor. The other artists arrived as well. Tim introduced us to the two I didn't know. Everyone said warm words about all the other work, of course. Creators don't have time for pettiness. They simply create—the best of them, anyway. I like being part of a group show. It introduces my work to viewers and buyers who might not otherwise see it. Always a plus.

Tim had featured Matt's portrait beautifully. "What do you think, darling?" I asked him.

"I think it's perfect, Kenny," he said. "I couldn't be prouder of you. Do I really look like that?"

"You did that morning in Chicago. If you let me photograph you for the rest of my life, Matt, then I'll show you everything I see in you."

"It's a deal," he said. Guests began to arrive. There was a considerable presence from *GLITZ*. They wouldn't be able to do much with the opening for future issues of the mag, but they had their Pride Month coverage on media. We greeted Tisha and Lisa. That was a pleasure. We also greeted Steve. Not so pleasurable. A staff photographer and Matt's new assistant videographer were also on the scene.

Tisha said, "Kenny, I've never seen this side of your work before. It's lovely. It's heartbreaking, really. I don't know if we'll ever be able to use anything this black-and-white in the magazine. Maybe next winter. Will you do a human cityscape for us? I don't know what I'm talking about. But I'll bet Lisa can cook up something stunning. Congratulations, darling. It's a beautiful show. And you're in excellent company."

I thanked her for the praise. Lisa grabbed me and said, "Kenny, this work is deliciously dark. I can see winter cityscapes with despair all around except for fashion models. They could be in color—but very low-key color—while the backgrounds are black-and-white. I'll call you next Monday so we can start working on it. I'm psyched!" I thanked her, and she headed off to the bar.

Can't say why I was so surprised, but I was shocked to see Dan and Caleb walk in with Elaine and Richard! It had never occurred to me that Dan's parents would come to the opening. I greeted them all warmly. I said to the Blackwells, "I couldn't be more delighted to see you two. I had hoped that Dan and Caleb would come, but I never thought to see.... Well, I hope you like the work."

Elaine kissed me and said, "When Danny told us you had an opening, we knew immediately we wanted to be here. We don't get into the city so often these days, but the chance to see your new work is reason enough. Richard, let's get a glass of bubbly." And that's what they all did. After a few minutes, they began to view the images. It made me a little nervous, because none of them had really seen my work before and because I hadn't told them to expect to see themselves—or my version of them—in the pictures. Never mind that there was some nudity and some very gritty reality here and there.

All four of them studied my work carefully. Elaine was the first one with feedback. She took my arm, led me toward the bar, and said, "Kenny, you've shown me your heart. I suspected there was some darkness there, but the light that shines through that darkness is nearly blinding. I think your vision of Montana is your best work. Richard and I will buy one, of course."

"I'd be honored," I said, "but not the portrait of you and Richard. I've already dedicated an artist's proof of that one—to the two of you. My framer has it. He'll ship it in the next few days."

"Well, then, the portrait of Dan and Caleb," she said. "It shows everything we love best about both of them. And Kenny, your picture of Matt is so tender it made me cry. I told you, didn't I? I said you could do it." It was my turn to be weepy. I embraced Elaine.

"You already have two sons, Elaine. Three really, counting Mary Ellen's husband. But will you take me on, too?" I asked.

"Of course," she said. "I always wanted an Italian son and never had one." We both laughed. The rest of the family joined us at the bar. We topped up our glasses. It was all festive, except for the fact that Matt was standing with Steve and some of the other *GLITZ* people across the room. Back hairs up again.

"Ken, your work has real balls," Richard said. "You take what you see, and you put it out there— along with your self. I think it's brave. I think it's honest. I think it's more real than what the rest of us see. And I think I'm proud to know you." I embraced him, of course. Another weepy moment.

Dan and Caleb had never seen their picture either. And I had never really thanked them properly for helping Matt to find his way home to me. "It's beautiful," Dan said. "We both loved the magazine photos you did, because they were charming and because they were respectful. But this work is ... and our portrait is ... well, it's extraordinary." Group hug.

"Thanks for being here," I said, "and for bringing the folks. You have no idea how happy you've made me. Could we have dinner sometime soon? Maybe next week?"

"Of course," Caleb said. "Text Dan. He's the responsible one in the family." Another hug and they headed off to see the rest of the show. Matt was still talking to Steve. I was still uncomfortable. Tim caught my eye and motioned to me to join him.

"Ken, I want you to meet Jeremiah Darnley, one of your most ardent fans. Jerry, this is Kenneth

Garda." We greeted each other. Tim said, "Jerry's been wanting to meet you, and now here we all are."

Jerry said, "Ken, this new work is your best, I think. I have three images I've acquired in the last couple of years. And I'm pleased to add a new one. Tim still had *Potential* 1/20 for me. I like to have the first print whenever possible. I think I see your model here tonight, and I think I understand your interest in him." I liked Jerry's smile. I also liked his attraction to my work, of course.

"Thank you for your kind words," I said. "Let me give you my card." And then I said to Tim, "Only in case he wants to take me to dinner, Timmy. I'm sure Mr. Darnley knows that all business arrangements go through you." We laughed.

Harvey Letterer—from Caleb's publisher, Scrive—arrived with a young guy in tow. "Kenny, I can't wait to see the new work!" Harvey said. "Jim, my boss, wants me to buy the portrait of the boys for him. But I want to see it all. Meet Len Turrow. This is Ken Garda." We greeted each other. He was cute, Len, in a delicate sort of way. I sensed that Harvey would be very kind to him, and I hoped he would be very kind to Harvey. I directed them to the bar. I knew they would find the literary, artistic, and magazine camps on their own.

It was a good evening. Tim had already told me the sales were even better than he had hoped. I would have been delighted, except for the uneasiness in my chest. Matt seemed to be always just out of sight. I did my part. I spoke to guests. I smiled at other artists. I drank champagne. I was visible. I participated. Most of all, though, I worried about Matt.

There was a small garden in back, out the door beyond the bathrooms. Tim used it mostly as a storage and staging area. So, only staff ventured there. When I looked for Matt and decided maybe he had gone to the men's, I happened to notice that the garden door was ajar. I investigated. When I looked out, I saw Steve pinning Matt to the garden wall. His hands seemed to be everywhere. Matt was trying to avoid Steve's advances, but without much success.

I called out, "Hey, Steve!" He turned to me, and I decked him. I had never slugged a man in my life. But I did that warm June evening, in the garden behind Tim's Chelsea gallery. Matt was in shock, but he was in better condition than Steve was. "Come on, Matt," I said. "We can leave him here with the trash." We headed back inside. There hadn't really been any visible commotion indoors. But scenes take on a life of their own, in my experience.

When we were back in the middle of the gallery, Tim asked me, quietly, "What's going on, Kenny?"

"Nothing, Tim," I said. "Just a little housecleaning. I hope I didn't upset any of your guests."

"No, Ken. But I'd prefer it if you keep your drama on paper."

"Will do, Tim," I said. He smiled, actually. I was relieved.

Matt said to me, quietly, "Kenny, I feel like a fucking idiot. I thought I knew all about flirting. But I never saw this coming. Promise."

"I believe you, Matt. Don't beat yourself up. It's not your fault that you're irresistible. Just promise me you'll be careful."

"I'll promise you more than that," he said.

Steve slid through the room and out the front door. Just then Tisha approached us and said, "I think I know what's going on here, and I'm *sure* I know how to deal with it. At *GLITZ* we have zero tolerance for harassment." I embraced her and thanked her, as did Matt. For just a moment I wondered if she might have been happier if there had been a videographer assigned to the garden. But that thought seemed so ungenerous that I released it immediately.

Harvey and Len walked over. We introduced Len and Matt. And then Harvey said, "So when are you two going to march down the aisle?"

I looked at Matt. He said, "Soon, I think. But that's up to Ken."

"Well, in that case," Harvey said, "I think you should book the preacher. Good timing! There happens to be one in the room." He beamed.

"Did someone propose marriage here?" I asked. "I'm confused."

"You're never confused, Kenny," Matt said. "That's part of why I love you so completely." He embraced me, and the Green-eyed Monster flew away to haunt a more willing victim. "When can we go home?" Matt asked.

"I'm always home when I have you in my arms," I said.

"Chelsea is nice, but there's a warm bed in Park Slope," Matt said. "Do you think Tim can do without you for the rest of the evening? Because I can't."

"I'll ask him."

The End

HOLIDAY NOVELLA SERIES
BOOK THREE
INDEPENDENCE DAZE
BRUCE K BECK

INDEPENDENCE DAZE

a holiday novella

by

Bruce K Beck

AUDACITY BOOKS
WE DARE TO TELL THE TRUTH

New York

Collecting is my favorite pastime, I suppose. It started when I was a child. On weekends when other boys were out playing ball, I was going to a flea market with my mother. She enjoyed the company, since it wasn't something that interested my father. Mom collected Staffordshire figurines, which left me a little cold. I collected blue-and-white porcelain, which I found exceptionally beautiful. I had a fairly good eye, it turned out. Some of the first pieces I bought—for a few dollars from my allowance—remain some of the best in my collection.

It wasn't until college that I took a real interest in photography. It started with an exhibition of George Platt Lynes's photos at the art department's gallery. There were fashion photos and celebrity portraits from his early career and of course lots of silvery male nudes from his two lives in New York and LA. Technically spot-on and heartbreakingly beautiful, I thought. While I doubted I could ever afford to own a Platt Lynes, the urge to collect beautiful photos was born in me.

After NYU and a degree in art history, I landed a job at the New-York Historical Society. I was mostly a gofer at first, but eventually I worked my way through the Audubon collection and period furniture to become an assistant curator in the permanent collection. And in that post, I got to work on temporary exhibits as well. I loved being in on decisions about how best to show pieces that were on loan. So my workday was always filled with beautiful things, both familiar and novel. I always thought we did a fine job of honoring the things we owned and the things we borrowed.

Despite all the beauty I worked with every day—or maybe because of it—I wanted to surround myself with beauty at home as well. I'm realistic about what I can buy on my limited budget. But I never acquire copies of things, and I've never bought a print that wasn't numbered and signed by the artist. This is all to explain how I happened to discover Kenneth Garda's photography a few years ago. It was at Tim Hart Gallery, in Manhattan's Chelsea neighborhood.

Tim had flawless taste in presenting artworks. I should know, since I was in the same line of work, really—only just from the not-for-profit point of view. I put myself on Tim's email list the first time I happened to be walking in that neighborhood on a quiet weekend and discovered his gallery. I also fell in love with the Kenneth Garda photos on view. And I made an appointment for the following Saturday, to return to the gallery to see more of Garda's work.

His photos spoke to my heart about the human condition. I admired the darkness of his vision—even the nudes—while at the same time I sensed hope as a constant theme. I wondered what it was about Garda's images that made me think of Platt Lynes. Surely their styles were decades removed and oceans apart in terms of surface polish. And yet, seeing Kenneth Garda's photos for the first time gave me the same shiver up my spine that I experienced when I first discovered George Platt Lynes.

The following week I purchased my first Garda at Tim's gallery. It's a sullen, brooding nude that reminded me of my ex. So I'll probably need to explain why I wanted to be reminded of my ex. Karl Dubinsky and I met at NYU. He was a year younger and a poli-sci major. But we connected on our first meeting. And our hearts connected shortly thereafter. Karl's feelings were fierce, whether it was his sense of injustice or his love for me.

He was feisty, and I often assumed the role of peacemaker. But when Karl made love to me, I felt alive for the only times in my life. And nothing could replace that feeling of wholeness. And nothing could keep me from wanting to maintain it. After about ten years of storms and quiet sunny days in roughly equal measure, Karl got an offer from a liberal think tank in DC. He was eager to accept the job. And I was genuinely pleased for him.

"Surely you can commute," I said. "They can't expect you to be there every minute. I know it's four hours on the train, but surely you can come home on weekends. Or every other weekend. Or so. Talk to me, Karl." He did talk to me, of course. But what he said was that he was ready to move on—that he wanted to create a new life in DC that didn't include me. He also said a few obligatory things about how much he loved me and how much he would miss our life together. Cold comfort.

I had a job to show up for every morning. Luckily. It threw a little structure into the void that Karl's departure had carved into my heart. So how did I cope with his absence? Badly, at first. I hardly slept at all the week after his departure. Without Karl in my arms, there didn't seem to be much point in being in bed. I also didn't eat much. Or smile much. My friend, Lucinda Warren, knew what was going on, of course. I had started sharing my heart with her shortly after she came aboard at the Historical Society.

"How long have we known each other?" Lucy asked me one Monday morning when I was particularly gray—emotionally and physically, too, most likely.

"I don't mark those things on my calendar, dear," I said. "What's your point?"

"My point is that I'm about to give you some advice," she said. "I've watched you navigate life and love for several years now, Jerry, and it's my considered opinion that you are not handling Karl's departure well. I think it's time for you to pull on your big-boy pants and get on with it. I'm tired of seeing your heart on your sleeve."

"Thanks, Cindy," I said, knowing full well how much she hated that name. "And what about you, dear? When was the last time you had a date? When was the last time you had contact with someone worthy of your love?"

"That's easy, Jerry," she said. "Daily. And you're going to take me to dinner tonight, so I think we can put the focus back on you. I don't like watching you mope, Jer. And I don't think it's good for you. Self-pity is a starvation diet. You've lost too much weight. I intend to fatten you up, starting with dinner tonight."

"Thanks, Lucy," I said. "If anyone can save me, it's you. What would you like for dinner?"

"Spanish, I think," she said. "I never tried to force-feed *paella*, but I'm willing to give it a try—in the service of a good cause."

"Spanish it is," I said. "Let's go directly from work." So that's how it happened that Lucinda and I went to dinner that Monday evening. We hadn't been out together in months. Karl and Lucy got on great, but Karl and I most often kept to ourselves. So I was having to relearn social skills that had grown rusty. And Lucy proved to be a great teacher.

"Why, Jeremiah Bradford Darnley," Lucy said at dinner, after we had downed a couple of glasses of dry sherry and two delicious *tapas*, "it seems you have an appetite after all."

"I could probably remember lots of functions," I said. "Thanks for your help, Lucy. I've handled this all so badly,"

"Hush, Jerry," she said. "This is not a test. This is your life, and I just think you should start living it again. Is that reasonable?"

"Quite reasonable," I said. That Monday dinner proved to be my turnaround. Over delicious *paella* and even better red wine, I resolved to put myself back into the game. And that's how I happened to go to Tim Hart Gallery's big Pride Month opening that June. Tim always had interesting art on view, but I had never attended one of his opening parties. I was feeling alive again as I dressed to go out—for the first time in how many months?

📖

"Jerry, it's great to see you," Tim said as he greeted me, "and I have a pleasant surprise for you.

Kenneth Garda is here tonight. I want you to meet him."

"Love to," I said. It wouldn't change my appreciation of his art, but it would certainly enhance my experience of the works I owned—and the ones I intended to acquire in the future. Yes, I was capable of becoming something of a fanboy under the right circumstances. But that had nothing to do with my critical faculties for judging the quality of art works. Surely.

It was a lovely exhibition. All five artists showed powerful and sometimes disturbing visions of humanity. Photography, painting, sculpture, and even video. The immediacy of the experience of the works was enhanced by the party atmosphere and the presence of all the creators—under the same roof at the same point in time. I vowed to accept every opening-night invitation from Tim in the future.

When Tim introduced me to Kenneth Garda, I found him very much as I had expected him to be. After years of experiencing his work daily, on my walls, I'd have been shocked, really, if he had turned out to be mousy and sexless. Instead, he proved to be handsome, winning, and very hot. No surprises, except that he greeted me warmly and offered me his card.

Garda made a joke about using his contact info strictly for personal purposes, since Tim was his exclusive gallerist. We all laughed, but I made a mental note to follow through on Ken's offer of an actual relationship. I had known instantly, as soon as I started viewing the collection, that I had to purchase one of Garda's newest works. It was a portrait, and

Tim had hung it quite close to the front door, in an exceptionally favorable light.

I went to Tim immediately and told him I wanted the first impression. I needed to own that image, but I also needed to own the first copy. Silly? Maybe. But I was quite moved by the tenderness of it. There was also an underlying eroticism that went right to my crotch. I was used to that. All of Garda's photos felt dangerously sexy to me, even the ones that were darkly scruffy. He seemed unable to lift his lens without releasing pheromones.

I didn't realize until after I had committed to the purchase that Garda's model was in the gallery that night, too. He was unmistakably the subject of the portrait I had just bought—even though he was in glorious Technicolor while my new photo was in black-and-white. Somehow I had sensed—or imagined that I had sensed—that his hair was a bright ginger hue. But the reality of it left me winded.

I hadn't felt so ... physical in a long while. Not since Karl left me. I hadn't felt much of anything, really. But there I was at Tim Hart Gallery on a warm June evening, surrounded by interesting people and remarkable art, and I began to feel that perhaps I could truly live again. I was sad that Lucy had been unable to join me for the opening, but I knew I would return, with her, probably on Saturday afternoon.

It wasn't until after I had seen all of the works on display, drunk my fair share of champagne, spoken to a few people I knew in the art business, and congratulated some of the other artists, that I finally saw Garda and his model together for the first time. They were not only stunning to look at individually but breathtaking as a couple. Yet there seemed to be a slight tension between them, as if there had been a kerfuffle of some sort.

I looked around and spied Tim, who seemed unflappable, as always. I couldn't help noticing a tall, slim, hot guy with a fat lip who made a hasty exit from the gallery. And I observed—because it was hard for me to take my eyes off Garda and his partner—a glamourous young woman who seemed to be comforting them. Since I have enough trouble trying to solve the mysteries in my own life, I simply thanked Tim, wished him a good night, and headed home.

Chapter Two

"What about the Fourth of July?" Lucy asked me at lunch the next day.

"What about it?" I answered.

"Don't be coy, Jerry. You know I'm asking if you've made plans. It's a Friday this year, so that gives us a nice long weekend. Want to do something?"

"That sounds like a great idea," I said. "You're so smart, Lucy. Why don't you come up with something fun? I'm easy."

"Everyone knows _that_," she answered. "I'll get on it."

"Lucy, we're planning the Fourth of July, but what about Pride?" I asked. "I pretty much ignored it last year, but Karl and I used to watch the parade on Christopher Street and then walk up Hudson to a little Portuguese restaurant that isn't there anymore. Great food. Cute owners. Who knew that Tarcísio is a first name? But he wore it well. As did Miguel. And I miss them. But not as much as I miss Karl."

"Well, dear," Lucy said, "we're not going to suddenly fix that today, but I think you should be proud of the progress you've made. And I think I'm going to leave it at that. Let me know if you want me to go to the parade with you. I'm willing."

Bruce K Beck

"Thanks, Lucy," I said. "Meanwhile, I want you to go to Tim Hart Gallery with me on the weekend, since you missed the opening. We could make a day of it. Brunch, and then the gallery. Or the gallery and then an early dinner. I haven't made any plans for Saturday or Sunday. I'll leave it to you." She agreed.

It was a quiet week. Mercifully. My only real excitement was in trying to find the perfect place for my new Garda photo. Tim had promised that I could pick it up on the weekend, after he had ordered the framing of 2/20, to take the place of mine. I'll confess I was excited about welcoming the photo into my home.

I was also excited about emailing Ken Garda to gush a bit about meeting him and about how much I loved the new image. I proposed that he and his model—I still didn't know his name—come for dinner some evening, so they could see the photo *in situ*. To my surprise and pleasure, he responded the next day:

Hi, Jerry,
It's good to hear from you. Yes, Potential is dear to my heart as well, so I'd love to see it in its new home. Matt agrees. We'd be pleased to have dinner with you sometime. We plan to be in town most of the summer – except maybe for the Fourth of July weekend – so give me a couple of dates, and I'm sure we'll find one that works.
Looking forward,
Ken

I opened my calendar and chose two Saturdays in the near future. I figured a Saturday evening dinner party would give me the day to cook—and clean. I wondered if I should invite Lucy. Probably. Having just Ken and Matt over felt a little dangerous. And a little boring for them when I had to attend to things in the kitchen. I emailed Lucy the dates and promised to confirm after hearing back from Garda.

Lucy and I had a lovely Saturday, starting with brunch at our favorite weekend spot. Eggs Benedict with smoked salmon in place of the Canadian bacon always starts my weekend off right. "These are such weird times," Lucy said. "Isn't it nice to have a job?" It was nice, indeed. I can take prosperity for granted as easily as the next boy, but I also know how to practice gratitude. Something to do with my childhood, I think.

Growing up in the suburbs was deadly dull—except when it wasn't. When Dad's drinking got out of hand, then the drama would fly. We only had the police to the house once. Had it become a regular occurrence, I might have retreated entirely into my shell, instead of mostly creating a life of my own. I discovered art there, so it wasn't exactly a loss. But money was always an issue.

Mother convinced her parents to pay for my college. That gave me a little stability from ages eighteen to twenty-two. Before that, I didn't exactly miss meals, but I also never knew exactly what I'd find when I got home from school. I'd have been sympathetic—I think—had Mother told me she was leaving him. It would have been disruptive but logical. That never happened, or at least not until many years later. Instead, I came home to the financial crisis of the day—which sometimes included a sudden move to a smaller house.

I didn't much care about houses and such. It wasn't as if I had a bunch of friends who liked to hang out with me after school. *Nothing* like that. Both of my parents were something of a disappointment to me, but books and learning never let me down. *They* became my friends and family. There were a few important teachers. Many troubled kids find that kind of support from adults in the education system. The ones who don't most likely go under, I always thought.

Once I headed off to NYU, I never looked back—as much as possible. There were some Christmases in Connecticut where everyone pretended nothing was wrong. Otherwise, I saw both my parents as rarely as I could. Karl never met them. I was careful about that. I jealously guarded the privacy of the little family I had built entirely on my own. I knew *Karl's* parents. They were warm and welcoming to the "shiksa" their son brought home.

Karl's parents seemed nearly oblivious to the fact that their son had fallen in love with a boy. The fact that the boy was a goy, now there was a matter of concern. But they got over it. I still hear from them now and then. Karl's mother, Rachel, always remembers my birthday. And his father, Isaac, always sends me Chanukah gelt. They'd have been pleased to see their son permanently partnered. But not as pleased as I'd have been.

The Saturday morning in June when Lucy and I brunched—exactly two weeks before Pride weekend—I was thinking less about the past than about the future. I was a little anxious about hosting Ken and Matt, of course, but I was becoming increasingly anxious about living alone. "This being alone business is getting me down," I said to Lucy.

"Tell me," she said. "The only man I've met in the last year I've wanted to date is my new veterinarian. And I'm sure his husband would disapprove."

"How is your pussy?" I asked.

"He's doing very well indeed, thanks. You should stop by and see him. He likes you, Jerry. But then he always responds to the male. I think he was a rent boy in another life. Come for dinner, maybe next weekend. I'll cook something you like, and you can catch up with Sylvester."

"Excellent idea," I said. "I'd love to." And then Lucy remembered she had made plans with her family for the following weekend. So we found a date in mid-July and left it at that. Lucy and I strolled to the gallery after brunch. Tim greeted us, and I introduced him to Lucy.

"Good timing," he said. "We were just about to pack up your picture. Come take a look. There's always time for buyer's remorse. I don't think Lucy's ever seen it, right?"

"No," I said. "But she's certainly heard about it." We followed Tim to the basement, where an assistant—a very cute fair-haired kid—was up to his knees in packing materials.

"Thanks, Seth," Tim said. "Mr. Darnley bought *Potential,* so I thought he might want to see it again before it goes under wraps." Seth smiled sweetly and produced the picture. I needed only a quick glance—since it was nearly mine. The lighting was good enough in the packing room so that Lucy got to really see it. She caught her breath in a slight gasp, I guess I'd call it.

"Stunning," she said. "Of course you had to have it, Jerry." She was visibly moved. I gave her a minute to recover.

"Don't bother much with packing, Seth," I said. "A couple of mirror corners will do it. We're only taking it a few blocks." He smiled and quickly proceeded to pad and strap the picture well enough to survive an ocean voyage. And then Tim, Lucy, and I headed upstairs with my treasure. But first, I thanked Seth and slipped him my card.

"Tim, I've had such a good time," Lucy said. "I've been here before, but I've somehow missed you *and* Kenneth Garda. I won't make that mistake again. I had a thought: We don't show enough contemporary works at the Historical Society, even though our mission is to document everything New York. I'm sure we're overdue for something new and fresh. And we've paid very little attention to photography lately, despite our considerable holdings. No promises, of course, but I'll develop a concept—with Jerry's help—for a show in the main gallery. Maybe next spring. It's hard to say."

"Just let me know if I can help," Tim said.

"Will do," she said, "since you know so many artists—the living ones especially. And Jerry knows all the dead ones. So I'm sure we'll make it work. And if we can advance this thing, then I'm sure we can find a guest curatorial spot for you. Thanks, Tim. What a treat this afternoon has been!"

It was that kind of day: Brunch with the person I loved most in the world (except for the person I couldn't have) followed by communing with beauty. Lucy and I thanked Tim for his hospitality. There were hugs all around, and then the two of us headed out into the warmth of the June evening. Seth had put a sort of handle on the package, so it was easy to carry.

Never mind Crossing Delancey. Crossing 14th Street is also bridging a neighborhood divide. We strolled toward the comforting familiarity of the Village. "Will you come in?" I asked Lucy. "I can feed you a little supper. And you won't go thirsty."

"Thanks, Jer. Not tonight," she said. "I'll come back when you have the new photo in the perfect place. Thanks for a lovely day." We embraced. "Besides, I have to get back to Sylvester. He misses the litter box when I leave him alone too long. Just like a man, wouldn't you say?"

I let myself in and stood the picture just below the space I had prepared for it—in the living room. There was no rush. I savored the thought of removing Seth's packaging on a quiet Sunday morning after coffee. I also savored the thought of Seth. I hadn't experienced a dose of youth and sweetness in far too long. Perhaps it was time. Perhaps Seth would agree. How little we know!

Chapter Three

When Ken emailed me with a date, it turned out to be the weekend before Pride. Lucy had promised to visit her folks in New Hampshire. A birthday, an anniversary—family stuff. So I cast my guest net a little wider. I lived in a part of the Village that had always been home to lots of NYU students. Karl and I took the apartment our last year in school, and I held onto it even after his departure. I liked the neighborhoody comfort of it—lots of good, cheap eats, and mostly all the other goods and services one could require.

I also liked my neighbor, Cornelius Randolph. Connie was tall and black and pistol-hot. It was the sweetness of his nature that always called to me the most. After Karl left me, Connie would drop off food and the occasional bottle of brandy. He never intruded on my grief. He simply offered his gift and then got on with his life. Karl and I didn't know him well, but I was aware Connie came from an old Virginia family. Maybe Southern Blacks understand the grieving process better than the rest of us do. They've surely had plenty of experience with loss.

I phoned him that Thursday evening and said, "Connie, I haven't really seen you in ages, but you've been so kind to me. I was wondering, can I take you to dinner some evening soon? Some place in the neighborhood, maybe. Something a step up from Mamoun's Falafel."

"Thanks, Jerry," he said. "That sounds like fun." We set a date, for early the next week, for our supper. My first thought was a little Spanish place called El Faro. And then I remembered it had been shuttered for several years. It seemed time for me to move into the present. I decided on Mary's Fish Camp. Not too radical. I hadn't been there in ages, and the prospect of enjoying really good fish-and-chips appealed to me. Or maybe some chowder and a lobster roll. Didn't matter.

As I dressed to go out that evening, I experienced a flood of memories. But then, when *didn't* I experience a flood of memories? Karl had asked me once if I'd be willing to invite Connie into our bed. The prospect was attractive in the extreme, but we had never done that—we had never added another man to our lovemaking. I hesitated. Perhaps Karl lost interest in the concept. Never mind the interest he had lost in me. It was one of those things that never happened. End of story.

MFC is a tiny place, but it does have a lot of windows—because of the corner location. The host offered us a comfortable table we were pleased to accept. So far so good. I ordered an Oregon pinot gris. Delicious. Connie and I both smiled a lot. We decided on some chowders to start and some mains. And then it was time for some reminiscence and some getting-to-know-you.

"I haven't thanked you properly for being so kind to me after Karl left," I said. "Those were dark days, Connie, and your sunny face did a lot to brighten them."

"I think you're selling yourself short, Jerry," he said. "I think you're entirely resilient. And I think you can handle anything. Just my opinion—but I'm never wrong. Just saying." I hadn't had such a comfortable time in years, really. Dining with Connie made me see how deeply Karl and I had slid into an uncomfortable comfort that offered little nourishment to either of us. It was a revelation.

Connie said, "I always wanted to go to bed with you, Jerry. Not Karl, really. He's handsome. He's sexy. I'd have made a sandwich with the two of you in a heartbeat. Had I been asked—instead of just flirted with. But it was always you."

"Goodness," I said. "I had no idea. What else have I been missing?"

Maybe that's enough history for one evening," Connie said. "I'm much more interested in the present. Will you come to my place after dinner?" I was startled, and I'm sure I looked it.

"Wow! Thanks, Connie, but not tonight," I said. "Will you ask me again?"

"Of course," he said. "I can be a patient man when I'm waiting for what I want."

Over coffee, I said, "Oh shit! I almost forgot to ask you. Connie, will you come to dinner on Saturday? I'm expecting two men—a brilliant photographer and his muse, I guess. I don't really know much about the younger guy. Connie, I've committed to dinner, but I can't do this alone. Will you help me?"

"Sure, Jer," he said. "Just tell me what you need. I'm easy." I had always admired Connie's smile, but never more so than when he flashed it at me that June evening in the Village.

"Bless you," I said. "Should we head home?" It was a school night, after all. I took Connie's arm as we walked along the narrow Village streets in the direction of our separate domiciles. When we reached Connie's building, we stopped, Connie took me in his arms, and he kissed me with such tenderness that I was afraid of going all limp—in the limbs, that is. Other parts of me were far from limp.

I accepted Connie's kiss, and then I offered one of my own—less elegant, more needy. He responded in kind. And then we looked at each other in the half light of streetlamps. I nearly asked Connie to take me inside. I wanted him. I wanted him to wrap me in warmth and affection. I wanted to surrender the pain of the past to the healing power of a living union. I wanted a lot.

But I did have to be up and off to work in the morning, after all. As did Connie. I gave him a last embrace. Connie thanked me for dinner, and we parted. I felt a little deflated as I let myself into my apartment and got ready for bed. *Why did I choose to be alone?* I wondered. Scotch helped.

📖

Connie came early on Saturday evening to help me set up. I said to him, "I've never been certain which I prefer seeing more, in the neighborhood— your smile or your ass."

"Two sides of the same coin," he said. "Take your pick, or you can have both if you want them."

"Both, I think," I said. We smiled a lot. I had told him what I intended to cook, and he had offered to bring the fixings for a big salad. I showed Connie all four of my Ken Garda photos. He was suitably impressed—moved, I'd say. "I don't know anything about this model except that he's a redhead and I think he's from Montana. It's one of those states I have trouble wrapping my brain around. Never having been there, I almost doubt its existence. Almost. But wait till you see him—this Matt."

"Goodness, Jerry," Connie said, "I can see how you write such compelling captions at the Historical Society. You can certainly spin a story."

"All part of the service," I said. "Let me pour a glass of wine. Red or white?"

"White, I think," Connie said. I poured. We clinked, we sipped, we smiled, we put the finishing touches on my apartment. It looked ready to receive guests after all. Yes. A dinner party. How long had it been?

Ken and Matt arrived only a few minutes late, bearing Campari and almond cookies—treats we rarely think to buy for ourselves. I started introductions, and everyone pitched in. Matt Flowers. Sweet name for a sweet man. "I love what you've done with my photos," Ken said. "I had nearly forgotten about that one," referring to the nude that reminded me of Karl. "He's not bad, is he?"

"He's a whole lot better than that," I said. "I love them all, but especially *Potential*." Matt blushed slightly.

"There's nothing like the perfect model," Ken said. "Jerry, you've hung them—all of them—with such care. They look as if they've become a part of your life. And that's always my goal. Well, maybe not so much while I'm shooting and editing. *That's* all about me. But once it's time to release an image, it's all about the viewer. You've made me very happy."

Ken embraced me warmly, for the first time, really. It was a lovely feeling.

I had decided on a cold supper—just in case the air conditioning refused to cooperate. One never knows in old buildings. We started with an avocado purée soup garnished with a few grilled shrimp. Delicious. "Connie, who are you? Besides tall, dark, and handsome," Ken asked.

Connie laughed easily and said, "Jerry and I have been neighbors for years, but we've never really been friends until recently. I also went to NYU, and I took a degree in social work. I run a food pantry, mostly. But there's so much hunger and other needs these days that we're all over the place. The days I have to spend at City Hall advocating for the poor are the most trying. I'd rather be begging for supplies and handing them out to people who need them. But we all do whatever has to be done."

I felt very grateful for the bounty under my roof. I think everyone did. For the main course, I had decided on that strange Northern Italian summer dish called *vitello tonnato*—veal braised tender and chilled, then sliced thinly and dressed with a creamy sauce (a mayonnaise really) flavored with good Italian tuna. It has to be the kind packed in olive oil and put up in a glass jar. Perfect.

Connie's salad was just right with the veal. "So, Matt," I asked, "you're from Montana, and you work with video?"

"I do," he said, "At *GLITZ Magazine*."

"But he used to be an EMS worker," Ken said, "so don't underestimate him."

"I wouldn't think of it," I said. "There was a beautiful, light brown woman at the opening—at Tim's gallery. Toward the end of the evening, she seemed to be ... I don't know, comforting you two. What was that about? Not that it's any of my business."

"Oh, that was Letisha Carmichael from *GLITZ,*" Ken said. "There was a new guy at the magazine who was hitting on Matt pretty hard. I'm not saying that Matt can't take care of himself, but it reached the point that I decided to hit back."

"So that's why the tall guy had a fat lip when he left the gallery."

"Pretty much," Ken said.

"How romantic!" I said.

"Not at the time," Ken said. "But we can laugh about it now. You don't miss much, Jerry. What's that about?"

"Oh, I started reading other people's moods when I was a child," I said. "Survival, I expect." I wasn't used to getting quite so close to the truth with people who weren't trusted friends. Or perhaps with anyone. It made me feel a bit off-balance.

"It's served you well. I just had a thought," Ken said. "What are you two doing for the Fourth of July?"

I looked at Connie, who mostly shrugged. "I haven't made any plans," I said.

"I'll have to check with them, of course, but remember my portrait of the boys who got married in Montana?"

"I certainly do. I nearly had to have it, but Matt called to me more loudly." Matt smiled broadly. Great teeth.

"Well, Dan's parents—who I love—gave them a big old house in New Jersey. And the boys asked Matt and me to come out on Friday. They also told us to feel free to invite another couple. There's plenty of room. I'm sure they'd be happy to have you join us. And then we can all come back together on Sunday."

"What do you think, Connie?" I asked.

"Sounds great to me," he said.

'Sure, Ken. If it works for them. What should we bring?"

"Just yourselves, I think. Or maybe something for a breakfast. That's always welcome."

"Let us know." It was a lovely evening. Matt and Ken were both very warm with their thanks and good nights. Connie and I finished clearing the table and organizing the kitchen. I said to him, "Connie, it's been far too long since I've kissed you. Can we remedy that?"

"Of course," he said, as he enveloped me in his warmth. Connie's kiss was even more welcome than I had imagined. I melted into his embrace. Soon I took Connie's hand and began to lead him to my bedroom.

"I don't think so," Connie said.

"But why not?"

"Because I've wanted to make love to you for ages, Jerry. But now I want your heart, too. And I know better than to go after things I can't have. Your heart belonged to Karl for all those years, and now? I don't know. I just know that it is *not* available." That shut me up pretty fast. Connie kissed me again, smiled sweetly, and said, "I'm heading home. Great dinner! Call you tomorrow?"

"Please," I said. And he was gone. I was still in shock as I brushed my teeth and got ready for bed. Alone. It was certainly not the night I had planned. But was it the night I deserved?

First thing in the morning, I remembered that Lucy had offered to make Fourth of July plans. Ouch! I waited for a respectable hour to call her on a Sunday morning. About 9:30. "I'm covered with shame," I said.

"What have you done this time?" she asked.

"I accepted an invitation to a house party for the Fourth of July weekend. I don't even know the hosts, but it sounds like an all-boys event. I could eat my head."

"I can't see how that would help," Lucy said, "though I'd love to watch. Instead, why don't we just let this one go. I can rethink the lovely weekend in Provincetown I had in mind. Don't mind me. I love being alone, and those holiday broadcasts with all the stars and fireworks are so entertaining."

"Lucy, you don't have to enjoy punishing me quite so much," I said. "To show how contrite I am, let me take you to dinner—anywhere you want to go—after the Pride Parade. Would that help?"

"It would be a start," she said. "How about Eleven Madison Park?" I would ask Connie to join us, of course, and after a quick calculation, I realized that I could nearly purchase a photo by Ken Garda for the price of dinner for three at Eleven Madison Park.

"Why don't we save that for some super special occasion, like your engagement?" I suggested.

"A person could get mighty hungry before then. Look, Jer, I have to meet a friend for brunch in a little while—Phyllis from furniture. Could I stop by for a minute after, so we can plan?"

"Of course," I said. "I'm not going anywhere today." That was certainly the truth. The thought of spending the whole day at home in an old silk robe felt delicious. I was enjoying the sensation of the silk against my skin when Connie phoned.

"How is the Host with the Most this morning?" he asked.

"Lazy, actually," I said. "And how is the Best Neighbor?"

"Holding up rather nicely, thanks. Jerry, I loved meeting Ken and Matt last night. Ken is so obviously the artist behind those beautiful works in your apartment. He's complex, physical, intensely sexy, and wonderful to look at. And Matt seems his perfect complement. Or did I imagine that?"

"I don't know what I was expecting," I said, "but I thought Matt was like an answered prayer. I thought he was sweet and cute and all of that, and yet he seems to offer Ken a foundation of strength to anchor his heart to. Or am I just making shit up?"

"No, you're spot-on, Jerry," Connie said. "But you're always right about others. I wish you knew yourself so well." That felt like a shot across the bow. I chose to ignore it.

"I spoke to Lucy a little while ago—you've met her, haven't you?"

"Just once, I think. Handsome woman. Obviously adores you, but then who doesn't?"

"Nevertheless," I said, "we were talking about Pride and having dinner after the parade, and I assumed you and I had agreed to make a day of it, but now I'm not so sure. Do we have a date for Sunday?"

"Yes, or at least we do now. And I'd love to see Lucy again. Where are you taking us for dinner?"

"To be determined," I said. "Any preferences?"

"Any restaurant that has you in it will suit me fine," Connie said.

"You go to my head."

"Good. Let me know when and where."

"Will do," I said, "and thanks for being ... for being you." I had a very warm and tender feeling throughout my body after Connie and I ended our call. I also had a fierce erection, which I decided to deal with later—after Lucy's visit. I took a nap.

📖

"Jerry, promise you'll never ask me to go to The Smith ever again, even if they open another dozen branches," Lucy said when she arrived. "My tolerance for stupidity at the hospitality desk is waning."

"Come in, dear," I said. "I love you, too. I think you need a proper drink. Gin?"

"Pink, please," she said. I deftly poured Lucy a stiff gin with some ice, a few dashes of bitters, and a splash of soda. I poured myself a glass of chardonnay. We settled in on the sofa.

"How's Phyllis?" I asked.

"Oh, she's fine. Enjoying some boyfriend troubles at the moment. Sounds like they'll patch it up. You know, Jerry, I'm also losing my tolerance for boyfriend issues that are not my own. I guess that makes me a bad friend."

"No, it makes you a self-aware individual. But speaking of boyfriends, how come you don't have one?" I asked.

"I might ask you the same question," she answered.

"Touché," I said. "Lucy, have you ever had an affair with a woman?" I asked.

"Uh … no, not really. Nearly, once. I've had sex with women. *You've* had sex with women."

"Not recently."

"There's something magical about going to bed with someone who understands your body. Why am I telling you this, Jerry? Of course you know exactly what I'm saying. Not only did you figure that out a whole long time ago, but it turned out to be absolutely right for you. I don't think it is right for me. I hoped maybe I was in love, once. I wanted it.

"She was amazing, Jerry. She was beautiful, she was tender, she was funny, she was thoughtful. And she loved me. But I couldn't commit. I suppose she waited for me to come 'round as long as she could. And then she gave up on me. It was like watching the death of something fine in slow motion. And yet I felt powerless to do anything about it."

I offered Lucy my arms, and she fell into them. "This business of being a grown-up is overrated," I said. We sat quietly for a while as I rocked her gently. When she had recovered enough to reach for her drink, I said, "And now to the matter at hand. I asked Connie to join us on Sunday."

"Oh, good," she said. "I only just met him once, you know, at an opening. He's stunning to look at, of course. And such a sweetheart! The truth is, Jer, I've often wondered why you haven't gotten together with him in the last few years. It certainly has logic on its side."

"Yes, but, since when does logic sway my heart? Let's make a dinner plan. Where would you like to go?"

"'Someplace bohemian, where we can have cocktails and be very gay, and you can make love to me. Perhaps then I'll learn to lose my inhibitions—I've shocked you. I must sound very depraved.'"

"Sorry, dear," I said. "*I'm* the only one who gets to do bad Bette Davis imitations around here."

"Quite right. It won't happen again."

"Good. Where should we have dinner?"

"Anywhere is fine, as long as it isn't The Smith," Lucy said. "I'll leave it to you. I'm heading home, Jerry. Sylvester is waiting. Thanks for the drink."

"Pull his tail for me," I said. A quick kiss, and she was gone. I returned to my lazy Sunday afternoon and the pleasure of silk against my skin. But then I got a text from Seth Greenly, the kid who worked for Tim Hart. I had thought of him, of course, since he packed up my new acquisition so expertly—in the basement of the gallery. When I gave him my card, I maybe even half hoped that I might hear from him. And that was all before recent developments with Connie. Whatever they might be. So I was flattered, but also a bit disconcerted by the reality of this new attention.

Seth wrote that he wanted to see me. He suggested that we meet on Tuesday for supper and then spend some time together afterward. I thought of a casual restaurant nearby, since I assumed I'd be picking up the tab. And then a short walk to my apartment. Very convenient. But was it sensible? That remained to be seen.

I texted Seth back to accept and to suggest a place and time. And then I stretched out on my sofa to enjoy the rest of my day off. I was keenly aware of the erection that Connie had inspired and that Seth had reinvigorated. Instead of taking it in hand, I made a conscious decision to save that energy for Seth.

Bedding him began to feel inevitable. And I wanted to offer Seth my best. I would be a considerate lover, of course. That was a given. But I also wanted to be a passionate lover. He was so young. I knew I was also young, but of a different decade. Would I be able to satisfy him? Did it matter? I tried to put questions out of my head so I could enjoy the rest of my day off. It mostly worked.

Chapter Five

Seth was every bit as cute as I remembered him,
when we met on Tuesday. Maybe more so. We ordered two draft beers and some snacks. And then
we began the getting-to-know-you dance. We smiled
a lot. It was all perfectly pleasant until I was obliged
to say, "Why don't you come to my place? It's only
two blocks from here." I hadn't been to bed with a
twenty-something since *I* was twenty-something.
Not since Karl, really. It seemed odd. Almost like
regressing.

I let us in. "These Ken Gardas look amazing in
your apartment," Seth said. "Of course you had to
have them." I led him to the bedroom. There was no
point in pretending we had any other business between us. First kisses are important to me. Seth
seemed in a bit of a hurry, but I slowed him down
enough to enjoy a deep oral union. Nice. So far so
good. We stripped and fell into bed.

Seth was all over me like white on rice. "Whoa,
Cowboy," I said. "This is not a race." Seth looked a
little sheepish. I kissed him warmly, and we fell into
an exploration pace that was comfortable. There was
a whole lot to like in Seth's sweet little body. I tried
my best to taste everything. And that included, of
course, his perfect round butt. I might have spent

the rest of the evening rimming him, had he not insisted on a change of venue.

Seth rolled me onto my back and got on top of
me. Not only did he kiss me deeply—which always
gets my attention—but he began to slide my dick into
the sweet spot that had been consuming my attention. Seth's body seemed to pull me in like a magnet.
When I was all the way there, Seth reared back and
whooped with pleasure. I put my hands around his
sweet ass cheeks—not because I intended to have
any say in the pace Seth chose, but because I loved
holding him.

Seth did what he did. At times I felt honored, as
though he were worshipping at the altar of Priapus—
as if my stiff penis were the most important part of
Seth's universe. At other times I felt used for his
pleasure. Both feelings were heady. I lasted as long
as I could. I didn't want the experience to end any
more than he did. But of course it doesn't work that
way. As he felt my body tighten in anticipation of the
climax to come, he doubled down on his efforts to
honor me.

Seth lowered his body onto my chest and kissed
me deeply. It was his kiss that started the series of
eruptions that followed. I gave Seth my best. He
accepted it with reverence. Seth continued to kiss
me as I recovered a bit. When all was stillness in my
bed, he slowly extricated himself from our union and
scooted his body forward until his own ample cock
was available to my greedy mouth. I took it like a
man who is starving—as indeed I was.

Seth soon honored me with his own explosion,
which filled my mouth with extraordinary sweetness.
Seth's offering was so ample that I invited him to help

me savor it. He was not shy about sharing the bounty. And then he lay beside me, our arms still entwined. I had nearly forgotten what it's like to have a real orgasm—a shared experience. I was a bit dazzled, actually. We were silent for many minutes.

Seth broke the silence to say, "I've never done that before."

"Oh, shit! Why didn't you tell me, Seth? I'd have been more careful!"

"No, I didn't mean *that*," he said. "It's just that I've never held another man in my arms and felt his heart beating next to mine. I guess I've gotten used to falling into bed with boys who want to get off quick. I've been okay with that, because most of them have been worth about that much of my time and attention. I knew there had to be something better. I just didn't know what it was. When I met you at the gallery, I thought, *He looks like a man who knows what he wants and how to get it. He looks like a man, actually. And I've had more than enough boys.*

"That was it, really," Seth said. "That's why I texted you, Jerry. I hoped you could teach me something. And you have." I wasn't so sure how I felt about being cast in the role of teacher. I had never sought a pupil or a mentee. But I accepted the responsibility, somehow. We lay together quietly for a while.

Then I said, "Maybe you think I've forgotten what it's like to be—23, is it?"

"21, actually"

"I stand corrected. Enjoy every minute of it— and make as many regrets as you can handle. I like you, Seth," I said as I stroked the perfection of his belly. The tiny trail of hair that led from his pubes to his navel began to fascinate me. "I think you're a good man."

"That sounds like goodbye," he said.

"Not at all."

"Can I see you again?" he asked.

"Sure," I said. "Whenever you like. Within reason, of course." I kissed him warmly, by way of reinforcing my invitation.

"Please don't tell Tim about this," Seth said. "He wouldn't approve of me dating a client."

"I understand completely," I said. "It will be our secret." I wondered if it might prove to be a bigger secret for me than for Seth: I wouldn't be likely to tell Connie about this encounter. Not any time soon, anyway. And while Lucy would probably enjoy hearing that I banged the cute kid from the gallery, the timing seemed all off.

"If we're going to see each other again, there's something you should know," I said. "There's a man— there's always another man, Seth, in case you didn't know—there's a man who wants my heart. And he won't share his body with me until I give him my heart. So I have decisions. And you're not making them any easier."

"Can we meet on Thursday?" he asked.

"Yes, but then comes Pride weekend, and I have plans."

"Of course," he said.

"Seth, will you sleep over?" The words just tumbled out of my mouth. I had no intention of speaking them.

"Yes," Seth said. And he snuggled in closer.

"Good," I said, though I doubted that was the truth. "I'll get you a toothbrush, and a towel if you want it. Let's turn in. I have an early morning." Seth smiled at me in a new way as he prepared to brush his perfect young teeth. I liked his smile. More than I should, I decided. We returned to my bed, Seth kissed me good-night, and I spooned him. His perfect little body in my arms felt warm and wonderful. His sweet round butt pressed against my crotch, and it easily got another rise out of me. But it was too late at night for such things. We slept.

I jumped out of bed at the first jangle from my morning alarm, skipping my usual ten-minute snooze. I made coffee and looked to see if I had anything breakfasty in the fridge. I toasted some good bread and opened the avocado in the bowl on the counter. It was about 90%—not bad for an avocado in New York.

Seth surfaced just as the coffee finished brewing. He was just as naked as I was, and he walked over and embraced me. I kissed him warmly. Then I held him at arms' length to get a good look at the sweet man I had inhabited the night before—dressed in morning sunlight now instead of in moonlight and newness. Except for his morning wood, which was decidedly grownup, Seth's pillow-head made him look like a little boy—as indeed he was in many ways. I was moved to tears, actually, but I quickly brushed them away and said, "There's sugar on the table. Do you want milk?"

"Yes, please."

"I'll warm some." We shared coffee and some decent avocado toast. We smiled a lot. I was running out of free time. "I have to shower in a minute," I said. "What are your plans for this morning?"

"I have to be at the gallery at 10:00," Seth said.

"Then you can take your time. I'll give you some clean shorts, and I'm sure I have a shirt in the back of my closet that's small enough to fit you. Or a polo, if you want. So you don't have to go home first. Where is home, by the way?"

"I have a tiny studio in the East Village. It isn't much, but it's mine. I almost have a view of the East River from the fire escape. It doesn't exactly bring me joy, but I had my fill of roommates in college." I didn't touch that. There didn't seem to be time. "You're at the Historical Society, I think," he said.

"Yes, and I'd better get my ass moving if I want to stay there."

"It's a very nice ass," Seth said.

"Thanks," I said, on my way to the bathroom. I stopped to kiss Seth warmly and to tousle his hair. And then I went into my morning routine. There were little DANGER signs that flashed in my brain as I showered. I mostly ignored them. I hurried through washing and dressing. It was a not-very-public workday for me, so I didn't have to put on a tie and jacket. Small mercies. I was ready. "I put out some things for you to try, on the bed," I said to Seth. "Just let yourself out when you're ready. The house lock is plenty secure. I'll tell the doorman I have a guest, so no one will bother you." One more kiss, a quick, "See you Thursday," and I was off.

I rather floated through the rest of the day. Lucy said I looked like a cat who's been licking the cream. Perhaps I did. I had dipped my tongue into riches I had nearly forgotten about, after all. I worried for a while about what I had gotten myself into, but then I resolved to simply enjoy the ride, wherever it might take me. A couple of hot dates with a sweet kid who wanted my body. No, he wanted *me*, actually. But how dangerous could that be?

37

Chapter Six

When Connie phoned on Wednesday evening,
I was delighted to hear from him, of course. I hadn't
spoken to him in a few days, and I missed him. I
also felt a little dazed from the time I had spent with
Seth. Mostly I had no idea how the one affected the
other—in my brain, of course. Connie and Seth
seemed polar opposites in most ways. And yet they
were each drawn to me as strongly as I was drawn to
them. Hmmm....

"You sound distracted," Connie said.

"Strange day at work," I said. "But then I'm sure
every workday is a trial for you. I respect that, by
the way, in case I haven't told you. We should talk
about Sunday."

"Yes, what's the dinner verdict?" he asked.

"Well, I decided the three of us should go to my
favorite Greek restaurant in Astoria. We can jump
on the 1 train at Christopher Street and then change
to the N at 42nd Street. It's not that far, really, and
the food is great. Are you okay with that?"

"Of course," he said. "I love Greek. And I've always wanted to share Greek with you. So here's our
chance."

"You're fucking with me, Connie," I said. "That
isn't nice." I loved Connie's laugh. He graced me
with peals of it.

"I don't know how to say 'poor little you' in Greek," he said, "but maybe I'll learn. Meanwhile, what's the plan for Sunday morning?"

"Yes, well, I want you to come here around 9ish. I'll get some smoked salmon and such from Russ & Daughters. And that should fortify us until dinner. Does that work for you?"

"Of course," he said.

"So I'll confirm all of that with Lucy. She's excited about seeing you again, by the way. Please be kind to her. But please make sure you keep your focus on me. If I lost you to Lucy I'd have to murder someone. And it wouldn't be pretty."

"Understood," Connie said. "I'm properly chastened for my improper thoughts. Get some rest, Jer. I think you need it. My Granny used to call me, 'my perfect little man-child.' Well, I think that's who *you* are now. I think you're as much child as you are man, I think you're perfect, and I want you to be mine. Just saying. Sleep well."

I tried my best to do just that—with imperfect success.

There didn't seem much point in elaborate courtship rituals. For our second date, Seth suggested that he bring over a falafel dinner for the two of us. I assured him I always had plenty of wine in the house, plus any condiments we might need. It was easy, and it had the advantage of getting Seth to my apartment without any niceties of invitation or delay.

"This is from Mamoun's," he said after I had greeted him with a kiss and we had begun to unpack the goodies in his bags. "Is that your neighborhood favorite? A friend told me it would be, since you live here."

"Used to be," I said. "I haven't been there in years. I'm glad it's still flourishing." We smiled a lot as we enjoyed the food, which was light and fresh and just as I remembered it. We drank chardonnay. We concentrated on each other more than our dinner. It all made me feel young and free, and I resolved to remember the feeling and to repeat it as often as possible. The meatiness and crunch of the falafels complemented the creaminess of the tahini sauce. We enjoyed hummus and baba ghanoush and some salady things.

"What's for dessert?" I asked. Seth stood and opened his jeans.

"You could start here," he said. Indeed I dropped to my knees before him, pushed down the fabric that was interfering with my access, and began to adore—not just his wondrous cock but all the treasures between his legs. I pushed some dinner things aside and sat Seth on the dining table as I stripped his jeans down to his shoes. He spread his knees to give me unfettered access.

I made real acquaintance with Seth's balls for the first time. The delicate blue veining of a pale scrotum has always been a thing of wonder to me. So fragile looking, and yet sufficiently strong to support not just what gay men crave but the seed of future generations. I quite liked both of the inhabitants of Seth's generous scrotum. A handsome pair, but very slightly mismatched. Fascinating.

Like the rest of him, Seth's balls were so available! Neither ever shied away from my tongue or my touch, even when I flirted with—not roughness, really. I hope you know by now that's not who I am. But I'll admit that I did maybe *pressure* his package beyond what I would have found comfortable in the same circumstance. Seth never flinched any more than his balls did. He never complained. He always waited impatiently for more.

I avoided my favorite part of Seth's anatomy for as long as I could. But then I picked him up, kissed him deeply, turned him around, and urged his chest down onto the clearance in the middle of the dinner table. I dropped to my knees again to savor the sweetness between his cheeks. It's not that I had my fill. That seemed an impossibility. But it seemed time to move on. I reached for the extra-virgin olive oil I had brought to the table for our salad, anointed both of us, and prepared to enter him.

It didn't feel like an occasion for romance. Nothing too gentle. Nothing tentative. Nothing polite. Our Thursday evening was all about lust—or so it seemed to me at the moment. As soon as I felt welcome, I entered Seth's body firmly and aggressively. "Yes," he said with my first thrust. "Harder," he said with the next thrust. "Don't stop," he said. I didn't. I stayed with Seth. I filled him up to the best of my ability and my anatomy. I gripped his shoulders. I leaned in to lift his head so I could kiss him, and I dropped sweat—and maybe tears—in the process. His angelic smile never wavered.

I shouted when I came as deeply inside Seth as I could manage to be. It was a cry that came up from my gut and would not be silenced. I'm sure I had never had an experience like that before. And I'm sure it knocked the wind out of me. I felt as if I had transferred all the energy in my body into Seth's. I was enervated. Seth seemed to spring to life.

He stood and said, "It's my turn." Seth urged my chest down onto the dining table. The scent of tahini sauce was a heady welcome to the submissive posture I assumed. I was ready for nearly anything. To my surprise, Seth explored me with such tenderness that I began to weep. His lips, his tongue, his nose, and even his playful nibbles made me feel ashamed for the force I had used on him. Or so it seemed at the time.

Seth eased himself into position to mount me. I wouldn't—I couldn't have resisted him at that point. He teased my sphincter. He made a few tentative pushes toward entry, and then he stopped and lowered himself down onto my back. He kissed me, and said, "No, not tonight. No, I don't even know if you want it. No, I couldn't bear to do anything that hurt you. No, Jerry. Not tonight." Instead, he humped me rather gently until he creamed all over my back and his belly. Warm. Nice. I was exhausted. Seth was merely sated.

When we had recovered a bit, Seth began to chuckle. So did I. He said, "You were an animal, Jerry. I wasn't expecting that."

"I'm so sorry," I said. "Are you okay?

"Don't apologize, Jerry," he said. "I loved it. And believe me, I know how to say, 'no.' I like every part of you that I meet. Will you show me the rest?"

"I'll try, but I think we should maybe straighten up a little first." We laughed, pulled up our jeans, and organized the remains of our feast. Seth gave the dining table a little extra polish. The wood shown like a mirror.

"Olive oil," Seth said.

"Body oil, more likely," I said. "But they're both therapeutic." I took Seth in my arms and savored the nakedness of his torso. I kissed him deeply. He kissed me back. In fact, he kissed me as if there was nowhere else on Earth he'd rather be. I was stunned for the umpteenth time that day. "Please tell me you'll sleep over," I said.

"Of course."

"How about a quick shower?" I asked.

"Nice." We stripped and headed for the bathroom. I had never showered with Seth before, of course. We were creating firsts left and right. We kissed more than we lathered and scrubbed. Our shared shower cleansed not just our skin but a lot of the fear that had been building in my heart.

Even so, my residual fear spoke next. It said, "Seth, you're trying to kill me."

Seth took my face in his hands, quite tenderly, and said, "No, Jerry. I'm trying to love you. I just don't know how. Maybe you can teach me." That silenced me really fast. We finished our shower and dried off. Then we headed to the bedroom. I welcomed the perfection of Seth's body into my bed again. I kissed him with the urgency of a lover who dares not miss a chance to express his devotion.

I thought I was too weary to sustain another erection. I was wrong. Seth said, "Oh, the animal is back!"

We laughed. "No," I said. "You're lying next to quite a different beast. A tame one. A pet who wants only to please."

"In that case," Seth said, "I have plans for my new pet." He plumped up some pillows and encouraged me to lie back on them. And then he proceeded to celebrate my body with his hands and his mouth and probably other body parts, too. I wasn't always certain what he was doing. But I always knew he was honoring me. No one had explored my armpits since, maybe, ever. Even Karl never took such an interest in my nipples. Or my equipment, really.

I surrendered to the pure physicality of it. As I got closer, it was only heavy breathing that gave me away. Otherwise, I never tensed a muscle; never gave into the urge to move into the mounting pleasure. I think Seth had at least one finger inside me when the spasms began. Maybe more. I practiced slow, deep breathing. I wanted my orgasm to be his, as indeed it was. I wanted Seth to feel every sensation I did. I wanted to gift him with my deepest self.

So much for exhaustion! Seth savored every drop of my offering that he could find on my belly and my chest, and then he lay quietly beside me. There was no need for words. I turned out the light and wrapped my arms around the perfection beside me. We slept.

📖

The morning was rushed, as before. But I found time to hold my naked treasure as close to my heart as possible. "I don't know what to do with you," I said.

"You could love me," he said. "That would be enough."

"Let's not go there this morning," I said. "Daylight and off-to-work make such a coward of me. Will you be patient with me, Seth?"

45

"Yes," he said. "And I'll bring back your clothes after I do laundry on Monday."

"Please keep them," I said. "I have plenty of shorts, and I'm sure the shirts look better on you than they ever did on me. I want you to have them."

"Thanks," he said. "I know you have a busy weekend, Jerry. When can I see you again?"

I did some quick thinking and said, "Would Tuesday work for you? We could make it a tradition."

Seth grinned and said, "Don't be late for work." I headed off into the bustle of the Friday morning commute, and it was nearly as if nothing extraordinary had just happened to me. Nearly.

Pride Sunday always fills me with—pride, I suppose. I've never been an activist. I've always let others fight for my civil rights. But one month a year, anyway, I pay attention to advances and regressions on the political front. Karl was probably the most secular person I've known, and yet he used to get on his soapbox occasionally to decry the complacency of Americans Jews, who think it can't happen again—who think there won't be another Holocaust.

And that harangue was always followed by, "And that includes faggots, too. Do you think you're safe? Do you think they won't come for you, just because some say they're in favor of marriage equality? Forget it! They can turn on a dime. You're living in the same fool's paradise as the Jews." I was properly chastened by Karl's warning. But it was really only in June that I chose to celebrate the freedoms that others had secured for me.

I got up early on Sunday morning and organized all the goodies I had collected for our Pride breakfast. The apartment looked good, and it would most likely be a beautiful, sunny day. I showered and slipped into tight jeans, a magenta T, and my rainbow vest— ready for its annual outing. Yes, a good day, surely.

My two favorite people were prompt. "Why do gay boys make such good coffee?" Lucy asked.

"Attention to detail," Connie said. "Why do you think we make such good lawyers?" I noticed that Connie didn't mention hairdressers or makeup artists or interior decorators. Lucy noticed too, surely.

"That must be it," she said. "So, Greek food tonight, Jerry. I don't think you ever told me about this place."

"Maybe not," I said. "It's nearly the same restaurant Karl and I liked so much. New management, I think. They spiffed it up a little, and the food is even better. Since we'll be there on a Sunday night, wait until you see all the families. They're so—Mediterranean, I guess it is: They obviously love to go out together and to eat good food. Three generations, at least. And they're so loving to the children. Show me that in Connecticut. I'll shut up now."

Connie and Lucy both laughed. They had their own family memories and issues. Who doesn't? "So what's the plan—for the parade?" Lucy asked.

"I thought we'd head over to Christopher Street about 11:00 or so," I said. "We should be able to find decent standing room before noon. That's when the parade starts, but it won't reach us for more than an hour. Karl and I always used to camp out in front of a bar I know—with bathrooms—that stays open all afternoon. Very convenient."

"I like a man who's practical," Lucy said. I had decided on two different salmon choices—my favorite Scotch and a cured one, also smoked, with an added pastrami spice coating. They were both delicious. I had bought more than enough of everything, so the three of us enjoyed a prideful feast that Sunday morning. Lucy loved the pastrami one. Connie was more of a purist, like me.

After breakfast, we put the leftovers away and headed out into the shimmering light of early summer. Yes, it would be a perfect day. Christopher Street was already abuzz with anticipation and joy. We staked out our territory for the next few hours. We also greeted friends and acquaintances, because it's impossible to attend the Pride Parade without encountering some of each.

The crowd's energy level began to soar as we waited for the opening "marchers," who were always Dykes on Bikes. They announced their imminent arrival with the now-familiar roar of motorcycle engines. Great shouts went up from the crowd on the east end of Christopher Street as the bikers rounded the corner and headed in our direction. Heady stuff.

The bikers were followed by a marching band, followed by a colorful float manned by very cute representatives of a favorite food charity serving homebound AIDS patients. In the course of the afternoon there would be Pacific Islanders, Brazilians, Latinos, other ethnic groups, plus banks and other businesses that prided themselves on their service to their gay clients; also nonprofits, gay/straight alliances, and community outreach programs.

Some bars had a presence. Hospital volunteers, groups of friends and business associates, and nearly every imaginable reason to march got people on their feet. Here and there were sprinkled exuberant crazies in fantastical outfits. The crowds were just as warm in their reception of these individuals as they were of the well-known institutions. It was a day of inclusion, after all.

That parade was in the days before the controversy over police presence in the march. So one of the crowd favorites was, for the umpteenth year, the NYPD in formation complete with marching band. I think most people sensed the symbolism in their annual participation. I certainly did. For me it spoke of a carefully nurtured relationship between the police and the gay community that had managed—through the years—to effect a 180° shift since Stonewall days. Instead of the enemy, police had become the guardians of the streets we walked and the businesses we frequented. More or less. It was certainly the case on Pride Sunday.

Probably because I drank too much coffee at breakfast, I was the first one to peel off and get in the bathroom line in the bar behind us. When I returned, Lucy decided it was her turn. Connie and I smiled at each other in an intimate way. "When you went to pee, Lucy asked me what we're up to," he said. "I told her it's all up to you. I told her the future is your choice. Lucy said, 'I always thought you two were meant for each other. But someone is stalling. You?' she asked me."

"And what was your answer?"

"I told her I'm as open as a daisy. I told her I've loved you—from a distance—for a lot of years. I told her I'm not willing to settle for anything that isn't complete."

"Thanks for the clarification," I said. Some twinges went through my body. I had no legitimate reason not to give my heart to Connie, and yet visions of Seth danced in my head. (Sorry, wrong holiday). I took Connie's arm and pressed closely against him. He kissed me. The crowd had given us the same feeling of intimacy that people experience in a crowded restaurant.

When Lucy returned, we made room for her between us. "That wasn't so bad," she said. "But I think we should have a drink in the bar before we go. It seems only fair."

"Very thoughtful," I said. It was an exciting and colorful afternoon. And then the three of us went to the bar for a glass of wine. Thus fortified, we were ready to push through the crowd—which was now headed toward the piers—to reach the subway station. A 1 train arrived shortly. The wait at 42nd Street for an N train was a little tedious. But we were in a mellow mood, so no one got antsy.

"Isn't the transit system a wonder? When it works, of course," Lucy said. She was right. All New Yorkers marvel at how easy it is to get from one part of town to another. Except when it isn't. A sick passenger or someone interfering with the third rail can bring the whole thing to a screeching halt. And then there's weekend construction. But let's not go there. Our Pride Sunday evening trip was uneventful.

The restaurant was welcoming, as always. I had made a reservation, for the sake of form. We were nearly an hour early. It didn't seem to matter. They found a table for us right away. I asked Connie and Lucy how they felt about *retsina*. They were both game, so I ordered a liter. So far so good.

I ordered an assortment of spreads and some fried squid to begin. I had been to Athens once and had noted the Greek preference for fried squid in thick pieces, rather than the dainty ringlets we're more accustomed to in the US. And that preference made its way to Astoria. I had learned to like the meatiness of it, and I hoped my companions would agree.

"The baby lamb in a fricassee with romaine lettuce is delicious," I advised them. "It sells out fast, though, so they may not have any more. The lamb in tomato sauce is also really good. I like everything I've tried. Nothing is better than a grilled sea bass, so we can also go up front and choose a likely candidate from the display on ice. But since it's Sunday, that might not be the best idea. Have I confused you sufficiently?"

"Quite," Lucy said. She chose the *moussaka*, and Connie decided on a chicken dish I had never tried. They had one last order of the baby lamb fricassee for me. The waiter was gentle and patient. He was also exceptionally cute, which is always nice. The families began to arrive. Within a half hour, all the eight- or ten- or twelve-tops they had prepared were peopled by happy relatives.

The dining room was filled with love and warm food smells—a good combination. "I adore this place," Lucy said after we had sampled the appetizers. "Why have you been keeping it from me?"

"It wasn't intentional, dear." And then, I don't know why I said it. I didn't intend to. But it tumbled out of me. I said, "Connie, you haven't met him, but Lucy did—the nice kid who works for Tim Hart at the gallery. His name is Seth. He wanted my advice on his future, so I had supper with him last week."

"So what did you advise that pretty little thing, Jerry?" Lucy asked. I knew she'd remember him.

"He wants to work in the arts, one way or another," I said. "I told him he could do a lot worse than to stay with Tim. I don't know a classier gallery in Chelsea. I also told Seth to consider nonprofits. We all know about those." And, indeed, all three of us were up to our armpits in serving public institutions. "And I told him if he really wants to learn a lot fast and take his belt in a notch at the same time, he should get a job in the management of a dance troupe."

"Quite right," Lucy said. "I'm sure he'll figure it out. He seemed very—capable." It was not a generous observation. Lucy did *not* say, "I'm sure he can look out for himself," or "I'm sure Seth knows how to get what he wants." She didn't have to. Her meaning was clear. Connie seemed a little sad about the conversation—about the direction it was headed in and the fact that it didn't include him, largely. Or maybe he saw through me.

And then I wondered why I had felt the need to create such an elaborate ruse to cover up my—peccadillo? Was that what I had been doing? Was I ashamed of having found such comfort in Seth's arms? Or was it the fact that I had fallen a little bit in love with him? I probably admitted it to myself for the first time, while I was enjoying a really good dinner with the two people in my life who were most important to me.

"I think they serve coffee these days," I said, "but it's generally considered polite to go to a café for coffee and sweets. Shall we surrender this table to the hungry people who are waiting for it?" And that's what we did. There was a café in the next block. The coffee was good, the sweets entirely too sweet—as expected. They capped our day perfectly. And then we headed home.

We all left the N train at 34th Street and transferred to the F. Lucy left us at 14th Street, and Connie and I continued on to W 4th Street. It was a beautiful evening, we had full bellies, and we both wanted to be together. It doesn't get much better than that. As we walked home, I put my arm around Connie, instinctively, and he put his arm around my waist. It felt warm and strong and reassuring.

"Are we going to New Jersey on Friday morning or Thursday evening?" Connie asked. "Either one works for me."

"I'm not certain," I said. "I'll check with Kenny and let you know."

We stopped in front of Connie's building in a combination of moonlight and streetlight. He kissed me sweetly. I kissed him back, of course. And then we looked at each other for a while. Connie seemed sad. I felt like a rat. We couldn't seem to find anything to say to each other, so another kiss and we parted. As I walked the last two blocks home I started to cry. Softly. Tears of self-pity, most likely. Unjustified, and yet quite real, nonetheless.

It was good to be back at work on Monday morning. The structure, the discipline of it felt reassuring. I don't know how productive I was, but I went through the motions. Lucy didn't have time to lunch with me. It was just as well, I decided. She could always see through any subterfuge I mounted. And I was not prepared to discuss Seth with her. I wasn't even ready to discuss Seth with myself.

I dreaded the thought of seeing him again the following evening. I also craved his presence in my bed. I was angry at myself for wanting Seth, and I felt guilty for the *way* I wanted him. Surely it was wrong to use his youthful sweetness to satisfy my carnal needs. What about spiritual needs? What about the youthful sweetness of building a lasting bond between two individuals who care for each other?

I nearly canceled our Tuesday date. But I couldn't do it. I wish I could tell you it was out of a deep desire not to hurt Seth, but that isn't the truth. I kept our date out of deep desire, period. I thought of another casual supper spot in the neighborhood— the sort of place I would be unlikely to run into Connie or Lucy. We met at 7:00.

Seth was his usual self—sunny, upbeat, easygoing, and thoroughly sexy. Any resistance I had harbored simply melted away. I smiled easily in response to his warmth. We drank a beer and ate some bar snacks—nothing memorable, believe me. And then we headed to my apartment. Wasn't that always the goal? As I turned my key in the lock, I wondered if it would seem routine, bedding Seth again. How much newness can there be in a sexual relationship?

I was about to find out. We stripped slowly, pausing to kiss often. When we slipped into my bed, Seth wrapped his arms around me and kissed me deeply. I responded in kind. And I realized that instead of the frenzy of previous matings, Seth was making love to me. There was nothing boyish or inchoate in his physical response. Instead, there was a beautiful young man beside me who wanted to share himself with my self.

It wasn't only the union of souls, however. Seth had learned a number of things about my body. He had learned how and where to touch me in order to deliver exquisite pleasure. I attempted to return his favors as skillfully as I could. Eventually, Seth eased me on top of him and wrapped his legs around my waist. It was a gesture not really of surrender but of total sharing. He gave me his body, trusting I would use it well. I accepted his gift.

That time I entered Seth quietly and carefully. We kissed throughout the process. As the two of us joined our bodies, we became as one—one being intent on not just pleasure but on an actual union. I truly couldn't tell where I ended and Seth began. It was the unit that mattered. We ceased to be individuals with individual needs.

When I started to get close to orgasm, Seth was with me. I knew he was. I knew we would explode in unison. I just didn't know if the top of my head would blow off at the same time. It did not. We both survived the experience intact, more or less. We still clung to each other and kissed deeply. Neither of us wanted to end our union. But it doesn't quite work that way, of course.

When, eventually, we had to accept that it was over and that we were but mere mortals again, there was a slight sadness to it. As we disentangled our limbs—and our lips—it took rather a long while before we began to smile, and then to laugh. "Seth Greenly, aren't you full of surprises!" I said.

"Jerry, you make me so happy!" he said. "You're perfect, really. I never thought ... well, never mind what I thought. Let's enjoy what we have." I got up to go to the john to pee. And as I stood above the toilet, I was suddenly hit with an attack of something like panic and something like guilt. Is there such thing as a panic/guilt attack? There is now.

When I got back to my bed, Seth was the same beautiful creature I had just left. I, on the other hand, was someone else entirely. He sensed it. I knew he did. But the change was made and could not be reversed. Seth reached for me warmly anyway. I think my response was rather icy. He decided it was his turn to visit the john.

When he returned to bed, I said to him, "Forget about me, Seth. I'm not worth it. I forgot how to love years ago. You need someone who can adore you for the rest of your life. Thanks for thinking that someone could be me. But I'm not the man you want. I'm not much of a man at all, really. More like a shell."

Seth got up and started to dress. As he was tying his shoes, he said, "I know what you're doing, Jerry. I'm not stupid. I know you think you can distance me so you don't have to feel your feelings. But it's not going to work. I know the truth." He finished dressing and headed for the front door. I followed him, pleading with my eyes, anyway, for him to stay.

On his way out, Seth turned to me and said, "Have a safe trip. I'll text you next week. Don't forget our Tuesday." A quick kiss and he was gone. I felt as low as a snake's belly. But surely I had to brush him off. Didn't I? I wasn't certain about much of anything except that I needed sleep. I forced myself to text Ken Garda for weekend instructions. And then I conked out.

📖

I texted Connie with travel info as soon as I heard back from Kenny. "It's Friday morning about 9:00. They rented a car that's big enough for the four of us. They'll pick us up here, if that's okay with you. I'm going to buy some breakfast things, otherwise we're not supposed to bring anything. Casual clothes. Swim trunks, unless you don't wear them. That's okay, too. I'm going to keep my options open, since I don't know our hosts. Questions?"

Connie responded later that morning: "Sounds good. I happen to like skimpy swimsuits, so I'll bring some. I also like swimming without them, but it's good to have options. And it's good to know I'll be spending the weekend with you." I was pleased, of course, that Connie was looking forward to our weekend together. I also felt dishonest. Surely I'd have to tell him about Seth. Wouldn't I? But when? How?

I passed the rest of the workweek in a kind of daze. I made weekend wardrobe choices and did my food shopping after work. Lucy had invited a sister to stay with her, so she had some things to do to get ready for the visit. I didn't see much of Lucy that week. It was just as well. If the whole Seth thing had to come out, then Connie deserved to be the first one to know. Didn't he?

Connie looked marvelous when he arrived about 8:30 on Friday morning. But then when didn't he look marvelous? I greeted him warmly. I liked the easiness of summer, but I suspected I might like him in sweater weather and parka time just as well. I had never walked in a snowstorm with Connie. But I hoped I'd get that chance in about six months. I hoped for a lot. I also wondered if I deserved to have any of my wishes come true.

"You didn't say anything about breakfast, so I brought two croissants stuffed with scrambled eggs and bacon," Connie said. "Could you eat a little something?" I could. I gulped down a few bites as I finished gathering my things for the trip. Connie, as always, was more measured and elegant. He took sensible bites and chewed them thoroughly. I liked the way he chewed—with purpose, strength, and with obvious enjoyment. I liked everything about him, of course.

"Speaking of breakfast," I said, "I hope the boys are happy with the one I'm going to make tomorrow— or on Sunday if that works out better." I had bought two dozen free-range organic eggs, breakfast sausages in several flavors, apples, and blue corn grits from South Carolina's finest mill. Or so the cute guy at the shop assured me.

"If they're anything like me," Connie said, "they'll be happy to have someone cook for them. Especially someone as handsome as you are." I decided that deserved a kiss. As always, Connie gave me much more than I seemed to be able to give him. Could that change? I wondered. "I brought a bottle of port," Connie said. "It's not very original, but I wanted to take them something."

"I think it's lovely," I said. "Let me get my wheelie from the bedroom. The boys will be here any minute." My things were ready. Packing had been easy—a few Ts, a couple of undershorts, a swim bikini with tropical flowers on it, and a light-weight hoodie in case it got cool at night in the country. The bare minimum of toiletries, heavy on sunscreen. Like that. I had a thermal hamper for the food. That was much more complicated than my wardrobe.

"Are you ready?" I asked Connie.

"I was born ready," he said. I believed him. We spent our last few minutes alone kissing, right up until I got the text telling me the Brooklyn boys were nearing my building. I neatened the apartment a little, and we headed to the street. They pulled up in a Cadillac SUV—spacious and super comfy.

"Isn't it amazing what you can rent these days?" Ken asked. There were hugs and kisses all around. Matt was driving. I figured if he could handle an EMS van, he could probably handle a passenger car. We loaded in and buckled up. There was excitement in the air. As much as New Yorkers love being at home, we also thrill to the occasional outing.

As soon as we had navigated our way to the Lincoln Tunnel, Ken turned toward Connie and me in the back seat and said, "I've never been to the house, but I fell in love with Dan's parents, so I'm sure their house is warm, generous, and welcoming. I don't know if we'll see them this weekend. I hope so. You'll love Dan and Caleb. I'm not sure what I told you about them."

"Not very much," Connie said.

"Dan is an editor, and Caleb is a writer. It works for them. I was hired—*we* were hired" (indicating Matt)—"to shoot their wedding. So that's how we all met. Apparently, Dan's parents, Elaine and Richard, gave the house to Dan and Caleb. So, *they're* trying to figure out what to do with it. They're not about to give up their apartment in Chelsea. And they can only get away for a long weekend in the country once in a while.

"Anyway, that's about all I know," Kenny said. "Maybe we'll learn more this weekend. You two look delicious in sunlight. I knew this would be a good weekend. Matt and I are delighted you could join us. And so are Dan and Caleb." We exited the tunnel, and Kenny studied a map app he pulled up on his phone, to figure out the best way to get to Rte. 17. The maze of highways and exits on the Jersey side of the tunnel is confusing. I doubt GPS could sort it out. We made it.

"Thanks, Kenny," I said. "I haven't left the city in months, and Connie and I never seem to manage to spend the weekend together. So this is a treat."

"No weekends together?" Kenny asked. "I'd guess it's time to change that. Not that it's any of my business." We all smiled warmly. Connie and I held hands in the back seat of that cushy Cadillac. I was nodding off, as we sped toward Ridgewood. Connie put my head on his shoulder. And that's where it stayed until we pulled up in front of the house.

_________ *Chapter Nine*

Two handsome men came out to the driveway to greet our arrival. "You made good time. I guess the tunnel traffic wasn't too crazy," said the smaller of the two. "I'm Dan Blackwell and this is Caleb Bromley. You must be Jerry. Welcome to New Jersey." We finished our introductions, and there were greetings and kisses all around.

"We're so glad you two could make it," Dan said to Connie as we gathered up our luggage. "This old house needs some new life in it now and then. Let me take that," he said to me as he reached for the thermal hamper. "Come in, everyone. We have coffee and mimosas. And a little lunch in a couple of hours." We all headed inside.

Caleb said, "I love the new beard, Matt. Very distinguished."

"Kenny keeps hoping it will make me look older," Matt said. Ken tousled his flaming red hair. And kissed him. Their affection was lovely to witness.

"Leave your things here," Dan said. "I'm taking beverage orders." There was plenty of room in the foyer for all our stuff. It was the sort of big, old house I had seen before, when I was growing up, but never spent any time in. My grandparents lived in a neighborhood with houses rather like that, but they all seemed formidable. Dan and Caleb's house welcomed us, or so it seemed. Or maybe it was the kindness of our hosts.

Everyone decided on a mimosa. We sank into comfy furniture in the living room. I let the holiday freedom wash over me. Connie took my hand, and I snuggled in close to his body. I felt safe. I felt loved, really. And the other two couples in the room completed the circle of warmth. "There's almost nothing to do here," Dan said. "We hope you appreciate that as much as we do. We'll go down to the pond and worry the ducks after lunch. And there's a badminton net we can set up in the back yard, if you like. That's about it."

"Perfect!" we guests all said in unison.

"Mom and Dad were going to stop by, but they got a rare invitation from my sister and her husband. They wanted to see you, but next time."

"I'm so disappointed!" Ken said. "I wanted the boys to meet them. Please give them my love. I don't want to make you jealous, Danny, but Mom likes me best."

"You're probably right," he said, "but that woman has a huge heart. I think there's still room for me." We had finished our mimosas. "Let's get you boys settled in. Caleb, why don't you take Ken and Matt to their room, and I'll show Jerry and Connie to theirs?" We roused ourselves and headed to the foyer to gather our things. Dan had already moved the hamper to the kitchen and put the perishables away. We headed upstairs.

"This was my sister's room," Dan said, "so it has the best bed in the house. I think you'll be comfortable here."

"I know we will be," I said. We had a sort of group hug. Dan was easy to like. And he felt good, too. The skin on his bare arms—and underneath his thin T, no doubt—was soft and inviting. I imagined Caleb making love to him. Now, that was an occasion where I'd truly like to be a fly on the wall.

"Why don't you two rest for a while?" Dan suggested. "Or take a nap, or—I'm sure you'll think of something. Come to the dining room about 12:30. We'll have a bite of lunch." We thanked Dan, and he was off. Connie and I decided we had nothing but our toiletries to unpack. So we found a place to stow our bags so we could live out of them for the weekend. Toiletries to the bathroom, and we were all moved in.

"Jerry, this is such fun having a getaway with you," Connie said. He kissed me. I kissed him back. It started a rumble in my shorts. I wondered how I'd survive the next few days. We tested the mattress. It was even more welcoming than our hosts. I slipped off my sandals and lay down. Connie joined me. He moved in behind me and pressed his body close. The warmth of the arm he put around me melted all my fears. Nearly.

📖

Lunch was a simple affair—cheeses, Italian cold cuts, good bread, a few pickles and relishes. There was also a crunchy salad and, of course, plenty of wine. I decided on white. It was an Alsatian pinot gris. Luscious. Connie chose a red—a California pinot noir, I think. He pronounced it delicious.

"I'm going to try for a real dinner on Saturday night—a recipe of my mother's," Dan said. "Other than that, it's going to be a 'help yourself' kind of weekend. Oh, and Jerry's breakfast! Let's make it Sunday. Followed by nap time, of course. A good way to end our holiday." It was hard for me to think that far ahead. I had the next day—and two nights—to survive.

We enjoyed some getting-to-know-you chat with our leisurely lunch. Connie and I learned, for instance, that Caleb was a pilot as well as a writer. "I won't make you two go up in a single-engine plane," he said to Connie and me. "I've already dragged Ken and Matt into the air—kicking and screaming. I won't inflict that on you," he told us.

"First," Kenny said, "I neither kicked nor screamed. And it was an honor being aloft with you, Caleb. I think you should initiate these two newbies. I think they deserve it." I wasn't so sure about that, but I smiled broadly.

"I'd love to go for a flight," Connie said. "I had a thing about planes when I was a kid. But they didn't seem to have black pilots then. Not with the commercial airlines. I could be wrong, but I never saw one."

"I'll take you up tomorrow if you want," Caleb said. "I'm sure I can reserve a plane on short notice on the holiday weekend. Let me know for sure in the next hour or so, and I'll arrange it." Connie and Caleb both beamed. I was less enthusiastic. The others were quite cheerful because they weren't going. We finished eating.

I helped Dan put the lunch things away. We loaded the dishwasher, and that was about all that needed doing to put the kitchen to rights. "Dan said, "I'm so glad the boys decided to invite you. I'm smitten with the both of you. So, what's the story? Do I hear wedding bells? I'll help ring them."

I blushed crimson, I'll bet. "I don't know, Dan," I said. "It's complicated." Dan seemed like a trustworthy guy. Like a gentle and loyal friend. I could almost imagine telling him about Seth. Almost. Surely I needed advice. And surely I didn't know where to get it. Could that change—that weekend? Maybe.

"Sorry, Jerry," he said. "I didn't mean to put you on the spot." Dan embraced me. I welcomed his touch, as before when he showed us to our room. I almost got a little weepy. Almost. "Let's go see the ducks," Dan said. "They get cranky when they're ignored. No people food, though, if you want to feed them. They're on a strict duck diet." Caleb had already led the others down the yard to the pond.

"What a gorgeous day," I said as Dan and I walked lazily down the low hill to join the others.

"Yes, and I think the whole weekend is going to be like this. But if it changes, we can always find indoor pursuits. We're all resourceful men, don't you think?"

"Indeed we are," I said. It was quiet and a bit cooler by the water. The only sounds were the occasional rustle of the willow tree on the far bank and the soft little throaty calls of the male mallards as they preened their iridescent feathers. The females were neither courting nor policing their broods, so they tended to be silent—except for the occasional loud quacks that announced a territorial dispute.

"I hated taking care of the ducks when I was a child," Dan said. "I don't know exactly how I'd feel about it now. But we're not here enough to look after them. So we have a 'gamekeeper' who stops in now and then—especially in the winter—to make sure they have what they need. He's cute, too, our duck boy. Very cute. But I don't think you'll get to meet him this holiday weekend. And early July is a quiet time for wildlife."

"Who wants a swim?" Caleb asked. "See down the way, on the right, where the bank is mossy? That's where it's best for swimming because it's deepest there. And that's where an artesian spring feeds the pond all year round. So the water is fresh—and cold actually. Reminds me of Montana. But not as much as Matt does," he said, affectionately. I had forgotten that they shared that bond. I almost wished I had a real friend from Connecticut who could understand my past. Almost.

"I'd love a swim," Connie said. "I'll just go back to the house and get a suit."

"We don't bother with that here," Dan said as he and Caleb led us to the prime swimming area. I had just enough wine left in me from lunch that I could shed my hidebound New England reserve and follow along obediently. And I began to strip, like everyone else. We put our clothes and sandals and espadrilles high on the pond bank, out of reach of the ducks, and hit the water. But not before I got a long, loving look at the men around me.

Never in my life had I experienced such beauty. Not in a locker room or even at an orgy—and yes, I've attended a few of those. I was stunned by the diversity in our little band of six. Matt was at the fair end, with his bright hair and pale skin with delicate blue veining. Caleb came in next on the color wheel—fair but not dramatically so. Dan and I held up the all-American middle, I suppose, while Kenny had that wonderful Mediterranean coloring called olive—not accurate, but appropriate. And then Connie completed our spectrum with the most glorious medium-brown skin I'd ever seen.

It wasn't just skin I noticed, of course. I was glad I got to see all the equipment *before* we took the plunge. Even the proudest endowments shrivel a bit in cold water. Not that it matters. It's all good. We splashed around. We whooped and roughhoused. We nearly organized a chicken fight, but the bottom wasn't even enough to support the standing soldiers. We settled for more surface play.

When we had had enough of piscine pursuits, we pulled ourselves out of the water and sat on the mossy bank to dry off. And as the sun began to warm our bodies, the equipment I had admired before our swim began to come to life. As did mine. Connie put his arm around me. And when he kissed me, we both came to full attention. I was embarrassed, but I needn't have been, considering that the other two couples were doing the same thing!

I had always assumed that Connie had a really big, really beautiful dick. It's a hunch we form at meeting, often. I'm rarely wrong about these things. But I was unprepared for the full glory of his manhood. It scared me, really—not because I'm afraid of taking a big dick but because I began to worry about whether I could satisfy him. Whether I could honor him properly. I tried to put fears aside and just enjoy the warmth of the sun and the beauty of the company.

"It's nearly cocktail time," Dan said. "We should probably go in." We slipped our clothes back on and headed to the house. Connie put his arm around me and said, "While you were helping Dan in the kitchen, I told Caleb I'd really like to take a flight tomorrow. He arranged it. Do you mind, Jerry? I'd love you to come with us, but you don't have to, of course. Please say you're happy about this."

"Naturally I'm happy, Connie," I said. "I don't know if I'll go along. Let me think about it. But I want you to have the experience. I thought you'd know what would make me happy."

"How could I know?" he asked. "You tell me so little, Jerry." I was stunned. Connie was right, of course. I had been stingy with both facts and feelings all the years we had known each other. It seemed time to change that. We went up to our room and relaxed for a while. We smiled at each other—a lot. And we kissed—a lot. And then we headed downstairs for drinks and dinner. So far, so good.

Dinner was casual, as Dan had promised. He served some soups from "the new food shop in the village" with some blanched vegetables with vinaigrette—for crunch and balance. The air conditioning was so effective that Dan and Caleb could burn lots of candles on the table without overheating us. Lovely.

"Sunsets are sometimes beautiful around here," Caleb said. "I'll keep an eye on the sky, so we can decide if we want to go outside. From the deck, the sun sets over the pond. I was never much of a sunset boy before I met Dan. But now it's my favorite time of day. We even go out there in the dead of winter— at about 4:30, of course. We have some extra sweaters and sweatshirts, in case someone gets cold." We assured Caleb we had come prepared.

It did turn out to be perfect sunset weather, with just a few low clouds on the horizon to diffuse the colors and direct them into a stately dance for our viewing pleasure. Connie held my hand. That was what kept we warm in the evening chill—not my hoodie. And when the sun had become nothing more than a tease of red on the edge of the pond, we headed inside.

Somewhere in the distance there were Fourth of July fireworks just getting underway. "Probably

Paramus," Caleb said. It was just festive enough to add to our sense of the holiday without demanding too much attention. We looked out occasionally at the sound-and-light show in the distance. But mostly we focused on the indoors.

Some of us helped to clear the table and put the dining room to rights. And some of us helped Dan put away leftovers and load the dishwasher. The cleanup was completed in minutes, and then we headed for the living room to relax and enjoy our shared company. I suddenly realized I hadn't seen a cellphone since Kenny navigated our trip to Ridgewood. It was a welcome feeling.

"There's a TV in here," Dan said. "It's hiding behind that picture. We don't use it much."

"If we're here for more than a few days," Caleb said, "we check in with CNN or MSNBC, just to make sure the world hasn't come to an end. Otherwise, we like being off-line."

"It's a rare treat," I said, "as is visiting your home, by the way. Thank you."

"'Halcyon belongs to its guests,'" Dan said in his best old-movie imitation. He reminded me of why I've always been attracted to gay men—for their charm, their humor, their accomplishment, their knowledge, their ability to love, their sense of play. The fact that most of them have a dick does no harm, of course.

Matt—at Ken's request—told us about the fall issue of *GLITZ Magazine* he was working on. So we were the first to learn which celebrities and which fashions were trending. Dan spoke of the publishing industry, and how lucky he felt to be working in a house that was firmly rooted in sensible products and sensible marketing techniques. Caleb revealed that he was about a quarter of the way into a new book.

Ken said, "You all know Tim Hart Gallery, I think." We did, of course. "Tim likes to open the fall season with a group show. So, I'm starting a new series. I think you'll find it more ... loving than most of my past work. I can't help it. It's how I feel since Matt came into my life." There were oohs and ahs all around the room. Matt blushed demurely. The flush in his face made his new beard look even more handsome.

"I wish I had good news to report on the hunger front," Connie said. "But unfortunately, things continue to get worse. Food insecurity is at levels approaching those of the Great Depression. We try to do our part. The city and state governments offer more encouraging words than funding. And the federal government does shit. Although Food Stamps help. I'll give them that."

It began to feel like my turn to speak. "Connie knows my colleague, Lucinda Warren."

"Indeed I do," Connie said. "Terrific woman."

"Lucy had the bright idea to propose a show in the main gallery at the Historical Society for this spring, one which features living New York artists— including present company," I said, indicating Kenny. "She asked Tim Hart to be the guest curator. I think it's going to happen, and I think it will be a remarkable show. And that's all I can tell you tonight."

Dan opened the bottle of port that Connie had brought and poured little glasses all around. It was delicious, but not as tasty as spending the day with five remarkable men. It was beginning to feel like bedtime. I both welcomed the chance to sleep with

Connie and feared the demands the situation placed on me. The *situation*—not Connie, of course. He was always patient.

We said our goodnights and made our way upstairs. "Breakfast is whenever you want it," Dan called out. He and Caleb headed for their room—the big bedroom on the ground floor, I guessed. I made a mental note to ask for a tour of the house. Connie and I approached our room. Matt and Ken stopped for an embrace and a goodnight kiss on their way to theirs. It had been a delightful day.

When we were alone. Connie and I stripped and shared a kiss. "We could probably both brush our teeth at the same time," I said. "That's a big bathroom. A little too pastel for my taste, but nice." Connie grabbed me and made a dive for my left armpit. Before I knew what was happening, he had managed to explore much of my upper body and arouse not just my nipples but everything south of the navel as well.

"I want you so badly it hurts," Connie said. "But I want all of you. And I won't settle for just your body, luscious as it is."

"Not likely," I said.

"You haven't a very high opinion of yourself, Jerry. Strange. Most handsome men think they're hotter than they really are. But you underestimate yourself, for some reason. I wish I knew why. If I had your looks and talent, I could conquer the world with both arms tied behind my back. Speaking of which, maybe we should try that some time. When we know each other better."

I dove into Connie's arms and held him with an urgency that terrified me. How could I need another man so desperately? What if I gave him my heart and he abandoned it? What if he grew to hate having to make love to me? What if he simply lost interest, as Karl had done? What if we learned—after moving in together—that we didn't really like each other all that much? What if? All the uncertainty exhausted me. I must have fallen asleep in Connie's arms.

Connie was still holding me when I woke in the morning. He was the same pillar of strength I had clung to the night before, only the pillar was now snoring softly. I disentangled myself as gently as possible so I could head to the john for a morning pee. When I returned, Connie was sitting up in bed and smiling at me.

"Why, Jeremiah Darnley," he said, "you look like the best thing God ever created. I've never seen morning look so good." I grabbed a pillow and swatted Connie with it.

"Didn't your momma teach you to be honest?" I asked him.

"And diligent, and kind, and loving. I'm doing my best over here."

I sat on the side of the bed. I touched Connie's face and gazed into the pools of sweetness that were his eyes. "Is that really what your momma taught? I never met her. I only have your word on the subject. Can I trust your word?"

"Yes, as a matter of fact," he said. "Always. You know, Momma will fall in love with you. Not at first, I'm guessing. She's known for a lot of years that she'll never have a daughter-in-law. She's accepted that. But a white son-in-law? That will take some getting used to." And then Connie suddenly pulled back and said, "Jerry, you're fooling with me. You're giving me hopes without any commitment. You've got me making plans for a future that can't exist."

I reached for him and said, "No, Connie, you're quite wrong. I want that same future. I just ... can you give me a little more time to sort things out? I don't mean to be ... difficult." I saw the same sadness in Connie's eyes as I had seen as we returned from our Greek dinner after Pride. I hoped it was the last time I'd have to witness that emotion. I hated seeing it, and I knew it was all my fault. Not fun.

After breakfast, Caleb and Connie got organized for their outing to the airstrip. I had decided against flying. I was having enough trouble maintaining my equilibrium on solid ground. "Have a wonderful time," I said to Connie as I embraced him. Caleb was flushed with excitement, and Connie had a new sparkle about him. Caleb threw him a heavy jacket, and they were on their way.

Kenny and Matt decided to go outdoors and take some photos. Dan and I sat down at the kitchen table to have another cup of coffee. I felt quiet and close to him. I took the plunge: "Could I talk to you, Dan?" I asked.

"Of course."

"I won't swear you to secrecy. I think that's creepy. But...."

"Enough said."

I gave Dan the capsule version of my affair with Seth. I wanted him to have a good sense of the time-line and just enough physical detail to make the story compelling. "I think we need a drink for this," Dan said. "Dad left some good *grappa* in his bar. This could be the right moment for it."

Dan retrieved the bottle. He poured. We sipped. He was thoughtful. And after some consideration he said, "Jerry, you have to tell him, of course. You have to tell Connie that this hot little twink—Seth?"

"Yes."

"That Seth fell a little bit in love with you, and that you, as a consequence, fell a little bit in love with him. These things happen, Jerry. Get it out of the shadows. If you don't tell Connie, your heart will never be free. And you'll never forgive yourself for shutting him out."

"But what if Seth is the love of my life?" I asked Dan. "What if he's handing me everything I've ever wanted and I'm busy trying to return it?"

"Men don't get more attractive than Connie is," Dan said. "Except for Caleb, or course. All I know is what I see, but Connie looks like the perfect man for you. Seth is twenty-one—is that right? And you're my age, Jerry, I think. Thirty-something?"

"Thirty-seven in September," I said.

"Seth will be just fine," Dan said. "No matter how mature he may be, he's still just a big version of a little boy. Jerry, surely you remember what it's like to be that age. You'll find the right way to let him down easy. He'll hate you for a minute. But in no time at all he'll thank you for being his first adult romance. And he'll cherish the memory of your love for the rest of his life."

Dan and I sat quietly for a while, sipping our *grappa*. And then Dan said, "So Seth has a college degree? At twenty-one. So he must be a hard worker. And he wants a career in the arts. Or did you manufacture that?"

"Not entirely," I said. "I believe he does want to find something meaningful for his life. He's very much aware of what's happening at Tim Hart Gallery."

"As well he should be," Dan said. "Tim is the finest gallerist in Chelsea. Look, Jerry, let me think about this for a little while. We'll talk again soon. I have some ideas I want to run by Caleb. Meanwhile, listen to your Uncle Dan. Release the boy. Seize the man. Whew! I'm glad I don't give advice! It's too exhausting—and dangerous. Jerry, will you help me with dinner, in a couple of hours?" Dan asked.

"Of course," I said.

"I'm going to attempt a pork chop thing that Mom's famous for. Maybe I thought her kitchen would do all the heavy lifting. But it's up to me— with a little help from my new friend." Dan embraced me. And he kissed me, which was very pleasant indeed. "You'll be fine, Jerry," he said. "Don't sweat the wrong things." He pushed my hair off my forehead, turned me around, slapped my butt, and said, "Go take a swim. But stay close to the bank! Mallards make very poor life guards."

I did as I was told. The late morning quiet was only interrupted by some insect calls. I knew I had heard them before, and I knew they were not June bugs. But what did I remember about summer in the Northeast? Not much beyond Washington Square Park. The water felt cool and refreshing. It helped to clear my mind—partially, anyway. I was on the edge of making a decision. And the time to make it was running short. Would I get it right?

79

When the boys returned from the airstrip, I was in the kitchen helping Dan with dinner. Both Connie and Caleb were animated. I kissed Connie and asked, "How's my new aviator?"

"It was terrific, Jerry. You have to come along next time. I know you'll love it. Caleb is a natural."

"I'll consider it," I said. I wasn't certain about the notion of flying in a single-engine prop plane, but I liked the idea of next time. I liked the thought of being invited back. I liked being in Dan and Caleb's home and feeling I belonged there. And I loved Connie, of course. There was no denying that. "Dan and I have a few more things to do," I said, "and then I'll come up. I'll bet there's time for a nap before dinner."

The flyboys headed to their rooms to change. Dan said, "I think we've got this, Jerry. Why don't you go upstairs, too?" He gave me a knowing look, and a part of me agreed it was time to tackle the subject of Seth. But the sinking feeling in the pit of my stomach didn't encourage my resolve. Still, I washed my hands and went to join Connie.

"There's something I have to tell you," I said once Connie had slipped into some shorts and a T. We sat together on the side of the bed. I took his hand. "At dinner in Astoria, I lied to you about the kid from

Tim Hart Gallery. Seth texted me because he wanted to go to bed with me. I accepted because I wanted to go to bed with him. It was supposed to be a one-off. But it turned into more than that."

Connie did not look shocked. Instead, he waited patiently for more information. "He fell in love with me, Connie," I said. "And I think that's why I fell a little bit in love with him. You'll probably meet Seth someday. I think you'll understand."

"I think I understand right now," Connie said. I searched his face for clarification. I was suddenly frightened. "Jerry, hearts aren't manageable things," he said. "If yours never went out to play I'd be worried about you. The important thing is how we feel about each other. I've been certain about you for a long time. If you're ready to offer me a commitment, that's all I need to know."

I reached for him. "Yes," I said. "Yes, Connie. Yes, if you'll have me. Yes, a million times yes." Connie embraced me with such enthusiasm that I could hardly breathe. It didn't matter. I had everything I needed. We held each other for what seemed like hours. Never in my life had I felt so completely in the right place at the right time with the right man. And I vowed to maintain that feeling permanently.

"I guess I'd better get back to the kitchen," I said. "Dan has a special dinner planned for us, but he's not much of a cook. Look who's talking! But together we'll pull this off." Connie kissed me.

"I don't want you to go," Connie said. "I want you in my arms always."

"My thought exactly," I said. "But it won't be for long. Come down for drinks about six." Another kiss, and I was off. When I returned to the kitchen,

I was the only one around. Dan and Caleb were probably in their room, and Ken and Matt were probably in theirs. I stood at the sink and looked out the kitchen window, marveling at the wonders of nature.

I was lost in thought when Dan put his hands on my shoulders. I spun around and met his inquisitive stare with a big smile. "Good," Dan said. "That's out of the way. Do you think we have to peel the asparagus?"

"Probably," I said. "They're very fat. Do you have one of those peeler things? I watched someone do it on television. I've got this, Dan. Why don't you deal with the mash?" We were a good team. By the time the others arrived for drinks, all we had left to do was warm the chops and blanch the asparagus.

It was a delightful menu: Elaine's Famous Pork Chops with Gingersnap Gravy—very retro and wonderfully satisfying—with the last of the season's New Jersey asparagus plus mashed garlic potatoes with celery root to soak up all the goodness. A chilled puréed soup to start. Some sorbets to finish. "This house hasn't seen a real dinner since Mom and Dad moved to the village," Dan said. "It's fun—as long as I don't have to do it often. Thanks, Jerry. You're a lifesaver."

"Thank *you*," I said. And I rose to my feet to propose a toast to our hosts. "Hear, hear!" was the response. It was a lovely evening. And an early one. We had shed our citified night owl habits in only a day and a half of country living. Connie and I announced our departure first, after a polite bit of cleanup assistance. Kenny and Matt wanted to talk remedies for Matt's sunburn. Dan sent them upstairs with a bottle of apple cider vinegar.

When we got to our room, being alone with Connie for the first time with a light heart was a liberating experience. He kissed me. "I love you, Jerry," he said. "Have for years. Always will."

One of the biggest thrills of my life was being able to reply, "And I love you, Connie. Have for years. Always will." We sank into the comfort of that amazing bed and began to express our love for the first time. Connie seemed able to caress every part of my body at the same time. I took a more regional approach to honoring him.

"Don't rush," Connie whispered. "We have a lifetime to get to know each other." He was right, of course. I relaxed into the sweetness of shared bodies. The fact of our being together was enough. We didn't have to *do* anything to improve our union. And yet I think we both sensed where we were headed. I think we both knew where our love would take us. I certainly did.

Connie was gentle but masterful as he held me, plumped some pillows, and then placed me on my back. Instinctively I wrapped my legs around his waist. He entered my body so carefully that I felt nothing but welcome. Instead of pain I felt joy. Instead of fear I felt love. I accepted Connie as a new part of my body, just as he had become a new part of my life. He filled my spirit just as surely as he filled my interior with his physical perfection.

I'd have been happy to spend the rest of our lives in that embrace. But it doesn't work that way, of course. Connie moved inside me. I tried my best to caress him with every interior muscle I possessed. His breathing grew heavier. I knew he would soon gift me with his liquid treasure. I wanted it. I craved it. I *needed* Connie's essence deep inside me to complete our bond.

I may have been focused entirely on Connie, but my body was not on automatic pilot. I needed to express myself physically just as keenly as he did. And when Connie erupted, so did I. I stifled a shout, successfully. Connie was more vocal. Great timing for "I love you!" I always thought. I believed him. Always will.

We lay together quietly while our breathing normalized, and then we began to chuckle. "That was the best thing that ever happened to me, Connie," I said. "I knew that making love with you would be great, but this was beyond all expectations. How did you do that?"

Connie roared with laughter, then quieted himself as he remembered we were not alone in the house. "I just followed my instincts, as I always do. If you were a polite little thing, you'd inspire polite lovemaking. But a tiger demands a worthy partner. And you, my dear, are my new favorite tiger. Please don't ever let him get away, Jerry. I want to see that look in your eyes whenever we embrace."

It was my turn to laugh too loudly. I checked myself. We lay together for a while. Speechless? Maybe. "Will you hold me?" I asked.

"As long as you'll let me," Connie said.

"Good," I said. "Should we say something? Should we make some vows? I haven't been in a situation even remotely like this since Karl. And we were just children. We got a lot of it wrong. I don't want to make those mistakes again."

"Hush, baby," Connie said. "We've already said everything we need to say tonight. Sleep now. Let me make everything right. Let me keep you warm.

Let me keep you safe." Who in his right mind would refuse?

📖

I had a huge grin on my face when I went to the kitchen to start breakfast. I could feel it, but I was helpless to control it. Dan embraced me. "I'm so happy for you both," he said.

"Dan, I can never thank you properly for your help," I started to say.

"Shush," Dan said. "You just needed a little push in the right direction. We all need that now and then. How can I help with breakfast?"

"You can crack some eggs. All of them." And that's what he did. When Connie joined us, he made the blue-corn grits. He remembered how to cook grits from his childhood in Virginia. I sautéed a selection of breakfast sausages and cored and sliced some apples to sauté in the sausage fat. Yum! I scrambled the eggs with lots of butter in the largest skillet in Elaine's kitchen. Caleb toasted some brioche. Dan found some raspberry preserves and orange marmalade in the fridge. We had a big, leisurely breakfast that would take the place of lunch.

Over the last of the coffee, and before everyone embarked on their afternoon pursuits, Dan said, "Caleb and I have been trying to figure out what to do with this house. We get here so rarely that it sits empty most of the time. If we could have weekends like this every week, it would be enough. But that's not going to happen, of course. You guys don't have that kind of availability any more than we do, I'm sure."

"We thought about turning it into a clothing-optional resort," Caleb said. "That would be fun. But we'd only get a few months of the year out of it—even if we put a thermal pool by the deck. This is hardly Palm Springs, so it's just not practical. And Dan and I are not looking for a new business venture, really. Are we, darling?"

"No, Caleb," Dan said. "I think we need to simplify. So we're trying to find the right formula for something that benefits people and takes some of the responsibility for this house off our shoulders. Caleb had a great idea a few months ago that we've been mulling over. He wants to turn the place into a retreat for writers. Or maybe all kinds of artists. That way the house has something to offer in all seasons.

"Funding is always an issue," Dan said. "We'll have to find a philanthropy with deep pockets. I don't know where we'll get the funding, but I think I know a young man who might be just the right one to run the program. Or at least to coordinate it from New York City. I just found out about him yesterday, so these are fresh thoughts."

I knew who the young man was, of course. I suspected Connie did, too. Ken said, "It's amazing that you two would be willing to give this up for the benefit of artists you don't even know. I'm a bit awed, really."

"We'll probably keep our bedroom," Dan said. "We need the occasional retreat, too."

"And the four of you will have first dibs on rooms whenever you want them," Caleb said. "We'd value your feedback. This is a big step for us. We want to get it right." I had no doubt that they would get it right, whatever they decided to do with the house. After breakfast, the three couples went their separate ways to enjoy the last of our holiday. Connie and I spent our afternoon in bed. I suspect the others did as well.

Dan ordered some sandwiches from his favorite food shop in the village. They afforded us a bite of early supper before our departure but without the cleanup. Nice. Connie and I hated to see our holiday end, but we both sensed it was time to return to our real lives, I think. We threw our things back into our bags and met the others in the foyer.

Just before we slipped into the rental car, Dan pressed his business card into my hand and said, quietly, "Tell Seth to call me this week." I assured him I would. And I was in the car and sitting as close as possible to Connie. It had been such a relaxing weekend that we were all quiet on the way home, like children returning from a day at the beach. I was glad that Matt was a competent driver. It allowed Connie and me to nap.

I said to Connie after we got home, "Please stay over tonight. I don't think I could sleep without you holding me."

"Of course," Connie said. "I'll have to head home early in the morning to get ready for work. I don't know how we're going to figure this all out, but I'm sure we will."

"And so am I," I said. "But on a more sober note, I promised Seth I'd see him on Tuesday evening. I think I have to keep our date."

"Of course you do," Connie said.

"I'm nervous about it," I said. "You don't know how seductive Seth is."

"No, I don't know Seth. But I know some things about you, Jerry. I know how smart you are and how kind you are. And I know you'll do exactly what's needed to resolve the situation. Jerry, you don't owe me an explanation. You don't owe me anything. But I'm proud to accept your love. And for as long as it's freely given, I couldn't ask for more."

"Come to bed, you," I said. And then I had Connie in my bed for the first time. It felt natural, as if we had been sleeping together for ages. "Welcome to my world, darling," I said.

"Thank you, Tiger," he said. "I like being in it. And I want you in my world, too. Will you come to my place soon? How about tomorrow night? No, maybe that's rushing things. Jerry, could I sleep over tomorrow night?"

"Of course, darling," I said. "You don't have to ask."

"You have an appointment on Tuesday, and then maybe you'll come to my apartment on Wednesday after work. My tiger in my lair. Yes, let's make it Wednesday."

"I'd love that," I said. He called me Tiger. I'd never had a nickname before. No one had ever found a term of endearment for me. Not my parents, certainly. No schoolmates. Not even Karl. Lucy called me Pookie once, but that was the extent of my experience with endearments. And yet Connie took what he liked best about me and fashioned a name from it. I was enchanted.

We got ready for sleep. Connie set an alarm for 5:00 so he could get home to prepare for his Monday morning. He put his arms around me in the same way as he had done the night before in New Jersey. And I felt just as complete. We slept. I didn't mind the morning alarm. I got up and made coffee while Connie was putting on some clothes and getting his things together. He only had time for a sip of my brew. "Have a great day, Tiger," he said. One deep kiss and he was on his way.

When Connie had left, I considered going back to bed for a quick nap. Instead I lingered in the kitchen over coffee and then started my morning in earnest. I looked around. I liked my apartment. I had carefully hung my art collection—principally my prized Ken Gardas—so that guests and I could see them to advantage. I liked my bed. I liked my bathroom. The thought of redoing all of that was daunting. I had never even seen Connie's apartment, though I was sure it was comfortable.

I had no bright ideas about how we would combine our households. I simply knew we would. A new place, maybe—a two-bedroom so we could have an office? Or could we make do with my place or Connie's? Or could we keep them both? That seemed a little extravagant, and yet, it might prove to be the best solution. I tried to put all of that out of my mind while I got ready for work.

Lucy was free for lunch. We met in the cafeteria. It was good to see her. We hadn't really spoken since Pride. "How is sister Evelyn?" I asked.

"Oh, she's the same, I guess," Lucy said. "She was always the sensible one in the family: went to business school, got a good job on Wall Street, married a hotshot broker, usually spends weekends at their house in Connecticut."

"She can keep Connecticut, as far as I'm concerned," I said. "I want you to know I wasn't idle this weekend, Lucy. I did some growing up."

"And did that include *waking* up?" she asked.

"It did," I said. "I finally accepted a future with Connie. I feel stupid for waiting so long."

"The important thing is that you did it," Lucy said. "I couldn't be more delighted. I'll text Connie right away to congratulate him."

"For?" I asked.

"For knocking some sense into your head. I love you, Jerry. And I love you and Connie together. Just keep it that way."

"Yes, dear," I said. I was quiet for a moment while I finished my lunch, and then I said, "You knew, of course, that I was having an affair with Seth."

"Of course."

"Thanks for letting me tell Connie in my own time," I said.

"It wasn't my secret to tell. How did Connie take the news?"

"Well. Better than you did. Lucy, I have a favor to ask. I want you to find something for Seth to do with the spring show—if it happens. Name him Tim's assistant, or let him assist *you*. He's capable."

"I'll bet."

"Don't be catty, dear. It doesn't suit you. Besides, I think you'll find Seth dependable and smart. And loveable, actually. You might just learn to like him. Stranger things have happened."

"I'll bet," Lucy said. "Look, Jerry, I don't mean to be snippy. Of course I'll try to find something for him to do."

"Good," I said. "I want Seth to have something positive come from getting dumped. I think it's only fair."

"You're a kind man, Jerry, and occasionally a smart one. Just keep it that way—the smart part, I mean. The kind part is a given."

"Yes, dear," I said. "I intend to." So, at that point I had told Connie about Seth. I had told Lucy about Seth. The only one remaining to be told about my new life was Seth. And I was most certainly not looking forward to it.

I chose a slightly nicer restaurant for our (last) supper than the dives Seth and I had met in before. We started with the predictable "How was your holiday weekend?" conversation. And then we fell silent. Eventually, I took the bull by the horns.

"Seth, we can't see each other anymore," I started, clumsily. Seth was silent. "This is not going to work for either of us. Thank you for the time we shared. I loved every minute of it, but it can't continue." Seth remained silent. "There are some people I want you to contact. This week if you want. They're expecting to hear from you." I gave him Dan's card and Lucy's contact info.

"You can't just push me off on other people," he said.

"Seth, I'm trying to do what I can to fast-track your life. I'm trying to help. Please don't fight me. You think this is easy for me? My guts have been in a knot all week. But, Seth, we don't have a future together. I told you—from the beginning—there was another man."

"But Jerry, I love you."

"And I love you, Seth. But then, you know that. How could I not love you? You're handsome, you're smart, you're kind and thoughtful, you're one of the hottest men God ever put on this Earth. I hoped maybe I deserved to have you by my side. But I'm not for you, Seth. I'm not your man. You'll find him. Soon, I expect, if that's what you want."

"I can't do this," Seth said. "I can't walk away from you, Jerry. Not like this. Will you let me go home with you? Will you let me stay the night? Will you let me hold you? If I promise to make a clean break in the morning?"

I took a deep breath. And then another. And then I said, "Yes, Seth. Of course. Come to my apartment." It felt perfectly ordinary, walking to my place with Seth. And yet there was a leadenness in my legs that felt like dread. I let us in. We headed for the bedroom. We stripped in silence and got into my bed. It felt natural, holding Seth in my arms again. Natural and terribly wrong at the same time.

"Your bed smells different, Jerry," he said. "It doesn't smell like us anymore." He was right, of course. My bed smelled of Connie and me. It smelled of the future and not the past. And still, Seth and I were celebrating the past. He kissed me. I kissed him back. When he clung to me, I embraced him with much of the same passion I had felt our first time. He hadn't altered, after all. I was the changeling.

"I want you, Jerry," Seth whispered. "I want you inside me. Fill me, one last time. Give me your love. Share your body with me. Give me your essence."

"No, Seth," I whispered back. "I made a commitment. Don't ask me to break it—if you love me." Instead of entering him, I simply held Seth firmly in my arms, as if he were a friend in need of comfort— as indeed he was. He clung to me for a long while. I don't usually think of poetry when I'm in a hot guy's embrace, but that night my head was filled with "Quoth the Raven 'Nevermore.'"

We were emotionally spent. We slept. I had set an early alarm. It roused both of us instantly. Seth rose and dressed. There was no conversation. He headed for my front door. I followed. When Seth reached the door, he turned and said, "Thank you." He kissed me sweetly, and he was gone.

As soon as I had started to brew coffee, I stripped the bed and put clean sheets on it. Appropriate, after all. I looked out my bedroom window, where I could see just a sliver of the Washington Square arch. The early morning sunlight promised a perfect summer day. And then I phoned Connie. I knew he'd be up. "Good morning, darling," I said. "I love you."

"Could we start every morning that way, Tiger?" he asked.

"Yes," I said. And I had never in my life been so certain of anything.

The End

GIVING THANKS

BRUCE K BECK

GIVING THANKS

a holiday novella

by

Bruce K Beck

New York

Chapter One

It's hard to say who missed Andy more, Rufus or me. Andy's death was so sudden. One night he was sleeping beside me in our bed, and the next night he was in the morgue. He looked so healthy that no one would have guessed he was harboring a fatal heart defect. No doctor ever detected it—until after the fact. Andy died of a broken heart. I thought perhaps I would, too.

I tried to explain things to Rufus. As Labs go, he was exceptionally intuitive. But I could barely make sense of it myself. Rufus was inconsolable. When he wasn't moping around and refusing to eat, he would park himself in front of Andy's clothes closet with his nose pressed against the opening at the bottom of the door. I gave Rufus one of Andy's leather sandals—the ones he always wore around the house. Rufus took the sandal to his bed and began the process of eating it—slowly, carefully, lovingly.

I would gladly have eaten the other sandal if the act could have restored Andy to my arms. The only thing that kept me functional—other than my responsibility to Rufus—was that I had a business to run. Andy had been so proud of me when I took an old furniture warehouse and turned it into Tim Hart Gallery—the chicest art gallery in Chelsea.

Bruce K Beck

I was proud that I had been able to attract a number of quality artists who wanted me to represent them. My personal favorite—and my best seller—was photographer Kenneth Garda. He was immensely kind to me after Andy's death. Sometimes he would come to the gallery with some interesting takeout food or something he had just cooked, and he'd sit with me. For an hour or two. Sometimes he'd insist that I eat something, and sometimes he'd just hold my hand. When I needed to greet browsers and try to turn them into customers, Kenny would just wait.

Not only was he my favorite artist, but he was the only one who truly understood my situation. Kenny had also lost a partner to a freakish cardiovascular accident. Ken's disaster predated mine by maybe five years. And while he had adjusted to the loss and found a new life and a new love, his grief was always simmering just below the surface. It was visible—to me, anyway—in every one of his pictures. Even the newest, most positive ones spoke to me of sorrow.

Kenny never suggested that I should pull myself up by my bootstraps and resume being the confident, energetic entrepreneur I had been before Andy's death. He knew better. "Timmy, you will survive this, you know," he told me one afternoon in August. "You're a good man, and a handsome man—which always helps—and someday you'll learn to love again."

I wasn't so sure about the handsome part or the learning to love again part. I was aware of *wanting to be* a good man. Andy said I was. Anything good in me I had learned from Andy. And I feared that his death had deprived me of the support, the example, the will to strive for a quality existence.

"Matt hasn't seen you in weeks. He misses you. Will you come for dinner some evening?" Ken asked. "You close early on Mondays, don't you? How about next Monday?"

"Thanks, Kenny," I said. "Yes, I'll be delighted to see you two on Monday—as soon as I feed and walk Rufus. He's the most important man in my life these days. Please give Matt a big, sloppy kiss from me. He's nearly as delicious as you are. I don't know if I ever told you, Kenny, how happy I was that you two found each other."

"You were very warm, Timmy," he said, "as you always are."

"It was Easter, wasn't it? When you came back from out West with Matty on your arm? I never saw you so happy, Ken. And Matt's sweetness and his ginger perfection made my heart flutter. Andy was still so very much alive then. I knew how blessed I was to have him by my side, but I'll never know if he understood how precious he was to me."

"Hush, Timmy," Ken said. "That doesn't help, believe me. Been there, done that. Andy worshiped you. And anything you wish you had told him he already knew. Jesus, Tim! How did you learn about guilt? You're not Jewish. You're not even Boston Italian."

"I'm gay," I said. "I think guilt is standard equipment—like a tight ass."

"You have an exceptionally pretty ass, Tim. I'm just saying. I've always admired it, but ... you were partnered when I was single, and now it's the other way around. Could we talk about something else? You're giving me an erection, and happily-partnered men are not supposed to get erections in the presence of their friends, no matter how much they love them."

"Kenny, I couldn't get through this without you," I said.

"Of course you could. But you don't have to," Ken said. "Come on Monday as soon as you can. Rufus comes first, of course. We'll have supper in the garden if the weather is decent and the bumblebees aren't dive bombing."

"Thanks, Ken. Sounds lovely." I hated to see him leave. The emptiness returned immediately. I would see Ken and Matt on Monday evening for sure. That was something. I took a deep breath and returned to my workday. I phoned my assistant, Seth Greenly, who was working downstairs in the packing room.

"Mrs. Gottlieb is picking up today, right?" I asked.

"I have her order ready," Seth said.

"Good," I said. "Why don't you bring it up? I need your help."

"Sure, Tim." Seth was a good kid. He was also pistol-hot with a pretty chest and the most perfect butt I've ever seen. From a distance, of course, and fully clothed. I would never touch an employee. And I never touched another man while Andy and I were together. Or rather, I never had *sex* with another man while I was with Andy. I don't judge those who do, but it wasn't for me. Nor for Andy, I think. Fidelity had recently become a moot point, and yet I needed to cherish the commitment that we had made and honored.

Seth's fair hair and winning smile made him a pleasure to behold. Memorable, even. Seth was not only cute but bright and ambitious. I had begun to count on his help more and more, especially since the distractions that followed Andy's death. The fact that Seth was highly decorative *and* skilled at charming our customers made him essential to the business. "Thanks, Seth," I said. "I wanted to talk about the Fall Show. I'm feeling a little overwhelmed by everything that needs doing."

"Of course, Tim," he said. "Some of the artists have sent in their work already. We could talk next week about wall coverings and colors. I can get the galleries prepped. I think you'll want to approve the placement of every piece."

"Yes, please."

"I can get the same lighting guy in—as soon as the decisions are made. And I can talk to the caterer about the opening party. The invitation list is auto-mated, subject to additions and omissions, of course. I can coordinate all of that with Maria. Tim, I've got this. You don't need to feel pressured."

"Thanks, Seth," I said. "I just realized I haven't really spoken to you in weeks. What's going on in your life?"

"I fell in love," he said. He didn't seem particu-larly pleased about it.

"Surely that's a joyous thing," I said. "What hap-pened?"

"I met a quality man who wanted to have sex with me. It was my idea, really. He only flirted with me once, so I'll never know if he would have reached out if I hadn't done it first. But we ended up making love. I fell for him completely. I've never felt like that before, Tim. And he also fell in love with me. At least a little. I know he did. I have that memory, anyway. But this quality guy *also* fell in love with *another* quality guy. And he judged *that* relationship to be his future. I can't say I wanted to die, but I also couldn't get too excited about living."

"Ouch!" I said. "If I gave advice, I'd probably tell you to keep your heart open to the possibility of love. But my own heart is so paralyzed these days that I can't be much of an example. Still, I think you understand my feelings, Seth, even though you're so young. And I think I'm exceptionally lucky to have you here to help me. I'm going to ask you to take care of the show—everything except the final placement of the art works, of course."

"Of course," Seth said. And he smiled so warmly that I nearly felt cheerful. Nearly. Everything would get done, surely. As always. Only this time it would have to happen with only half of my attention. Could I count on Seth to pick up the slack? He had been with me for nearly a year, so he understood my brand, surely. I had never known him to do or say anything that made the gallery look less than elegant and accommodating.

When I locked up and headed home that evening, I felt a little shudder at the thought of walking into an apartment that lacked Andy in it. Often, in the last few years, Andy had worked late and then swung by the gallery to accompany me home. Sometimes we'd stop off for dinner or takeout, and sometimes we'd head straight home, open a bottle of wine, and take leftovers out of the fridge.

It never mattered to me much the particulars of what Andy and I did together—except for making love, of course. That was always a sacred act. All the secular occasions were interchangeable, as far as I was concerned. Being with Andy was always enough. Everything I knew about devotion and faith

I had learned from him. And then one day the deity I worshiped was headed for the crematorium.

When I arrived home that August evening, Rufus greeted me warmly—even though I was alone. It seemed he had completed his period of mourning and resigned himself to having only me at the center of his life. He loved the young woman who looked in on him during the day, but Rufus knew the difference between Dog Walker and Daddy.

I poured myself a glass of wine, took off my work clothes, sat on the floor, and invited Rufus to join me in play. He was all over me. I avoided his kisses as much as possible, but I accepted his affection gladly. I wanted Rufus to have a normal life, even though I doubted I would ever again experience one myself.

We roughhoused for a while. Rufus gave at least as good as he got. And then I held him tightly to calm him before his supper. When he had settled into my arms, I said, "Well, Big Man, would you be okay if Daddy fell in love again?" He licked my face. I took that as a "yes."

Chapter Two

The sky was indeed clear on Monday. I had
only been to Ken's apartment in Park Slope once or
twice before. I wondered how the addition of Matt to
Ken's life had changed things. My Uber driver made
good time getting us from Chelsea to the tunnel and
then under the Harbor and on into Brooklyn. It was
a charming neighborhood, just as I remembered it.
Stately old residential blocks punctuated by business areas that offered mostly all the goods and
services one could desire.

The boys greeted me warmly. "You look terrific,
Tim," Kenny said. "Please come in. Do you want red
or white? We have both open." I indicated the white
and gave them the liqueur I had brought. "I'm so
glad the weather's holding. And the bumblebees are
so obsessed with those big bushes in the back with
the tiny white flowers that I think we'll be safe from
aerial attacks." We took our wine out to the garden.
It was a perfect, lazy, late-summer evening—still, yet
shimmering with the promise of a rosy sunset.

Ken got a phone call—from his sister in Boston—
so he headed back inside to deal with his family. I
doubt I had ever been alone with Matt. His hair
glowed like spun copper in the horizontal light of a
receding sun. It was difficult to decide which was
more arresting in that light—Matt's hair or his

sparkling green eyes. I had thought him exceptionally pretty, but then I'd expect nothing less of Kenneth Garda's mate. Matt's calm manner was maybe his greatest charm, though. Matt said to me, "Tim, it's wonderful to have you here. Ken adores you, and I know why."

"It's entirely mutual," I said. "Matt, I probably never told you how pleased I was when you two found each other. I've loved Kenny for a lot of years, and I wondered if he'd ever find someone to fill the void in his life after Patrick's death." I regretted having gone there. I didn't need to relive loss any more than Matt needed to hear about it. He was gracious. He took my hand and we sat quietly for a while, savoring the stealthy transition from day to night.

Dinner was remarkable. Ken had made one of his grandmother's specialties—a rather elegant take on veal scallops. There was a small portion of pasta to start, flavored only with lemon zest, pepper, butter, and some cheese. Exceptional. Ken served some veggies with the veal, and then a bit of salad and a perfectly ripe gorgonzola. It was a feast. I tried to beg off dessert, but Matt served me sorbet and some *amaretti*, just the same.

During coffee and lots of contented sighs, Ken said, "Timmy, I want you to see the pictures I'm working on. I value your input. It's your show, after all, so if you think some of them would work better than others ... I'll do it your way. Maybe." We laughed. We went to the living room where Ken's laptop was set up, and Matt began to bring in the dinner things from the garden and busy himself in the kitchen. Ken opened the images he was considering. They were extraordinary. His best work, I thought. His complex vision of humanity was deeper and kinder than ever.

My favorites were a new portrait of Matt—intensely erotic and yet almost gritty in its frankness—and a cityscape peopled with homeless New Yorkers. I was once again dazzled by Ken's vision in all its complexity and beauty. Yes, they would make for a stunning part of my Fall Show. "Beautiful, Ken," I said. "I love all of them, so you choose."

"There's one other shoot I want to complete before making final choices," Ken said. "I asked Seth to model for me, Tim. Are you okay with that? Matt said he didn't mind having a naked model in our apartment, so I scheduled our shoot for Thursday since that's Seth's day off. He's a pretty thing, of course, but he has a quality that's hard to describe. There's a steeliness in his spine and a lust for life that maybe only the camera can capture. The camera or the eye of the beloved."

"Of course, Ken. Seth is free to do whatever he wants when he's not at the gallery. I think you're right. I think you'll find something heartbreaking in him." Had I perhaps discovered that same quality on my own? Maybe. Matt brought out a bottle of grappa and some glasses. We sipped, we laughed, we drew the family circle tightly around us. I felt nourished. I felt safe. And then it was time to go home. Alone.

"Seth, will you have dinner with me tonight?" I asked him on Tuesday as we were wrapping up the day's business. I hadn't been certain that I would ask. I'd been apprehensive all day about the possibility of a "date." And yet I had arranged an extra walk for Rufus—just in case I might not arrive home at my usual time.

"Sure, Tim. That sounds nice."

"I don't know what you like," I said. That was faintly awkward.

"Pretty much everything, I think," Seth said.

"Good," I said. "There's a Thai place near here that serves a great duck in green curry sauce. They always seem to have a table, even on short notice. I guess they do more takeout and delivery than dining room business. We could go there."

"Sounds great," Seth said. "Give me five minutes to turn out the lights downstairs and check the bolts on the back door." He finished up, and I activated the security system. We headed out into the sultry August evening. I liked walking to the restaurant with Seth. We could be silent as we came down from the pressures of the workday. Seth was self-sufficient and didn't require entertainment. A nice quality. It reminded me that we had never been out together.

Dinner was delicious. The duck was never better. I was feeling a little adventuresome, so I ordered it with the *red* curry instead of my usual green. I became a big fan of both. Seth had appetite—an important quality in a man. He was not afraid to order dishes he had never heard of, and the explosions of unfamiliar Southeast Asian flavors in his mouth made him smile with genuine enjoyment.

We ordered green tea and a mango ice cream thing to share. We talked business for a few minutes. The Fall Show was under control. I called a halt to shoptalk. It didn't seem fair to let our dinner be an extension of the workday. Seth smiled a lot. I think I did, too.

As we were finishing up, Seth said, "Ken Garda asked me to model for him. Do you mind?"

"Not at all," I said. "I think of Ken as my brother, and if he gets to see all of you then it's pretty much the same as if I got to see all of you."

"Tim, I'll gladly show you all of me," Seth said. "How about tonight?"

"Would you really come home with me, Seth?" I asked. "Would you come to my bed and warm it?"

"I'd do anything for you, Tim. I hoped you knew that."

"Please, give me some time, Seth. I can't do this tonight, as much as I'd love to. I'm not ready. And you deserve ... a 'quality man,' as we know—a man who can give you his undivided attention. I can't be that man. Not now. I might be able to heal enough to become that man in the future. Will you give me time?"

"Of course. Take all the time you need, Tim. But I'm wondering what you might want from me—someday. In your bed, I mean."

"I've been wondering myself. I didn't think much about roles for a lot of years. Maybe in my heart of hearts I'm a top. Maybe. But Andy and I were so ... balanced, I suppose I'm trying to say. Sometimes I needed to top him, and sometimes he needed to top me. Sometimes we just needed to hold each other. But we were always one body when we were together. So the particulars of whose what went where seemed irrelevant. I don't know if I'll ever find that kind of love again. But I won't settle for less."

Seth looked a little weepy. He shook his head as if tossing his pretty hair could clear his thoughts.

"Tim, you're amazing. It's as if you just went inside my heart and taught it everything it needed to learn."

"If only life were that simple," I said. "Thanks, Seth, for making me feel almost alive again. You're in the East Village, right? Let's grab a taxi, and I'll drop you off on my way home." And that's what we did. Rufus was glad to see me, of course. And I was delighted to see him. We shared an extra-long midnight walk. And then I got ready for bed and reexperienced the loneliest time of the day.

Going to bed alone always made me feel cold and ... worthless, really. I might have let Seth share my bed that night. He wanted to, didn't he? I might have had human warmth beside me instead of the void I felt all around. I might have said yes to life and to a remarkable young man who was brimming with it. And yet, somehow, I just couldn't do it. Tomorrow? Who knew?

Chapter Three

The preparations for the show were going smoothly. There were the usual headaches—artists who were late with their submissions, outsized pieces that seemed not to fit anywhere, and issues with getting decorating supplies delivered on time. But for this show I had Seth to share the responsibilities. I could concentrate on the art itself.

I always approached the group shows as a curator plans museum galleries. Three times a year—the Pride Show in June, the Fall Show, and the Winter Show—we transformed Tim Hart Gallery from a place of commerce into a cultural gift to the City. The fact that guests also had the opportunity to become patrons of the arts did my bottom line no harm.

I was acutely aware, from the first day I opened the gallery, that it offered me the unique opportunity to enrich the public _and_ talented artists while lining my pockets at the same time. A satisfying combination. Andy loved what I was doing, but then he loved everything I did. Or so he said. Andy had been by my side for a dozen years, and then one day he wasn't anymore. Some days I doubted the reality of my memories.

Lately I had felt like Dolly Levi asking her dead husband for permission to live again. Did I pray to Andy? More or less. Did I ask him to release me?

Never. I had no desire to be released from Andy's embrace, even though it was no longer physical. But I did yearn to return to the land of the living. Did I ask Andy for a sign of his approval? That I did do. I offered to wait for that sign before I dared to consider extending my heart to Seth.

That afternoon in early September, our attorney phoned to tell me she had found a letter among Andy's papers—a letter addressed to me. "Sorry to be so long with this, Tim," she said. "It wasn't part of the new wills I drew up for each of you two years ago. He entrusted the letter to me the year before that, but it slipped my mind, I suppose. Anyway, the estate is in probate. Moving forward. No hitches expected. You'll remember we were very careful to make both of your wishes clear."

"Thank you, Judy," I said. "We've always appreciated your diligence."

"Not this time, it seems. Tim, I'm going to stop by the gallery this evening on my way home. You should have had this letter six weeks ago, and I want you to have it today. And it will be good to see you. Not since the memorial, I think. About 6:00, I'm guessing. Does that work for you?"

"That's fine, Judy," I said. "I'll be here until 8:00. Thank you."

"Thank *you* for your patience." A letter! How bizarre. Andy wrote lovely letters. I received a few—email missives, mostly—when we were courting and one of us was traveling on business. I had trusted Andy to be our social secretary all the years we were together. He always knew exactly how to address success or failure, congratulations or bereavement.

A final letter from Andy! I asked Seth to watch the floor so I could go to the john and have a private cry. It didn't last long. My crying jags were relics of the past—before the numbness had set in. I was fine for the rest of the afternoon. When Judy arrived, I was reminded that she was a handsome woman and a skilled advocate. "Tim, this gallery is more exciting every time I see it. And so are you," she said as she kissed me. "How are you?"

"Surviving," I said. "How is Sylvia? I haven't seen her in at least a year."

"Sylvia is perfect," Judy said. "That's right: she was out of town on the day of the memorial. But there will be a fall show, yes? Of course. We got our invitations last week. We'll be here, and you can see Sylvia for yourself. I'll tell her you asked for her. Tim, I could eat my head over this letter."

"Hush, Judy," I said. "I probably couldn't have read it before today. Thanks for guarding it—and for delivering it safely."

"Andy was so special," Judy said as she put her hand on my cheek. "He thought the sun rose and set with you. And of course for him it did. Be good to yourself, Tim. Andy would want that. I'll keep you informed. Call me if you need anything." Another kiss and Judy was on her way home. I put the letter in my bag. I didn't dare read it at work.

When I got home that evening, I greeted Rufus, poured a glass of wine, and hung up my work clothes. Usual stuff. I had some leftover beef stew in the freezer, so I transferred it to the microwave. Some play with Rufus, and it was time to eat. All the major food groups, I assured myself. The stew was fine, but I was eating it alone, so I didn't much care whether it was tasty or not.

And then I retrieved the letter from my bag and returned to my perch at the kitchen counter. Did my hands tremble as I opened it? Slightly. I used the dullest knife in the kitchen, knowing that this would be the last letter I would receive from Andy. It deserved to be opened cleanly and properly. I poured myself another glass of wine. And then I read:

Dearest Tim Bear,

I'm looking forward to a long and fruitful life with you by my side. Even so, I wanted to pause to tell you how very much our years together have meant to me. My heart aches at the thought of losing you, and yet we have so little control over the future.

I want to renew my commitment to you, Timmy. Every day you make me full to bursting with pride at your accomplishments and with the joy of sharing my life with you. I couldn't find a more perfect mate, nor would I care to search for one.

In case we don't make it to the old folks home together—with matching walkers, I hope—I wanted to be certain you know how very much I love you and the life we've built. And if something happens to me, then I'll expect you not only to carry on but to find another man—someone who is worthy of you. You have so much love to give, Tim. Thank you for sharing it with me.
Your devoted Andy Bear

Rufus jumped up on my lap and lunged for the letter. He would have been happy to eat it, but I made certain to hold it out of his reach. Shit! Was that a sign, or what? I might have become prostrate with grief—literally. I could have simply taken to my bed with my tears—plus a bottle of brandy. Except that Andy insisted that I live and love. Well, of course he did! He had always valued my happiness above his own. He said once that he found his satisfaction in mine.

Maybe I had found that a sweet declaration without really understanding it. But it didn't much matter whether we were deciding what color to paint the kitchen or where to go on holiday or what form our lovemaking would take. Andy always deferred to me. And I always decided on what I hoped would bring him the most pleasure. Was I any good at that? He seemed to think so.

I didn't really understand our relationship until that moment. I thought I did. I thought we had been two fortunate men who happened to love and like in equal measure. I thought we had made all of our decisions together. I thought we had shared the responsibilities and the pleasures equally. But I suddenly realized that Andy had created a universe for us that revolved around me. And he was content to be the brightest moon in our planetary system.

I had hoped I was all out of tears, but that wasn't the case. As I got his leash and prepared him for our walk, Rufus tried his best to lick away the tears that ran down my cheeks. I preferred to keep them. I had earned them, after all. It was dark enough on the street at night so I could be as pitiful a jackass as I wished without attracting attention. Rufus never judged.

I wasn't sure how to proceed with my decision to rejoin the living. Seth deserved to be wooed, surely.

He was so achingly beautiful—and so young. I wouldn't call it toughness—the place his strength came from. But I feared Seth had never known the tenderness that everyone deserves. "I can do that," I told myself. "I can give Seth what he needs. If, indeed, he wants what I can offer. I'll have to find out."

I resolved to do just that. We had about three weeks until the Fall Show. It seemed an odd time to start a new romance, but I wasn't willing to put it off for long. I would be closing the gallery the week before the opening party. That way the decorators could have unfettered access to the wall space in each area. And then Seth and I could start to place each artwork.

I set a goal. "Tim," I told myself, "you and Seth should be lovers when you hang this show together." I couldn't argue with the logic, even though Seth's mouth had often distracted me in the past. Would we get any work done between kisses? I decided to put conjecture aside and take a forward leap.

"Seth," I asked him, "will you go out with me on Monday?"

"Sure," he said.

"Good. We could have an early supper, and then I want you to meet the man in my life." That seemed a little mean, so I added, quickly, "I don't think Andy ever brought Rufus to the gallery. He's a chocolate Lab. I know he'll fall in love with you. He has excellent taste in men."

"Obviously," Seth said.

"So we'll have an early dinner on Monday and then go to my place. Good. Would you like to choose a restaurant?"

"No, thanks, Tim," he said. "Anything you like is fine with me." I thought carefully about the perfect venue for seduction—romantic, but not too obvious. Good food was most important. Nothing too spicy. Nothing too filling. Eventually I decided on my favorite neighborhood Japanese. I knew we could order some sashimi and a roll or two and feel properly fed without being overstuffed. Yes.

Chapter Four

Seth looked so delicious in the soft glow of the restaurant lighting that I wanted to leap over the table and ravish him. I restrained myself. Seth said he liked the seaweed salad. We also shared a small order of mixed tempura. I'm always happy when I'm eating something expertly fried. The sashimi selection was stellar—each piece moist and brimming with its own unique flavor. The dragon roll gave us the unctuousness of avocado and eel in each bite— my idea of the perfect dessert.

When we got to the apartment, I was pleased to see that Seth understood dogs. He crouched and offered his hand to Rufus palm down. When Rufus had had a sniff and then licked Seth's hand, I knew we would be okay. "I promised you coffee," I said. "Will you join me in the kitchen while I make it?"

"Sure." I set up my coffee maker, and then I turned to Seth and smiled. He came to me and put his arms around me. And he kissed me. I kissed him back, of course. Rufus watched patiently. He didn't seem worried. He had never missed his dinner in the past, after all. Seth and I kissed for a while. It had been months since I had felt so alive.

"Will you come to the bedroom with me?" I asked.

"Of course," Seth said. I took his hand and led him in the right direction. I kissed Seth deeply. He responded with equal passion. But when I began to undress him, Seth froze. Suddenly.

"What's wrong?" I asked.

"Tim, I'm sorry, but I can't do this."

"Why?" I asked in near exasperation.

"Because I'm not Andy."

"No one expects you to be Andy. Seth, you're your own beautiful self. *You're* the man I invited to my bed."

"Not tonight," Seth said. "I'm about to cream in my shorts, but I can't do this. You asked me to give you time. I'm asking for the same."

"That's fair," I said. "Let's have a coffee." We went back to the kitchen. I poured, we sipped. Rufus watched. Eventually, I said, "Let me give Rufus his dinner." And that's what I did. He was an eager eater. And when he had finished, I wiped his mouth and said to Seth, "Will you come with us on our walk?"

"Yes, I'd like that," he said. And the three of us headed out into the heaviness of the late summer air. It was as close to being underwater as is safe for humans. There would be a thunderstorm soon. But not before we all got safely home, surely. As we walked along and Rufus paused to investigate all the street smells he found irresistible, Seth said, "I thought Andy was a wonderful man. I loved watching you light up when he walked into the gallery. He was so in love with you, and no one thought that relationship wouldn't go on forever."

"Seth, we don't need to talk about the past," I said. "Not now, while we could be considering the future. I want a future. I want a future with you, actually."

Seth said, "I never considered falling in love with you, Tim, while Andy was alive. I'm not stupid. I knew I wouldn't stand a chance. Maybe everything's different now. I'm not so sure. I know I can't replace him. And I'm thinking the last thing you need is a wannabe Andy. I don't have his looks. I don't have his calm grace. I don't speak the way he did or smell the way he did, and I'll never be able to honor your body the way he did. I don't have a decade of history with you."

"Hush, Seth," I said as I embraced him. Rufus pulled on his lead. I ignored him. "Andy is the most important part of my past, but I'm ready to create a new chapter. Will you write it with me? Please?"

Seth melted into my arms. I drew in his scent as it filled the nearly liquid air around us. I decided I loved the way the back of Seth's neck smelled best of all, where his hair curled softly. And yet, I still knew so little about his body. My heart ached to know more. My *dick* ached to know more.

"I'm going to head home," Seth said. "I'll jump on the crosstown bus, and I'll be there in ten minutes."

"Do you have an umbrella?" I asked.

"I don't think I need one."

"Come back to the apartment with us," I said, "I'll give you an umbrella. I want you to be safe and comfortable." He protested, but I insisted. And we had already made our way, by a circuitous route, nearly back to my building. Seth waited—on the sidewalk, with Rufus—while I dashed upstairs to find an umbrella for him.

"Get home safely," I said as I pressed the umbrella into his hand. "Seth, I love you," I said. There was a rumble of thunder that was not so distant. "I had to tell you," I said. "You don't need to respond."

Seth looked a bit off balance. He said, "Look, Tim, you don't have to court me."

"I think you're quite wrong," I said. "I think you deserve to be courted, Seth. I think you merit careful attention. I don't want you to miss out on anything. And I don't want to miss out on the chance to know you. *And* I don't want you to be caught in a downpour. Will you kiss me?" He did, of course. And then he was on his way home.

As I took Rufus upstairs and the two of us settled in for the night, the storm began to boom and crackle. I invited Rufus up on the bed—which Andy and I never did—so I could hold him close, to calm him. His fear wasn't so intense as his reaction to the fireworks on the Fourth of July, but a robust late summer thunderstorm could also set him off. I'd have preferred to have *Seth* in my arms, but Rufus needed me, after all. He would have to be enough.

The next morning, as I opened the gallery, Seth said, "I'm sorry, Tim."

"Don't be," I said. "You have to follow your heart. I just hope that someday it will lead you to me."

"It already has," Seth said. "I'm not really sure what happened to me last night. I was so certain I wanted your body more than anything else on Earth, Tim. But then when you held me, I panicked. I won't do that again. Will you give me another chance?"

"How about tonight?" I asked.

Seth laughed and said, "Perfect!" I was relieved that we had cleared the air before we started our workday. It made everything feel lighter. But the thought of having Seth in my bed that night left me giddy with expectation. It was a quiet day at the gallery. Early September was always like that. People seemed to need time, after Labor Day, to say goodbye to summer. And then the phenomenon of Autumn in New York could begin—right after the Jewish holidays.

I always scheduled the Fall Show to capture the excitement of the season. That's why it would debut the first week in October that year. I had set out, five or six years earlier, to make the opening party one of the first and most anticipated events of the social season. I had succeeded—beyond my dreams, really.

Talented artists trusted me with their newest works, and I displayed them flawlessly to an eager crowd. Being part of a seasonal show at Tim Hart Gallery guaranteed artists fancy eyeballs on their work, not to mention sales. Opening night purchases had increased steadily over the years, and word-of-mouth brought other buyers to the gallery in the weeks that followed. Win/win/win.

My professional life was simmering along at a generous pace. My heart was a different matter. After weeks of indifference to life, I had made the choice to rejoin the human race. And yet Seth had rebuffed my advances. More or less. Hadn't he promised a change that very night? Maybe.

I didn't fret over dinner, that afternoon. All my careful planning for the previous evening had seemed to backfire. After we locked up and set the alarms, we strolled to the Greek restaurant about two blocks away. The air was still hot, but the storm the night before had cleared it, mercifully. I put my arm lightly around Seth's shoulders. He automatically put his arm around my waist. It felt natural. It felt right.

We had a light supper—some salady things and a shared grilled whole fish. We were both more interested in getting to my place, I think. I know I was. We walked into the apartment, greeted Rufus, and then headed for the bedroom. That time, Seth was just as ready as I was. His kiss was deep, and our clothes seemed to fall away from our bodies. Removing shoes is always a pain, but we managed to get naked with very few interruptions to our kisses.

As we fell into my bed, I began to fully appreciate Seth's beauty. I already knew about his pretty eyes and hair and lips—his lips most of all—but much of him was new to me. I marveled at the breadth of his shoulders and the fragility—plus strength—of his throat. I paid a visit to his front half, admiring the perkiness of his nipples and the ripple of each individual muscle beneath his velvety skin. I vowed to devote an hour or so to his armpits. Someday.

Meanwhile, Seth was conducting his own tour. With one hand he held my head close to his, so that we could kiss as often as possible. And with his other hand he seemed to discover all my erogenous zones except for the ones he couldn't reach from that position. As much as I hated to be deprived of Seth's kiss, I struck out on a downward path. I needed to meet his dick. I knew it would be fine. I had no idea how fine.

Seth's dick was straight and proud—generous, but not scary; rock-hard, and yet soft to the touch. When I took him in my mouth, it was just as sweet as his kisses. I wondered if his glans was maybe the same color as his lips. It didn't seem to matter much to me which I kissed, as long as I could have access to both in perpetuity.

I rolled Seth over and caressed the strong V of his back, which led to the glorious ass I had always known he possessed. You can't hide that kind of perfection, even if you hire a terrible tailor. I stroked Seth and petted him, and then I spread his cheeks and went for the sweet spot. It only occurred to me later—when my addiction to Seth's body was complete—that here was a *third* pink zone for my delectation. Delicious.

It really didn't matter to me which part of Seth I got to savor, but he took a particular interest in my dick. I like a good blowjob as well as the next man, but I've always preferred to be *doing* something. I reached for his shoulders and urged him to move up my body so he could kiss me. As Seth lay on top of me, he said, "Tim, I didn't tell you last night how much I love you. I want to tell you now." I stopped him with a kiss.

As I threw my arms around Seth and held him, probably a bit too firmly, he began to lead our bodies into the arrangement he wanted. Almost before I realized what was happening, Seth eased me inside him. We lay there for a while, our bodies joined in what felt like a perfect union. I started to weep. It had been so long since I had been so close to another man. And *this* man was like no other I had known.

I renewed our embrace—and our kisses—as Seth began to move slowly and carefully. I resisted the urge to grab his ass cheeks and to force myself inside him to maximum depth. For our first time together, I wanted Seth to have exactly what *he* wanted. I had never thought of myself as an instrument of pleasure, but I vowed to become just that. Seth seemed almost trance-like as he received me and experienced me and caressed me. I surrendered totally.

I could feel the changes in Seth's body as he approached orgasm. His breathing became husky and his muscles tensed—seemingly in spite of his determination to remain relaxed. And when it was all beyond his control, Seth suddenly reared up, sat back—taking me as far inside him as I could go—and shouted, "Oh, Tim! Oh, Tim! Oh, God!" as he released a torrent of sweetness that splashed all over my chest.

That was all that was needed to trigger a chain reaction. I gave Seth the best gift I could create. He received it with reverence. *Ecstatic* reverence, I suppose. "Yes, Tim," he said. "Yes, Tim. Give me your love. Give me your self, Tim. I want all of you. Thank you!" And then we were both truly spent. Seth eased his torso back down onto mine, and we lay together, quiet except for our panting.

When I began to feel like a mere mortal again, I kissed Seth and said, "I have no words to describe how much I love you. Maybe tomorrow."

Seth laughed and said, "I knew it would be good, Tim, but I had no idea how good. And that's all I can say tonight."

Eventually we got up and headed for the kitchen. "Let me feed Rufus," I said. "Will you walk with us?"

"Sure."

"Good," I said. Rufus became suddenly animated when he heard the dinner things. He ate quickly, as always. "Good boy!" I said as I wiped his mouth. "Seth, let me give you some shorts. We don't need anything else. I don't usually take Rufus out for a late walk with cum all over my chest, but I'm making an exception tonight. I won't wash it off—not until morning. It's your first gift to me, Seth, and it's too precious to lose." Seth kissed me.

We slipped on shorts, and Rufus brought me his leash. I hooked him up and we headed out. Of course I hoped I wouldn't run into anyone I knew—in our condition. I had never gone out for a walk in the neighborhood bare-chested, much less while sporting clear evidence of lovemaking. But it was dark, after all. And it didn't much matter anyway. I waved to a dog-walking friend from half a block away and kept going. That was about it. And then we were back home.

I showed Seth the dog treat routine Rufus and I had created, where he sat and froze while I balanced a biscuit on his nose. He always waited patiently until I clapped, at which signal he would flip the biscuit into the air and catch it in his mouth. It's hard to say which of us enjoyed the ritual more. Seth roared with laughter. Rufus was even more pleased with himself than usual.

"Seth, you have to sleep over. You have to stay in my arms. I won't give you up," I said.

"Tim, it's not that simple," he said.

"Of course it is. I have an extra toothbrush and an extra razor and anything else you need."

"Tim, I don't have anything to wear to work tomorrow. My shirt is totally soggy from this heat."

"No problem," I said. "I'll give you some briefs and socks and a shirt of mine. You'll look terrific. Seth, please don't fight me. I'm going to win, you know." And I did.

Lucinda Warren, from the New-York Historical Society, called me the next week. "Tim," she said, "I hope you remember we talked about an exhibition of contemporary New York art in the spring—at the Society."

"Of course," I said. "How are you, Lucy? I don't think I've seen you since June. Or Jerry, for that matter."

"Summer doth make sloths of us all, I fear. But Tim, this show I invented while Jerry and I were here in your gallery is actually going to happen. If you agree to be a guest curator, of course."

"Lucy, that sounds wonderful," I said. "I'd be honored to work on it with you."

"Good," she said. "Can we get together next week? I could come to you some afternoon, if that's convenient. I know this is a bad time for you to leave the gallery, with your Fall Show coming up and all."

"Of course," I said. "Let me know what works for you and I'll clear my calendar."

"Let's say Tuesday around 1:00. Will that do?"

"Of course," I said.

"And could Seth Greenly join us?" she asked. "Jerry believes he'll be the right point man to help us coordinate the decisions."

"That sounds fine, Lucy" I said. "I'll look forward to seeing you on Tuesday. And I'll ask Seth to join us."

"Perfect," Lucy said. "Jerry is bringing me to the opening. We're both excited about it. But I'm pleased I'll get to see you even before then. Have a great weekend." And she hung up. This was exceptionally good news. Public-private collaborations create a sense of authentication and prestige that is always good for business. And no one had ever asked me to translate my skill at choosing quality art into a professional curation. The part about Seth, however, gave me pause. I don't like being in the dark.

"Seth, do you have a minute for me?" I asked when I phoned him.

"Of course, Tim. I'll be right up." He joined me on the main floor.

"I just got a call from Lucinda Warren, from the New-York Historical Society. You met her, briefly, in June. She came here with Jerry Darnley, who was picking up his latest Ken Garda purchase. You were just packing it, and I asked you to show it to them before the image was hidden."

"Of course, Tim. I remember."

"Just before they left the gallery, Lucy got an idea for a spring show at the Society. Contemporary New York artists. Well, it's really going to happen. And she wants me to help curate it."

"That's great!" Seth said. "Congratulations, Tim."

"Thanks, Seth. Lucy is stopping by on Tuesday at 1:00, to fill me in. And she asked that you join us. Any idea why?"

Seth looked a bit taken aback. He took a deep breath and said, "Tim, I didn't tell you at the time.

The man I fell in love with, in June, was Jerry Darnley."

I said, "Why did I suspect that, I wonder? Jerry's handsome, and he's most certainly a 'quality guy.' I can imagine falling in love with him. Why shouldn't you?"

"Because I met him on the job, Tim. I would have told you—if it had gone somewhere. But when it ended, I just let it go."

"With everything that's happening in the world—even just in our own little worlds—I don't think anyone should apologize for falling in love. What do you think, Seth?"

"I think that what I felt for Jerry was more like puppy love. My feelings for you, Tim, come from somewhere else. They come from deep respect because you've demonstrated your kindness and your honesty over and over. My feelings come from the place in my heart that admires beauty and yearns to be worthy of it. My feelings come from a deep desire to give the best in me to the man I love. And you're also hot. I'm a lucky guy."

"Not nearly as lucky as I am," I said. "If you'll come home with me tonight, I'll try to show you how lucky I feel." Seth agreed. I floated through the rest of the day. I was trying my best not to overthink my new relationship with Seth. I never said, "Please move in with me." Instead, I invited Seth to my place every night, and most of the time he accepted my invitation. After the opening, perhaps we could sort things out.

I did feel exceptionally lucky, after all. Work was going well, and Seth brought me the kind of joy I feared I'd never know again. Andy had been my age, bright, playful, accomplished, and exceptionally handsome in a slightly funny-looking way. Seth was much younger, eager, smart—but sometimes untutored—and so radiantly beautiful that he often took my breath away. Andy and Seth could hardly have been more different, and yet each brought me the gift of love. Lucky, indeed.

That evening, Seth and I stopped off for some takeout on the way home. Rufus greeted us with his usual enthusiasm. In fact, I wondered if Seth didn't get a warmer greeting than I did. I was obviously not the only one who had grown accustomed to having Seth around. We set out our purchases on the dining table and dove in. The food was adequate. Sharing it with Seth was better.

I realized I hadn't turned on a TV in quite a while. I got my news from the CNN bulletins on my phone. At home, I wanted no distractions, especially when I had Seth in my arms. That evening, Seth was particularly playful. He was bouncing all over my body—touching, and tasting, and tickling. I was a bit surprised when he rolled me onto my stomach and began to work his way from my shoulders all the way down my back.

When Seth reached my butt, he kneaded my cheeks for a while. And then he spread them and dove in. I hadn't been tasted in ... a few years, maybe. It was something that Andy and I had lost the habit of doing. Seth explored me eagerly with his tongue and his lips. He even nibbled gently, here and there. I started to slip into a realm of consciousness that only registered physical pleasure.

When Seth was satisfied that he had done what he could with his mouth, he asked—quietly, bashfully—"Tim, may I?"

"Do it, Seth. Please," I said. He moved carefully into position to top me. I hadn't expected to receive Seth's perfect dick inside my body. I hadn't considered the possibility, really. I had assumed that if anyone was going inside it would be me. And yet I was entirely ready. Seth presented himself, and I accepted him as easily as if I had been performing breathing exercises for hours.

Seth knew exactly what he wanted. He went deep. He held me, lifted my head, and kissed me. His tears mingled with mine. Seth was tender, even delicate with me. My love for him expanded beyond what I had assumed was my capacity. I had no idea my body could experience such intense pleasure. We had discovered a new definition of home. I had no desire to leave it.

When Seth's muscles began to tighten in anticipation of the eruption to follow, I was as ready as I could be. I welcomed the offering his body was preparing for me. I wanted to be a worthy vessel. I wanted to accept his deepest essence into my deepest self. I wanted to serve my beloved to the best of my ability.

And then all hell broke loose. Seth shouted, "Tim, I love you!" I felt every pulse, every drop of Seth's offering. And then I came all over the bedsheet, with Seth still deep inside me. It was glorious. We lay together, still locked in that embrace, until our breathing had stabilized and we both knew it was time to move on. Seth eased himself off my back. I rolled onto my side so I could see him better. We kissed.

"I'm yours now, Seth," I said. "No returns."

"No returns," he said. "Good thing I chose wisely. Did you mind, Tim?"

"Of course not, Seth," I said. "I love you. I'll do anything with you. Nearly. Test my limits and I'll let you know."

"I just had to be inside you, Tim," he said. "I'd have done anything to be there. I needed the warmth of your body. And I needed to share your strength. I needed to be part of you. I won't do it again. Promise."

"Hush, Seth," I said. "My body is yours. You can do whatever you want with it."

Rufus needed some attention, so we repeated our shirtless dog walk. Rufus seemed to love the extra company. I loved whatever I was doing with Seth. There wouldn't be too many more sultry September evenings when we could head out nearly naked. I didn't tell Seth that his luscious package was peeking out of one leg of the little gym shorts I had given him.

If we stopped to talk to fellow dogwalkers, I'd probably have to tell Seth—so he could rearrange himself. Otherwise, I welcomed the sight of as much of him as possible. Soon we'd have to find a different routine. I could imagine going for walks while Seth and I were wearing sweaters or even down coats. Rufus always seemed perfectly comfortable in his own coat, whatever the season.

When we had gone back inside and completed the dog biscuit routine, Seth and I sat at the kitchen counter while I poured us a brandy. I smiled a lot. So did he. And then I said, "I hate to bring it up, darling, but I'm, what, fifteen years older than you are?"

"Good," he said. "Boys don't interest me. They have nothing to offer and nothing to teach me. And they come too fast. Who needs them?" We both laughed, and then we kissed for a while.

"So, you don't like boys," I said. "Does that mean I'll have to prove to you, regularly, that I'm a man?" I asked.

"You've given me all the proof I need," Seth said. It had been a remarkable evening. One of many, I hoped. We did minimal cleanup—including taking a damp towel to the cum stain on the bottom sheet. And then we turned in. I asked Seth to spoon me. We hadn't yet established a sleep routine. Maybe that was it. It felt perfect to me.

Chapter Six

The next morning, as we were heading to work, I said to Seth, "I haven't quite sorted this all out, but I'm wondering if you'll camp out with me until after the opening. I mean, you could just bring a few things and plan to stay with me. I don't want to sleep without you, Seth, but I don't want to ask you to commit to living with me. Not today. Not with so much work to distract us. It wouldn't be fair to you."

"Thanks, Tim," he said. "Of course I'll 'camp out' with you. I'm ready to make a commitment, actually. But I understand what you're saying. Let's do it your way. As long as we can be together, it doesn't matter what we call it." I stopped right there on the sidewalk and embraced him. He certainly had a way of getting right to the point.

When Lucy came to the gallery the following Tuesday, we were rather well organized. "You make it look so easy, Tim. I know better," she said. "Hi, Seth, it's nice to see you." She was a bit dismissive of him, but she managed a kiss anyway. "Let me get right into this so I don't waste your time: For the spring, the committee decided on a survey of New York art over the centuries. We're going to make the exhibit chronological. We have some exceptional Colonial and early nineteen-century pieces by New York artists or owned by New York families. I'm sure you remember the strange portrait of a woman who may or may not be Edward Hyde, Viscount Cornbury, for instance."

"Of course," I said. If Seth didn't know it, he soon would.

"We'll include that for sure. And a half dozen of the other favorites, probably. Some portraits from the Peale family. Maybe two early Asher B. Durands—presidents, most likely. From the mid-nineteenth century we have a lovely Frederick Church or two, and that amazing Thomas Cole series, The Course of Empire. I think our members expect to see that.

"In late nineteenth and early twentieth century, we have two William Merritt Chase portraits, an Arthur Dove, two John Sloanes (I think), several Maurice Prendergasts, two George Bellows, a John Marin, a dozen iconic Alfred Stieglitz photos, and two Childe Hassams I love. Those flags flying on Fifth Avenue at the end of World War I always bring me to tears.

"I wish we could borrow the Robert Henri portrait of Gertrude Whitney from the Whitney, but that's not likely. Maybe they have something else to lend. We have a good relationship with them. Our mid-twentieth century holdings are a little weak, but we can probably borrow to fill in. But getting to contemporary, I'm not sure yet how much gallery space we'll have. In a month or so I'll know better. And that's where you guys come in.

"We want to show the finest art that's being produced in New York right now. We'll have to consider the pieces 'on loan'. But at the end we intend to purchase as many as we can afford. The show will hang

for three months—maybe four—so it's great exposure even for artists who don't make a sale. Those
buying decisions are not up to me. The committee
will choose. Jerry and I can only suggest. Does this
make sense?"

"It does," I said. "Every artist I know would be
pleased to be in the permanent collection of the New-
York Historical Society. And they'd also be pleased
to be part of a major exhibition there. You're making
our work easy." Seth was quiet. But I knew he
would soak up knowledge like a sponge as we went
along.

"Good," Lucy said. "I won't take up any more of
your time. I just wanted to be certain this is doable
and that we're all on the same page."

"Absolutely," I said.

Lucy rose to leave. She kissed me and said, "Let's
talk about this again in a month. Can't wait for your
opening!" She also kissed Seth—almost warmly, I
thought—and she was off.

Seth said, "Tim, I didn't understand a word she
said."

"I know," I said. "Doesn't matter. You will. We'll
go to some museums together before we meet with
Lucy again. And I'll find some websites to help you.
You're lucky. You only have to master the entire history of American art as it pertains to New York City."

Seth forgave me instantly for teasing him. I could
tell he did. I wanted to kiss him so badly I felt weak
in the knees. But that would have to wait until we
got home. Our home? I wanted it with all my heart.

43

Bruce K Beck

We had planned a lot of white for the gallery walls. I knew from experience, for instance, that a stark white background would make the subtle range of gray tones in Ken Garda's photos pop right out of the frame. Something dark—or worse, something moderate behind them—would make them look subdued.

In the interest of variety and of differentiation, we also chose some colors. One of the painters worked in a palette of brilliant primary colors. For her wall space, we chose a pale celadon green. It would lend a feeling of calm to balance the excitement of the paintings. And that's how we did it.

As we approached the last week, it truly felt as though the disparate pieces were falling into place. My office assistant, Maria, said to me, "It's always nice to have a week off, Tim, but are you sure you don't need me?"

"As long as you're ready to process lots of sales on opening night, then we'll be fine. Have a good week, Maria. And don't forget to bring that beautiful husband of yours to the opening. You two will be as decorative as anything on the walls."

Maria swatted me with a stack of papers and said, "Tim, you're impossible! Good thing I understand bad boys. I have two of them at home. And they're enough."

"I haven't seen the baby in almost a year," I said. "He must be all grown up by now. Bring him in some day this fall. We'll find something for him to do. I play a mean horsey. And Seth and I can teach him the gallery business. He could do worse."

"Much worse," Maria said. "I'll bring him to work with me some day soon. He's still talking about his last visit. And Fabián is looking forward to the opening party. You're always so kind to him, Tim. He gets it, you know."

"Hush, Maria," I said. "Go home and have a great week with your beauties. And come back with your charge machine finger well rested."

Maria finished arranging and putting away the last of the papers on her desk. Seth was deep in the gallery, checking the spaces where we would install the new show, starting in a few days. Maria said, quietly, "Seth is family now, isn't he?"

I embraced her and said, "Go! Before you make me cry." She went.

The following morning, Seth and I put the last of the pieces from the previous show into the vault. It seemed a shame to hide them away, and yet they were easily available for viewing or for return to artists who decided they needed them back. I approved the final arrangement of the partitions that would create rooms and define the various gallery spaces. The decorators came in about 10:00 and began to prep the surfaces, according to the agreed plan.

I was always nervous about background color choices and about the flow of the show from front to back, or from back to front for those viewers so inclined. This time, I felt more confident because I had Seth to help me. He had a sharp eye, and he was not afraid to make suggestions. If anything didn't quite work, we could always pivot.

I never promised artists that I'd tell them exactly how far from the front door—or how far from the bar—their works would be. They trusted me to show them in the best light, and we rarely had disagreements. I asked all five of them to stop by a day or two before the opening so there would be no surprises.

By Thursday morning the perfect blank spaces were ready. I hired a couple of guys who worked in the neighborhood to help Seth bring up the new works and place them in the areas where we would install them in the next few days.

Every show has its stars, and I fully believed that Ken Garda's new portrait of Seth would be one of them. It would have pride of place, for sure. Maybe next to his new portrait of Matt. One of my favorite artists was a sculptor whose work I had long admired. The smaller sculptures that were wall-mounted were just as exciting as the big freestanding pieces. They all begged to be fondled.

Bronze is so cool to the touch, and yet Jan created a sense of heat in the contours of the metal. It didn't matter whether the shapes were phallic or otherwise organic or geometrical in their inspiration. From tiny to room-sized, Jan's sculptures were all human-sized. And in a gallery—as opposed to a museum—touching is encouraged. Jan loved watching gallery-goers who couldn't resist reaching out to experience his work with their hands. And *I* loved having Jan as a client.

When Kenny dropped off the new portrait, he said, "This should be everything. Let me know if you need anything else. Don't unwrap it now. Tell me on opening night what you think of it." He kissed me, and he was off. I called to Seth and asked him to join me. Together we unwrapped the photo and took it to the window to be sure we had lots of light.

I caught my breath in a little gasp, I suppose. It was so obviously a Ken Garda photo, and yet it was pure Seth. "Do I really look like that?" Seth asked.

"Absolutely."

"But the man in this portrait is beautiful."

"That beautiful man is you, darling," I said. "Didn't you know that?"

"I'm not so sure," he said. "I'm not used to compliments. I certainly didn't get any at home. And tricks mostly told me they liked my ass."

"You have a highly likeable ass—by the way—but Seth, I fell in love with all of you, as did Ken's camera. He has an amazing way of finding the truth, whether he's shooting individuals or groups or cityscapes. Didn't you know that's why he asked you to model for him? Pretty boys are everywhere in New York. Ken asked you to model because you're special. Because you're beautiful."

Seth embraced me and put his head on my chest. I don't think I had ever seen him in full-out tears. But he shed them that day. I tried my best to kiss them away. Eventually, I said, "Well, young man, we have a lot of work to do this afternoon." And we got to it. Surely I would have to ask Seth questions about his childhood. Surely he would want to ask me questions about mine. But not then. Not with the Fall Show looming. It could wait, couldn't it?

Chapter Seven

Men are such peacocks, aren't they? Especially black and Latino men, I always thought. That's not fair. Mediterranean men run a close second. When Maria and her husband arrived for the opening—early—Maria was dressed quietly and elegantly. She would be working, after all. Fabián, however, was pure exhibitionism. And he had a lot to exhibit. His tight slacks showed off his bulge and his butt to equal advantage. Cowboy boots with high polish completed the lower half of him. Pure sex.

Fabián's top half was lightly draped in a sheer merino sweater—V-neck—that floated over his torso like a silk handkerchief in a slight breeze. It also exposed the beauty of his throat, as well as the richness of the gold chain around his neck. Every carefully gym-toned muscle was evident. Nice nipples, too.

When I greeted Fabián, I kissed him on both cheeks, as always, and I made it a point to bump his bulge—to acknowledge it. Far from being phobic about gay men, Fabián welcomed our attentions. We knew who was hot, after all. "Thanks for coming," I said. "I told Maria she'd better bring you. And you've grown even more handsome since the last time I saw you. How did you manage that?" Fabián flashed his dazzling smile. He also blushed a little.

"Tim, If I weren't so in love with Maria, I'd take you in the back room and ... well, never mind what I'd do."

"Sounds like fun," I said. "But it seems we're both spoken for. Maybe in another life. Get a glass of bubbly, Fabián. But pace yourself. It's going to be a long night." Fabián was so obviously sexy. Seth, on the other hand, was merely beautiful no matter how he dressed or preened—or didn't. I had given him a silk shirt to wear to the opening. It had fit me perfectly when I bought it—less perfectly in recent years. Too many bench presses, probably. "Seth, you take my breath away," I had said to him as we dressed for the event. "Let's head for the gallery before I change my mind."

I hadn't unlocked the doors yet when Seth walked over to me, looking serious. "The caterer just texted me," he said quietly. "The van was sideswiped. They're in the middle of a police report. He thinks they'll be about forty-five minutes late."

"Well, it is what it is," I said. "When they get here, will you help them load in as discreetly as possible?"

"Of course," Seth said.

"Fortunately, the bartenders are here and the champagne is on ice. That's the first priority. Welcome to show biz, darling." I embraced Seth. It would probably be my last chance before we got home that night. I was not overly disturbed about the caterer. I had learned years before that it's good to get the disaster out of the way early, so everyone can relax a little. I just hoped *that* would be the only disaster.

Our first guests were two older women from the neighborhood who were good clients. Seth greeted them. He blushed charmingly as they flirted with him. Seth got them glasses of bubbly and took them to see the latest offerings from their favorite artist. Yes, Seth was almost as good for my business as he was for my heart.

When the caterer arrived, tail between his legs, I said to him, "Forget about it, Jimmy. These things happen. I hope you have an easy time with your van repairs. Seth's going to help you load in and set up. Don't make yourselves crazy. No one's going to starve."

When Kenny and Matt arrived, Ken said, "Tim, I hope you're happy with the new portrait of Seth. I hope *Seth* is happy with the new portrait of Seth. Where is he?"

"He's helping the caterer with setup. Long story. He'll be out front soon, and you can ask him what he thinks. As for me, I've had a few good cries over that photo already. You've taught me things about Seth that I hadn't even imagined, Kenny. I don't know how you do it, but don't stop! Matt," I said, "I'm glad you're part of this new collection. Are you here to-night as a model or as a staffer at *GLITZ Magazine*?"

"Mostly as Ken's date, I guess," he said. "Tisha and Lisa should be along shortly. We never miss an opening at Tim Hart."

"Good. Let's keep it that way," I said. The cover-age I got from *GLITZ* was invaluable for my business. Since their Internet presence had grown in recent years, they could cover any event and have images and even videos up on the website within hours. No more waiting for the next monthly issue of the mag-azine. They were arbiters of taste for a lot of readers. We had foot traffic every day from people who discov-ered us at *GLITZ*. Especially tourists with a need to keep in touch with Big Apple events and trends.

When Jerry Darnley arrived with Lucy and with his new boyfriend—presumably—I realized I hadn't met Jerry's partner. It felt odd, seeing for the first time the man Jerry had quit Seth for. I was glad Seth was still busy helping the caterer set up. "Tim, please meet Cornelius Randolph," Jerry said.

"Call me Connie," he said as his generous, warm right hand enveloped mine.

"He loves my Ken Garda collection almost as much as I do," Jerry said.

"Obviously a man of exquisite taste," I said, including Jerry in that observation. Connie was tall and stunning, but he also showed a quiet comfort in his skin. I decided he was the exception that proved the rule—about black men being peacocks. Instead, Connie was effortlessly charming and seemed to know exactly who he was without the need for display or reinforcement.

Lucy obviously adored Connie nearly as much as Jerry did. She said, "It took some doing to get these two together, but it worked. And I'm delighted." *I* was delighted that Seth was not present to hear that.

"Jerry, I want to thank you for what you're doing for Seth," I said. "He'll want to thank you himself. I'm sure he'll catch up with you in a few minutes. Please look at the Ken Gardas first, in case there's one you find you *must* own." We laughed. I wasn't so certain how grateful Seth was feeling toward Jerry. We had talked about his presence at the opening. It was a given. But I sensed that Seth was still a bit raw over the way their affair had ended.

It was early, and the gallery was still sparsely populated, so Jerry and company soon found Ken and Matt. I wondered which Ken Garda photo Jerry would purchase that night. Surely he would make a purchase. I hoped it wasn't the portrait of Seth. Or perhaps I hoped it *was* the portrait of Seth that he would need to own. I could understand his need to own it. And I could feel entirely generous as long as *I* owned the original. And then I felt like a complete asshole for imagining that I could own anything on Earth, especially Seth.

Once Jimmy had the food service under control and the wait staff had begun to circulate with trays of beautiful bite-sized goodies, Seth returned to the main room. I said to him. "Kenny and Matt were asking for you. Ken wants to know how you like your portrait. And Jerry Darnley is here—with his partner and with Lucy. You can't avoid them. Sorry, darling."

"I've got this," Seth said, and he headed in their direction. I saw him shake Jerry's hand, and then Connie's—after their introduction. Lucy kissed him, rather convincingly. My heart ached for Seth's situation, but I couldn't live it for him. He knew he would have to handle it himself, and he did. I tried to busy myself with my arriving guests.

I wasn't spying on them, but I did notice that Connie and Lucy peeled off to view the work in the galleries, leaving Seth and Jerry alone together. That I *couldn't* watch. I felt like a parent forcing himself to allow his child to navigate deep water on his own. And I hated myself for feeling paternal when all I really wanted from my life was to have Seth as an equal partner.

"Tim, you've outdone yourself!" It was Dan Blackwell, the editor, with his husband, Caleb Bromley, the writer. I was delighted to see they had brought Dan's parents with them, Elaine and Richard Blackwell. I had known Dan for years, from the gallery, but I remembered them all keenly from the Pride Show in June. I still thought of Ken Garda's portrait of Dan and Caleb—in a jacuzzi on their wedding night—as one of his best.

"What a treat it is to have you all here!" I said. And I meant it. "Come in! We have to get you a glass of bubbly. You'll notice I've hung the Ken Gardas right up front, as always. But I hope you'll look at everything."

"We always do," Caleb said. His embrace reminded me of how delicious men can be—the ones who are quality inside and out, of course. The family all headed for the bar and then for the galleries.

When they had had a careful look around, the Blackwells recharged their glasses and came to see me. Richard said, "Tim, my man, if I had your presentation skills, I'd be rich today—instead of just comfortable. But my business—or what's left of it—could still use an injection of fresh blood. Let's talk." I embraced him. As older, hetero, suburban white guys go, he was exceptionally warm.

Elaine said, "Tim, I thought your June show was stunning, but the collection here tonight is even more exciting. Richard and I want one of each, but we're going to settle for a Ken Garda. I'd love his work even if I didn't love him, I'm sure. And speaking of love ..." Elaine paused and put her hand on my cheek. She looked me straight in the eye and said, "Tim, you're in love! I think that's wonderful!" I'm sure I blushed. "Who's the lucky person?"

"I'm not sure how lucky he is, but I don't think you've met him, Elaine," I said. "I'll fix that. I'll bring him to meet you as soon as we get a chance."

Shortly after the Blackwell clan arrived, I was greeted by a plump, middle-aged guy I couldn't quite place. "Harvey Letterer," he told me, "from Scrive." Of course, he was from Caleb's publisher. He had been at the Pride Show in June. And he'd purchased Ken's portrait of Caleb and Dan for his boss. "Please meet Len Turrow," he said.

I greeted both of them. Len was cute, in a delicate sort of way. They looked happy together, the two of them. With all the misery in the world, happiness is always cheering, I think. "Enjoy the show, gentlemen," I said. "The bar is just ahead. And be sure to try the crabmeat thing. It's a winner." They smiled appreciatively and moved into the flow of guests.

I caught Seth's eye, and he joined me near the front door. "You don't have to tell me, darling, but I'm wondering what you and Jerry had to say to each other."

"Yes, well, Jerry said, 'I'll always feel guilty about the way I ended our affair, Seth. Can you forgive me?' So I said, 'Of course, Jerry. You were quite right. We're not suited for each other. I know that now.' And that was about it."

"When did you get to be so fucking smart?" I asked him.

"Since I went to bed with you, Tim. Smart by injection, I think." I had promised myself I would keep my hands off Seth all evening, but I couldn't resist holding him close. And then we both went back to work.

When my lawyer and her wife arrived, Judy looked terrific in a kind of dark pantsuit thing that was much too elegant for the office. "Thanks for coming, Judy," I said. "You look amazing. Howdy stranger," I said to Sylvia as I kissed her. "You look edible." She did, really. She was simply clothed in a lightweight cashmere dress—persimmon-colored, as I remember it—that clung to every curve in her very nice body.

"I'll bet you say that to all the girls," Sylvia said.

"No, just to the ones who look edible," I said. "Do grab a glass of bubbly, ladies. And there's some food circulating. Be sure to try the cheese puffs. And don't worry, Judy, the caterer is insured."

"Good," she said. "And so are you." They headed into the middle of the party. Seth was introducing a potential client to the sculptor whose works Seth and I had placed with particular joy a few days before. They were Jan's best to date, for sure. When Seth had completed the introduction, I signaled him. He joined me in the front.

I said to him, "Seth, I'm going to take you to meet the Blackwells. You remember the Ken Garda portrait of Dan Blackwell and his husband, Caleb Bromley. They're here tonight with Dan's parents, Elaine and Richard. Elaine wants to meet you. She guessed, darling. I couldn't deny that I'm in love."

We headed to the Blackwell camp. I introduced Seth to Elaine. "Ah! The young man in Ken Garda's best new portrait," she said. "I should have known." She embraced him sweetly.

Richard returned from the bar with some glasses of champagne. I made introductions. He said, "Jesus, Elaine, is this another one of your matches?"

"I had nothing to do with it, Richard," she said. "Tim and Seth are quite capable of figuring these things out on their own. I only spring into action when people need a push. These two managed it all by themselves. Which is always better. Now you two boys run along [indicating Richard and me]. I want to speak to Seth." We did as we were told. Richard headed in the direction of the sensual paintings by

Liz Hernandez, the artist with the big ass. I headed to see how Maria was doing.

Maria was confident that we were breaking all previous sales records. I was delighted, of course, but I was even more pleased that Seth and I, together, were presenting quality art in a welcoming setting. I got a little teary thinking of the laws of hospitality. I wondered if I could explain it to Seth— the host's sacred obligation to care for his guests. I concluded that I could explain anything to Seth.

When I returned to where Elaine and Seth were talking, I happened to be standing with my back to Dan and Caleb. They had their backs to me and didn't notice that I was there. At a party, guests tend to speak a little louder than they would in a quiet space, of course. I eavesdropped. Dan said to Caleb, "I think Jerry made the perfect choice. He had nothing to offer Seth beyond affection. Whereas Tim can teach him things and build a real partnership. And I've never seen Tim look happier."

I put my hand on Seth's shoulder, smiled at Elaine, and slipped away to see how I could make my guests more comfortable. The party was humming along. There was no shortage of cold champagne or warm food. Guests reached out to say, "Great show, Tim," or "Wouldn't miss one of your openings," or "It wouldn't be fall without this show, Tim." When I returned to the main space, Elaine signaled to me. She was still standing with Seth. I joined them.

"Seth tells me you two haven't made any Thanksgiving plans," Elaine said. "In that case, you have to come to New Jersey, to our house. Well, it's Dan and Caleb's house now, but they invited us to join them, and I said, 'Only if I do *all* the cooking.' They agreed, so it's all set. "Danny," she called to her son, "I just invited the boys for Thanksgiving."

Dan and Caleb joined the conversation. "That's a great idea, Momma," Dan said. "Of course you should come," he said to Seth and me. "It's a wonderful holiday house, and it doesn't get much use these days. Yes, come out on Thursday morning and then stay over. You can stay the weekend if you can get away. There's plenty of room. Think about it—the weekend, that is. Thanksgiving is all arranged."

I decided Dan had learned a lot from his mother's example. And his father's, too, for that matter. I wondered if maybe the acorn doesn't fall far from the tree. And then I thought about my own family and wondered how much of who I was—beyond my physiognomy—I owed to them. Not much, I hoped. I also wondered a little about Seth's family of origin. We would have plenty of time to explore all of that, surely. But I developed warm and gooey feelings for the entire Blackwell clan.

It was always fun to see Letisha Carmichael and Lisa Turner from *GLITZ*. They arrived with a photographer and a videographer in their wake. I was pleased that Matt was not on video assignment that evening. It was Ken's night almost as much as it was mine, and Matt deserved to share it with him.

"Timmy, you've done it again," Tisha said. She wrapped her long, creamy brown arms around me and reminded me why she and Dan Blackwell had fallen in love once and remained besties through the years.

I said, "Tisha, I'm always delighted to have you here. You *GLITZ* girls certainly know how to dress up a room!" I introduced them to Seth, who commandeered some glasses of champagne and some nibbles. Lisa made a big fuss over Seth, especially after she saw Ken's portrait of him.

Lisa said, "Tisha, I just had a terrific idea. Seth, do you ski?"

"Uh, no. At least I never have."

"Doesn't matter. It's the *après-ski* fashions we're interested in mostly. We're casting a winter fashion shoot. Tisha, look at Seth. He's gorgeous. And we already know the camera adores him. He wears clothes like a model. He's young. We can pair him with that Filipina girl. Sparks will fly! We'll get them into a hot tub in very skimpy swimwear. Perfect. Seth, we pay well, and models usually get to keep the clothes. What do you say?"

Seth looked to me for feedback. "You're on your own, darling," I said.

"Do I get to think about it?" Seth asked.

"No," Lisa said. "If you wait until tomorrow, you'll have to audition with your résumé and your portfolio. Tonight, the job is yours. Your call."

Tisha laughed and said, "Seth, we're not scary. If Lisa didn't come on strong, we wouldn't get anything done. I think she's right. I think you're perfect for our shoot. We'd like you to come aboard."

"Yes," Seth said.

"Good!" Lisa said. "Now we can all relax and enjoy Tim's opening. These egg things with the asparagus tips are amazing." She happily downed another one. "Tim, we'll try not to inconvenience your business too much, but we need Seth to come to the office in the morning for some test shots and contracts. Seth, just wear jeans and a T. If we need any other looks, we'll find them for you. You don't mind posing in a micro bikini, do you? Good!" And it was all settled.

About halfway through the evening, there was some noise on the sidewalk out front. It didn't *really* affect my guests, but I was very much aware of it. And it might deter latecomers from deciding to enter the gallery. It seemed to be a homeless guy who had become very animated. The last thing I wanted was a police presence in the middle of the opening. I hoped the crazy would simply move on. He didn't.

Fabián noticed, too. He said to me, "Let me take care of this." I didn't see many other options. I had nearly forgotten that Fabián worked in security. He walked outside—quietly—put a hand on the crazy guy's shoulder, and led him down the block. The incident seemed to be over.

When Fabián returned, looking unruffled and just as sexy as ever, I said to him, "What did you do?"

He said, "I just told him to move on. I also gave him the address of the nearest shelter with mental health counseling. And I told him if he came back, I'd kill him. He got the message."

"Would you? Kill him? If he came back?"

"Probably," Fabián said. "We're talking family here, Tim."

"Thanks, Brother," I said. "But let's try to keep violence to a minimum." For the umpteenth time that day I felt truly blessed. The evening moved along smoothly. The guests were happy. The artists were happy. Seth seemed happy. And that made *me* happy.

The Blackwells kissed us goodbye. Judy and Sylvia had an early morning. Ken and Matt went off to a midnight concert in Grand Army Plaza. The *GLITZ* group stayed as long as the joint was jumpin'. "Timmy, we had a lovely time, as always," Tisha said. Lisa had an especially warm goodnight for Seth. I thought she was going to grab his ass, but that would have been abusive, after all. Instead, she kissed him and reminded him of the office address where he was expected at 10:00 AM sharp.

"Tim, what a treat," Harvey said as he and Len were about to leave. "I couldn't help noticing that you and Seth are very much in love. Now, don't deny it."

"I couldn't," I said.

"Let me give you my card," Harvey said. "I'm an ordained minister. I perform ceremonies. I married Dan and Caleb, by the way. I'll be happy to marry you and Seth—when you're ready." I was too tired to do anything but smile, thank the two of them for coming, and to promise I would put Harvey's card in a safe place.

When the last of our guests and artists had left, I locked the door behind them and lowered the lights a bit. Jimmy and his crew quickly broke down all of the catering setups and loaded out. Seth promised he'd get us ready to close up for the night. I started yawning. I knew business had been good. I had noticed all the red dots throughout the galleries.

"Tim, I'll give you a final report tomorrow afternoon," Maria said.

"Thank you—both—for being here tonight," I said. I kissed Maria and said, "Noon, tomorrow, I think. No, make it 1:00. We've all earned some rest. Try to keep that handsome mate of yours in line!" She gave me a knowing look.

When I kissed Fabián goodnight—on the lips instead of ceremonially on the cheeks, as usual—I made it a point not only to bump his bulge but to grab his ass as well. "Thanks, Brother," I said.

He flashed his delicious grin and said, "I'll do anything for family." And they were on their way home. I suddenly wondered if I had just crossed a red line. Lisa had been so careful not to touch Seth inappropriately. And there I was groping a hot guy whose wife worked for me—because I thought he wanted it. Who was I to decide what Fabián wanted? I felt like a jerk. I felt like a failure as a man, really.

I was a bit of a mess when Seth came to me to tell me the bolts were thrown and everything in the back of the house was secured. "Timmy, you seem so sad," he said. "I thought you'd be as happy as I am." I grabbed him, too forcefully, probably.

"If I were any happier, I'd probably explode. Please, take me home, Seth." And he did. As we prepared for bed, did I feel a little apprehensive about the opportunities coming Seth's way? Yes. But I had to trust that our love would get us through it. And if it didn't, then I'd have to conclude that I had overestimated our love. I'd have to be adult about it. I'd have to find a new kind of sinew to bind up by heart. When we lay together and Seth held me close to *his* heart, I had to believe that the beauty beside me would always warm my nights as well as my days. Wouldn't he?

Chapter Eight

The next morning, we slept in—until 8:00. We had earned some extra rest. As I was making coffee, Seth came to me, embraced me, and said, "Timmy, I'm terrified of this *GLITZ* gig."

"Of course you are," I said. "I would be, too. But since when do we let our fears rule our lives?"

"Since never."

"Damn straight!" I said, "pardon the expression. You'll be fine, darling. Lisa and Tisha will put you at your ease. You'll share your beauty with them, and they'll pay you handsomely. Sounds good to me." Seth kissed me. "Please, come to the gallery whenever you finish. It doesn't matter when. I'm not expecting much foot traffic the day after the opening. And Maria will be there."

"What about my work at the gallery, Tim?" he asked me. "I have no idea how much time this project will take. I guess I'll find out today."

"Don't worry about it, darling." I said. "You're good for my business. Almost as good as you are for my life. But I can get a part-timer to fill in when you have to be away. There are plenty of art students who can use some gallery experience and a little pocket change—like the guy who came in and helped you after the Pride Show. I've got this." I didn't talk about all the time Seth would be away from me when he became the go-between for the spring exhibit at the Historical Society. I wasn't ready to face that.

Seth's modeling gig would probably help to ease me into the reality of the situation: After a year in which I could count on Seth's support for my business nearly every business day, I would have to learn to make it work without him. "You can handle this, Timothy," I told myself. And, of course, I could. I offered Seth some yoghurt and granola. He thanked me, ate, and then headed to the shower.

Rufus walked over, sat, and put his head in my lap. I massaged the special area behind his ears that always sent him into a blissful zone. He'd have purred if he had known how. *Thank God for Rufus,* I thought. And then I felt foolish for not having thought, *Thank God for Seth* first. There were no endings going on, after all. Just changes. So, what else was new?

Seth looked properly casual as he prepared to leave the apartment for his appointment at *GLITZ*. He also looked so delicious that I got a little misty. "Have fun!" I said to him. "That's the important thing." Seth kissed me deeply, and then he headed for the door. I followed him. I smacked him on his perfect butt, and then I said, "Oh, sorry, I shouldn't damage the merchandise." Seth laughed, kissed me again, and then left Rufus and me to fend for ourselves.

I wasn't planning to reach the gallery before noon, so I went back to bed and napped for a half hour. It helped a little. Rufus and I went for a walk, and then I took a shower. It was all quite unremarkable, except that I felt a nagging sense of abandonment. It was nothing like the torture I experienced after

Andy's death, of course, but it was there. Irrational but real.

                         📖

"Hi, Maria," I said as she arrived at the gallery—early, as always. "So, you'll have the good news for me soon?"

"Sure, Tim," she said. "The software we use keeps running totals, but I want to double check each purchase and reconcile the charges and the cash. Just when you think cash is a thing of the past, it surfaces again. We took in about four thousand dollars in big bills last night."

"Good," I said. "Take your time, Maria. I don't expect we'll have a lot to do today." I had decided to bring Rufus with me. I didn't do it often, but it seemed like the right day for it. Despite his being such a big guy, Rufus never got in the way. Mostly he napped in the sun just inside the front window. Maria greeted him. He was grateful for the attention, as always.

"It was a great opening, Tim," she said. "I don't mean the sales. I mean it was a good party. You have a nice clientele. They like to have a good time, but they don't get crazy. They obviously feel welcome, and you make it look effortless."

"Last night certainly didn't *feel* effortless. Please thank that husband of yours—again—for getting rid of the homeless guy. You know, I had completely forgotten that Fabián works in security. He's a good man to have around."

"He *is* a good man—and a good father. And he thinks you're terrific."

"I adore him, but I think I got out of line last night. Fatigue and champagne are not a good combination. Do I owe him an apology?"

"Not that I know of," Maria said. "He's pretty up front. But I'll ask him if you want me to."

"Yes, please," I said. "It occurred to me that I need advice about security. The value of our inventory keeps growing. I'm sure Fabián can teach me what we're missing here. Please ask him if he'll consult with me—if I promise not to grope him, of course."

"Sure, Tim," she said.

"Openings are great, but I'm glad we don't have to do that again for a few months." Maria smiled and got to work. I felt a bit of relief about having overstepped boundaries with Fabián. I hoped I had learned something. I took a quick look around to be certain there wasn't any party residue lurking anywhere. The galleries looked clean and inviting, just as they had looked before the first guests had arrived the night before. I was glad Jimmy understood the level of cleanup we needed after a party. There was no evidence of food or drink anywhere.

I had to admit that it really was a remarkable show. My artists continued to up their games, and Seth and I had done a classy job of displaying their art. Working with Seth—the two of us together, caring for my business—had been exceptionally sweet. Or would it become *our* business? I'd have been feeling nothing but pride, had I not been experiencing some low-grade loneliness.

I was glad we could keep the exhibit together for a while. We always asked purchasers of paintings and other unique items to let us keep them in-house for two weeks or more. Photos and prints and even some sculptures that were created as editions we could release on the weekend, after we had the next-in-series printed, signed, and framed (or cast) and ready to replace the opening night piece.

When an artwork was sold—or sold out—it was always a simple matter to consult with the artist and choose a replacement. My galleries always looked of-a-piece—never cobbled together. I knew what I was doing. At least until I fell in love with Seth. Falling in love with him had nothing to do with knowledge or skill. It was all about deep yearning that welled up from a place in my soul that was inscrutable. And it changed everything.

When Seth arrived at the gallery, shortly after 2:00, he greeted Rufus, gave me a kiss, waved at Maria, and said, "Timmy, what a day!" Seth was ... flushed with excitement? Not exactly. But he was energized, for sure.

"I want to hear all about it," I said.

"Well, the shoot is the first week in November. In Aspen, probably. Or maybe Telluride. I have to go to the office next week for any fittings that might be necessary. They say I'm a pretty standard Medium, so they don't expect much in the way of alterations."

"There's nothing standard about you, darling," I said. Seth kissed me. "How long will you be away?" I asked. That was my principal concern, of course.

"Just a week—unless there are some issues with the weather and it takes a little longer. They think a week."

"I'm glad I have a couple of weeks to plan for your absence." And then I changed the subject because I was sick of thinking about being alone. "What would you like for dinner, darling?"

"It doesn't matter," Seth said. "I'm easy." I laughed and kissed him. Rufus stirred, briefly, and then resumed his nap. It was a perfect afternoon.

Maria came to me with the final sales figures. "Best opening night ever," she said. "I'll contact all the artists tomorrow, and then I'll cut checks on Thursday, if that's okay with you."

"Of course," I said. "As soon as the funds clear, I want the artists paid."

"Will do," she said. Seth and I locked up at 6:00. We strolled toward my place, enjoying the slight autumn chill in the air. Fall was Rufus's favorite season. Mine too, I suppose. But lately I had come to crave any season with Seth in it. We stopped at a restaurant near home for some takeout. I went inside to order while Seth and Rufus played on the sidewalk. I was a happy man.

When the three of us got home, Rufus bounded in, recovered his favorite toy, and presented it at my feet. He also stood guard over it with the concentration of a pointer. I grabbed the toy, suddenly, and tossed it across the room. And then the games began. Seth was even better at it than I was. He was willing to feint and tease and fall to the floor with the toy beneath him so that Rufus had to pounce on him to recover the prize. I got a little weepy—a lot weepy, actually—as I watched our family at play.

Were we a family? I hoped so with all my heart. Over dinner, I said, "Tell me more about today, Seth. Did you have a good time?"

"I was too nervous to have a good time, but I realized I didn't exactly mind it—having a bunch of people studying my body. In fact, I kind of liked it."

"Good," I said. "We don't get very far in life if we're afraid to display who we are." I meant it, of course.

I was delighted that Seth was learning to own his beauty. But I also felt a gray fog rising in my heart as I pondered the longevity of our relationship. Seth was so young. And so vital. How could I possibly earn his devotion? How could I possibly satisfy his needs?

Chapter Nine

"The vault is secure, but otherwise you're exposed," Fabián said after he had thoroughly examined the premises. In daylight and in casual clothes, he looked every bit as desirable as his puffed-up, cologne-drenched evening presence. More so, I think. Of course that's only my opinion, but I'll take the natural man without the window dressing any day.

"Well, then, please create a system," I said, "when you can get to it, and then teach Seth and me how to use it. I won't ask for an estimate. I know you'll be fair. Just present an invoice, and Maria will pay it."

"I like Seth," Fabián said. "I think he's a good guy. And he obviously loves you—like the rest of us." I had promised myself to keep a physical distance from Fabián. I bent my new rule enough to embrace him. His hug was warm and comforting, and while I could feel the stirring in his sweatpants—I had always assumed there was a great hooded wonder swinging between his legs—it was more friendly than challenging. Fabián kissed me lightly on the lips and said, "You know I'll do anything for family, Brother. We're going to make this gallery as secure as Fort Knox."

"Good," I said. "I've been wondering if I need a human security presence here, too. I've never been held up, but I was thinking about opening night: If you hadn't been here, the situation with the crazy guy out front could have gotten nasty."

"I was just about to get to that. You can't ever be here alone, Tim. I'll find you some guys who look like customers or assistants. No uniforms or pistols on their hip. I know Seth is here a lot of the time, but he has work to do deep in the gallery and downstairs. It's not enough that he's here, too. There have to be two men up front at all times—or one of my guys, when you're showing a customer around."

"I see your point. I hoped I wouldn't need to go there—the expense and all—but I think it's time. You're a wise man, Fabián. And a good man. I'm so glad you and Maria found each other. She's precious, and she deserves to have a quality man by her side." I liked Seth's notion of a "quality man." So, I appropriated it. Another embrace from Fabián, and I was starting to feel quite randy.

"I'll stop by tomorrow with my locks-and-alarms guy. And we can start the process. It may take a little longer to find the perfect security guards for your business, but we'll make it work. Another thing: I think your hours are too long. I know you don't open until 10:00, but 11:00 is probably better. I feel certain your customers expect to visit you in the afternoon. Let's ask Maria for a sales breakdown by time of day.

"I'll bet you do almost no nighttime business—especially in the winter. The hours after dark are the most dangerous for a quiet business like yours—unless you're having an opening with a few hundred guests. I think you should decide on 11:00 to 6:00—

11:00 to 5:00 in the winter—and close on Mondays," Fabián said. "You need some time for your life, Tim. You need some time for Seth." He flashed me his delicious grin. I melted.

"You're probably right," I said. "I'll have to think about it. And I'll have to talk to Seth about it. I value his opinion."

"Of course you do," Fabián said. "The thing about your brand, Tim, is that you have to be here. If you're busy, or having lunch, you can pass customers off to Seth—or someone else who's knowledgeable and attractive. But if you're not visible in the front of the house, then *estás jodido*."

I wasn't certain what Fabián had just said, but I got the message. I was sorry that Seth had gone to a fitting. I would have much preferred that he join me to hear Fabián's analysis. I would also have preferred that he never left my side. But it couldn't be helped. I thanked Fabián for his wisdom, embraced him as fraternally as I could manage, and sent him on his way.

After supper, I said to Seth, "You've shown me everything I really need to know about you, darling, but we haven't talked much about our experiences. I want to know everything about you—every little detail. I'm happy to go first."

"Yes, please, "Seth said.

"I grew up in an old house in a pretty little New England town in western Massachusetts, near the Vermont border. I hated it I hated the predictability of it. I hated the emotional coldness of my family.

No one really abused me—except maybe my cousin Robert, who used to take me out to the shed and fuck the shit out of me. The rest of it wasn't awful, but I wouldn't exactly call what I got nurturing.

"I know current wisdom suggests that gay kids now have role models and peer support. Pardon me, but I don't believe it. I don't think it's ever easy to grow up gay. And I don't see any signs of a grand change. Anyway, I retreated into a world of books. I devoured all sorts of disciplines and genres. Eventually I chose art history as my favorite. So by the time I was ready to choose a college, I had an academic plan as well as a strong desire to get out of town."

I poured us a brandy, took a deep breath, and got back to my story. "I knew it would have been wise to go to Harvard, but I couldn't bear the thought of being that close to home—too easy to spend weekends and holidays there. I considered UC Berkley, but I guess I'm too much of an Easterner to take that leap. Eventually, I chose NYU. My parents weren't thrilled, but I was resolute. The day I moved into my new dorm room, I said to myself, 'Tim, you're home.'

"I loved it. I loved New York City, I loved my coursework, and I loved the classmates I met. And when I met Andy, I began to love life. We made love—as much as two nineteen-year-olds can manage that. I would have insisted that we move in together, except that Andy had to go home and help his family with some sort of business crisis. When he returned to school two years later, I think we were both better prepared to build a life together. And that's what we set out to do.

"We both took grunt jobs to keep our little boat afloat while Andy was finishing college. Didn't matter. I had everything I needed when Andy was in my arms. Our lean years were as happy as any we shared. Then Andy landed a good job on Wall Street. I began to seriously consider the gallery business. Andy found my investor—a low-key guy who was willing to share the risk and to accept a sensible annual return.

"I never met the guy, even though proposals and counterproposals flew back and forth. We came to an agreement, and I found the space in Chelsea I wanted. And the rest—as they say—is history. There's been tons of hard work, but it's paid off. And I have such a warm spot in my heart for this investor that I look forward to paying him his cut. When Maria calculates it, quarterly, I always handwrite the check. If he walked into the gallery, I'd drop to my knees and give him the best oral service I could manage."

"I thought your best oral service was reserved for me," Seth said.

"It is, darling, but allow me to be hypothetical. Seth, what I'm trying to tell you is that I lived a charmed existence right up until the night Andy died." I fell silent.

"Do you want to talk about that—the night Andy died?" Seth asked.

"No, but I probably should," I said. That took several deep breaths and another small brandy. "We were getting ready for bed. I was sitting, checking to make sure that my alarm was set. Andy walked in from the bathroom, slipped off his sandals and sat on his side of the bed. And then he just collapsed. I grabbed him, of course, talked to him, and maybe I shook him a little. And then I sprang into action.

"First, I called 911, then I called down to ask the doorman to send our guests right up. Then I put Rufus on his lead and tied him up in the kitchen. The EMS people were prompt. I only had a few minutes to cradle Andy and to rock him in my arms. I could tell he was no longer there. All I could hold onto was his *body*. But I still needed the closeness. I nearly forgot to remove the ring I had given Andy when we were first together. As I was doing that, the doorbell rang. I threw on a robe, answered the door, and directed them to the bedroom.

They quickly took Andy's vitals, which were non-existent, of course. I don't know if they were used to attending handsome, healthy, naked young men who had died suddenly in bed. But they eased him, respectfully, onto a stretcher and covered him with a blanket. They had him out the door and on the way to the hospital in a few minutes. Rufus howled. I'd have howled, too, if it could have done some good.

"I considered jumping into the back of the EMS van with Andy—Andy's body, really. But I couldn't see the point in it. I knew he was gone, and I had already said my last goodbye. Instead, I focused on Rufus. He was agitated and disoriented. I held him and tried to comfort him. I also tried to persuade him we would get through it. Eventually he was calm enough to wander off to his bed. It wasn't until I had turned off my bed lamp that the tears set in."

Seth took me in his arms and held me until I could let go of the trauma of the evening that had thrown my entire life into a tailspin. Maybe I had learned something in the retelling. Or maybe I had simply learned that it was time to move on. "Seth, I'm sorry to be such a big baby," I said. He held me a while longer. And then I poured a little more brandy and it was Seth's turn:

"I grew up in South Philadelphia," Seth said. "I didn't think of it as a bad neighborhood. It was just home. But I *was* aware that my parents hated each other. I couldn't figure out why they stayed together. But they did—right up until about two years ago. I look a lot like my dad, so Mom hated me, too. I accepted that early on and stopped looking for anything warm and fuzzy from her. Dad mostly connected with the flat of his hand. When he wasn't slapping me around, he mostly ignored me.

"By the time I was five, I was parenting myself. I learned how to get to school on time. I learned how to put some food together. I wouldn't call it cooking, exactly, but I managed to assemble something like lunch that I could take to school and something like supper that I could take to my room--to avoid the folks. I did my homework every evening. I even did the laundry every other week.

"My story is quite different from yours, Tim," Seth said, "except that I also had a cousin. I don't think he was as nice as your Cousin Robert. Mostly he wanted to hurt me, and he was good at it. I was twelve the first time he came to my room—it must have been after school when there was no one else in the house—and he threw me on my bed and nailed me. I was scared, of course, and he has a huge dick, so it hurt like hell. But by the third time he fucked me, I was a willing participant.

"This went on, once or twice a week, until just after my fourteenth birthday. Suddenly, I decided that stupid affair was over. Jack didn't take it very well, but what could he do about it, really? Other than hitting me. But that time he went beyond his usual abuse and scared me more than ever. When he took out a pocketknife and prepared to carve his initials on my ass, I developed superhuman strength. I decked my cousin, and then I dragged him out of my room and pushed him down the stairs. He never bothered me again.

"When Mom asked, 'What happened to Jack?' I said, 'I don't know.' 'What was he doing here?' she asked. I said, 'I don't know. You gave him a key, didn't you?' 'You must have heard something,' Mom said. "No, I had headphones on all afternoon, listening to music in my room.' Mom gave up on getting to the bottom of the story. Like so many other situations in our lives, she really didn't give a shit about what happened to anyone but herself. So she let it go.

"Cousin Jack was the least of my problems. I knew I had to get out of that house. I had a school-teacher who took an interest in me—thank God. She never pressed me for info about my home life. I think she sensed that it was hopeless and that the future was more important. She created a reading list for me. I read—for hours a day and into the night. When I was sixteen, she called me into her office:

"'Seth, you're a bright guy,' she said. 'There's a community college nearby that will take young students with incomplete high school credentials. I would be pleased to recommend you for admission. I'm guessing you'll be finished with your remedial studies by the end of the first semester. If you maintain an excellent record—and I'd expect nothing less from you—then you can take an associate's degree and then transfer anywhere.'

"It was like a dream come true, but then reality set in. I said, 'Thanks, Miss Flannery, but I don't know how to pay for this, and I don't want to involve my parents if I can help it.' She said, 'Never worry about money, Seth. It's just an energy that flows through our lives. I'm confident you'll be accepted, and—If you want it—I'll start the process of getting you a free ride. You'll have to continue to live at home, at first, but I don't want you to even consider a part-time job for the first year. Making a good academic start is crucial.'

"It often seemed too good to be true, but it all fell into place. So, at age seventeen I headed off to college every morning instead of to high school. My parents barely noticed. I shared as little as possible with them because I knew they were not really interested and because I wanted my new life to be mine! I transferred to the University of Pittsburgh and took a business degree. I was interested in the arts, but I couldn't quite see the point. Tim, it's late, and I'm running out of energy. Can we continue this some evening soon?"

'Of course, darling," I said. "Will you come to bed? I want to learn just how close I can get to you. Very, I'm hoping." My heart had swelled with extra tenderness and pride as Seth and I began to learn about each other. *How do humans do it?* I wondered as I got ready for bed. *How do we even survive childhood, much less learn to thrive?* I had no answers.

Chapter Ten

In the weeks that followed the opening, some mornings I woke with the warmth of Seth's embrace still enveloping me and wanted nothing more than to extend it as long as possible. Some mornings I made love to Seth with an urgency that was new to me. And some mornings I simply gazed at him in the soft light of sunrise as he slept beside me. Or I explored the perfection of his skin with my hands as gently as I knew how. Seth accepted whichever Tim greeted him at first light.

On one of the mornings I needed desperately to get as close to him as possible, Seth woke enough to throw his legs around my waist and invite me in. I wept softly as I claimed his body for my own. Seth took me in his arms and held me close with the same intensity I felt toward owning him. We became one creature that morning. I could swear to it. I had no idea where my body ended and Seth's began. And he seemed to feel the same way. That was the miracle of it.

We shared one orgasm that morning. Did I fill him up, or did he fill me? Who came on our bellies? Seth's semen tasted very much the same as mine. I had no idea which we were savoring that morning and no desire to differentiate. When we finally had to separate—to get on with our day—I suddenly felt as if half of me were missing.

The real world intruded on our love nest, of course. Rufus needed a walk every morning, and we had to get ready for work. And Seth had to get on with his project that didn't concern me. By the time he headed off to Aspen for the photo shoot—the first week in November—I was prepared, as much as possible, for being alone. It would only be a week. Yes? And we both had "unlimited talk and text," after all.

I hated being alone every bit as much as I expected to. But I had a business to run and a dog to care for. Fabián sent me some candidates for the security guard position. I quickly hired three part-timers—two men and a woman. I didn't have to worry about their credentials, thanks to Fabián. I only had to decide which guys looked like they belonged in an elegant gallery and which ones I felt I could work beside for a whole business day. The process seemed less daunting than I had feared.

When Seth returned from Colorado—looking flushed and fit—I was more than ready to ease myself back into living with him. He had already unpacked by the time I closed the gallery and headed home that evening. "How's my Adonis?" I asked.

"Tim, I wouldn't have missed the experience for anything short of you asking me not to go."

"Why would I do that, darling?" I asked him. "I'll always want you to take advantage of opportunities that come your way."

"But not all men are as generous as you are, Tim. Some guys would be threatened by all the attention I've been getting."

"Some guys are not me," I said. "Let's get some dinner." And that's what we did. After we had fed and walked Rufus, we got ourselves ready for bed.

"Timmy, it was torture being away from you," Seth said. "It was amazing being in the middle of all that fashion energy, but I'll *never* do it again. Modeling is for people who love it. If I took another job, it would mean that some professional who needed the work and the exposure would be losing out to an amateur."

"How did you get to be so smart? And so kind?" I asked him.

"Everything I know about life I've learned from you, Timmy," Seth said. "Could we turn in? I need to hold you." And that's what we did. I relaxed into the rightness of Seth in my bed. His embrace warmed me all the way to my core, and his presence gave me a feeling of safety I had sorely lacked while he was away. I slept.

Lucy stopped by the gallery the following Wednesday with an update. "About thirty-five pieces," she said. "Forty if some of them are smaller. We usually include no more than two works by the same artist, in the interest of variety. Does that work for you? I could send you pictures of the wall-space, but I suspect you're better off seeing it firsthand. You close on Mondays now, right? Why don't you and Seth stop by next Monday and take a look? I'll buy you some lunch in the café. The new chef is doing a great job."

"Thanks, Lucy. That sounds lovely," I said. "I'll run it by Seth to make sure it works for him, but it should be a go. Does noon sound good?"

"Perfect." I had a positive feeling about that spring exhibition at the Historical Society. It required very much the same skills I had been exercising for the past five years at Tim Hart. And now that Seth had begun to help me, I felt more confident than ever. I even felt lighthearted about all the hours the job would take Seth away from me. Surely I could cope with the occasional time when I might not see him all day. Couldn't I?

Thanksgiving had long been a favorite holiday for me—ever since Andy and I had begun to celebrate it together. This would be my first Thanksgiving in more than a decade without him. But then, life had become a series of firsts. Each one had to be experienced and accepted. I tried to think of it as my first Thanksgiving with Seth, rather than my first one without Andy. That mindset mostly worked.

Seth had a rather jaundiced view of holidays. His matching view of family was fairly earned. But since we were building a new family of our very own, Seth was open and optimistic. The Monday before—after our luncheon with Lucy at the Historical Society—we began to gather the dainty offerings we wanted to bring to Elaine and Richard for their Thanksgiving table. Wine and spirits, muscat grapes and Italian pears. Like that. Yes, we could add to the festivities.

On Thursday morning, we threw a change of underwear into a wheelie, along with a change of shirts and two light sweaters. Those, along with our winter jackets, would serve us well. It would have been fun to stay the weekend, but it didn't seem practical. I had long closed the gallery on Black Friday, but the weekend after Thanksgiving was rich with possibilities for small businesses catering to affluent shoppers searching for just the right holiday gift.

Ken and Matt had rented a car—a minivan, really—to transport six of us to New Jersey— themselves, Seth and me, and Jerry and Connie. I would have preferred not to travel with Jerry and Connie—for Seth's sake—but there was no real reason for us to be anything but grateful for the lift.

There was a bite in the air, like a rehearsal for the winter holidays to follow. I knew there had been a dusting of snow the night before in Bergen County. But the roads were completely clear all the way out Rte. 17. Other than navigating our way to the right highway after surfacing from the Lincoln Tunnel, the trip was uneventful.

Dan and Caleb rushed down the driveway to greet us in front of a handsome, big old house made of red brick and white clapboard. It had become *their* house, after all. I was pleased that Elaine and Richard would be in it for the holiday weekend. I'm sure the boys were, too. "Dad is mulling some cider, but I convinced him it can wait until noon—after you guys have settled into your rooms. There's still time for a nap. Follow me, troops!"

We went inside and greeted Elaine and Richard, who were both flushed with activity—the culinary kind for Elaine and the holiday cheer kind for Richard. They both seemed pleased with our offerings. Dan and Caleb led us upstairs to our rooms. "We moved back into my old room for the holiday weekend," Dan said. "We put you two in the bedroom next to ours. We hope you find it comfortable.

"Jerry and Connie are across the hall, in my sister's old room. It has the best bed in the house. It's sort of theirs now. Kenny and Matt are down the hall in a room with a great view of the pond and the woods beyond. That room has become theirs. Feel free to stake your claim. This house needs people in it." I sensed that Dan had much more to say, but I also sensed that it would have to wait for the right moment. We did decide to take a nap, after putting our toiletries in the bathroom and deciding we were all moved in.

I relished every opportunity to have a naked Seth in my arms. The bed was slightly smaller than the one at home, but welcoming, nonetheless. The comforter was thick and puffy. I imagined we'd be grateful for its warmth come bedtime. We snuggled, we napped, we resurfaced just before noon. And then we dressed, ran a brush through our hair, and headed downstairs.

"Tim, my man," Richard said, "will you have cider? Seth?" We both accepted. "This has applejack in it. You know, the same New Jersey family has been distilling it since the seventeenth century. The government couldn't quite shut it down during Prohibition, so applejack became a popular spirt in Manhattan. Jersey lightning, it was known as."

I had been in generous old homes in the Northeast before. This one was remarkably welcoming. The architect and the family who inhabited the house had both added layers of comfort to the design. "Elaine's great-grandparents built this house around the turn of the last century," Richard said. "The kitchen has been redone twice and some bathrooms were added, but that's about it. We never thought we'd live here, but then we could never find a house we liked better."

Richard seemed almost lost in thought for a moment. And then he concluded his introduction to what was every bit the holiday house Dan had told us to expect. "Elaine and I were comfortable here until after Danny and Mary Ellen were both out of the nest. Gradually, there didn't seem much point in the two of us rattling around in this big old place. When Dan and Caleb agreed to accept it, we were delighted to move into an apartment in the village last winter. It suits us."

I could tell he meant it. I could tell that he and Elaine had moved on—clear-eyed, unsentimental, forward-focused. I wondered if I'd ever learn to live in the real world the way they did. "Danny and Caleb are making plans for this place. I'm sure you'll hear about it later. And I'm sure they'll do the right thing. Do you have children, Tim?"

"No, it never seemed to be my path."

"It's not for everyone. I'm glad we did it, though I'm not so certain I thought that every minute along the way. Seth, I think you'd be a good father. I think you'd make up for everything yours did wrong. Consider it." We were both a little nonplussed, but Richard had a way of speaking his mind. "Let me talk to some of the boys," Richard said. "Tim, I haven't forgotten what I said to you at your opening. I'll get back to you in the morning." And he was off to pour cider and chat with the others.

Elaine appeared from the kitchen and said, "Tim, can you peel a potato? Of course you can. I'm so used to dealing with Danny and his sister, Mary Ellen. Neither of them inherited the culinary gene. But it's just as well, I suppose. They have other qualities and other talents." I joined her in the kitchen. Seth joined the others in the living room. "Would you start on these potatoes?" Elaine requested. I assured her I would. Elaine got on with the business of preparing a cream sauce for the pearl onions she had carefully peeled. I worked on the sack of potatoes she had given me, putting each one into cold water to prevent discoloration.

Elaine said, "Dan told me you've had a rough year, Tim."

"Yes."

"How are you surviving it? I'm always amazed at survival skills. I think I'm strong, as suburban housewives go...."

"Elaine, I've never included you and 'suburban housewife' in the same thought. And besides, I've known for years that women are stronger than we are. Many men don't like to accept that. But it's true."

"Richard and I both are in excellent health," Elaine said, "but we've all watched life turn on a dime. My first pregnancy ended in a miscarriage. And when that didn't kill me—only the little boy Richard and I were so excited about welcoming into our lives—we decided to try it again. Mary Ellen was such a pretty, healthy little thing. And then we got our baby boy. And Danny has been magical ever since."

"If Seth hadn't come into my heart," I said, "I guess I'd have resigned myself to living alone with my memories. It would have been nearly enough. Nearly. But I'm not the sort who settles, any more than you would be. Elaine, I need Seth so much. It scares me sometimes."

"Never forget, Timmy, that Seth needs you every bit as much as you need him. If you hadn't come into his life, he'd still be the promising kid from ..."

"South Philly."

"... from South Philly who never quite figured out what to do with all that promise. No, you two are perfectly balanced. And whether you get another day together or six or eight decades more, you will have done it right." We continued our work in silence. I welcomed the quiet after having gone about as deep as I was willing to go for one Thursday afternoon.

Dan walked into the kitchen and greeted his mother with a kiss. "Thanks for doing all this, Momma," he said.

"Hush, Danny! Did you help your dad set the table?"

"Yes, Momma. The dining room is ready. What time should I tell everyone to expect dinner?"

"Four o'clock, I think," Elaine said. "You should take our guests out for a walk—everyone but my helper, here." I felt proud to have been selected. "It's a beautiful day, and they can work up an appetite. Make sure they take jackets. It's colder than it looks."

"Will do, Momma."

After Dan left the kitchen, I asked Elaine, "How did you do all this?"

"I have a system. For instance, I rolled the pie shells on Monday and put them in the freezer—so I could just fill them and bake them first thing this morning. If you're interested in baking pies, Timmy, always use Pyrex pie plates and bake them in a 350° oven on the bottom rack. Not the floor of the oven—they'll burn there—but on the lowest rack. That way you don't have to bother with prebaked shells and all that nonsense. Too much information?"

"No, not at all," I said. "I'm always fascinated by people who know what they're doing. And the rest of it?"

"I made the cranberry relish on Tuesday. It needs a couple of days for the brandy to work its magic. I also brined the turkey on Tuesday. I like a weak brine and two days. I think it improves the flavor as well as keeping it moist. The turkey went into the second oven this morning—hot to start and then moderate for the rest of the roasting time. It will have at least an hour to rest before it goes to the table. Richard is a good carver, but if we're feeding more than four people, I like to carve half the bird in the kitchen so we can get on with dinner before everything gets cold.

"I boiled and mashed the sweet potatoes yesterday. They're all blended with butter, maple syrup, and crystallized ginger. I'll put that in the oven a little later. It takes seconds to crush saltines, layer them with shucked oysters, add some cream and mace, and dot with butter. I'll put the scalloped oysters in to bake last thing. Oh, and I made stock yesterday with the turkey neck and the giblets.

"I've been collecting bread for dressing all season and storing it in the freezer. Maybe you can help me slice some onions and celery and an apple or two. We'll sauté them in too much butter and toss in the bread and just enough stock to moisten. Do you like sage? Good. We'll add some, and thyme leaves, and some chopped parsley. Let's get on that and get it in the oven." And that's what we did.

When Elaine released me from my kitchen service, there was still time before dinner for Seth and me to head to our room. "What do you think, darling?" I asked him. "Are you glad we're here?" He embraced me firmly. I took that as a yes.

Chapter Eleven

Our Thanksgiving feast was warm and wonderful, just as I had expected. Richard seated me between Connie and Jerry. Seth was across the table, flanked by Ken and Caleb. Dan completed their side of the table, and Matt completed ours. It was undeniably a handsome group—a little white, certainly, except for Connie, but still deliciously diverse. Richard gave a sort of nonsectarian blessing before he began to serve up the turkey. It was all about gratitude. There were amens all around.

The food was remarkable, as I was certain it would be. Even the turkey was delicious. The mashed potatoes were pillowy ("Boil one tiny garlic clove and one or two peeled white turnips with the potatoes, then drain and toss over heat until the potatoes are dry and floury, and then add *hot* milk with the butter while you mash," Elaine explained). It was all rather American, and yet there was a welcome balance of flavors and colors and textures, including a salad of blanched green beans, watercress, thinly sliced raw mushrooms, and a sprinkling of sweet corn kernels just sliced from the cob. A handful of pomegranate seeds strewn on top made it extra festive.

We all overate, of course. How could we not, given the quality of the food and the company? I noticed early on that Seth had surrendered himself entirely to the holiday experience. I wondered if I could ever offer him that kind of festivity all by myself. Our first Christmas together would be coming up in about a month. Could I handle it? I wondered.

Over coffee and dessert, Caleb said, "Richard and I are going to rent a single-engine plane in the morning and take a spin. There's room for one more. Any takers?"

"Yes," Seth said automatically.

"Good," Caleb said. Of course, he was a pilot. I had nearly forgotten that his memoir-like first novel—*ABOVE THE CLOUDS*—was mostly about flying. I was glad that Seth had volunteered for an adventure. I wanted him to try everything. I wanted him to have the freedom to soar, though it hadn't occurred to me that he might soar quite so literally.

Richard presided over after-dinner drinks while Dan and Caleb cleared the table and Kenny and Matt went to the kitchen to help Elaine put away leftovers. Once the dishwasher was loaded, they all joined us in the living room. I noticed immediately how carefully they had hung Ken's portrait of Dan and Caleb on their wedding night. Exquisite. I went with Richard to the cellar to retrieve a bottle of vintage port.

"Richard, you're so easygoing about 'alternate lifestyles,'" I said. "How did that happen?"

"Oh, please," Richard said. "I was in the Navy. Do you think sailors don't take comfort in each other's arms? I won't tell you if I ever took a dick in my mouth, but I will tell you that I saw the power of human connection at an early age. And I vowed not to judge anyone. And I've done a decent job of keeping that vow through the years.

"But I doubt I gave Danny the acceptance he needed. It wasn't because I judged him. It was because I worried about his safety—and his future. Not only were hate crimes common—then as now—but the AIDS epidemic was still red hot when Danny was growing up. If Elaine and I had lost him to a virus, I think we'd have lost our way." I embraced Richard, probably too firmly. He seemed okay with it. We took the port and rejoined the others.

I saw Caleb and Matt talking together, and I remembered their Montana connection. But it was more than that, of course. They had both managed to build new lives in NYC—and intertwined lives at that. I realized that I hadn't really spoken to Connie all day. I found a place to perch next to him. I said, "I won't ask how business is. I'm certain it's entirely too good." I had learned that Connie managed and advocated for a food pantry/soup kitchen/community outreach program in the East Village.

"You're right, Tim," he said. "Business is better than ever. We've had an especially busy time these last two weeks getting organized for our Thanksgiving event while trying to provide the usual staples for the food-insecure in our community. I'm feeling a little guilty about traveling on such an important day. But I couldn't bear the thought of *not* spending Jerry's and my first Thanksgiving together. And I have a terrific team who insisted I take this time off. I hope I can make it up to them."

"I'm sure you make it up to them every day," I said. My heart leaped toward the extraordinary man sitting beside me. I kissed him on the forehead. Any gesture more intimate than that and I might have groped him. Connie rewarded me with a dazzling smile. "I've known Jerry for a few years now," I said,

Bruce K Beck

"and I've never seen him what I'd call truly happy. I know he had a partner once. So did I. I think I get it. And I'm certain you've made all the difference in his life. *And* I'm certain you cherish him. He deserves it."

Connie embraced me and filled my senses with his scent and his sweetness. Ken and Matt were the first to head to their room. We kissed them good night and then started the good night process with our hosts and with Jerry and Connie. It had been a long, delicious day. And it would be followed by a long, delicious night with Seth holding me close to his heart. Grateful? Probably more so than I had ever been in my life.

On Friday morning, when Seth and I headed downstairs to join the others, Elaine was wearing an amazing silk dressing gown with splashes of rose and lime green. She gave us coffee and toasted raisin bread with butter and marmalade. The various houseguests took their breakfast to the living room or the dining room and settled in with a book or a newspaper. "Elaine," I said, "that robe is exquisite."

"It was a Christmas gift from Caleb and Danny last year. It's the most elegant thing I own—except maybe for the mother-of-the-groom dress Vera Wang made for me last spring. I'm sorry you and Seth weren't there. It was such a fun wedding."

"I heard the *GLITZ* girls arranged the whole thing," I said, "so I know it was perfection. And Kenny's cover shot of the boys eating wedding cake was priceless."

"*Tisha* is priceless," Elaine said. "She came to the house once, when she and Danny were dating—in their early twenties. Did you know about that?" I indicated that I did. "It seems so long ago," Elaine said, "and Richard and I had to think long and hard about welcoming a black daughter-in-law into our family. But we realized that our children's happiness was the only reality that mattered. Fortunately, they both have excellent taste in friends *and* mates."

"Rather like their parents, I think." Elaine embraced me. "What are you up to today?" I asked her.

"Oh, not much. I'll dress and go out for a walk in a little while. Soup for lunch, I think. Something light. Danny and Caleb would love it if you two could stay the weekend, but maybe another time. Richard and I are driving home to the village this evening, so we'll drop you two at the bus stop on our way. And I'll make turkey sandwiches for you before we leave, so you don't starve. Should I add dressing and cranberry relish?"

"Yum!"

"Seth, be sure to wear a sweater under your jacket. It gets cold up there—I'm told." Seth responded warmly to a little mothering. I kissed him, and he went to our room to dress for his excursion into the wide blue yonder. When he and Caleb and Richard had left for the local airstrip, the house seemed much quieter without them.

Jerry said, "Tim, why don't we take a walk down to the pond? I don't think you've met the ducks."

"Sounds good," I said. "Let me put on some shoes and grab my jacket." And that's what I did. I didn't know why Jerry wanted to be alone with me, but I had always enjoyed his company. I had also enjoyed flirting with him through the years, even though we had never gone beyond flirtation. Well, maybe a kiss or two in the back of the gallery. But he was a client, after all, and I was happily partnered. So our relationship was mostly businesslike.

As we walked down the hill, Jerry said to me, "I envy you, Tim."

"Whatever do you mean, Jerry?" I asked.

"I envy you because it turns out you're the perfect man for Seth. That's who *I* wanted to be. But I couldn't do it. Connie is fine and loving, and my heart is totally his. But I'll always regret my failure to commit to Seth. I thought I'd always wonder if things could have been different. Until yesterday. Seeing you two together, I knew that everyone made the right choice."

We embraced. "You're a good man, Jeremiah Darnley," I said. "Connie is exceptionally lucky to have your love."

"I think it's the other way around," he said. We embraced again. I could feel the stirring in Jerry's groin. It matched mine. We can't help it, we gay men. It's who we are. Jerry and I continued our walk, and he introduced me to the ducks and to the weatherproof box in the shed that housed duck feed. The mallards were a little daintier than Rufus was when it came to a snack, but they were just as enthusiastic.

Dan and Connie walked down from the house and joined us. "It's such a nice day," Dan said. "It's good to be outdoors. Kenny and Matt went to their room. That's good, too. And the lack of cloud cover should be perfect for the flyers. Dad always wanted to be a pilot. Did you know that?" We didn't, of course. "I had no idea until the folks met Caleb last December.

Of course I also had no idea if they would fall in love with him, as I had. But they did."

I said, "How could they not?" It was the picture-perfect morning after Thanksgiving. Connie embraced Jerry and kissed him sweetly. They wandered off along the edge of the pond in the direction of the mossy bank about a quarter of the way around.

Dan pointed it out and said, "That's the perfect swimming hole in the summer. There's an artesian spring that feeds it, so it's always fresh and cool. I hope you and Seth will come back then. Actually, Caleb and I hope you'll come back often. I don't mean to be mysterious, Tim, but we've been thinking long and hard about the future of this house. We want to talk to you and Seth about some ideas we've put together. We could probably find some time to meet this afternoon, but I think it's better to get together next week, after the holiday shimmer has faded."

"Of course, Dan," I said. I was a bit mystified, but not anxious.

"I could take a long lunch—maybe Wednesday? Caleb is mostly writing at home or at Starbucks these days, so he should be able to get away. If Seth is available, then Caleb and I could stop by the gallery—around noontime Wednesday?"

"I'm sure that will work fine," I said. "But we'll talk before then. Dan, I'm so grateful to you two— and to your parents—for opening your home to us. Everything between Seth and me is so new, and I can't imagine a better first Thanksgiving."

Dan embraced me. "The first of many," he said. "Enjoy all your firsts, Tim. But remember: it can keep getting better if you stay open to the possibilities. I'll shut up. You don't need advice from an old married man." I kissed him, and we headed back to the house arm in arm. When the aviators returned, they all three looked younger—and happier—than before they left for the airstrip.

Seth said, "Tim, you should have come! Oh, I guess it would have been a tight squeeze for the two of us in the back of the cockpit. But I like tight squeezes with you." He kissed me. I melted into a puddle of gooey happiness. It was that kind of afternoon. It was quiet, it was warm, it was unpressured, it was intimate, it was familial. In short, it was exactly what days off should be and rarely are.

When it came time for goodbyes, I felt twinges of separation anxiety even as I reminded myself how grateful I felt for the chance to connect with some remarkable people. Elaine made fat, luscious turkey sandwiches for us, as promised. When she and Richard pulled over on Rte. 17 to drop Seth and me at the bus stop, I said to her, "Elaine, this has been such a treat. When will we see you again?"

"Well, I know I'll dance at your wedding, but I expect we'll get together even before then. Safe home." She kissed me. And then she reached for Seth. I heard her say, "Be very good to him," as she embraced Seth. Even in the harsh mercury-vapor streetlight on the side of the highway, I could see a tear in Seth's eye.

"Tim, my man," Richard said as he embraced me, "we never got to that business meeting. Oh, well. Soon." And it was time for the bus to arrive. We walked forward to the little bus shelter with just our little wheelie, now that the holiday gifts had been given. Richard and Elaine drove away. I felt as if I were parting from fond parents—a feeling I had yearned for as a child but never actually experienced. Seth seemed to be on the same wavelength. We didn't talk about it on the way home. We didn't need to.

Chapter Twelve

The following week, we were thinking about how to celebrate Seth's twenty-second birthday—on Christmas Day! I didn't know quite how to approach it, considering that we still had to attend to our workday at the gallery, plus preparations for the Winter Show coming up in February and the spring event at the Historical Society. Finally, I just asked Seth what would bring him the most joy.

"Truth?"

"Truth."

"Timmy, the best gift I could receive is if you agreed to marry me." Did I burst into tears? More or less.

"Darling, please don't kill me before we can get to the altar. Of course I'll marry you, Seth. There's nothing I'd love more. But I would never have asked you. I would never have presumed to think you could give up your youth and your freedom in exchange for the love I have to offer. Are you certain it's what you want?"

Seth kissed me deeply. "I won't be giving up a thing," he said. "I'll be gaining the friendship I always wanted, and the partnership I always wanted, and, of course, the ready sex I always wanted. And you make me laugh." I tousled his hair. Seth's grin melted any fears I had been harboring. Most of them, anyway.

"If we're really going to do this, we have to figure out when and where," I said. "This is a complicated time, with the Winter Show coming up and the Historical Society in the spring, followed by the Pride Show in June. How about the Fourth of July? I'm thinking we could just about make that work."

"Perfect," Seth said. "I'd love to marry you on Independence Day."

"Do you want to tell anyone?" I asked. "Dan and Caleb are meeting with us on Wednesday, you know. Should we tell them?"

"I don't know, Timmy," he said. "I haven't gotten that far yet."

"Exactly," I said. "Let's sleep on it." I slept badly that night, despite the warmth of Seth's embrace and the romantic glow that enveloped us. I had a serious case of the What-ifs. What if Seth grew tired of me? What if I couldn't satisfy his needs? What if he were hit by a bus? Such things happen. What if he developed some virulent cancer that claimed his life in less than a month? Such things happen, even to twenty-somethings. I had no shortage of disaster scenarios.

Eventually I grew too exhausted to continue my self-torture. Seth was still holding me when I woke in the morning, and I was still madly in love with him and full of fears, maybe in equal measure. Over coffee, I said to him, "What if we have a cocktail party at the gallery during Christmas week? We could announce our engagement to our friends then."

"Yes, Tim," he said. "That sounds perfect. When we get to work, you could go over the calendar and chose a date. Actually, I'm sure Jimmy is really busy this time of year, so give me two or three dates, and I'll figure it out. Timmy, I've got this. Please let me take care of it. I don't want you to stress." Of course, I would do just that.

this time of year, so give me two or three dates, and I'll figure it out. Timmy, I've got this. Please let me take care of it. I don't want you to stress." Of course, I would do just that.

⌗

"I'm glad you two had a chance to experience the house," Dan said when he and Caleb came to see us at the gallery that Wednesday. "I grew up there, so I'm the wrong one to evaluate it accurately."

"I think it's a welcoming house," Caleb said. "I find it exceptionally relaxing. No matter how stressed I am, I always begin to unwind as soon as I walk through the door. It's a great place to do absolutely nothing, and it's also a great place to work without the distractions of the outside world."

"I think you're absolutely right," I said. "But what does this have to do with us?"

"Yes, well, we've known since last winter that we have to find a real use for the house and grounds," Dan said. "If we go there one weekend a month, it's a lot. That's nice for us, but it does nothing for anyone else. And a house that isn't lived in starts to decay."

"We've been thinking for months about turning the place into an artists' retreat," Caleb said, "but we can't quite visualize it. That's where you two come in."

"You have different skills, gentlemen," Dan said. "We figured Tim will know how to configure the space to make it conducive to both relaxation and creativity. And we figured Seth will bring a fresh, young perspective to the project that will keep it vital. And the fact that you, Tim, know everyone worth knowing does no harm."

"We know that funding a nonprofit is a complicated business," Caleb said. "I'm sure we can talk to Connie about it at some point, but first we need to figure out just what we're doing. Will you two help us?"

I said, "I'd love to ..."

"But?" Dan asked.

"But there's so much work for us to accomplish in the next few months. I'm a little overwhelmed at the thought of taking on another project."

"Tim's right," Seth said, "but I think we can focus on your blueprint after the Winter Show opens in mid-February. What do you think, Tim?"

"Sure," I said. "If you guys can give us two months to wrap up our other commitments, then we should be able to focus on your plan—which, by the way, I think is a great idea. And, of course, we'll be thinking about it and comparing notes when we should be focused on other things!"

Dan and Caleb looked at each other with the silent shorthand that married couples develop. "That sounds great. We'll get out of your way," Dan said as they rose to leave. There were kisses and holiday wishes all around.

"Seth and I are going to have a little pre-Christmas cocktail party," I said. "Actually, we have to set a date today. You'll hear from us shortly." And they were off. "You're so smart," I said to Seth. "Or is it a smart-ass?" Seth laughed and kissed me. "Okay, let's nail down this party business before Jimmy has his whole year booked up." And that's what we did.

Not everyone was available on such short notice, but most of the people we loved were able to at least stop by for a cup of cheer. Early in the party, when most of our guests were still present, Seth made our announcement. We had set up a portable PA system for the occasion. He quickly called for quiet in the room—and got it.

"Dear friends," Seth said, "we wanted you to be the first to know that Tim has agreed to make all my dreams come true. He said he'd marry me, and I'm going to hold him to his promise." A great cheer went up all around the room. That plus the general feeling of holiday joy made it unlikely that I could manage quiet for a few words of my own. So I gave up trying and just savored the moment.

Ken greeted me first. He started to laugh. "Timmy, that's the best thing I've heard since Matt told me he loves me. I couldn't be more delighted. I'll shoot the wedding. And the honeymoon. But, Tim, we'll never be able to sell those pictures, you and I. Too personal!" Matt embraced Seth warmly.

"We can't do anything as splashy as we did for Dan and Caleb," Tisha said, "but when the owner of Tim Hart Gallery marries his assistant—who also happens to be one of our models—then I think that's newsworthy. We'll do something fun and try to stay out of your way at the same time. Agreed?"

Lisa said, "Tim looks very Yves Saint Laurent to me. Their rep is generous. And Seth needs to wear something cutting edge. Something Dries van Noten, only younger. A black designer, I think. We'll figure it out."

Jerry and Connie had recently arrived with Lucy. Jerry was very physical—with me and with Seth.

Lucy was also warm and congratulatory. Connie said, "I just had a thought: If you stage the wedding at my community center, I can guarantee you an enthusiastic audience. All of our regulars love a good love story—and a good meal. It would certainly be something different for *GLITZ* to cover. It could be good for them and good for our visibility, too, since we're always fundraising."

Tisha said, "Connie, that's a terrific idea! We don't do enough coverage of people and places that are not chic. We'll make yours the hottest soup kitchen in the country!"

Lisa said, "I can see the decorations now: Handmade, except for some very expensive flowers. Like a village wedding in Mexico with a little haute couture thrown in. Gorgeous!"

I had been disappointed when Dan told me Elaine and Richard couldn't make it to our party. I wanted them to be among the first to know. Dan took care of that. He handed me his phone.

"I told you I'd dance at your wedding," Elaine said. "When will it be?"

"The Fourth of July, I think."

"Good," she said. "Timmy, you're going to have a wonderful life together, you and Seth. Please put him on." I did, of course. They spoke briefly. Seth smiled a lot. And then he handed the phone back to me.

"Tim, my man," Richard said, "you're going to love the old ball and chain. Best decision I ever made. I'll get you out here to look at my business someday, but first things first. Put Seth on. I want to talk to him." I did, of course. Richard had never seemed that interested in talking to Seth, so I was curious about the conversation I was not privy to—and Elaine's as well.

Later, when the party had quieted down a bit, I asked Seth, "What did Elaine have to say?"

"She told me I had made the best decision of my life and that it would bring me great happiness."

"And Richard?"

"He said if I hurt you, he'll hunt me down and cut off my balls. I believed him. Fortunately, it's not an issue." I couldn't resist giving Seth a kiss, even though I disapprove of airing one's clean linen in public. I hoped our guests would forgive the eagerness of the newly engaged.

Judy and Sylvia were warm and congratulatory. "We'll have to draw up a prenup, of course," Judy said, "but it can wait until spring. As long as it's signed before the ceremony, we're good."

"You know, my sister bakes wedding cakes," Sylvia said. "They're beautiful and they're delicious. Let me arrange it. All you have to do is tell me how many guests. And the cake will be my wedding gift to you two." I wasn't expecting to get weepy just at that moment, but I did. I thanked Sylvia as warmly as I could. And she and Judy headed on to another party. It was that season, after all.

"Well, Mr. Preacher Man," I said to Harvey, "Will you save the Fourth of July for us?"

"With pleasure," Harvey said. "You know, Len is creating custom invitations these days. He could design one for you." Len smiled sweetly. How could I say no?

"Sounds lovely," I said. "Thanks to you both."

"If you're certain about the Fourth of July, then we can send out a 'Save the Date' right after the holidays," Len said. "And then you can wait until March to focus on the actual invitation."

"Whatever you say, Len. We'll put ourselves in your capable hands." What else could I say? The party was winding down, for certain. I was looking forward to some down time at home with Seth.

"Tim, is the date certain—the Fourth of July?" Jimmy asked me. "I want to put it in my schedule."

"Yes, Jimmy. The date is firm. And thanks for doing this for us tonight. I wouldn't have sprung it on you at the last minute if we hadn't needed to make an announcement. You're a good sport. And an excellent caterer, by the way. You have the February date locked in?"

"I do. And congratulations to you both!"

"Thanks, Jimmy." Maria and Fabián were the last to leave. Except for Fabián's security guard, of course. He would help Seth and me lock up. Maria embraced Seth—perhaps for the first time. She seemed moved by our news. Fabián then hugged Seth. His kiss looked a bit too passionate for my taste, but then I would have to continue to learn to share Seth with the world.

Fabián said, "Tim, I wondered if I'd ever see you happy again, after ..." Neither of us needed to be reminded of Andy. Not that evening. "I'll get to work on your bachelor party," Fabián said. "I shouldn't ask, but will you let me stand up for you? It would be a great honor."

"Of course, Fabián," I said. "I would have asked you—if I were thinking straight these days. Which I'm not." When Fabián embraced me, he pressed his equipment against mine—not intentionally but rather more like unavoidably, considering the scope of his endowment. I had always assumed it was there but never actually experienced it so closely. "Engagements always give me a hard-on," he said. "Can't help it, Brother."

"Don't apologize," I said. "But please get Maria home safely." And that's what he did. Seth and I finished up with the security settings and headed for the front door. The guard—my favorite: the cute one named Jason—walked out with us and waited while we locked up. And then he wished us a good night.

As Seth and I walked home—briskly because the wind had picked up—I said to him, "You know, Fabián said engagements always give him a hard-on. I guess my brother and I are more alike than I thought, Seth. I need to get you home and show you how our engagement is affecting me."

"I guess I'm a brother, too," Seth said. "I'll race you to our bed!"

The End

This is Bruce K Beck's **Holiday Novella Series**, which includes *A BUCKSKIN CHRISTMAS*, *MY EASTER MIRACLE*, *INDEPENDENCE DAZE*, and *GIVING THANKS*. Also by Bruce K Beck are his **Tolerance Trilogy**—*SUCH A GOOD MAN, IT'S THEIR WAY,* and *THIS IS GOD'S COUNTRY.* Look for the **Obsession Trilogy**—*INK OBSESSED, OPERA OBSESSED,* and *LOVE OBSESSED.* And the **Love Trilogy:** Volume 1, *YOU'RE SURE TO FALL IN LOVE*, is set in Provincetown, MA, in the summer of 1976. *LOVE AND THE EPIDEMIC*, set in New York City in 1986, is Volume 2. Volume 3, *AND LOVE ENDURES*, is set in the early 1990s. For updates, and for occasional gifts and offers, please subscribe at:

www.audacitybooks.com/#subscribe

Many thanks to Walter Maas for his generous wisdom. And to Richard Kutner for his classy edits. Tim Barber of Dissect Designs (www.dissectdesigns.com) signed on as a cover designer for my first novel and then became a friend. You're Sure to Fall in Love, indeed. This journey would not have been possible without the example and the teaching of Joanna Penn at www.thecreativepenn.com. I am delighted, Joanna, to add this volume to your long list of books you have enabled. No doubt you will hit your one million mark any day now!

Bruce K Beck is both a writer and an accomplished chef. His novels—including the **Love Trilogy,** the **Obsession Trilogy**, and the **Tolerance Trilogy**—are available online and wherever books are sold. Before turning to fiction, Beck authored ***PRODUCE: A FRUIT AND VEGETABLE LOVERS' GUIDE***, which was called "gorgeous" by ***The New York Times***, "a dazzler" by ***Bon Appetit***, and "the most spectacular food book of the year" by ***The Boston Globe***. His next book was ***THE OFFICIAL FULTON FISH MARKET COOKBOOK***, which was called "invaluable" by Jacques Pépin, and "a treasure" by Irene Sax of ***Newsday***. And Rex Reed said, "... you'll love this book. It's like a movie!"